"*And They Called It Camelot* is the book club pick of the year. Stephanie Marie Thornton brings an American icon to life: Jackie the debutante, the First Lady, and the survivor who at last becomes the heroine of her own story."

—Kate Quinn, *New York Times* bestselling author of *The Huntress*

"An extraordinary profile of the courage and grace of the indomitable Jacqueline Bouvier Kennedy Onassis, *And They Called It Camelot* is impeccably researched and richly drawn. Readers are instantly transported to Jackie's version of Camelot as they immerse themselves in the fascinating and tumultuous history of the times. An unputdownable read."

—Chanel Cleeton, *New York Times* bestselling author of *Next Year in Havana*

"Jacqueline Kennedy Onassis leaves an enduring (and intimidating) legacy; for a writer, finding something new and meaningful to say about her is a daunting task. Thornton harnesses her immense talent for historical fiction and combines it with a biographer's immersive research to create a rich portrait that is both intimate and thoughtful while also wildly addictive." —Steven Rowley, author of *The Editor*

"Addictive, dishy, and emotionally haunting, this novel paints an intimate portrait of a tumultuous marriage that played out on the world's stage and ended in national tragedy. Vivid, engrossing, and utterly unforgettable, *And They Called It Camelot* is Thornton's best work yet."

—Stephanie Dray, *New York Times* bestselling coauthor of *America's First Daughter*

"Stephanie Thornton has compellingly and sympathetically humanized an American icon. Well-researched and beautifully written, *And They Called It Camelot* is compulsively readable historical fiction!"

—Laura Kamoie, *New York Times* bestselling coauthor of *My Dear Hamilton*

"Even if you think you know the story of Jacqueline Bouvier Kennedy Onassis, you're in for a rare behind-the-scenes look at the former First Lady's life. This book is nothing short of magical."

—Renee Rosen, author of *Park Avenue Summer*

"This book grabbed me from page one and wouldn't let me go. A multidimensional imagining of the trials and triumphs of Jaqueline Bouvier Kennedy, *And They Called It Camelot* will make you rethink everything you thought you knew about this remarkable First Lady. Full of glamour, scandal, and heartache, this is a novel you will want to discuss with all of your friends."

—Kerri Maher, author of *The Girl in White Gloves*

"A sumptuous, propulsive, scandal-filled peek behind the curtain of American royalty."

—Erika Robuck, national bestselling author of *Hemingway's Girl*

"Jackie steps out of the pages a convincing, three-dimensional character, complete with contradictions and self-doubt. It's like reading her private diary—witty, warm, and full of color."

—Gill Paul, author of *The Lost Daughter*

"Lush, smart, and sumptuously elegant, *And They Called It Camelot* captures Jacqueline Bouvier Kennedy's life in all its many complexities, drawing back the curtain on a legend to reveal the all-too-human woman beneath. A beautiful portrait of an American icon."

—Bryn Turnbull, author of *The Woman Before Wallis*

"Simply spellbinding. This intimate story of Jacqueline Bouvier Kennedy Onassis portrays a woman finding her way in a landscape dominated by men, and, with grace and astounding resilience, forging an identity the world will never forget. A tale of love and devastation, greatness and sacrifice, this remarkable novel will grip readers until the last page."   —Kristin Beck, author of *Resistance*

PRAISE FOR
AMERICAN PRINCESS

"As juicy and enlightening as a page in Meghan Markle's diary."
                                                              —*InStyle*

"Skillfully woven and impeccably researched, *American Princess* brims with scandals, secrets, and the complexities of love in all of its wondrous, maddening forms. A vividly imagined portrait that mesmerized me from the first page to the last."
                          —Kristina McMorris, *New York Times* bestselling author of
                                                        Sold on a Monday

"A rare behind-the-scenes tale of a spunky woman who relies on her independent spirit to face down each challenge with courage and grace."   —*Woman's World*

WRITING AS STEPHANIE MARIE THORNTON

American Princess

And They Called It Camelot

WRITING AS STEPHANIE THORNTON

The Secret History

Daughter of the Gods

The Tiger Queens

The Conqueror's Wife

AND THEY
CALLED
IT
CAMELOT

·····

A NOVEL OF
JACQUELINE BOUVIER
KENNEDY ONASSIS

STEPHANIE
MARIE
THORNTON

BERKLEY
NEW YORK

BERKLEY
An imprint of Penguin Random House LLC
penguinrandomhouse.com

Copyright © 2020 by Stephanie Thornton
Readers Guide copyright © 2020 by Stephanie Thornton
Penguin Random House supports copyright. Copyright fuels creativity, encourages diverse
voices, promotes free speech, and creates a vibrant culture. Thank you for buying an authorized
edition of this book and for complying with copyright laws by not reproducing, scanning, or
distributing any part of it in any form without permission. You are supporting writers and
allowing Penguin Random House to continue to publish books for every reader.

BERKLEY and the BERKLEY & B colophon are registered trademarks of
Penguin Random House LLC.

Letter on pages 86–87 used by permission of Pete Mark, Kennedy Collection.

Library of Congress Cataloging-in-Publication Data

Names: Thornton, Stephanie, 1980– author.
Title: And they called it Camelot : a novel of Jacqueline Bouvier Kennedy Onassis /
Stephanie Marie Thornton.
Description: First edition. | New York : Berkley, 2020.
Identifiers: LCCN 2019039584 (print) | LCCN 2019039585 (ebook) |
ISBN 9780451490926 (paperback) | ISBN 9780451490933 (ebook)
Subjects: LCSH: Onassis, Jacqueline Kennedy, 1929–1994—Fiction.
Classification: LCC PS3620.H7847 A88 2020 (print) |
LCC PS3620.H7847 (ebook) | DDC 813/.6—dc23
LC record available at https://lccn.loc.gov/2019039584
LC ebook record available at https://lccn.loc.gov/2019039585

First Edition: March 2020

Printed in the United States of America
4th Printing

Cover art by Bettmann / Getty Images
Beach © CO Leong / Shutterstock Images
Clouds and sky © suns07butterfly / Shutterstock Images
Cover design by Emily Osborne
Book design by Kristin del Rosario

This is a work of fiction. Apart from the well-known historical figures and actual
people, events, and locales that figure in the narrative, all other characters are products of
the author's imagination and are not to be construed as real. Any resemblance to persons,
living or dead, is entirely coincidental. Where real-life historical persons appear,
the situations, incidents, and dialogues concerning those persons are not intended to
change the entirely fictional nature of the work.

To Stephen & Isabella,
because you are my everything

PART ONE

. . . . .

For one brief shining moment
there was Camelot.

JACQUELINE BOUVIER KENNEDY
NOVEMBER 29, 1963

PART ONE

November 22, 1963

The pink pillbox hat and Chanel-inspired bouclé suit awaited her on the bed. The shouts of "Jack-ie!" still rang in her ears, and her headache had scarcely dulled after yesterday's constant cascade of blinding flashbulbs. Yet she'd braved the crowds as she had so many other times over the past ten years, and with her husband's reelection campaign looming, her false smile was guaranteed to become a permanent fixture in the months to come.

So she tugged the watermelon wool skirt over her silk slip and buttoned the jacket's gold buttons, the deafening roar of applause from downstairs causing the walls to tremble, while John F. Kennedy shook voters' hands and kissed their chubby-cheeked babies in the ballroom below.

A few more minutes alone, she thought to herself. Just a few more minutes.

There were never enough minutes. And there was never, ever enough time alone.

"Are you ready, Mrs. Kennedy?" Her Secret Service agent entered in his crisp black suit, for once not wearing his ubiquitous dark sunglasses. Her personal secretary swept in behind him, faithful steno pad in hand. "The president needs you at breakfast."

She would normally have had an army of excuses ready—I'm too tired, I have to call the children—but things had changed in the weeks since she and her husband had emerged from their blackest month, forged anew and made stronger than before, although they'd forever bear that brutal shared scar.

He needed her. And she needed him.

She smiled and held out her wrists to her secretary in a silent request to assist buttoning her short white kid gloves. "Of course." Once finished, she straightened the jacket's navy silk collar. "Let me just get my hat."

She didn't usually care for hats, but this simple pink pillbox put to shame those jowly Texas matrons with their overwrought concoctions of flowers and feathers. She'd worn it before to several private events, but after today's public spectacle, it would likely be featured in Cosmopolitan *next month, with identical replicas in store windows in time for Christmas.*

Christmas, when they would be home with the children. Together, they would build a family of snowmen and tumble inside afterward with snowflakes still tangled in their hair to sip hot chocolate and nibble cinnamon toast together beneath a fairy-tale Christmas tree. Caroline and John Jr. would clamber into their laps and laugh with glee over their dolls and model planes.

But first, Texas.

God, how she couldn't wait to get out of Texas, with its hateful demonstrators who spit on Lady Bird Johnson the month prior and the airport spectators who waved picket signs reading HELP JFK STAMP OUT DEMOCRACY. *If a man's manners were the mirror in which he showed his portrait, then the Lone Star state was a Jackson Pollock painting.*

She glanced in the mirror, supposed she was camera ready enough for the interminable motorcade to come. "Oh, Mary," she said to her secretary with a rueful smile. "One day in a campaign can age a person thirty years."

"That would make you the best-preserved sixty-four-year-old anyone has ever seen." Mary clasped a delicate gold bracelet around the First Lady's left wrist and handed her a navy pocketbook. "You're picture-perfect, Mrs. Kennedy."

The First Lady cast a lingering look at the quiet oasis of the hotel suite before settling her shoulders. "I'm ready, Mr. Hill."

Moments later, the elevator bell chirped their arrival at the Grand Ballroom, and she braced herself when her vision went spotty from the pandemonium of klieg lights. A brick wall of applause hit upon her entrance, but her husband waited with boneless grace behind a lectern on the dais, so she kept her steps measured, reminded of another time she'd walked down an aisle to meet him. He was a beacon then, as he was now, the air crackling around him.

"*Two years ago,*" he said into the microphone, his voice everywhere all at once, "*I introduced myself in Paris by saying that I was the man who accompanied Mrs. Kennedy to Paris. I'm getting somewhat that same sensation as I travel around Texas.*" The crowd chuckled, and he glanced approvingly at his wife's pink American-made ensemble. "*Nobody wonders what Lyndon and I wear,*" he added, and the crowd's chuckle turned into a good-natured laugh as she joined him at his side. It was where she belonged, for over a decade now.

"*You look smashing.*" His breath was warm against her ear, and she marveled that he still had the power to make her flush with pleasure. "*I'm glad you let me persuade you to wear that suit again.*"

"*And you look like the most powerful man in America.*" She dared wink at him, actually winked. She, Jacqueline Bouvier Kennedy, who had been her husband's twin iceberg for all those years, cold and untouchable. They were icebergs no more. "*It's a good look on you.*"

The remainder of the breakfast passed with bites of bland hotel food between fielding inane questions from the press about whether Lyndon Johnson would remain on the ticket as vice president (of course), or whether the president had given support to Communist-inspired race riots (absolutely not). She heaved a sigh of relief when the clock struck ten thirty and her husband pulled back her chair.

He took her hand with real warmth, the kind she'd craved for so long. "*To Dallas?*"

She smiled when they strode hand in hand across the ballroom and into the November sunshine.

"*To Dallas,*" she said, and pushed headlong into the storm that was already hanging in the stars.

CHAPTER

January 1952

The market seems to be recovering from its recent drop." John—my fiancé, although the word was still too slippery to make sense of—stood on the curb, oblivious to the bustle of people retrieving luggage from the trunks of yellow taxis and tail-finned Cadillacs. He wore his omnipresent gray flannel work suit, fingers twitching as if hovering over a calculating machine. "I really think the railroad division is going to carry the rest of the market, and American Telephone and Telegraph has been performing well in recent weeks too."

"You don't say?" I tried to summon a single iota of interest to recapture how endearing his stock market talk had been on Christmas Eve when we admired a shop window on Madison Avenue, how the crisp pennants of our breath in the cold air had mingled together before he'd asked me to marry him.

I'd invited John to Merrywood, my stepfather Hughdie's second estate outside Washington, DC, the better to convince my harridan of a mother—and me, if I was being honest—that I'd made the right decision. Instead, John spent most of the weekend debating Wall Street investments with my stepfather while I'd retreated unnoticed to the oak-paneled study. Normally the room's rich scent of antiquarian books and Oriental carpets and tobacco was the one place I could truly relax in this home that wasn't really mine, but I verily twitched with annoyance as I flipped the pages of *Sybil*, a novel written by Hughdie's cousin about a spirited woman who resigned herself into the necessity of marriage and thus settled into being a vegetable wife.

She became humdrum and boring, like broccoli.

I hated broccoli.

"That's it," I'd announced to my younger sister Lee—who had been christened Caroline, although no one ever called her that—as I slammed shut the book. "If I marry John, I'll become one of those dull country club wives who can only converse about the progress of their children's teeth. My entire future will be spent as Sybil Husted."

Lee had recently snagged a position as an editor's assistant at *Harper's Bazaar* and scarcely glanced up from the magazine's latest issue, its cover touting resort fashions with a breezy blonde whose legs stretched for five miles beneath her cotton shorts. "I thought you'd be Jacqueline Husted," she mused, waving a hand with fingernails bitten to the quick, "but I suppose you can change your first name, too, if you'd like. Very bohemian."

Jacqueline Husted.

Not for the first time, I worried that in marrying steady, number-crunching John Grinnel Wetmore Husted Jr., I'd be not so much settling down as *settling*. Not because he wasn't the gloriously wealthy New England husband my mother envisioned for me (even if his family was listed in the *Social Register*), and not because marrying him might mean bidding au revoir to trips to Paris, fox hunts with my New England friends, and my passion for journalism. But because before I'd met John, I'd been prepping Givenchy models for a shoot on the banks of the Seine—part of my short-lived stint for an internship I'd won at *Vogue*—and my stern-faced editor had warned me that, at twenty-two, I was teetering on the precipice of spinsterhood's fatal abyss, and I'd felt a chill go through me.

I didn't want to marry any of the young men I'd grown up with, not because of them but because of their sedate lives. Still, had I accepted John's proposal for fear that I'd be left on the shelf?

I scoffed, for surely I wasn't so mundane. Was I?

I'd paced Merrywood's opulent study, ready to climb the walls as my fingers drifted over the beloved leather-bound volumes that I'd read countless times—Oscar Wilde's *The Picture of Dorian Gray*, Baudelaire's *Les Épaves*, Dostoevsky's *Crime and Punishment*, Hugo's *Les Misérables*. I'd cringed when my tall, supposedly urbane fiancé admitted to scarcely recognizing the first-edition titles on the mahogany shelves, preferring his stock columns and account books instead.

I loved books and words more than my horses; could scarcely imagine a life devoid of stories and drama. My heroes were Mowgli, Robin Hood, Little Lord Fauntleroy's grandfather, Scarlett O'Hara. . . .

Not Sybil Husted.

Now, with the last of winter's icy cold seeping through my wool jacket, John retrieved his newly purchased suitcase from the trunk of my blue Chevrolet Fleetmaster and pressed a dry kiss to my forehead. "In fact, it looks like corporate bonds will remain steady—"

"John."

He blinked, my voice drawing him away from the elusive chimeras of stocks and bonds. It was perhaps a bit overdramatic to think it, but John might well be nattering on about American Telephone and Ford and General Electric ten, twenty years from now. "Yes, dear?"

Dear. It was so blasé, so tame. So John.

I recalled a different man I'd met once, who had made me feel so alive, as if everything under the golden summer sun was possible. I banished the thought, for that had been nothing.

There was no doubt that if I married John Husted, I'd live a languid, comfortable life for the rest of my days.

But I wanted more than comfort. I needed something—anything—more than this.

I pulled my hand back, tugged the sapphire-and-diamond sunburst ring from my finger and slipped it into his flannel pocket. "I'm sorry, John. I'm well and truly sorry."

He blinked. "I don't know what you mean. Sorry for what?"

I stepped back, needing to put space between us. "I'm afraid I can't marry you." From the way his expression fractured, I almost wished I could pluck the words from the air. Except that if I capitulated, ten years from now—or maybe even next year, or next month—I'd hate myself for it. And John would learn to hate me too.

"What do you mean, you can't marry me?"

"Exactly that. I wish I could, but I just—"

"Is it about the money?" He squared his shoulders. "Because you can tell your mother that seventeen thousand a year is a decent amount for a stockbroker."

I'd tried informing my aristocratic, chain-smoking mother of that already, but she'd only shaken her cigarette at me, sprinkling ash upon the Aubusson carpet as she paced and railed against my stupidity.

"No, it's not that—"

"Was it too fast?" John held the sparkling ring between his thumb and forefinger, his handsome face turning a splotchy shade of red. "You said you liked spontaneity, but I ruined it, didn't I?"

I drew a deep breath. "It's none of that, John. You and I are too different to be a good fit," I said because I owed him my honesty. "You deserve a woman who can make you far happier than I ever will."

And I deserved someone who could talk about something besides corporate stocks and bull markets.

I didn't wait for a response, only hesitated long enough to touch his cheek. "Good-bye, John. I'm really very sorry."

I didn't look back when I fled to the driver's side of my Chevrolet, instead slammed the door behind me and shifted into drive, intent on returning to Merrywood, where I planned to stay up until dawn reading a biography on Louis XIV to avoid thinking about what I'd just done.

All I want is a man with a little imagination. Is that too much to ask?

I was already twenty-two—a leftover daughter who couldn't live off her stepfather's generous goodwill and fifty-dollar-per-month allowance forever—and at twenty-five, society would deem me spoiled goods. It was no use railing against the firm rule that well-bred girls must make a good marriage if they wanted to continue living their lives. I was willing to play the game, but only on my terms.

Jacqueline Bouvier, I thought to myself as John shrunk away in the rearview mirror. *You narrowly escaped making the biggest mistake of your life.*

Or had I in fact just doomed myself?

I adjusted my white evening gloves, glanced up at the imposing Georgetown mansion, and repressed a thin shudder.

Another dinner party.

Every bit of me screamed to retreat the way I'd come, to shuck off the black peep-toe heels I'd borrowed from Lee (that were a size too small), and hightail it home before the last golden drops of May sunshine dissipated into hazy twilight. I'd tried to beg off from tonight's dinner after Charley Bartlett informed me there was a friend he wanted me to meet. Following my broken engagement, it seemed every Jack and Jill now had a friend, cousin, or neighbor they needed to introduce me to.

I was no fool. This was an ambush.

To make matters worse, Lee had recently proposed to Michael Canfield, a handsome Harvard-educated veteran of Iwo Jima, which made it impossible to ignore that while my sister was seizing each day by its throat, I was merely treading water. It was perhaps the first time she'd bested me at anything—save the time as girls when I'd hit her with a croquet mallet and she'd retaliated by pushing me down the stairs—and I didn't care for the feeling.

I ran a hand over my newly cropped hair—it was some small consolation that my mother no longer cracked three raw eggs over my head to rub the yolks into my long curls each night—before drawing a steadying breath and ringing the bell.

Afternoon teas, dinner parties, and then what? I thought as footsteps approached from inside. *What are you going to do with your life, Jacqueline Bouvier?*

I banished the question to the deepest, darkest corner of my mind. I'd worry about that later. Namely when I wasn't about to be enfiladed by Charley's stuttering, stamp-collecting cousin or his recently widowed former college roommate.

"Jackie, darling!" Spectacled and buttoned-down Charley enveloped me in a stifling hug before helping me shrug off my coat. "So glad you could make it!"

"I wouldn't miss one of your dinners for the world." I smiled despite myself, for as my journalistic consigliere, Charley had gifted me with late-night writing advice before several of my deadlines for my new position at the *Washington Times-Herald*. That had been my answer to the chasm of spinsterhood yawning before me, to get a job, and while I loved the work—and its twenty-five-dollar-a-week paycheck—I worried it wasn't enough.

Charley let me kiss both his cheeks, a habit I'd picked up while in school at the Sorbonne. Then in his rapid-fire mumble, "I have someone I want you to meet."

Just like his editorials, I thought. *Straight for the jugular.*

Charley raised an arm and gestured into the crowded living room. "Jack! Over here."

The room's sudden electricity raised the hair on the back of my neck as a tanned man with a mop of sandy-brown hair and a smile more powerful than an atomic bomb blast returned the wave. He wended his way toward us, looking as if he might have strolled straight off a Hollywood movie set.

Dear God, I thought, unable to stop myself from biting my lip. *It's him.*

He looked just as he had a year ago, except he'd traded his tuxedo for tonight's black evening suit with *brown* shoes. But even that sartorial mishap was endearing as I admired how well his shoulders filled out his dinner jacket and the way his smile crinkled the corners of his eyes in a most attractive way.

I wondered if *he* remembered that other dinner party from long ago.

Charley introduced us, beaming like a proud papa. "Jacqueline

Bouvier, meet Congressman John Fitzgerald Kennedy. Although he's about to trade up and become Senator Kennedy."

One of the Hyannis Port Kennedys, I imagined my mother whispering in my ear. *Staunchly Catholic. Politically aggressive. More ill-gotten money than the Rockefellers.*

"My friends call me Jack," he said by way of greeting. His voice was unique but not unpleasant, the Bostonian accent so thick that his *r*'s all but disappeared. He held out his hand and I shook it, surprised when he didn't give it the usual dead-fish treatment most men did, as if worried they might break poor, delicate little me. There was power there, and confidence, too, so much that I couldn't help the grin that spread across my face, despite the fact that Jack gave no indication that he remembered me.

And why would he? He's Jack Kennedy, who just dethroned Rock Hudson for the title of America's Most Eligible Bachelor. You're just Jackie Bouvier.

That meant I had nothing to lose.

Toy a little while with the debonair congressman who acted last time as if he walked on water. See if that gets his attention.

"Are you *the* John F. Kennedy?" I asked as Charley disappeared on cue, leaving just Jack and me. "The same one who gets mistaken for a House page and recently addressed the floor of the House with his shirt untucked?" My grin deepened when Jack arched an eyebrow at me. "I read the article about you in the *Saturday Evening Post.* 'The Senate's Gay Young Bachelor,' wasn't it?"

And the *Post* was right: Jack Kennedy did have the innocently respectful face of an altar boy at High Mass. Although the wicked spark in his stormy Irish eyes would have sent many an altar boy to confession.

"That depends. Are you *the* Jackie Bouvier, who I once asked out for drinks, only to discover I was already the third wheel?"

A ripple of some foreign pleasure passed over my skin at the sound of him saying my name. I much preferred the French pronunciation of Jacqueline—*Jack-leen*—to plain old American Jackie, but Jack could call me Gertrude or Hortense for all I cared. "So you do remember."

He cocked his head as if to study me, allowing me to admire the chiseled angle of his jaw. There was no denying Jack was an impressive specimen, and my fingers itched for a typewriter to describe the slant of his easy smile. "I didn't want to spoil Charley's fun by telling him we'd already met."

"Another day, another dinner party." I laughed, forcing myself to appear impervious to the perceptive gaze that tried to pin me in place, like some sort of exotic butterfly. "I'll never forget the look on your face when you opened my Chevy's door to find John sitting in the driver's seat."

Or the fact that I'd had to convince John that Jack escorting me to my car hadn't meant a thing. Which it hadn't. Or had it?

Jack glanced over my shoulder. "Whatever happened to good old John? I assume he took you out for drinks?"

"He did." I rubbed absently at the empty finger on my left hand. Compared to Jack, John Husted seemed rawboned and prosaic. "So, the Senate?" I asked, searching for safer topics of conversation. "The House too dull?"

"Perhaps." Jack guided me toward the table as tuxedoed waiters filed in with silver tureens of soup, clam chowder from the smell of it. It was an intimate sort of dinner party, the kind with Billie Holiday crooning from the record player instead of a well-dressed string orchestra playing in the corner.

"So Charley tells me you're writing for *Vogue*?" Jack asked as he held out my chair, everyone around us settling in.

"Charley is behind the times." Amber-hued sidecars waited by our plates as we took our seats, little strips of orange peel dangling from the crystal rims. I took a sip to give my hands something to do, enjoyed the citrus notes among the Cognac. "Now I write a column called 'The Inquiring Camera Girl' for the *Washington Times-Herald*."

It was a column I was proud of, challenging traditional women's roles with questions like "When did you discover that women are not the weaker sex?" and "If you went on a date with Marilyn Monroe what would you talk about?" while reflecting on concerns of the day by asking whether people thought bathing suits were immoral and whether the rich enjoyed life more than the poor.

Charley perked up at the mention of his name. "You know, Jack here's a writer as well, covered the British elections with me for Hearst in forty-five and published a damn fine book, too, a few years back."

Now that was interesting. I'd never told anyone, but I sometimes fantasized about writing the great American novel. To spend all day stringing together sentences and painting scenes with Technicolor paragraphs . . . I loved words—by age six I'd eschewed naps to read Chekhov's short stories and scrawled my own poetry at age twelve—so the idea of being a published author was intoxicating. "What was the book about?"

"The failures of the British government to prevent World War Two." The iron set of Jack's jaw shouted that he didn't relish this sudden spotlight. I wondered why.

"That same war made Jack a hero." Charley held up a hand, ticked off his fingers one by one. "Purple Heart, American Defense Service Medal, and a whole slew of other pretty baubles."

"Next you'll be telling me that he took out Hitler too." I turned to Jack. "Let me guess. Blindfolded and with one hand tied behind your back?"

Jack shrugged, saluted me with his glass. "Naturally."

Charley laughed, unabashed. "Tell her how you became a hero, Jack."

"It was easy." Jack's flat tone told me he'd played this game before and he didn't enjoy repeating it. Suddenly I wanted Charley to disappear, to leave me to talk to Jack on my own. "The Japanese cut my PT boat in half."

"In the Solomon Islands, right?" The tale came back to me now, for the entire country had heard snippets of Jack's war feats since the newspapers had loved the war-hero-turned-congressman angle. "You guided your crew to swim to an island three miles away—"

"It's not as impressive as it sounds. I lost two men—" Jack said, but Charley cut him off with a wave of his soup spoon.

"But you single-handedly saved the rest. Why, you pulled one of your crewmen by the strap of his life jacket. Between your teeth!"

Jack rubbed the back of his neck. "That might have been part of it, yes. Gave me a hell of a toothache."

I wondered whether his reticence was an act, one he'd practiced with dozens of women before. If so, it was working.

This was no John Husted seated across from me. In truth, the idea of Jack's published book left me more in awe than his daring wartime rescue, but there was no denying he was someone who, although only in his thirties, had already *lived*. I felt small in comparison and found myself jealous of Jack Kennedy then. Undeniably, green-about-the-gills jealous.

Jack only managed to shake off his discomfort over the conversation when Charley suddenly became engrossed in a discussion with his wife. "You're at an unfair advantage, knowing everything about me," he said as he reached for the asparagus. "I think it's only equitable that you let me take you out for a drink sometime to even the score. I seem to recall you owe me."

I studied Jack, hard. If I had to describe him for a *Washington Times-Herald* column, I'd have written that his expression was lodged somewhere between laughingly aroused and intelligently inquisitive. When he flicked an irreverent eyebrow in my direction, I wished I could take his snapshot in that exact moment, even as I was aware that we were surrounded by a table of people pretending not to listen to our every word. "I think I'll step outside for a moment," he said when I didn't answer right away. "Bit of fresh air and all that."

He lingered for a hairsbreadth, long enough for me to know that this wasn't a dismissal.

An invitation then.

I counted to twenty before I excused myself, pausing only to drop a few words into my mentor's ear. "You are incorrigible, my friend."

Charley patted my hand. "I'm also brilliant. Go make Jack realize how much he needs a camellia beauty like you instead of all those blond airheads he collects."

A chill ran through me, for I was far from beautiful, with my freckles and boyish physique, the masculine hands and feet my mother was always critiquing. Charley's well-intentioned words reminded me that Jack was swimming in an entirely different ocean than me when it came to everything that mattered: age, money, connections . . .

Everything except my illustrious Bouvier ancestry, although that was a fanciful tale my mother had spun from mostly sugar and air, given that the real Bouviers had been humble French shopkeepers before the Revolution.

But Jack was larger than life, and I enjoyed that intensity. What other reaction was there to a man who laughed so easily and seemed to make each room a hundred degrees hotter?

Jack stood waiting on the Bartletts' front stoop with his back to me, the ember from his cigarette a pinpoint of orange light along the fingertips of his silhouette. I wondered then what a man like him thought about as he fell asleep each night, what ideas tumbled about in that mind as I watched him now.

Well done, Jack, I thought. *I'm sure as hell not bored.*

"So tell me." I leaned against the porch and accepted the cigarette he offered, doing my best not to think about how his lips had just touched the same paper. Instead, I focused on the pattern of smoke from my exhale as it swirled around the sickle moon. "Once you've been elected senator, what will you do next?"

His gaze flicked to me in a way that warmed me despite the cool night air. I suspected he knew exactly the power those twin beacons possessed, an alluring combination of green and gray. "Is this an official interview or off the record?"

"Off the record."

"Well, I suppose I'll just have to become president."

"Is that all?" I almost laughed, but his expression grew serious. I handed him back the cigarette. "I thought you were going to say something exciting like summit Mount Everest."

He took a long drag, teeth glinting in the moonlight. Despite the darkness, that smile threw shadows. "I *would* look rather dashing standing on top of the world."

This time I did laugh. Sure, I conducted interviews for the *Times-Herald*, but I'd never considered myself politically minded. That Jack was so focused on politics made him only that much more exotic to my eyes. "So, the presidency?"

"It's been my father's dream to see one of his sons in the White House—the first Catholic president and all that, you know—since he himself lost the chance."

Daffodils are yellow . . . I recalled the way my mother had *tsk*ed under her breath over wartime headlines as she'd lambasted Jack's father, a man everyone had once believed might run for president. That is, until he'd made a critical error. *But not as yellow as Joe Kennedy.*

I shifted uncomfortably in Lee's black peep-toe heels. "Did your father really suggest that Roosevelt and Churchill capitulate to Hitler during the war?"

"Not my father's finest moment," Jack admitted. "The taint of treason has proven difficult for him to shake."

New England Catholics are a small circle, I remembered Mummy saying, *and Joe Kennedy's betrayal is a betrayal of us all.*

Jack cleared his throat, as if he could hear my train of thought. "My father raised us all to be public servants, and we're expected to leave America a better place than we found it. Anyway, it was Joe—my eldest brother—who was always supposed to be president, but he went and got himself killed in the war. Since then, all Dad's hopes are pinned on me."

"And what do you want?"

Jack dared meet my eyes. "I don't want to fade into oblivion like my brother; I want to be president so badly I can taste it. America should be that shining city upon a hill—a place to dream the impossible and make it happen, to overtake the Soviets and become the world's brightest beacon of hope. If I win this election, I might just have a shot of getting us there."

I dared to lift a beckoning strand of sandy hair from where it had fallen across his forehead, let it fall through my fingers like water. It seemed as if Jack's bumper crop of sandy brown hair always fell over his eyebrows so he looked as though he'd just stepped out of the shower. I imagined such a scene, felt my cheeks flare crimson. "I think you might have a chance too. If you get a haircut, that is."

He stubbed out the cigarette with a laugh, and I found I liked that deep, throaty sound. Liked it too much, given that I'd only wanted to have a little fun with him tonight.

"So, about that drink?" he asked.

It was obvious that Jack Kennedy wasn't the type any woman should get serious with—everyone knew he had a hundred girls on a string—but a little voice inside my head urged me to accept.

Have some fun and live a little with this man who dreams of being the most powerful leader in the world. One drink with him won't hurt anything.

"Perfect." I flashed an impish smile. "And this time I promise not to have any beaus squirreled away in the front seat."

Jack arched an eyebrow, then retrieved a gold-capped fountain pen and paper from his jacket pocket. "Jot down your address and I'll pick you up tomorrow. Seven o'clock."

I hesitated, wondering how many other women had written their information with this same pen that probably cost more than my entire monthly allowance. "Make that three o'clock," I said, "and you've got yourself a deal."

Jack crossed his arms, leaned back against the stoop's brick wall. "I don't think I've had many three o'clock Monday drink dates."

"Afraid to try something new?"

"Never."

I wondered for a moment if letting John F. Kennedy break my heart would be worth the pain, but I had only my lukewarm relationship with John Husted for comparison, and that was akin to the dullest shades of gray. Better to keep my guard up.

One drink is all you get, Jack, I thought as I jotted down Merrywood's address.

After all, what was life without a little fun?

. . .

still think three in the afternoon is an odd time for an after-dinner drink," Jack said when he arrived at Merrywood the following day. White clouds scudded across the sky like summer swans, and the breeze was so mild I'd slipped into a pair of strappy stilettoes for the first time this season. Fortunately, I was the only one home as my mother and Lee were out shopping for Lee's bridal trousseau, so I'd kept all mention of Jack secret and had been able to avoid the inevitable barrage of feminine questions from their corner. I could well imagine Mother's eyes lighting up if she knew the handsome scion of one of America's wealthiest families was pulling up for me—a Bouvier who wasn't descended from French nobility for all Mother's finessing of our family tree. The plain truth was that for all the prestigious boarding schools I'd attended and all my stepfather's wealth, I was just the leftover daughter of a philandering stockbroker who lived off another's man's charity, hardly a match for a Kennedy, and I had no desire to see a simple daiquiri date hedged in from the start by my mother's iron-clad expectations.

"You're really taking me to rob a bank, aren't you?" Jack asked as we strolled down the vast drive.

"I'm fairly certain bank heists are a federal offense, Mr. Senator."

"That's Mr. Almost-Senator, but I appreciate the vote of confidence."

I ignored Jack's open convertible door and instead ducked into my reliable old Chevrolet, then smoothed the skirt of my black sheath dress and unlatched the passenger door for him. "Get in."

Jack cocked his head and hesitated, but I only tapped my wristwatch, sounding more confident than I felt. "The clock's a-ticking, and you don't know where we're going."

Jack shrugged and locked his convertible, then folded himself into the Chevy's passenger seat. "I would know, if you told me, that is."

"Sorry. Classified information."

I eased my foot off the clutch and we were off, the windows rolled down while I guided the Chevrolet around curves at breakneck speeds that had both of us laughing like hyenas and praying there were no police around.

"Don't worry," Jack said when we finally hit the city limits. "If you get pulled over I'll tell them I'm on official congressional business."

"Does that work?"

"You'd be surprised." We arrived with only minutes to spare. Jack gave a low whistle when he glanced up at the stately brick building as I pulled my ten-pound Graflex camera from its home on the Chevy's back bench. "Well, I'll be damned. I didn't realize Harrison Elementary School was the hot spot to get daiquiris at three o'clock in the afternoon."

"Work first, then drinks." I swung out of the car, pencil and notepad in hand. I pondered the bulky Graflex and then changed my mind—too intimidating for this job—and dropped it into the backseat. "This is Mamie Moore's school."

"Eisenhower's niece?"

"I want Mamie's take on her uncle's run for president for the *Times-Herald*." After all, I hadn't accepted Jack's invitation to be just another one of his lollipop girls. I'd show him that I had brains behind my finishing-school reputation.

More than that, I'd prove to myself that I wasn't just a mundane debutante. I was Jacqueline Bouvier, who could scoop a story while impressing Capitol Hill's most popular congressman.

"School lets out for the summer today." I tucked a tuft of hair behind my ear when the school bell heralded the end of the day. "So this is my last chance."

"Get to work then, Bouvier."

I felt Jack's gaze on my back as I navigated the cascade of students in blue plaid jumpers streaming down the steps. At twelve years old, Mamie Moore was all odd angles with a mouth full of orthodontic braces, and from the way she perked up when I held out my press badge, I could tell she was the sort who enjoyed the spotlight.

"I'm Jacqueline Bouvier from the *Washington Times-Herald*." I glanced to where Jack was watching me from the car. "I was wondering if you wouldn't mind answering a few questions about your uncle."

The interview was quaint but original: the foods Ike preferred while campaigning (quail hash and frosted mint delight, although not at the same time), if Heidi—his droopy-eared Weimaraner—would enjoy chasing squirrels on the White House lawn (she would), and whether Mamie thought her uncle would make a good president (she did, of course). I let her go with a firm handshake and a promise to send her a copy of the interview and the illustrations I had planned when it went to print.

"Now I'm ready for that daiquiri," I said as I approached the Chevy, barely batting an eye to see that Jack had switched to the driver's side.

The type who likes to be in charge. Duly noted.

"You made that look easy," he said as I swung inside. "That girl didn't know you from Lizzy Borden, but I bet she'd have let you read her a Nancy Drew novel before bedtime if you'd asked."

"People like to feel important, no matter their age." I waggled a finger at him. "Remember that the next time you're talking to voters."

Jack saluted, his eyes sparkling. "Any other assignments we need to take care of on the way to that drink?"

"Not tonight." Interviewing Mamie Moore was enough for today. Although . . .

"Just so you know," I said, "I have every intention of interviewing you when you clinch that Senate seat."

Jack's wink would have made me weak in the knees had I not already been sitting down. "With a promise like that, I'll have to try twice as hard to win, now won't I? Your article about me might win you the Pulitzer, and me another date with the one and only Jackie Bouvier."

If you'd have flicked water on one of my cheeks, I'm sure it would have sizzled; I suddenly found the federal buildings outside my window of the utmost interest.

Voltaire had once written that illusion is the first of all pleasures.

It might have been an illusion that Jack Kennedy was interested in me, but in that moment, basking in the warm glow of his undivided attention, I didn't care one whit, for I planned to dance the jitterbug in every minute of that divine pleasure.

I've never felt this way about anyone, I thought as Jack eased the car along the wooded outskirts of the National Zoo. The way Jack Kennedy looked at and talked to me, as if my thoughts were worth knowing and I was capable of accomplishing great things? That was far more seductive than any kiss.

And the idea of Jack kissing me tangled up every thought I'd ever had in my head. When I made the mistake of glancing over at him, it was impossible to pull free from the undertow of his eyes.

A man like Jack came about once in a century. People said it later—I was thinking it in 1952 in the front seat of my Chevy on our first date.

Why on earth had I thought one drink with him would ever be enough?

CHAPTER

2

November 1952

did have that drink with Jack—a daiquiri with extra mint he ordered at the Shoreham Hotel—and eagerly accepted his subsequent invitations to a carnival and then his campaign speeches in Quincy and Fall River. However, I was shocked to find him on crutches at the first speech event.

"What in heaven's name did you do?" I asked over the drone of the crowd. I didn't know how to help him and instead busied my hands straightening the turned-up collar of his slate-gray suit jacket that matched the clouds overhead.

A voice from behind interrupted me. "No need to worry, Miss Bouvier." A very tan man with the beginnings of a middle-aged paunch adjusted the adorable round spectacles perched high on his nose. "It's just that Jack's old PT boat injury hit the same spot he blew out playing football for Harvard. It gives him grief now and then."

"Dad, this is Jackie." Was Jack pleased to introduce me or was it seeing his father that made his smile go supernova? "Jackie, meet the infamous Joe Kennedy."

So this is the legend who had charmed actress Gloria Swanson into a torrid affair and hoped to single-handedly reconcile the Axis and Allied powers during World War II.

I remembered my mother's tart comments about the former ambassador, but to my consternation, I somehow found myself wanting to impress him.

Jack's eyes tightened as he maneuvered on crutches toward the stairs. "My father's right; it's nothing to worry about." Yet he struggled to ascend even the first step toward the speaker's platform. "It flares up every now and then."

He looked so vulnerable then with his hair flopping over his forehead that I wanted to help him, but he shed the crutches into his father's waiting arms before he hit the top step, and through sheer force of will, strode across the stage. His speech should have been dull and political, but it was as if a switch flipped inside him when he assumed the podium.

His father stood beside me as we listened, and I could feel him studying me, judging the cut of my skirt and the way I held myself. Was this some sort of test?

"Jack has the charisma to turn a funeral into a party," Mr. Kennedy finally said to me, and I nodded in agreement.

"Jack holds everyone in the palm of his hand," I murmured with no small amount of awe. This might be the first crowd I'd seen him address, but I remembered how he'd been the center of the room on the night we'd met, how he'd become the effortless hub of Charley Bartlett's party. No matter the size of the audience, from a party of fifteen around a gramophone to a hall of fifteen hundred, Jack knew how to speak to it. "Crutches be damned."

Truth be told, Jack held *me* in the palm of his hand. I listened with rapt attention as he spoke of the need for a more assertive America until I was persuaded to march down the Korean Peninsula myself. I marveled at the fact that although he was in pain, he was willing to subvert all that in order to do good for his country. Just how much was he willing to hide?

"You might be my son's good luck charm," Mr. Kennedy said to me when Jack finished and was nabbed by reporters before he could finish the agonizing journey back toward us. Was I the only one who noticed the way his laugh masked the pain, how his jaw clenched while he listened to their questions? "Jack certainly perks up when he talks about you."

Now that was a welcome surprise. "He talks about me?"

Mr. Kennedy removed his spectacles to rub the lenses on his jacket, gave a sage nod. "You have no idea."

Jack rejoined us then. "That went well," he said, but there was no mistaking how he clasped his father's arm for stability, the crutches set aside and hidden from the glare of the press. "The Boston papers have dubbed me the first Irish Brahmin."

I laughed at his audacity, but Jack's confidence wasn't misplaced. For he didn't just win the second Massachusetts seat a few weeks later. He carried it by seventy thousand votes.

Maybe I *was* good luck.

Perhaps Jack was *bonne chance* for me as well, for my steps had been lighter and my laugh easier since that dinner at Charley Bartlett's.

Maybe this isn't merely a fling. Could it be something deeper? For both of us?

I'd never thought the handsome scion of one of America's wealthiest families—to whom I was surely just one debutante among many—would be courting me.

Was Jack? Courting me?

I thought perhaps he was, but then the deluge of our dates dried into a biblical drought. Days that Jack didn't call turned to parched weeks, which stretched into a bone-dry month.

I told myself he was busy transitioning from congressman to senator, but that did little to soothe my bruised feelings.

"Charming scoundrels always come sniffing around when there's a pretty girl involved," my father reassured me when I mentioned the quandary over a New York City dinner. Though I rarely saw him now—due to his lack of finances and my mother's animosity toward him—Black Jack Bouvier had encouraged me as a little girl and my sister, Lee, to ride handle-free bikes and indulged my desire for a pet rabbit by letting it live in his bathtub in his Park Avenue apartment.

Today he had treated me to a rare day of shopping and insisted I stock up on books and splurge on a single elegant white wool dress before we headed to the Empire Room of the Waldorf Astoria for caviar and *le potage à la tortue*. I'd have been happy eating off the card table in front of the fireplace of his one-bedroom apartment, but I didn't dare bring up his finances when he'd dressed for the occasion in a midnight-blue suit of the finest imported silk embellished with a scarlet tie. His hair shone with a double dose of Vitalis hair tonic, and his debonair Clark Gable mustache twitched between spoons of turtle soup. "You, my dear Jackie, are the prettiest pixie this side of the Mississippi, and this Jack of yours sounds like he could charm the dentures out of an old lady's craw."

In fact, Jack's dangerous charisma reminded me more and more of my father, who was the walking definition of a scoundrel. I'd always loved Black Jack Bouvier all the more for being a bon vivant, but he was wrong in thinking Jack Kennedy was *my* Jack, no matter how much I might have wished it that way.

"I enjoyed it while it lasted," I said. "I suppose there must be someone else out there for me."

"Is that what your heart tells you?" My father gestured to a tuxedoed waiter, who topped off his glass of Chardonnay. His fourth glass, if my count was right, following the tumbler of whiskey he'd downed while we'd waited for our table. Another of my father's many talents was his ability to get boiled as an owl and somehow still traipse his way home each night.

"I don't think I can trust my heart to make decisions for me."

"Nonsense. Better a bad decision today than a good one three weeks late."

By that rationale, I could justify anything, just as my father had done all his life. I refrained from mentioning that as he continued, this time waving his soup spoon. "Life is full of life-enhancing or life-diminishing people. This fellow sounds like he's the former, a fox-hound who loves the chase. Play hard to get, my dear, and he'll be howling outside your door in no time."

Maybe my father was right, for only a few afternoons later I almost dropped Merrywood's telephone when I heard Jack's voice crackling on the other end. "Jacqueline Bouvier, I'm hoping you're about to make me the luckiest man alive," he said by way of greeting. *Why*, I wondered, *do I still love the sound of my name when it comes out of his mouth?* "Are you free the night of January twentieth?"

Still dressed in my black jodhpurs and snowy cravat after my morning routine in the woods with Danseuse, my favorite Thorough-bred in my stepfather's stables, I sank onto the formal sitting room's butter-toned velvet settee and wrapped the phone cord around my finger. I knew better than to ask where Jack had been the past month, why he hadn't called. Let him think I hadn't noticed—or cared about—his absence. "Why should I be free on January twentieth?"

"Because I need the best-dressed woman in town on my arm for Eisenhower's inaugural ball."

I paused in the midst of toeing off my riding boots, waiting for Jack's punchline. When it wasn't forthcoming, I could only conclude he was serious.

Best-dressed woman in town . . . You are a conquistador of the highest caliber, Jack.

I knew I should say no, but the very thought of the sheer royalty of it, not to mention the idea of Jack turned out in a tuxedo, set my heart thudding. "Well, I had important plans to alphabetize Merry-wood's collection of antique books that night. . . ." I hesitated, doing my best to sound serious, all the while failing miserably. "I suppose I can reschedule, but only if you promise to introduce me to the president."

"Deal. I'll pick you up at eight."

On Jack's arm that star-spangled night, I felt like Scheherazade acting out someone else's fantastical story, despite the wry twist of my mother's mouth when I'd told her who was escorting me to the inaugural ball. I'd worry about why she wasn't over the moon about Jack's interest in me later; right now my mind was agog at all the nattily turned-out DC politicians, Supreme Court justices, and foreign ambassadors as Jack squired me around the dance floor on nimble toes.

"God, I must be boring you; I'm boring myself." Jack stopped mid-sentence after I'd asked him about his plans for the Senate, which had launched him into a diatribe about French colonialism in Indochina. "We should talk about how stunning you look tonight, not Ho Chi Minh and the Indochinese Federation." He stared at me, those greenish-gray eyes turning to quicksilver. I'd borrowed a beaded white floor-length gown from Lee for tonight, the better that I might stand out among all the pinch-lipped matrons in their dour winter dresses, and I'd enjoyed the way Jack's eyes had grown smokier as they lingered on my trim waist and the way the silk pulled across my hips. "And you are stunning. In fact, I'm rather enjoying the many jealous stares thrown my way by every other man in attendance."

It was stupid for beauty to matter, but my throat tightened at his words even as I brushed away the compliment. In truth, Jack could have read the telephone book and I'd have hung on every number with rapture, dressed as he was in a perfectly tailored dupioni-silk tuxedo. With *black* shoes this time, thankfully. "Actually," I cleared my throat, "I studied France's Asian holdings for a history course at the Sorbonne. I still have a few of the books, if you'd like to borrow them. They might help with your Senate speech."

Little did he know that I'd since devoured every book about French history I could get my hands on, and could probably teach both him and his Senate colleagues a thing or two about Indochina. Every warning I'd ever heard growing up drummed in my head. *Men don't like smart women, only a pretty face. A husband is a greater asset than any college degree.*

Jack chuckled, a sound that made the room suddenly too warm. "Let me guess. The books are all in French, aren't they?"

I forced myself to focus on his words and not the way his hand rested on the small of my back or the feel of his shoulder muscles beneath my hand as he guided me effortlessly around the crowded dance floor. To count the plethora of presidential seals hung amid clouds of white silk bunting to keep the heat from spreading across my face. Still, being with him—touching him—seemed the most natural thing in the world. "That *is* the language they speak in France."

"I'm a fish in a tree when it comes to languages. May as well be in Polish."

Now probably wasn't the time to tell him that I was proficient in Polish, along with being fluent in French and Spanish. It was difficult to imagine red-blooded, rough-and-tumble Jack sitting still long enough to master his *mercis* and *s'il vous plaîts*. I pretended to brush something from his pristine lapel, avoided his gaze. *"Je pourrais faire la traduction."*

Jack's eyes crinkled at the corners. "You just called me an illiterate imbecile, didn't you?"

"How did you know?" Our dancing came to a sudden and inopportune halt as the Marine Corps band blasted the first notes of "Hail to the Chief" and Eisenhower entered the balcony with his pink *peau de soie*–draped wife, Mamie, on his arm, arousing a thunderous round of applause. I leaned in to whisper to Jack. "I said I could translate for you."

"Beautiful *and* brilliant. Watch out, Jackie, or I may never let you go." Jack clasped my hand and gave it a squeeze, so I only hoped he couldn't feel the thundering crescendo of my pulse. Thankfully, he didn't glance my way as Ike and Mamie waved to the crowd. "You know," he murmured. "If I play my cards right, that could be me in a few years."

Everyone else stared in rapture at Eisenhower, but I studied Jack through my eyelashes instead, his succinct movements as he clapped and the way his foot tapped with pent-up energy. There was no doubt that Jack Kennedy lived his life as a race against boredom.

Like called to like, or so they said.

Against my will, everything in me called to Jack. I could envision a future with him rolling out before us, this daring trapeze artist willing to hurtle his way through life for the chance at glory.

Perhaps if *I* played *my* cards right, I might share with Jack the future he imagined.

Was that what I wanted?

I gave a mental shrug as the band settled into a waltz and we began to move again to the music, Jack tugging me closer until we were pressed together. How could I bear such delicious torture?

The night held its breath when he dipped his head toward mine, brushed his lips against mine. It was only a whisper of a kiss, but I gasped aloud at the promise of that gentle touch.

He smiled at my shiver and bent to murmur in my ear, his warm breath making my blood turn molten in a way no poem or sonnet could ever truly capture. "I haven't forgotten our deal, you know. I promised to introduce you to the president—and the First Lady—before the night is out."

Kissed on the inaugural ball dance floor by America's most handsome senator, making the acquaintance of the President of the United States . . .

I almost tripped over my feet at the realization that I was falling for Jack Kennedy.

No, not falling.

Fait accompli—I'd already fallen.

This was what I wanted, and it was Jack whom I needed.

Who knew what our future might hold? I didn't care how far Jack's aspirations took him in that moment; I only cared that he choose me, this man whose love of history and politics rivaled only his passion and dreams, who was brash and daring and vulnerable at the same time, who could make me feel as if I were the center of his expanding universe with one errant glance.

Content and happy in Jack's arms as we passed beneath a balcony hung with Eisenhower's presidential seal, I didn't know what our ending would be.

I only cared that Jack be at my side for all the chapters in between.

• • •

Jack Kennedy filled all the empty spaces in my mind so it was all I could do to think of anything else. He even pervaded my work as I accepted his interview offer for a story about the young Capitol Hill pages who delivered correspondence and took messages for the senators.

Still, I didn't want Jack to think he was the sun I orbited—at least, not yet—so I also interviewed the pages themselves, and Richard Nixon too, who had recently ascended from the Senate to the hollow office of the vice presidency.

Nixon offered me tea in the living room of his house on Forest Lane. "I noticed that the pages were very quick boys with a definite interest in politics," he said as he passed me the cream. I wondered if he was bored in his new position, now that he had time to grant interviews to inquiring camera girls from the *Times-Herald.* "I always thought they would receive ideal political grooming watching the Senate's daily sessions."

Competent, but, kindly though he was, Nixon was no Whitman or Longfellow.

However, I could hear Jack's laughter between his words, imagined him conspiring with his own page as my fingers flew over the keys to type up the interview.

I'VE OFTEN THOUGHT THAT THE COUNTRY MIGHT BE BETTER OFF IF WE SENATORS AND PAGES TRADED JOBS. I'LL BE GLAD TO HAND OVER THE REINS TO JERRY HOOBLER. I HAVE OFTEN MISTAKEN JERRY FOR A SENATOR BECAUSE HE LOOKS TOO OLD.

To which sixteen-year-old Jerry had responded:

SENATOR KENNEDY ALWAYS BRINGS HIS LUNCH IN A BROWN PAPER BAG. I GUESS HE EATS IT IN HIS OFFICE. HE'S ALWAYS BEING MISTAKEN FOR A TOURIST BY THE COPS BECAUSE HE LOOKS SO YOUNG. THE OTHER DAY

HE WANTED TO USE THE SPECIAL PHONES AND THEY TOLD HIM,
"SORRY, MISTER, THOSE ARE RESERVED FOR SENATORS."

I chuckled, for I could well imagine the scene, Jack's sandy hair standing out like a beacon among that egg-bald crop of politicians.

Jack had come through on his promise of a good article, and now came my opportunity to give him a leg up.

I greeted the dawn several nights in a row while translating chapters from five dog-eared books on Southeast Asian politics, including a couple I'd asked old friends from Paris to send to Merrywood. I felt a warm rush of pleasure when Jack sent a thank-you note on his newly monogrammed Senate stationery, along with five more books.

My first Senate speech has to be perfect. I hate to ask, but can you do these ones too?

Clever women learned to conceal their intelligence from men, but here was Jack, aiming a blinding spotlight on my talents. And I loved him all the more for it.

I realized then that with Jack I wouldn't have to be ashamed of my real hunger for knowledge, something I had always felt I had to hide from the other men I'd dated.

So I transcribed more French histories until I was bleary-eyed and my fingers cramped over my Royal typewriter. My every nerve jangled as if I'd drunk ten cups of coffee when I zipped to Jack's Senate office to surprise him with the latest installment of my work.

I bit my lip and hugged the books to my chest, the staccato tap of my heels falling silent as I hesitated halfway down the Russell Senate Building corridor. Jack was twelve years my senior, a powerful senator who could have any woman he wanted. And who was I?

Je m'en fiche.

I was Jacqueline Bouvier, and I wasn't going to doubt my worth. Not anymore.

I straightened my shoulders and arrived at Jack's office, only to have his secretary glance at me through her harlequin glasses and gesture me toward a wicker rocking chair. "I'm afraid the senator is out to lunch. You can wait as long as you like."

So I sat and stared at the stark white walls, perused the bookshelf freshly unpacked with law volumes and topped with models of graceful sailing ships and military airplanes. Nearly an hour passed until I wondered if this was penance for all the times I'd made men wait for me, often under my mother's strident instructions. I was ready to leave when Jack's infectious laugh echoed down the hallway.

"Hello, Jack," I said when he entered, before the words turned to stones in my throat. I could neither swallow nor speak as I took in his companion's familiar sylphlike silhouette and glossy honey-colored hair, everything about her so opposite my own flat-chested physique.

From the way they leaned toward one another, casually touching in so many places, it didn't take much to imagine what they were to each other. What a fool I'd been to believe Jack might be thinking of me exclusively just because I could think of no one but him.

"Jackie." Jack's arm fell from the woman's flared waist. "What a pleasant surprise. This is Inga Arvad."

As if that explained everything.

She fluttered manicured fingers at me, had the audacity to wink. "Fancy meeting you here, Jackie."

I clutched the books I held, hard. "Hello, Inga-Binga. I thought you were supposed to be attending a press conference today."

For Inga, too, worked at the *Washington Times-Herald*, although *worked* might be too generous a term. The paper's owner and our mutual employer, publishing magnate Cissy Patterson, preferred to hire the pretty girls around town, claiming they landed the best stories since everybody only wondered one thing about them.

Do they? Cissy would always waggle her eyebrows here. *And with whom?*

Well, Inga did. With every decent-looking man under sixty.

I almost asked if Jack knew that Danish-born Inga (who was currently on her third husband) was rumored to have had an affair with Hitler's Reichsmarschall, Hermann Goering, and that she'd more recently undertaken an Olympic-sized tour of sleeping with the *Herald*'s entire male staff, including one reporter old enough to be her great-grandfather.

What did I know? Her expansive experience probably made her even more attractive, whereas I hadn't even properly kissed Jack yet.

"I brought the translations for you." I practically threw the books and their typed translations on his desk, wanting to slap Inga's hand when she took up perusing them. "*Bonne chance* on your speech."

Bonne chance *and au revoir, John Fitzgerald Kennedy. I knew you were too good to be true.*

"I owe you, Jackie." He seemed intent on saying more before his secretary interrupted and pulled his attention away, although he continued to glance over his shoulder at Inga and me.

"Did you know Jack and I dated at the beginning of the war?" Inga's announcement was made with that purr of a foreign accent that grated on my last ragged nerve as she thumbed through my translations. "We're still close—quite close—but you two just met. Yet you did all this for him, Jackie? Why?"

I answered with a one-shouldered shrug. "Oh, you know," I said flippantly. "So he'd marry me."

Sometimes it was easier to hide behind the truth than think up a lie.

I was surprised when Inga leaned forward. "I've always thought you were cute, Jackie." I must have scowled, for she only attempted to smooth my hair, which made me jerk back as if I'd received a mild electric shock. "Don't take it as an insult. You'll make a perfect little wife for an ambitious man like Jack."

"Inga." Jack's face had turned a shade of carmine I'd never seen before, the business with his secretary forgotten. *Dear God in heaven*, I thought. *I hope he didn't hear my comment about marrying me.* "I don't think this is a conversation—"

Inga dared touch one finger to Jack's lips. The very lips that had once kissed me. "Sooner or later," she said to him, "you are going to need a wife."

And sooner or later, Inga-Binga, you are going to need a muzzle. Or maybe a good case of syphilis.

I didn't speak, only paused when Jack leveled a glare at her that might have frozen the Potomac, before he guided me by the elbow toward the door. "Are we still on for dinner this Saturday?" He acted nonchalant, as if he always planned dates with one woman in front of another. Which he probably did. "Martin's Tavern?"

"I meant to tell you that I have to cancel." I picked up my handbag, feigning insouciance. "The Nixons invited me to lunch."

That wasn't strictly true, but I *had* interviewed the vice president, and the Earl Grey tea he'd offered me rounded up.

"That's too bad." Jack said. "I had something special planned."

"Next time," I said sweetly, before turning on my heel and walking in a calculated pace down the hallway, feeling Jack's gaze hot on my back, the tension between us verily crackling in the air.

There wouldn't be a next time.

I didn't care if his asking me out in front of Inga meant I was more important to him, or if it had some other meaning I was supposed to divine. I swore then and there that I'd never see Jack Kennedy again, no matter how much I enjoyed his company or whether he brought the world into perfect, vibrant clarity.

"Good riddance," I whispered as I stepped into the fresh onslaught of rain outside, wanting to scream and rage at my own stupidity even as hot tears coursed down my cheeks and frigid water soaked into the new black suede kitten heels I'd bought just for today.

I was making the right choice—the only choice.

Then why does my heart feel so damned hollow?

Quit your pacing or you'll ruin the rug." My mother interrupted what had been a quiet afternoon in Merrywood's library when she barged into my refuge and perched on the overstuffed leather sofa, dressed in pearls and one of her exquisitely tailored suits, always in the same shade of a brown forest mushroom. "You need to do something more than mope over Jack Kennedy."

Not for the first time I wanted to kick myself for confiding in my mother about Jack and Inga-Binga. It had been a moment of mawkishness fueled by a heady glass of Champagne, for my sister Lee had just been married, and in her billows of Parisian silk my sister had looked more exquisite than Queen Nefertiti as she swore her vows alongside her handsome groom who was believed to be Prince George's illegitimate son.

Lee had a prince.

I had no one.

Lee and I had always competed for everything—clothes, grades, our parents' affection—and while I was accustomed to winning, she'd trounced me soundly this time, had even tossed me her bridal bouquet to punctuate the fact that she'd won this round.

There's no place in society for an unmarried woman, I'd thought when I'd waved my sister into the getaway car for her honeymoon. *No matter how intellectual she might be.*

I missed the new way Jack had made me feel, like I was important and necessary.

As much as I hated to admit it, I missed Jack.

Without the planning of Lee's wedding to distract her, my mother had finally noticed my dour mood. I'd been perplexed when she took my side after I told her about Jack, for I'd thought the Kennedy bank accounts—the clan was worth at least $500 million and Jack lived off a $10 million trust fund—would have made her rue the day I'd cut ties with him. "I know, Mummy," I said now as I sat beside her. "But he's all I can think about."

"His father is a notorious philanderer, and I have it on good authority that Jack had assignations with married women back when he was a congressman. If a man can't be faithful, he shouldn't be married, and he certainly shouldn't be with one of my daughters."

I winced and curled deeper into the sofa. Apparently, my mother had done a little digging after I'd told her about Inga and found plenty of further evidence against Jack. I'd told her I didn't want details.

"All men are rats, Jacqueline." My mother's petite frame and patrician bearing belied an iron-fisted temperament better suited to a fascist dictator, so it surprised me when she enveloped me in a rare Shalimar-scented embrace. "And men like Jack Kennedy are the biggest rodents of them all. You can quote me on that."

To speak to Mother is to interrupt her, Lee and I used to say. To argue? A death wish.

Still, I couldn't help myself, not when I already felt so raw and battered.

"What about your relationship with Hughdie?" I asked. "Is he a rat?"

My mother waved a hand. "Hughdie is benign. That's why I married him after your father ran my heart through a meat grinder."

I didn't care to endure another tirade about my lying, cheating father, who had transformed her heart into a charnel house. I still recalled nights when I was young, peering with Lee through the banister while my mother screeched at Black Jack Bouvier and he knelt before her with his collar askew, a torrent of apologies tumbling from his lips. I could hardly fault my debonair father for his straying, especially when my mother could have taught Franco or Mussolini a lesson or two. "But you loved Father."

I knew because I'd seen grainy, fading photos of the two of them that had long since been banished to the attic. My mother alongside my father and always smiling, as if her face was lit by some hidden fountain of joy that threatened to bubble over.

"That doesn't mean I should have married him. Think of the run-in with Inga-Binga as a blessing, and we'll find you someone sensible to marry. Someone stable, like I found with Hughdie."

While my stepfather was a club man and serious bibliophile whose vast Merrywood library had introduced me to stories of America's founders, Lee and I had snickered and called him a magnum of chloroform behind his back. While kindly and perhaps exactly what my mother wanted now, Hughdie was as exciting as the dull tweed suits he favored.

I had already had that sort of relationship, with John Husted. I refused to become a vegetable sort of wife.

I shot my mother a warning look that made her lift her hands in a sign of détente, her arched eyebrows promising that we'd discuss this later. I plucked a leather-bound copy of Tolstoy's *Anna Karenina*—a bleak Russian read fit my mood perfectly—from the shelf when the telephone down the hall jangled.

"It's for you, Miss Bouvier," the maid announced. "It's Senator Kennedy. Again."

My mother shot me a side-eyed glare. "Weakness isn't something you're born with, Jackie; you learn it. Don't be weak just because Jack Kennedy makes your knees tremble."

I studiously ignored her, just as I'd ignored Jack's calls almost every day since the run-in with Inga-Binga. Which had had the strange effect of making him more persistent.

Did I misread him? Surely Jack can't be the horror my mother claims. . . .

Perhaps the conversation with my mother was the reason I accepted this time when he invited me to dinner at Martin's Tavern in Georgetown.

"Where are you going?" my mother asked when I returned and replaced *Anna Karenina* on the shelf. *Some other time, Tolstoy. Probably tomorrow after Jack breaks my heart. Again.*

"One last date with Jack."

My mother straightened the book so *Anna Karenina* was exactly one inch from the edge of the shelf, perfectly in line with the other alphabetized volumes. "You could do better. Far better, with your education and your lineage—"

"A false lineage. Maybe I could do better." I shrugged as I headed upstairs to change. "Maybe not."

I slipped into a smart white dress belted at the waist and added a string of faux pearls Lee had left behind in her jewelry box, before going downstairs to wait. The clock on the mantel crawled closer to seven o'clock, every ticking second making me worry that I was committing a terrible mistake. My mother's scowl deepened into a glare when a silver convertible pulled into the drive. "Your left stocking is crooked," she snarled. "Fix it."

I grimaced to see that she was right.

"Good night, Mummy." To my dismay, she may as well have been my shadow as I tugged the offending stocking into place just as Jack rapped on the door. My breath hitched in my throat to see him looking so windswept in a crisp navy suit, then it caught again at the show-stopping bouquet of showy white Asiatic lilies and frothy blue statice in his hand.

Flowers do not an apology make, I wanted to say, but stopped when he offered the fragrant blossoms past me. To my mother. "For you, Mrs. Auchincloss," he said. "My mother enjoys fresh-cut flowers during all seasons, and as these were especially lovely, I hoped you might enjoy them too."

My mother seemed as taken aback as me but recovered her aplomb when Jack offered me his arm. "Thank you, Senator Kennedy," she said. "They'll look lovely in the sitting room."

Why on earth is Jack bringing my mother flowers? What game is he playing now?

"I'll have her back by eleven o'clock," Jack called over his shoulder as if we were in our teens instead of grown adults. "Scout's honor."

My austere, courtly mother could have borrowed a page from Medusa's playbook and turned Jack to stone with the arch of one elegantly penciled eyebrow. "See that you do."

I believed this proved that John F. Kennedy wasn't the demigod everyone thought he was; that is, until I glanced behind me to see my mother's nose buried deep in the blossoms, her eyes closed in rapture.

My mother's defenses might have cracked, but I held myself aloof during the brief drive to Martin's Tavern in Georgetown, trying not to breathe in the glamorous French scent of Jack's pinewood cologne while I answered his questions about whether I'd read *Marlborough* by

Sir Winston Churchill (I had), and hearing for the first time about his many childhood illnesses—including bouts of diphtheria, appendicitis, and whooping cough that had almost killed him—which had prompted him to read every book Churchill had ever written while he convalesced.

Against my will, my staccato replies softened with each of Jack's smiles, as if his warmth could melt the ice that had formed around my heart following his display with Inga-Binga. By the time we'd parked and a waiter escorted us to a cozy candlelit booth, I was doing my utmost to avoid admiring the way his broad shoulders tapered to narrow hips, how he greeted all the waitstaff by their first names and the way they grinned back at him. Yet there was a tenseness to him as we sat down, his normal frenetic energy punctuated by an occasional snap of his fingers against his thigh. As if my chilliness had finally given him pause, perhaps even made him nervous.

A well-bred woman keeps the conversation flowing. Boarding-school admonitions drummed through my mind. *The weather, sports, music, but never politics.*

I'd acquiesced to this evening's date, so I supposed it wouldn't do to sit here in silence. Nor would I ever shy away from interesting topics. "So," I asked after we ordered, Welsh rarebit for Jack and oyster stew for me. "Did your speech impress the Committee on Foreign Relations? I hope you included some of my notes on the Viet Minh's initial goals of independence from the French Empire."

Jack blinked, as if his mind had been elsewhere, and it took a long moment to reel it back into place. "I didn't embarrass myself." The slow crawl of his smile made my blood simmer. "Which is due in large part to your translations. My father was impressed with your work, by the way."

I lifted my wineglass, let the dim candlelight dance along the stem before taking a sip of Chardonnay. A long one. "Your father?"

"I showed him. Not even he knew that much about Indochina until he read my draft." Jack leaned back and cocked his head, studying me. "He already liked you, but now he's convinced you're a queen among women."

I refused to allow heat to creep into my cheeks under his scrutiny, smoothed the linen napkin in my lap instead. "I'm glad my notes were helpful."

"You know, I missed you all this time."

I scoffed. "How could you miss me?"

Wasn't Inga-Binga keeping you company? I wanted to add but bit my tongue.

"You were avoiding me," Jack said.

"I was not. In case you hadn't noticed, I happen to be a very busy woman."

He arched an eyebrow. "You mean to tell me you had a headache every single time I called? Because if so, I have an excellent physician you should visit."

I rolled my eyes.

"Actually, I more than missed you." Jack rested his chin on his steepled fingers. "And I realized one critical thing every time you made some paltry excuse not to see me."

I caught myself picking at my nails, forced myself to stop by clasping my hands on the table. "And what is that?"

"I love you, Jackie."

I'd seen the words in print, read them in stories a thousand times, but it was an altogether different thing to hear them said out loud. To *me.* The words felt so right, as if I'd been waiting a lifetime to hear them. Yet it didn't seem possible that they were for me, coming from him, but instead it was as if I'd been cast in the wrong role in someone else's play.

"Don't lie," I said, but the words came out a whisper.

I won't say I love him. I won't.

Hurt flared deep in those mercurial gray-green eyes as Jack reached for my hands. "I'll never, ever lie to you. I'm in love with you, Jackie, truly, madly, deeply." He rested his forearms on the table and wound his fingers around mine, sending a familiar jolt of heat straight to my heart. "And that brings me to my next question." He took a deep breath and that traitorous heart of mine actually stopped beating, hovered on some unseen precipice. "Jacqueline Lee Bouvier, will you do me the honor of marrying me?"

I blinked and forced myself to keep breathing as starbursts of light exploded all around me, drowning out everything except the tiny universe contained in this cozy leather booth. This had to be a dream, a most wonderful and terrible dream. "What?" was all I managed to eke out.

"I told you I'd planned something special that day you came to my office," Jack said. "I just had to postpone a little when you canceled on me. Lunch with the Nixons, my ass."

"You had this planned?" I swallowed, hard, willed my voice to work. "That day with Inga?"

He must have heard the sourness in my voice when I choked out her name. "I wanted to throttle her that day."

"You dated her?"

He sighed. "I did once, a long time ago—it's no secret that I've dated a lot of women—but you're different, Jackie. You're everything I want, everything I need. You're the woman I want at my side for the rest of my life."

"Say it again," I whispered, my vision narrowed to a pinpoint filled only with Jack. And he knew exactly what I meant.

"Jacqueline Bouvier." He grinned, the gesture filled with such happiness and assurance. "Will you marry me?"

I wanted to draw out that moment forever, to savor it as one would a rare vintage of French wine, before I finally answered. I wanted to shout yes to the heavens until Saint Peter himself laughed with the joy of it.

But something important held me back, demanded my attention. Something I couldn't ignore.

I've dated a lot of women—but you're different, Jackie.

Was I? I wanted to believe him, but was this the moment I'd regret thirty years from now, just as keeping John Husted's starburst engagement ring could have been the most monumental mistake of my life? This time, I refused to rush into anything.

"I don't know."

Three honest, awful words in exchange for three words that had spun a fanciful world of dreams and promises mere moments ago.

Jack released my hands, putting enough empty space between us so I wanted nothing more than to grab the terrible words by their roots and pull them back as if they'd never been said. Instead, I clasped his hands, running my thumbs over the calluses there.

"I love you too," I finally said. "But this is sudden, and marriage is forever."

Or at least it was supposed to be. I had no intention of winding up like my mother and Black Jack Bouvier, even as my mother's warning about Jack echoed in my mind.

Don't be weak just because Jack Kennedy makes your knees tremble.

I sighed. "I need a little time to think about it."

Jack recovered a dim shadow of his prior smile, transforming once again into my daring trapeze artist as he pressed a kiss to the back of my hand. Not for the first time, I wondered what thoughts lurked behind those stormy eyes. "Of course," he said. "Just remember, I'm not the world's most patient man, all right?"

couldn't make up my mind over the demands of my heart, found myself blown about like a leaf in an autumn storm between which answer was right and which was a mistake. My father had said better a bad decision today than a good one three weeks late, but somehow, I didn't think that advice applied to marriage proposals.

What I needed was to run away, somewhere far from Jack and my mother's watchful eye.

I found the perfect escape when a family friend asked if I'd accompany her daughter to England for Queen Elizabeth's coronation, and when I mentioned the opportunity to my editor at the *Washington*

Times-Herald he requested I airmail daily articles with sketches on our neighbors across the pond. I left Washington like a thief in the night, only daring to telegraph Jack my plans when the ship was readying to depart.

My *Mayflower*-in-reverse crossing was blessedly uneventful, and coronation day dawned so gray and dreary that people on the street had donned their leather wellies, as if England had decided to swathe herself in everything decidedly British. I finished my tea and hurried down the hotel's staircase that morning, only to have the dapper desk clerk halt me with a tray of fresh cinnamon scones.

"Miss Bouvier!" He held up a finger, and I waited for him to lambaste me for the delivery of a crate of history books I'd purchased the day before, many of which were gifts I couldn't resist purchasing for Jack. *If I say yes, that is. If I say no . . . I suppose I can always give them to Hughdie.* Instead, the clerk surprised me by riffling through the wooden caddies behind the desk and retrieving a yellow Western Union telegram. "This arrived for you a half hour ago."

I tugged my wool jacket tighter. "I wasn't expecting a message today."

"Mind you, take an umbrella to the coronation," he said in that musical British accent as I tore open the envelope. "The weather is utter rubbish."

He might have said more; I couldn't hear anything over the words that echoed in my mind—all the *r*'s doing their best to disappear—as I read the telegram at least ten times before tucking it into my bag. The queen was being crowned today—a rare moment in history— and I would cover it, no matter the message that had already seared itself in my mind.

I found a place beneath an awning along the coronation route in time to sketch the queen's elaborate coach as it passed by, her breathtaking white gown shining like a beacon beneath the dull skies; the silk I knew was festooned with the floral emblems of her realm: the Tudor rose, Scottish thistle, and Welsh leek alongside several others.

Although Queen Elizabeth was already married to Prince Philip, she seemed a nervous young bride ready to wed her realm instead of a mere mortal. A cascade of flashbulbs erupted, yet she never flinched.

A royal bearing, I scribbled around the errant raindrops that spattered my notepad. *The queen was impervious to the trivialities of rain and cameramen. This was a moment for the ages, and she knew it.*

Then her coach turned a corner, and Elizabeth II was gone just as quickly as she'd come, bound for the austerity of Westminster Abbey.

I wished I were inside the Abbey, but only thirty journalists—all men—had been chosen to view the spectacle inside from the loft above the organ, which meant that I, a mere twenty-three-year-old woman, was left shivering in the morning cold. All this despite the fact that I'd read so much English history that I could have waxed poetic about the Imperial State Crown with its four pearls believed to have been the original Queen Elizabeth's earrings, or the coronation ring being slipped onto the new queen's finger that had been worn by every British monarch since William IV. (With the exception of Queen Victoria, whose fingers were too small.)

Instead, I waited.

My thoughts wandered then to Jack's easy smile and ready brilliance, the way the world seemed poised to fall at his feet. His telegram from this morning threatened to scorch my pocket.

JACKIE,

IT'S NO USE. I WAKE UP IN THE MORNING AND THINK OF YOU. I STUMBLE OVER MY WORDS DEBATING TRADE RESTRICTIONS ON KOREA WHILE MY MIND IS FULL OF A CERTAIN DARK-HAIRED NYMPH. I GO TO BED, AND GUESS WHAT? I THINK OF YOU.

HAVE I TOLD YOU THAT I LOVE YOU, JACKIE BOUVIER?

PLEASE DO YOUR PATRIOTIC DUTY AND PUT THIS POOR SENATOR OUT OF HIS MISERY.

WHAT'S YOUR ANSWER?

YOURS,
(I HOPE . . .)

JACK

I'd read enough novels to believe being in love meant being willing to do anything for the other person—starve to buy them bread and not mind living in Siberia with them like Raskolnikov's Sonya—and I'd always thought that every minute away from them would be hell.

Well, every minute away from Jack during this trip had been hell. Maybe I was supposed to spend the rest of my life with him.

You could be happy with Jack, a voice in the back of my mind murmured. *Confidante and companion to a powerful politician. God knows you're not made for a mundane sort of man.*

Yet could I—could any woman—be happy with the Gay Young Bachelor? Marrying Jack meant opening myself up to the possibility that he might stray, as most husbands did. Was I dooming myself to walk in my mother's shoes?

Stop it, Jackie. You are not your mother.

Jack and my father might be a pair of charming scoundrels, but my father had been driven away by my mother. I was *not* Janet Bouvier Auchincloss, and I'd prove it by never driving my husband away as she had.

History would not repeat itself.

After all, Jack was different than the other men I'd dated, the only one who challenged me and didn't make me choose between my intellect and love. I knew then that, for better or for worse, Jack had spoiled me for all other men. I found myself suddenly impatient to be home so I could see him again.

This time when the queen emerged to make her procession back to Buckingham Palace, draped in a rich purple velvet robe edged with cloudy puffs of ermine and glittering gold embroidery, it was my turn to smile.

I, Jackie Lee Bouvier, was witnessing history, and I thirsted for more, to be surrounded by important men and women, to watch important moments unfold.

I'd always believed being a reporter seemed a ticket out into the world, but John F. Kennedy would open that same door. A man like him could set the world on fire, and I'd be at his side every step of the way.

Because I couldn't help loving him.

I spotted Jack the moment my Pan Am flight touched the tarmac at Friendship International in Baltimore. I hadn't told him when I was returning, had no idea how he'd figured it out, yet here he was, waiting for me.

And I loved him all the more for it.

His thick hair ruffled like golden seagrass in the setting sun as the jet plane approached, and I envied his apparent nonchalance as he tucked his wayward silk tie into his jacket and raised a hand to wave, as if he somehow knew which tiny window was mine. Yet I recognized the way his fingers snapped against his thigh, the only tell that he wasn't quite so assured as he otherwise appeared.

I wanted to be the first one down the stairs, but I made myself allow every other passenger to disembark before me.

Make him wait, I thought to myself. *Jack's the kind of man who needs the chase.*

"This month has been torture," he said when I finally stepped onto the tarmac. "I need an answer, Jackie. I can't wait anymore."

Make him wait.

And I did, counting ten slow measures before I lifted my gaze to his bright eyes, filled with the same swirl of emotions I suspected was on my face. I'd always wanted to choose my moment, and this was it.

"Yes, Jack." I spoke softly, words meant for only him. "I'll marry you."

He surprised me by whirling me around once, then slipped a ring onto my finger with perfect precision, as if he'd spent all my time away practicing for just this moment. The ring was breathtaking, a diamond I guessed to be nearly three carats next to an emerald of equal size, bookended with glittering baguette diamond accents.

Unique and unexpected, just like the man himself.

"I'll never go swimming again," I murmured in awe, well and truly stunned. With Jack as my husband, no more would I be reliant on my stepfather's goodwill and fifty-dollar-per-month allowance. I'd be a Kennedy. "I'd sink straight to the bottom."

"I never do anything in half measures." Jack's gaze warmed as he drew me so close that I could feel the heat of a small sun radiating from him. "I'm going to make you the happiest woman in the world, Jackie. Stay by my side and you'll be the envy of every woman from here to Timbuktu. Hell, I'll even buy you the whole of Timbuktu if you want."

In that fairy-tale moment, I believed him. I would be like Queen Elizabeth, only instead of being draped in regal purple robes, I was poised to assume the mantle of the Kennedys.

And that meant that suddenly everything was possible.

The Kennedys' seventeen-room white clapboard villa in the affluent village of Hyannis Port had a commanding view of Nantucket Sound, yet the house itself peered down at me, as if sizing me up and finding me wanting. I'd expected a family flush with cash to own a classic and well-ordered estate, yet there was little that was appealing about this sprawling compound at Hyannis Port. Save for the American flag that flapped in the salt breeze on the tall pole outside and the small vintage World War II plane on the lawn, it felt like an empty shell of a house, nothing beautiful or inspiring about the plain tile and white walls. Surely a family with more money than the Pope could hire an architect. Or a decorator.

Safe upon the solid rock the ugly houses stand . . .

I ignored the flutter of Edna St. Vincent Millay's poem and the nerves tunneling deep into my belly as Jack helped me out of the car, his hand lingering on the small of my back. I'd met Jack's parents already—I liked his father, and his mother had been coolly polite at an earlier campaign rally—but who knew if I'd measure up in the rest of the Kennedy eyes?

It seemed I was about to find out, for the front door swung open and Mr. Kennedy—the man who might have run for president once—burst onto the veranda. Jack's father would have been as at ease on a tennis court or the Senate floor as he jogged our way, one arm raised in greeting and his glacial blue eyes twinkling.

"It's about damn time! I see you've finally decided to share Jackie with us." It was easy to trace Jack's boundless energy and enthusiasm as Mr. Kennedy enveloped his son in a hug that might have broken a lesser man. He rested one hand on Jack's shoulder, the other on mine. "She's a winner, isn't she, son?"

Jack flashed a matching smile, one that seemed to parse some secret message between father and son. "Only the best for us, Dad."

"We don't want any losers around here," Jack's father informed me. "In this family we want winners. Rose and the others are eager to meet you, kiddo, and then we'll have the photo shoot. The photographers want a shot of you kids on the sailboat."

Perhaps I'd heard him wrong. "Photo shoot? Sailboat?"

Jack, too, seemed caught by surprise. "Dad . . ."

Mr. Kennedy threw up his hands. "It's just a little cover story for *Life*. I suggested they call it 'Senator Kennedy Goes A-Courting.'"

The last thing I wanted was to be put on display for the Kennedys and all of America, but I supposed this came with the territory when marrying a senator. Rather than frown in dismay, I reminded myself that there had always been at least two Jackies: the puckish and spon-taneous free spirit who loved raucous foxhunts and could converse about any topic at the most sophisticated cocktail party, and the soft-spoken Vassar scholar who preferred solitude and reading about those same parties from the pages of her favorite books. It was the free spirit who spoke to Mr. Kennedy now.

"I haven't had a photo shoot since I was a debutante. It sounds like the perfect way to spend an afternoon." I offered a vibrant smile to Mr. Kennedy even as I squeezed Jack's hand. "I'm so looking forward to meeting all of Jack's siblings."

"This way then, kiddo." Mr. Kennedy winked, his hand on my elbow as we walked up the circular driveway. The *Life* crew waited on the side lawn with their cameras and nearly broke their necks to catch a glimpse of us. I recalled that Mr. Kennedy had run several Holly-wood film studios back in the 1920s; it was obvious he had passed on that star-making expertise into politics. It was an odd sensation, being the center of such rapt attention. I wasn't sure I enjoyed it.

I hadn't noticed Rose Kennedy waiting on the broad porch, her chair hidden by a low retaining wall and her face further hidden by a floppy sunhat. "It's a family ritual," Jack warned me in a low voice. "No one arrives at Hyannis without first greeting my mother."

The tiny matriarch—Rose—stood and removed the clip-on shades from her eyeglasses. I was almost disappointed there were no famous quotations pinned to her sweater, which Jack had warned me she memorized for use in future dinner discussions. She extended a limp hand, her iron jaw set. "Welcome again, Jacqueline, this time to the family." Her strident voice reminded me of a duck with laryngitis, even as she scarcely deigned to touch my fingers. However, her words of welcome were friendly enough, and I liked the way she pronounced my name in the French manner: *Jack-leen.*

"Thank you, Mrs. Kennedy. Believe me when I say I'm so pleased to be here."

I wondered for a moment what it would have been like having this woman as a mother. Jack had told me that she was difficult, but I'd imagined Rose Kennedy as the silent heroine of her family's saga, losing her eldest son in the war against Germany and then her favorite daughter in a tragic plane crash, followed by the incapacitation of her daughter Rosemary, who had been committed to a psychiatric hospital. I knew better than to ever bring her up.

Jack might have been tougher than barbed wire to survive his PT boat accident, but in the story I'd written in my mind, his mother would outlast the diamonds I now wore on my left hand.

The remainder of the Kennedys awaited inside. Whereas the house itself was unimpressive, the entire windswept family shone in their white linens and summer tans, assembled on tasteful chintz couches as if they were a tableau arranged for a portrait of the perfect American family.

I might as well be a gypsy next to them. A dark-haired, flat-chested, penniless gypsy.

"Allow me to introduce my daughters." Rose prompted three young women with impossibly long legs and great manes of hair like Shetland ponies to nod to me in turn. "This is Eunice. Patricia. And Jean."

Their gazes flicked over me, assessing and scrutinizing. Passing judgment. "We hear you were Queen Debutante of the Year back in 1947," one who might have been a female version of Jack said. Perhaps Eunice.

I brushed away the empty accolade, made my voice soft. It was a trick my mother had taught Lee and me whenever our emotions threatened to run away with us. "I believe your debuts were quite successful as well."

"We hope you're good at tennis, Jackie," the youngest chimed in. "Kennedy women are more than just pretty debutantes."

Ah . . . so this was a test. Or a game. Either way, I didn't plan to lose.

"I'm passable on the court," I said. "And wasn't your sister Kathleen dubbed the Debutante of 1938 by the English press, back when your father served as ambassador?"

The youngest Shetland pony retreated a little into her chair. *Touché.* Mr. Kennedy cleared his throat, and I almost thought he winked at me. "This here is my boy Ted," he said, prompting the young man with the square face next to me to rise and offer a hesitant nod. These Kennedys were all made from the same clay—hair, teeth, and tongues from the same reserve.

"And I'm Bobby." Jack's handsome middle brother spoke with more bombast than the rest, as if he was accustomed to being over-looked. He might have passed for Jack's twin, save that his eyes were a glacial blue instead of gray-green and he was slightly smaller, but with a presence equal to Jack's. Bobby perched on the arm of the sofa, leaned forward with one hand outstretched to shake mine.

Jack gestured toward the pretty woman with a brown bob and prominent teeth sitting next to Bobby. "This saint here is Ethel, who is well on her way to birthing an entire precinct. She's given me a niece and a nephew, with another on the way. How she puts up with my runt of a brother, I'll never understand."

Bobby preened like a rooster at sunrise while Ethel tilted her chin at me. "Did you always wish to be a debutante, Jackie?"

I gave an impish half smile. "Actually, when I was little, I dreamed of being a ballerina."

Ethel's gaze fell to my wedge heels. "With those feet, you'd have been better taking up soccer. You'll fit right in with the Kennedys, who love any sport that involves lobbing a ball about a field."

I forced myself not to shift in my size 10A heels at her bluntness. Saint, indeed. If Ethel was trying to make me feel more comfortable, her attempt had failed miserably.

Bobby turned his full attention to me, perhaps to deflect the conversation away from his wife. "Well, Jackie, I'm glad to see that my big brother took my advice to nab you while he still had the chance. Dad and I both agreed you're the perfect senator's wife: good-looking, elegant, Sorbonne and Vassar educated. . . . And you're willing to put up with Jack." He gave a wry chuckle. "He should have married you on your first date."

I started at that. Had Jack chosen me because I'd help him win elections?

No, he loves me. I'm sure of it.

"I'm afraid that's quite a lot of expectation to live up to." I cleared my throat, unsure how I felt about learning that the Kennedy men had sat around and discussed me, as if I were a component of some battle strategy. "I hope I won't disappoint."

"With Jack's energy and your polish, you two will be unstoppable." Bobby lifted both hands to frame Jack and me, as if taking a long angle shot. "This country is bored with stodgy Roosevelts and Eisenhowers, and I can already imagine you two on the covers of *Life* and *Time*."

I'd been warned by Jack that I'd either love or hate his younger brother; that people claimed he was an arrogant prick born with a silver spoon in his mouth. So far, I liked Bobby with his forthright manner and open smile. Still . . .

Is politics all these Kennedy men think about? I wondered to myself.

I'd soon discover the answer was yes, with very few exceptions.

Rose clapped her hands. "We're on a tight schedule, and the photographers are waiting. Eunice, take Jackie to find something more appropriate to wear on the water."

I glanced down at my white summer dress and pearls, hating that Rose was right about them being out of place on a sailboat. I shot Jack a lingering look as Eunice beckoned me to follow, but he was already deep in discussion with his father. The words *Korea* and *Panmunjom Declaration* came up, so I suspected he wouldn't surface for air anytime soon.

Sink or swim, Jackie. The whole family—and probably even Jack—is testing you.

"She's pretty enough," one of the other sisters said behind my back, just loud enough so I could hear it.

"For a vintage deb," the third whispered. "Nineteen forty-seven was a long time ago."

I forced myself to swallow my ire and smoothed my expression into marble as I followed Eunice, accepting the sleeveless gingham shirt and soft cotton shorts she wordlessly offered.

I surprised myself by actually enjoying the photo shoot. The *Life* crew started in the house, snapping staged shots of me gazing at the wall of Kennedy family portraits interspersed with photos of Mr. Kennedy as ambassador, posing with a potpourri of the world's royalty. I envisioned Jack with various kings and prime ministers in pictures that might one day adorn this same wall, wondered how many would show me at his side.

"It's time to head onto the lawn," Rose commanded the photographers. "We've always been a very active family. I'm sure Jackie can keep up."

With my soccer-sized feet? You bet I can.

Together, Jack and I tossed a football on the lawn and tested my softball batting skills. I quickly discerned that the Kennedys were the rough-and-tumble type who reveled in touch football matches that ended in near-concussions. Thanks to my father, I could hold my own on most playing fields, but it was with some relief that we finally put aside the balls and bats and headed down to the Kennedy's private beach to skip rocks in the surf.

"Fluent in every language under the sun, a walking encyclopedia of history, more athletic than my sisters, and stunningly beautiful to boot," Jack murmured as he passed me the perfect skipping rock. "Is there anything the amazing Jaqueline Bouvier can't do?"

"I'm horrible at crocheting. And don't even ask me to sing."

He leaned in close as if to tell a joke, both of us keenly aware of all the eyes on us. "You have no idea how badly I want to kiss you right now."

To which I gave an impish grin as the camera clicked away, even as my insides turned molten. The very thought of Jack's kisses turned my knees to water, for I'd discovered that the touch of his lips to mine set off a veritable bonfire over every inch of my body. "I'll hold you to that later."

His raised eyebrow asked only one question. *Promise?*

To which I answered with a playful jab in his ribs. *You better believe it.*

I reveled in this secret language we suddenly seemed to possess, as if we were meant for only each other. He grinned so I could almost hear his voice in my head. *I can't wait.*

The outdoor yard shots were fun, but even more, I loved leaving the rest of the Kennedys on shore so I could watch Jack maneuver with ease around the deck of the sailboat. He, too, had changed into khaki shorts and his white shirt collar was unbuttoned, allowing me a rare glimpse of his carefree side when he tossed off the mooring line to set us free from the pier.

"So, Jackie," the reporter asked as we skimmed over whitecaps, the briny ocean breeze tumbling both my hair and Jack's as the photographer snapped an avalanche of pictures. "How does it feel to be engaged to the handsomest young member of the U.S. Senate?"

I glanced at this man I was soon to marry, both of us beaming and laughing with sheer happiness, and wished this afternoon would never end, that we might stay suspended in this time and space forever. "So far it's an amazing adventure!"

After the photo shoot, we found ourselves alone in the formal dining room, the rest of the family on the lawn finishing a game of pigskin while my stomach rumbled at the faint aroma of the famous Kennedy seafood chowder wafting from the kitchens. I reached down to tousle Jack's hair from where he already sat at the table, not realizing the *Life* crew was still there until I heard the camera clicking away.

The photographer grinned. "That's going to be my favorite shot." He retrieved a card from inside his jacket pocket. "You two are both so photogenic; feel free to contact me anytime you have a story idea."

I contemplated tossing the card in the rubbish bin, instead tucked it into my pocketbook as Jack showed him out. One never knew when a friendly member of the press might come in handy.

I was gazing out over the lawn, watching the Kennedy vigor—or *vi-ga*, as they all pronounced it—on full display when Bobby did a victory dance following a touchdown. Just watching all their Irish energy wore me out, but I liked the Kennedys' refreshing contrast to my own reserved upbringing.

Rose joined me at the window, hands folded before her and her voice so quiet I had to strain to hear her. "I've lost two children to two separate plane crashes, Jacqueline," she said without preamble, "and another to incapacitation. Jack is our eldest now—our golden boy, as his father calls him." Her gaze never flickered from her sons out tussling over the ball, where Jack had joined in for the final down. "He needs someone—a proper Catholic girl with both her feet on the ground—to keep him from burning himself out, to help him soar without letting him crash into the sun." She crossed her arms, finally needled a glance at me. "Are you that woman, Jackie?"

Her lips were twisted so tight they almost disappeared, but I detected a cold glimmer of fear in the eyes of the tiny, birdlike woman before me. In the story that unfurled in my mind, Rose Kennedy was scared—terrified even—of losing another child as she'd lost three others before. I refused to take offense at her pointed question, reminded myself that she was only protecting her son as any mother would.

I drew a steadying breath, watching Jack intercept the ball and run full tilt toward the makeshift goal on the darkening lawn. "Jack's not fragile," I said. "I love him, and he loves me. That's all that matters."

"And you believe that's enough?"

"I do." I touched her elbow in a gesture of solidarity. "I really do."

I was thankful when the rest of the clan chose that moment to tumble red-cheeked and sweating into the dining room. Rose clapped her hands to motion us all to the table and allowed a servant to ladle chowder into the waiting bowls from a giant silver tureen. "I assume you've resigned from the *Washington Times-Herald*?" she asked before unfolding her serviette onto her tiny lap. "Journalism is terribly raffish for a well-bred girl. Don't you agree, Jack?"

When Jack didn't answer and instead fell into conversation with Bobby, I wanted to tap him—hard—upside his beautiful head with the silver soup ladle. Until he glanced in my direction, that is. And winked.

He's leaving me to fight my own battles. He trusts me to hold my own, even against his mother.

I took a demure bite of chowder, my mouth filling with the salty

tang of the Atlantic before dabbing my lips with the starched serviette. "I plan to work until just before the wedding." Part of me wished
I could continue after we were married, but that just wasn't done.
"I've enjoyed all the travel opportunities the *Times-Herald* has af-
forded me."

Truth be told, I was going to miss seeing my work in print. The
Times-Herald had featured my sketches of the coronation on their front
pages at least three times, and I'd carefully pasted them into a scrapbook of all my work, including my interviews with Eisenhower's niece
and the young Senate pages.

Later, Jack tugged me into the empty sitting room, took my hand,
and pressed it to his lips. "I'll take you to the far side of the moon and
back if that's what you want, Jackie. All you have to do is say the word."

"So you *were* listening."

"Always." He pressed my palm to his cheek. "I'll get our coats."

I waited in the darkened room, perusing a wall of family pictures
when Bobby's silhouette darkened the doorway. "Mind if I join you?"

"Of course."

He popped the top off a bottle of Budweiser and pocketed the cap.
"You're fierce, Jackie, and you're a good Catholic girl who has won
over both my parents, which is a goddamn victory in and of itself."
He took a long draft of the beer. "I hope you know what you've signed
up for in agreeing to marry Jack."

I frowned. "I'm marrying the man I love."

He gave me a wistful smile on those lips that were so like Jack's.
"I've never seen my brother so besotted. Don't get me wrong, I think
you're exactly what Jack needs, but you should know what sort of man
he was before he met you."

Another test in a day already full of them.

"I know about the women," I said to Bobby. "And that's not Jack,
at least not anymore."

It did give me pause that Bobby—who had so enthusiastically endorsed our engagement—was now trying to warn me of his brother's
flaws. Yet I was starting to believe—or at least, to hope—that falling

in love with me was crafting Jack into an entirely different man than Bobby now felt the need to caution me about.

"Don't say you weren't warned."

Jack arrived then, my wool jacket slung over his arm. "Just what are you two talking about that has you looking so serious?"

Bobby gave an innocent whistle. "Oh, you know, domestic affairs and the state of the dollar."

Jack cocked his head as he helped me into my coat. "Really? The state of the dollar?"

Bobby laughed, ran a hand over the back of his neck. "Well, I might have been betting your fiancée a dollar that she'd realize what a pain in the ass you are and call the whole thing off."

"You'd better bring that dollar to St. Mary's on September twelfth." I laughed. "I'll be the one in front wearing the white dress."

Bobby surprised me by hugging me first, and then Jack. "Congratulations, you two," he said. "I couldn't be happier for you both."

"I think Jack's a topside fellow, but he's lucky to get so lovely a girl as his bride," Mr. Kennedy said when he hugged me good-bye. "See you at the wedding, kiddo."

I tipped my chin at them and flashed my most blinding smile as I took Jack's hand, my eyes flicking to Bobby's. "That you will."

I'd rise to this challenge, and every other challenge this family threw at me.

Because while the closed-off Kennedy clan didn't settle for second best, they'd soon learn one thing about me.

Neither did I.

You look daintier than Dresden porcelain, Jacks. I'll bet the society columns will even use the word *timeless*." Lee, my matron of honor, adjusted my rose point lace veil that our grandmother had once worn while the rest of my bridesmaids chattered like spring chickadees around us. "There's never been a lovelier bride," Lee added. "Except me, of course."

I rolled my eyes heavenward. I loved the new gleaming single-strand pearl choker at my throat, and the antique veil was tolerable, but I hated—no, absolutely loathed—the silk taffeta dress I'd let Mother bully me into choosing, a shade of unflattering ivory with a portrait neckline and tight banding on the bodice that emphasized my washboard chest. Even the skirt was ugly, with clumsy circles of tucked taffeta better suited to parlor curtains.

I threw up my gloved hands. "Timeless, *mon cul*." I glanced around to ensure no one else had heard the profanity. In my mind, it was fine to curse, so long as it wasn't in public. And cursing in French hardly counted, although my mother would never agree. Thankfully, she was seeing to my other bridesmaids at that moment. "I look like a lampshade."

Lee chortled with laughter. "A very expensive lampshade."

A demon grappled with my stomach as I let my fingers trace the diamond and pearl bracelet Jack had sent over this morning, tiny nautical ropes carved into the white gold that called to mind his love of sailing. The day had dawned bright and windy, and St. Mary's imposing stone walls hummed with the expectations of the eight hundred guests crammed into the sanctuary. I straightened my shoulders and grasped the bouquet of pink orchids and gardenias, focusing on the graceful curve of their velvety petals as I willed my hands to stop trembling.

Only one song left until Mendelssohn's "Wedding March" . . .

"You're going to be so happy with Jack," said Lee, but she bit her lip in a way that made my heart stutter.

"What is it?"

"Mother didn't tell you, did she?" Lee tried to distract me by spritzing a luxurious dash of my favorite fragrance—Joy by Jean Patou—into the air, beckoning with a lift of her knifepoint chin for me to walk through the decadent mist of jasmine and roses.

"Tell me what?"

"Daddy can't walk you down the aisle."

I was almost relieved that some calamity hadn't befallen Jack, but it was impossible to imagine that my father—rascal though he was—wouldn't be at my side on this momentous day, cracking jokes the entire trip down the aisle. "What? Why?"

My mother surprised me by clearing her throat behind me. "Because your miserable excuse for a father imbibed himself into a stupor last night after I informed him that he wasn't invited to the rehearsal dinner at the Clambake Club."

So that was why I'd missed my father last night. My mother's ability to hold a grudge was relentless, but on my wedding day? "Mummy . . ."

She held up a hand against my growl. "Black Jack Bouvier drank Scotch all night into this morning. He won't be fit for human consumption until at least tomorrow, as he's currently passed out in his room at the Hotel Viking."

"He was probably drinking out of misery and loneliness," Lee said, and I agreed with her. "It's not his fault."

"Do not make excuses for that man." Mother pressed two fingers to the bridge of her nose, and I could imagine the force of will it took to keep her from launching into a tirade about the drinking and womanizing that had led to their scandalous divorce. Despite her warning against Jack before our engagement, she'd surprised me by giving her grudging support to our marriage. Miraculously—perhaps only because this was my wedding day—she sighed now, one hand falling to her side while the other beckoned impatiently to someone waiting on the other side of the door. "Hughdie will give you away instead."

I tried not to let my disappointment show as my chubby-cheeked stepfather peeked around the corner. Hughdie was kind and gentle, with an endearing stutter, yet I still yearned for my dashing rounder of a father who had sped to my Vassar dormitory bearing gifts of movie magazines and gardenias. Of course, Hughdie hadn't boasted to me that he'd had all my friends' mothers, when I was ten years old, while standing in the school yard with him during Parents' Day at Miss Porter's School.

All men are rats.

God above, I'd die if Jack and I ended up like my mother and father. *But that will never happen,* I thought to myself, repeating what was fast becoming a personal mantra. *Because Jack is not a rat. And I am not my mother.*

My sister seemed to read my turmoil of emotions as the organist punched out the initial vibrant notes of the "Wedding March." "That's your cue, Jacks." She grasped my shoulders and turned me toward the sanctuary as if she were the older, wiser sister. "Better not leave your handsome prince waiting for his fey princess."

Her words were a strain of soft music that soothed me. I breathed in the scent of my bouquet to calm my nerves, then took Hughdie's waiting arm as the rest of my bridesmaids filed into place.

My heart thudded a staccato beat as the sanctuary doors swept open and the hundreds of assembled celebrities, diplomats, and Washington power brokers rose in unison, expectant faces all swiveling in my direction. My gaze fell on Jack waiting for me at the altar and stayed there until the organ music subsided, leaving just the two of us in the entire world. The recent story in *Life* claimed that Jack was like any young man in love, but they were wrong, for Jack could never be ordinary. Today he outshone even royalty in his morning coat and pinstriped trousers, the exquisite sunlight from the glorious rainbow of stained-glass windows painting him with the hand of God. I could hardly tear my gaze from him as I stepped in sync with my stepfather down the white satin runner, passing stone arches and columns bedecked with creeping vines and hothouse orchids to where a silent army of ushers flanked Jack.

An insistent flutter near Jack's side demanded my attention as my flotilla of bridesmaids assumed their positions.

Bobby Kennedy seemed out of place among the cluster of florid and beefy men in bright blue suits, a wide grin on his face and a crisp dollar bill waving from his pocket. I almost smiled, especially as he mouthed a silent message to me. *You win.*

I swallowed a chortle of laughter, then lifted my gaze to Jack as Hughdie gave us his blessing. I wasn't the staunchest Catholic—

although my mother had made sure that as girls, both Lee and I attended Mass regularly and volunteered three times a week at the Helper of the Holy Souls convent—but there was no doubt that God had brought Jack and me together for a reason. While it was anyone's guess what course our lives together would take, ours was a story yet unwritten. A beautiful blank page.

Joyous laughter bubbled in my throat, and my heart soared to the heavens when Jack clasped my hands and the archbishop began the ceremonial High Mass with a special blessing from Pope Pius XII.

Are we really going to do this?

To which Jack only lifted both brows, eyes sparkling. *Sure. Why not?*

I'd wanted someone to set my life on fire and Jack Kennedy was going to fan those flames. A man like him could turn a trip through hell into a lark, but instead, we were going to soar our way toward the sun.

Together, we listened to the benediction and repeated our vows, Jack's bold and assured, and mine in a voice so tremulous with joy I doubted whether the front row could hear me, much less God himself. Finally, the archbishop motioned for us to turn to the guests still seated in their pews.

"Throughout this ceremony, John and Jacqueline have vowed, in our presence, to be loyal and loving toward each other, and have given themselves in holy wedlock. What God has joined together, let no one put asunder." He looked to Jack, his solemnity breaking way to reveal a smile of blinding happiness. "I now pronounce you man and wife. You may kiss your bride!"

Kiss me he did, in a glorious tempest I wished would never end.

The day remained sunny and windswept as we retreated to Hammersmith Farm for the reception, Danseuse and the rest of the horses in the pasture doing their utmost to ignore the fourteen hundred Gatsbyesque guests that mingled beneath the palatial white tents on the back lawn behind the gabled Big House. I did my best to ignore the swarm of reporters in the sound-and-light spectacle that Mr. Kennedy had insisted upon, overruling both Mother's and my objections, but their cameras clicked away nonstop. Still, not even the torrential cascade of their flashbulbs could mar my happiness.

We ate, we laughed, we danced.

How I wished it would never end!

The final notes of "I Married an Angel" had scarcely faded away before Jack clasped my hand and tugged me past the windmill toward the wooden fence at the edge of my parents' estate, both of us laughing as if we'd tippled too much wedding punch. A gust of wind picked up my veil just as Jack looked ready to say something, then seemed to decide against it.

"What is it?" I asked, ignoring the cameraman who had followed us, the rapid-fire sound of his Arriflex capturing this moment forever.

Jack shook his head. "I was just thinking that I truly did marry an angel, that you're my raison d'être." He laughed at my surprise. "Was that right? Because I asked Bobby to look it up, and so help me, if he taught me to say you're my wrinkled raisin—"

I pressed a finger over his lips, nodded over the sudden tightness in my throat. "It's right," I whispered. "It's perfect."

You're my reason for being.

Jack had actually said that. To me.

Jack held my hand over his heart. "I'm far from perfect, Jackie, but I hope I can make you ecstatically happy, that all our dreams come true."

Dreams.

I took his words as a sign from above. And I smiled, even as I pressed a piece of heavy cream parchment into his hand. "Your wedding present. It's not as elegant as your gift to me"—I raised my wrist bearing his tennis bracelet—"but I mean every word."

He unfolded it to discover the poem I'd labored these past weeks to write, agonizing over every line. I watched as he read, flushing with nervous pleasure as he read my favorite bit aloud.

Meanwhile in Massachusetts Jack Kennedy dreamed.
Walking the shore by the Cape Cod Sea
Of all the things he was going to be.
On a green lawn his white house stands . . .

The words trailed off, but then he repeated that final line as if in a daze. "'On a green lawn his white house stands . . .'"

"You're going to do amazing things, Jack," I whispered and touched his nose to mine. "And I'm going to be beside you every step of the way."

For this was his dream. And now it was mine.

CHAPTER

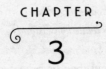

3

September 1953

cherished our honeymoon, the smattering of days we spent in a darling pink villa perched atop red-clay cliffs overlooking Acapulco's ocean. I'd first seen the memorable house as a girl, while traveling with Mother and Hughdie, had mentioned how I'd loved it to Mr. Kennedy. He astounded me by locating the villa and arranged with the owner—a former president of Mexico—to rent it. This was my first inkling of what it was like to be a Kennedy, to possess an endless fortune that could fling open previously locked doors. Jack and I spent our days sunning ourselves like godless heathens at the beach, Jack's boundless energy goading me on as we waterskied around the bay, me laughing while Jack leaped over the wake behind the boat like a lifeguard on the Riviera.

And the nights . . .

We spent the nights worshipping each other, until I finally understood the meaning of the word *honeymoon*, and laughingly nicknamed my husband Bunny for his appetite and stamina.

"That's not a very masculine nickname," he growled one night in the dark. "I'm not sure how I feel about that."

"Too late." My laughter turned to a gasp of pleasure as he worked his magic up the inside of my thigh. "I swear it will stay our little secret."

Those moments were indeed sweeter than the clearest honey, but I had only a week, not a full month, before we had to abandon our sun-drenched private paradise for reality, bound first for a bullfight viewing in Mexico City and then to California, where it seemed everyone wanted to claim a piece of Jack's time.

I blinked, and our honeymoon was over.

"You're going where?" I asked Jack from the open-air pool patio of Beverly House—the storied mansion had once belonged to publishing magnate William Randolph Hearst—on our final day. I felt like I'd hardly seen Jack since we'd landed in California. Oh, we'd been together in this land of golden honeyed sunshine but usually surrounded by a cadre of his old shipmates, whom he'd telephoned as soon as we'd arrived in town. It felt as if he was shuttering something away after the wedding, as if he needed to keep some integral part of himself separate from me.

And I hated it. Loathed it with everything in me.

"We're off to a football game." He shrugged into a camel-colored sweater, then ran a hand through his hair, mussing it the way I liked. "Don't worry, I've asked one of the wives to show you around. Try not to get into too much trouble."

I hesitated. Which Jackie should answer him, the free spirit he'd courted or the scholar-turned-picture-perfect-wife? *Neither.* The disappointed wife won out, for while I didn't want to seem petulant, neither could I hide my dismay. "It's our last day, Jack."

"We have our whole lives together." He stuffed a set of keys into his pocket. "It's not every day I can sit at the ten-yard line with my old friends from the war."

Was I already turning into one of those wives who harped on their husbands? Like my mother?

I suppressed a shudder. No, I was Jacqueline Bouvier Kennedy, and I'd never before needed a man to keep me entertained. *Nom de Dieu*, I wasn't going to start now.

I banished the disappointed wife and forced the free-spirited me to give Jack a winsome smile and tilt my cheek for a kiss. "Try not to miss me too much."

"Impossible." Jack surprised me by kissing my lips instead, tasting of the autumn strawberries and Champagne we'd nibbled for break-fast, so my blood sang and my toes curled in their silk bedroom slippers.

Until a car honked from outside, three long blasts that heralded the raucous arrival of his football-loving former shipmates. I shivered when Jack pulled away, holding my breath and hoping there was a chance he'd change his mind and stay with me.

Instead, he shoved his arms into a black gabardine sports coat. "I'll see you tonight, kid."

Even his new pet name for me—"kid," so similar to his father's—reminded me that my husband had lived a full life before we'd met, that I lacked over a decade of experience compared to him.

But tomorrow we'd be back to Washington, to the Senate and our families. . . .

His family. Whom he'd proposed we live with upon our return.

Mon Dieu . . .

"I'm going to make some calls about finding a house to rent back home." I rose and zipped his jacket, my fingers idly brushing his collarbones. The thought of living even for a few weeks with his parents made me cringe, of missing the chance to be proper newlyweds.

"I'm sure you'll find a perfect one," Jack said.

Perfect be damned, I thought as I watched him go, envying his self-assured swagger walking down the drive, as if he expected the world to fall at his feet, which it so often did. While I wouldn't mind sharing a house with Jack's father, I'd have sooner lived in Poe's macabre House of Usher than with Rose and her lemon-lipped daughters.

And I did find a perfect dollhouse of a rental in Georgetown, only it wasn't available until after New Year's. Which meant we went from our honeymoon to sharing the holidays with Jack's family at Palm Beach.

God help me.

Here we are," Jack said as we pulled into the drive. "La Guerida."
The unseasonable Florida humidity made me feel in need of another shower despite the early hour. I cast a critical eye on the Ken-

nedy's vaguely Spanish villa, which I'd heard described as Bastard-Spanish-Moorish-Romanesque-Renaissance-Bull-Market-Damn-the-Expense.

Not even Shakespeare could have penned a more apt description.

I was glad I had on my sunglasses, since the garish house with its mildewed, peeling paint threatened to make my eyes bleed. Still, Jack had many fond memories within these walls, and with a little luck, we'd make some memories of our own on this trip.

Jack opened the car door for me, his thumb brushing my wrist in such a sensual way that I almost missed the wince that passed over his face.

"Are you all right?"

"Fine." He rubbed his lower back, and I wondered if that lingering injury spurred his endless energy, since his distaste for sitting still seemed directly correlated to the level of pain in his back. "The plane ride felt unusually long."

I slid my hands beneath his jacket and used my thumbs to knead the muscles along the base of his spine, wishing there wasn't a shirt in my way. "Well, now we're here."

"Welcome to paradise." He kissed my nose. "Our home away from home."

I followed him down the wide lawn surrounded by squat palm trees and listened as he pointed out the tennis court and turquoise swimming pool. Then he gestured to a wooden structure, its door opened to reveal benches along the inner walls. "Whatever you do, don't go in there."

"Why?"

"My father calls it his bull pen." He waggled his eyebrows. "He uses it to sunbathe in the nude."

That explained Joe Kennedy's perpetual tan. I covered my mouth with my hands, but a peal of laughter burst free as Jack grinned and shook a stern finger at me. "Consider yourself warned. Our room is over there." He pointed to a ground-level room with French doors that opened onto the sprawling tennis court. Not much in the way of privacy, but I was starting to realize the Kennedys were open books, at least among each other.

"Jack!" Rose Kennedy's strident voice made me jump as she stalked across the pristine stone walkway. "We expected you a half hour ago. Didn't you receive the schedule I sent?"

To which Jack only shrugged. "Our flight was delayed."

In truth, Jack had driven me past every palm tree and grain of sand along the scenic route to his parents' compound, so I knew he must have seen the schedule in question.

Now Rose pursed her lips until I feared she'd swallow them. "You're looking thin," she said to her son.

Jack blinked as if he'd never heard his mother comment on his welfare, but then he polished his features into his close-the-deal smile. "Don't worry, it's nothing serious. Just Jackie's cooking."

To which I poked his ribs. "Jack's taking a speed-reading course at Georgetown, so I enrolled in a class on French cooking. Unfortunately, my soufflés sometimes resemble crepes."

In fact, to my surprise, Jack had even joined me once in the kitchen to measure flour and separate eggs, for I'd discovered that above all, one of my husband's best traits was his bottomless curiosity. Whatever I was interested in, Jack became interested in. After my recent absorption with French furniture, Jack had beamed with pride to recognize a Louis XVI console table, had also snatched my recent read on the eighteenth century and learned all of Louis XV's mistresses before I had.

So many men just wanted to talk about themselves, but Jack? He wanted to learn and know everything, so I sometimes teased that if I was to sketch him I'd draw a tiny body with an enormous head.

Rose's nostrils actually flared. "I see." She turned on a heel. "Jack," she snapped over her shoulder at us, as if we were faithful dogs instead of her son and daughter-in-law. "You're due to talk to your father from now until four o'clock, followed by drinks in the main room. Jackie, you'll sit with Ethel and me. Dinner is at seven fifteen, which does not mean seven sixteen."

And like that, we were reduced to recalcitrant children. I knew I should hurry after Rose, but it was a small act of rebellion to fall purposefully far behind.

Fifteen days until our house would be ready in Georgetown . . .

I awoke a few days later to an unnatural Christmas morning full of sun and the sound of the ocean surf, sans snowmen, sleigh bells, and pine trees. How I longed to don my heaviest wool jacket, saddle up Danseuse, and lose myself amid the silence of gently falling snow all afternoon. Instead, I slipped into a festive crimson sundress and tugged hard at an obstinate dark curl before the mirror, closing one eye and imagining myself with a mane of lustrous Kennedy-blond hair.

Jack came up behind me, nuzzled my ear. "Ready for the Kennedy gift exchange?"

"Actually . . ." I retrieved a brightly wrapped package from where I'd hidden it in a suitcase. It had been difficult to choose Jack's gift, given that the Kennedys didn't go in for snuffboxes, Fabergé eggs, or Persian rugs and instead spent their money on buying votes. My gift was humble, but heartfelt. "Will you open mine now?"

He cocked his head. "Are you daring me to break my mother's ironclad rules?"

I gave him an impish grin. "All the more reason, don't you think?"

"I like the way your mind works, kid."

It was easy to imagine Jack as a boy on Christmas morning as he eagerly tore the silver ribbon from the package.

"Paints?" he asked after he'd torn away the paper. I'd sometimes caught Jack doodling—often sailboats—in the margins of his Senate papers, and this wooden box of watercolors was the best money could buy, the vibrant palette inside like drops stolen from a leprechaun's rainbow.

"This is my cunning way of making you sit still for more than two minutes." I bit my lip, realizing how silly the gift seemed. "I thought it was something we could use together."

Jack scratched his chin. "I don't think I've painted since I was in kindergarten. Maybe not even then."

He doesn't like them. . . .

Flustered, I reached for the paint set, wishing I'd chosen diamond-plated cuff links or a year's supply of Cuban cigars, anything to impress a man who'd been born with everything. Aside from writing, I loved to draw and paint, and had hoped to share that passion with him. "I'll get you something else."

But Jack dangled the watercolors just beyond my reach. "I do like them." His free arm snaked around my waist. "And I love you for thinking of them. It's a very thoughtful gift."

In fact, he loved them—loved *me*—so much that we were late arriving to his mother's specified hour of the Kennedy gift exchange. The sour expression on Rose's face was almost as priceless as Jack's throaty chuckle had been the second time I'd pulled him back to bed.

I was surprised after our happy morning to find that I actually enjoyed Christmas day, playing tennis with the Rah-Rah Girls—my secret new nickname for Jack's sisters since they enthusiastically took to everything in life, except me—and settling around the huge dining room table for a dinner of honeyed ham and scalloped potatoes, both of which my Jack covered in enough salt to choke a deer. Uninterested in the Rah-Rah Girls' talk of the upcoming cinema release of Marilyn Monroe's *The Seven Year Itch*, I turned my attention to Jack and Bobby's discussion of foreign investments with their father.

"Don't let these two fool you, Jackie." Mr. Kennedy laughed as he slathered a dinner roll with butter. "Listening to my sons talk about business is like listening to nuns talk about sex."

Bobby roared, and I couldn't help a little chortle, too, that is until Jack stood, his face pale.

Bobby laughed good-naturedly. "Sit down before you hurt yourself, Jack."

Jack did, but he scarcely managed a bite of potatoes before he excused himself. "I think I'd better go lie down."

I rose to follow, but Bobby gave a terse shake of his head. "Stay and enjoy dinner, Jackie. I'll take care of him—I'm an old hat at this since his PT boat accident."

I watched Bobby follow after his brother and tried to do as he said, but once the after-dinner cigarettes were lit and talk turned to New Year's plans, I burst into the fresh air outside and hurried in the direction of the tennis court. Yellow lamplight banished the murky darkness on our patio, Jack's voice a low murmur as I approached the French doors.

"It hurts like hell, Bobby. The worst it's ever been."

Even without seeing him I could envision my husband's face contorted with pain. Jack had never admitted to me how much anguish he was in, but if what he said was true, he must be in agony, considering that the last time he'd had major back problems he'd been swimming across the Pacific with a man's life jacket strap clamped between his teeth.

Why hadn't he told me?

Bobby's footsteps crossed the floor. "Have you seen a doctor?"

A silent nod. "He says I may have permanent damage; that the football and PT boat injuries will only get worse with time. I worry how this will affect Jackie too. It's not just me I have to worry about anymore."

I stepped closer, hesitated at Bobby's next sentence.

"Don't worry about Jackie." The bed springs creaked as Bobby sat next to Jack. "She looks delicate, but she has a hide of Teflon if she puts up with you."

I smiled from my place in the shadows. At least I had one ally among the Kennedys.

Still, it was time to end their little tête-à-tête. I silently backtracked several steps before humming "Jingle Bells" and waiting for the brothers' conversation to veer toward the horsepower in the newest line of Jaguars, making me wonder how much practice they'd had at cover-ups over the years.

Jack was lying flat on his back when I poked my head inside, his dress shoes still laced and his silk tie snug around his neck. Even in

pain, he managed to affect the nonchalant air of a Renaissance aristocrat waiting for Botticelli to paint him, but I wasn't letting myself
be fooled. "I came to see how you're feeling," I said.

"Just another flare-up," Jack said. "Playing Harvard football and
being a war hero are finally catching up to me in my old age."

He might be flippant, but there was no denying the way his eyes
flicked to his brother, as if for confirmation of something vital. I wondered then who else knew what Jack truly suffered. Perhaps Mr. Kennedy, but I suspected the truth didn't reach outside that sacred trio.

Until now.

I gave Bobby a pointed look, and he cleared his throat as I untied
Jack's shoes one by one. "I'd better get back to Ethel," he said. "Merry
Christmas, you two."

I waited until Bobby had gone before I turned on Jack. "How can
I help?"

"It's nothing, Jackie, really—"

"You told me you'd never lie to me." I jutted my chin toward the
porch as I tugged off Jack's shoes, letting them fall one at a time to the
parquet floor. "I heard you talking to Bobby."

Jack's eyes turned to dark storm clouds, but he banked them so
quickly I thought I'd imagined it. "It's more than my back," he admitted, his gaze on the ceiling. "My family has always joked that if a
mosquito bit me, the mosquito would get sick. But there's nothing you
can do. I didn't want to worry you about it."

"Oh, Bunny—"

"Shh . . . just lie next to me, Jackie. Please."

The *please* did it, coming from this man who grabbed life by the
throat and wouldn't let go. He seemed so weak, so exhausted as I fitted my body to his.

I won't push anymore, I thought to myself. *At least not tonight.*

Still, I knew in that moment that I'd do anything in my power to
help Jack, to heal him.

But nor would I let him fool me.

. . .

Jack insisted on attending the opening of the second session of the
83rd Congress, and I fairly twitched with worry to see him seated
like a statue at his polished mahogany desk down on the floor. Only
his family, his secretary, and I knew that the back brace he wore beneath his suit forced him to sit ramrod straight, for his condition had
rapidly deteriorated after we'd moved into our newly rented Georgetown house on Dent Place. He wouldn't leave that Senate desk until
everyone else had filed out for fear that word—or worse, a photo—of
him on crutches would leak to his constituents in Massachusetts.

"He can't even bend down to pick up a pen or piece of paper he's
dropped," his secretary, middle-aged and married Evelyn Lincoln,
had confided to me one morning over the phone. "It's getting worse
with each passing day."

But Jack did go on, mustering that colossal will of his and forcing
his body to obey his commands, for a few months at least.

Until one summer day when we had to cut short our tour of Civil
War battlefields during Congress's August recess. Jack's face had lit
up like a boy at a three-ring circus as he pored over the hallowed
grounds of Bull Run and Spotsylvania, but even the sight of the grassy
hill where Stonewall Jackson famously rallied the Confederates
couldn't fully sweep the glaze of pain from his eyes.

"Jack," I said as I helped him hobble back to the car. "This is getting serious."

"It'll pass," he said between gritted teeth. Yet the sheen of sweat
that marred his tanned face claimed otherwise.

This time I insisted that we head to his parents' house on the Cape,
where I hoped that the briny sea air and slower pace would allow Jack
to heal.

Then came the night he couldn't get out of bed, even to vomit.

"That's it," I said after I'd cleaned up the mess. "You're seeing a
doctor."

"I know what's wrong with me," he snapped. His face was paler than a January moon as he eased onto the pillows like a man twice his age, switching off the lamp in a vain attempt to hide his weakness. "It's my damn back and the Addison's kicking up again."

"Addison's?"

"My adrenal glands don't produce enough cortisol. Never have. Why do you think I tire so easily and eat so much salt?"

"You knew all this?" I flipped the lamp back on. "And you never told me?"

He winced. "You're my wife, Jackie, not my physician. I don't want you to see me like this."

"Exactly. I'm your wife. And I'm saying enough is enough."

Jack opened his mouth to argue but withered as the next onslaught of pain crashed into him. "Fine." I could barely hear him when he whispered, the fire in his eyes banking so quickly my throat constricted. "Call the doctor."

The prognosis was grim. So grim, in fact, that it seemed ripped from someone else's life.

"You're facing life in a wheelchair, young man." The surgeon at the Hospital for Special Surgery in Manhattan demonstrated how Jack's vertebrae were fusing together, a result of his injury from playing football for Harvard and the disc he'd ruptured during his PT boat incident. Jack had tried to have me wait outside during the appointment; I'd refused. "Your Addison's is compounding the problem, since your immunity is shot to hell and back. You need surgery, and quickly."

"And then?" Of course, only Jack was brave enough to voice the question I couldn't bear to ask.

The physician steepled his fingers. "This is a very risky procedure with an extremely high chance of infection during recovery, only a fifty percent chance of survival. You will never be the man you were before your football injury or the PT accident, but I guarantee that if you don't have this surgery, you'll never walk again."

A very risky procedure. You'll never walk again.

I couldn't imagine my robust husband confined to a wheelchair; and there was no doubt in my mind that Jack was too young and too full of energy to die on an operating table. Yet one look at the surgeon and I knew he meant every word.

"I can't go on like this." Jack's fingers dug into the sides of his upholstered chair. "I'd rather die on the operating table than live this half-life. Schedule the surgery, but don't let word get out."

I knew what he was thinking, that he'd appear weak to his constituents and his political adversaries if this news broke. I arranged my features into a reassuring smile, never so thankful as I was now for the Kennedy fortune, which meant we could afford the best surgeons available. "Franklin Roosevelt hid his polio for four terms," I said, playing to Jack's ego and love of history. "No one will know about your surgery unless you inform them yourself."

I expected Jack to rebuff me when I reached for his hand, but instead his storm-tossed eyes met mine and he squeezed my fingers in a way that made my heart ache. For the first time, there were cracks in that veneer of self-assurance, cracks he had finally allowed me to see.

Jack's surgery was a scant week and a half later.

It was a week in which he deteriorated before my eyes until I could imagine him as an old man, even as the remaining days slipped away faster than grains of sand in an hourglass. I forgot to eat and hardly slept, too distraught over what sort of horrors might emerge for us on the other side of Jack's surgery. We'd only been married eleven months.

"I'll see you in a few hours, kid." Jack had finally settled onto the hospital gurney after glowering heatedly at the thing while I'd finished signing his admittance paperwork. A barrage of nurses and orderlies waited to wheel him in to the surgical theater, where a team of four specialists would perform the operation. I waited as Mr. Kennedy and Bobby shook Jack's hand; out of all his family, only his father and brother had come today.

And me.

Unable to trust my voice, I kissed Jack, wondering if this brief brush of his dry lips against mine and the hospital's clinical smell would be my last memories of my husband. Unable to stop myself despite all the onlookers, I ran both hands through his thick hair, let my fingers linger on the sides of his skull. "I love you, Jack. Fight like the Irishman you are."

He smiled, so gaunt and pale compared to the rugged and vigorous man who'd courted me. "I will. Kennedys aren't quitters."

His father cleared his throat, placed a steadying hand on my back as the orderlies helped turn Jack onto his stomach. "Damn right."

"Give 'em hell, Jack," Bobby said.

It was the constant pressure of Mr. Kennedy's hand on my back and Bobby's on my shoulder that kept me from shattering into a thousand pieces when the orderlies wheeled Jack behind the surgery doors, his face down and one stoic hand lifted in a final good-bye. "You look like you could use some breakfast." Mr. Kennedy cleared his throat. "And a smoke."

I lost track of how many Pall Malls we three burned through in the hospital cafeteria—our tasteless ham sandwiches and applesauce untouched on trays before us—as time seemed to move in reverse. The relentless seconds ticked into unbroken minutes, those minutes into never-ending hours.

What are they doing to him right now?

I've never felt so helpless in all my life. . . .

Is Jack even still breathing?

I must have muttered that last thought under my breath, for Bobby only gave me a wan smile. "Jack's never done anything quietly. You'll know when he goes."

I wasn't sure if I found that comforting, but I supposed he was right.

Finally, Dr. Wilson appeared, weary around the eyes. "He's awake and in recovery," he assured us. "But he's not out of danger yet. Things often get worse before they can get better."

I let the dire warning roll off me, for I thought the worst had passed, but things did get worse. Much worse.

Everything fell apart one terrible afternoon, when I slipped out into the sterile waiting area after a nurse came to review Jack's vitals. It broke my heart to see him laid so low, an oxygen mask over the lower half of his face and Gordian knots of IVs hooked into his bruised arms. He had a urinary tract infection and it embarrassed him to have me in the room when they checked his catheter, so I always slipped out on some pretense—usually to call my mother, who demanded regular updates—to allow him some semblance of privacy. It would be a few hours before Mr. Kennedy and Bobby came by for their nightly visit, so I thought to get Jack something to drink and a fresh magazine to read. I returned from the hospital cafeteria with a plastic cup of tepid apple juice in time to hear him call my name in a weak voice.

"Jackie . . ."

I tried to enter, but two orderlies barred the door. "I'm sorry, Mrs. Kennedy," one said, "but you'll need to wait outside."

Over their shoulders I could see the terrible tableaux unfolding: the surgeon and two nurses moving with quick and efficient movements. Jack pale and fragile between them. His eyes shuttered while the cold machines hooked to him wailed terrifying sirens.

"Mr. Kennedy." The surgeon pulled up one of Jack's eyelids and shone a penlight at his engorged pupil. "Mr. Kennedy, open your eyes."

Yet Jack wouldn't—couldn't—open his eyes.

I shoved at the orderlies, apple juice splashing onto my hands. "Let me in!" I begged, then choked on the sudden garrote of panic around my neck as they slammed the door in my face.

I was alone then. So terribly, horribly alone.

I composed myself enough to call Jack's father from the hospital pay phone, then dissolved into a storm of helpless tears. There was something soothing about Mr. Kennedy's beige trench coat and his dapper hat spattered with raindrops when he arrived, a reminder that life went on beyond these walls. Yet the wind sobbed outside, and beneath his spectacles Mr. Kennedy's kindly eyes were frantic. I wanted to reassure him that everything was all right, that Jack had woken up and was requesting a bowl of Kennedy seafood chowder. Instead, I could only shake my head as he shook out his umbrella.

"Don't worry, kiddo." Mr. Kennedy pulled me into a tobacco-scented embrace before we sank together onto the uncomfortable mustard-colored couch. "Kennedys don't die in hospitals. They're far too mundane for our tastes."

I tried to laugh, but it came out a strangled mess. Jack's father wrapped a heavy arm around my shoulder and together we clung to the shreds of our hope, reciting the Lord's Prayer and glancing up sharply every time a nurse or doctor passed through the room.

Until a haggard surgeon came to brief us and a rill of cold sweat ran down my back.

"There's an infection in his central nervous system." He looked me straight in the eyes as he spoke, speared me through the heart with his next words. "I'm afraid he's slipped into a coma."

I might have drowned as a sudden wave of panic and hysteria crashed over me.

This isn't how our story ends. This isn't when our curtain drops.

How could this happen? How could a man who was larger than life be fighting for that same life at this very moment?

I forgot that this had happened before to Jack, that he'd spent his childhood in sickbeds and almost died twice before, once from scarlet fever and again during the war. But his father remembered.

"I'd like the hospital chaplain to say last rites." Mr. Kennedy's words sounded curled up and wounded. "Once the rest of the family arrives."

I gasped, sitting stock-still even as I flailed like a drowning woman inside. "Last rites? You'd let him die?"

Mr. Kennedy's ravaged eyes were brimming, reflecting like mirrors as he gazed at me, the jovial father suddenly replaced by a broken old man. It was akin to seeing straight into his soul, one wrecked by years of pain. "Two of my children died without last rites, and this will be the third time I've listened to a priest say them for Jack," he said. "I'd take his place if I could, but seeing to his immortal soul is all I can do."

Everything ached, as if I was nothing more than a living, beating bruise. "I'm sorry." My hands fluttered uselessly at my sides. "I'll call Rose and Bobby—"

Mr. Kennedy rose with a wooden shake of his head. "Stay with him. Jack needs you to remind him of where he belongs. Here, with all of us."

So I sat by Jack's side, murmuring into his ear every memory I had of him, every scrap of our grandiose hopes and dreams. Anything to keep him tethered to this life. I stayed while his father made the barrage of phone calls from the hospital's rotary phone, and I remained a silent sentry as the battalion of Kennedys arrived.

"For you," Bobby said quietly as he handed me a lavender Bergdorf Goodman's hatbox that must have belonged to Ethel. I peered inside with bleary eyes to find an assortment of my sweaters and skirts all tucked together with impeccable folds. "I thought you might like a change of clothes," he explained. "There's a pack of cigarettes and a flask of vodka in the bottom too."

I squeezed his hand in silent communion as the rest of the family filed in, constellated together from Mr. Kennedy and Rose, the three sisters, all the way down to Ted. In this moment, Jack had become the sun we all orbited, and my knees trembled when the black-garbed chaplain entered, his very presence seeming to suck the life from the air. Mr. Kennedy must have noticed, too, for he took my free hand, steadying me as we silently bore witness to the chaplain anointing Jack's forehead with oil in the sign of the cross and absolving him of his sins.

Rose cleared her throat immediately after the chaplain finished. "I'm needed back at the Cape," she said, picking up her handbag. "And then I'm off to Palm Beach to see that the roof repairs are being done properly."

I whirled on her. "You'd leave him? Like this?" It was an unforgiveable outburst, but the man I gestured to looked so weak in that bed, so broken. As if he needed all of us there, fighting for him.

"There's nothing I can do." Rose's sniff was colder than a distant star, especially as she avoided glancing in Jack's direction. I wondered if she recalled the other times he'd almost died, if those memories snapped too close at her heels now. "He's in God's hands now."

I watched her leave in mute shock, horrified that a mother could even think of leaving her son's deathbed. Was she really so cold-blooded, or was it just too much for Rose to bear, watching another of her children battle for his life?

Rose left, but I remained after they'd all trickled home with promises to return, even Bobby, leaving only Mr. Kennedy and me.

That smear of oil on Jack's forehead taunted me with its finality, until I used the sleeve of my sweater to scrub it away. "Don't you dare leave me," I whispered in Jack's ear, my hands on his shoulders, pressing him into the hospital bed as if to anchor him here, to this life. "You're too damn young to die and you have too much left to do to give up now."

When I straightened, it was to find Mr. Kennedy looking at me with a queer expression. "Go home, kiddo," he said. "Get some sleep."

I shook my head. "It's easier to be here, not having to wonder how he's doing, whether he's still—"

My voice broke and I was unable to finish the thought. Mr. Kennedy only patted the couch next to him, removed a cigarette from the silver case in his pocket, lit it, and drew a long drag. "You know, you remind me of my eldest daughter, Kick. My other girls . . . Well, I've never really understood them. Kick was the only one I could ever talk to."

"Jack told me about Kick. I wish I could have met her."

"Me too." Mr. Kennedy wore a ghost of a smile. "I believe I owe you an apology."

"An apology?" The dense fog around my weary brain couldn't make sense of his words. "Whatever for?"

"I pushed Jack to marry you to put to bed the speculation of why someone his age wasn't married. I thought you were a cut above the rest of his girls du jour, but only a cut, mind you. Less silly and empty-headed, but still concerned only with china patterns and the latest fashion of hat. Yet here you are after all the others have gone, a well-dressed sentinel guarding my son while life falls to pieces around your ears. I misjudged you, Jackie, and for that, I apologize."

I looked to where Jack lay on the cold hospital bed, helpless in a way I'd never seen anyone before. "Any wife would do the same."

Joe's eyes flicked to the empty hallway, and I knew we both remembered the image of Rose's retreating back. "No," he said thoughtfully. "No, they wouldn't. I believe you'd crawl on broken glass down Pennsylvania Avenue for my boy. That makes you and me captains of the same team."

I leaned my head against his shoulder. "We'd both crawl through hell for Jack, wouldn't we?"

"You can say that again, kiddo." I could hear the smile in his voice. "Promise you'll stay with my boy. Always."

"Always."

Mr. Kennedy and I became fixtures in Jack's room all that night and the next, too, taking turns mopping his brow and reading aloud poetry and the day's newspapers just in case some part of him could hear us. Winter sunlight streamed through the blinds as I slipped woolen socks on Jack's cold feet and opened a well-worn leather volume to read him his favorite Frost poem, "Nothing Gold Can Stay."

> Nature's first green is gold,
> Her hardest hue to hold.
> Her early leaf's a flower;
> But only so an hour.
> Then leaf subsides to leaf.
> So Eden sank to grief,
> So dawn goes down to day.
> Nothing gold can stay.

I brushed the tears from my eyes. Frost's stark poem only reminded me that Jack had been my Eden and my golden dawn, that I needed more than the hour we'd been granted.

I set aside the poem and yawned my way through the business section of the *New York Times* when I felt something flutter next to my fingers on the bed.

Jack's fingers—moving.

I gasped, then my fingers flew to my mouth to see gray-green eyes peering at me from above the oxygen mask that obstructed his nose and mouth. His gorgeous eyes.

The sight knocked the breath straight from my lungs.

I yelped for Mr. Kennedy, for a nurse, for the very saints and angels who'd answered my prayers. "Don't you ever do that again," I commanded Jack, wild tears of relief streaming down my cheeks as footsteps pounded our way. "Or I swear I'll make you regret it."

Jack hardly had the strength to lift his hand, but he gave a meager attempt at a wink and lifted three fingers. *Scout's honor.*

In the days that followed, Mr. Kennedy left only to make arrangements for Jack's return to the Senate and to place special orders for half a dozen North Carolina oak rocking chairs to aid Jack's recovery. I never left; my entire universe was contained in this white-walled hospital room, and I refused to leave its microcosm.

"Read to me," Jack gritted out through clenched teeth one morning after he'd refused a higher dose of pain medication.

I shook my head, instead rummaged through a box Bobby had brought over and found what I was looking for beneath a game of checkers. "I've already read you enough books to fill the New York Public Library." Better all those books than the poem that Jack requested I read over and over: Alan Seeger's "I Have a Rendezvous with Death," which was far too macabre for my tastes. Yet no matter what I read, Jack fidgeted through every chapter, so I knew he was only thinking of how badly his back still hurt. "Today you're going to paint."

Jack scowled at me like I was mad, which maybe I was. He turned his glare to the canvas and set of Christmas watercolors I laid on his lap. "And if I don't want to paint?"

"Then I'll go find some other handsome fellow to share my lime Jell-O tonight."

I was half shocked when Jack propped the canvas on his breakfast tray, then shook a paintbrush at me. "I'm the only fellow you get to share lime Jell-O with, you know. The lemon, on the other hand, you can share with whomever you wish. That stuff's wretched."

Watching the way he bit his lower lip in concentration before dipping his brush into the cup of water I prepared and then the vivid turquoise on the palette, I allowed myself to relax for the first time in ages. I plucked up a spare canvas and lost myself in sketching a fanciful imagining of the White House's early days complete with a happy couple strolling on the front lawn, garbed in an old-fashioned Victorian suit and day gown.

The White House . . . That dream seemed so far away now, as if it belonged to someone else.

"What's the subject of your masterpiece?" I asked Jack after I'd finished shadowing in the couple. I set the canvas aside and stretched along the hard cushions of the hospital couch.

"Happy memories." He swiveled the canvas for me to see, and I smiled at the crudely rendered seaside vista, reminiscent of the beach from our honeymoon in Acapulco.

Was that really only a year ago?

I glanced at the dour clock above the door—as if it might possess the answer to time's capricious ways—then frowned and riffled through my purse. "Don't forget," I said as I applied a fresh coat of Arden Pink lipstick in the tiny hospital room mirror. "You have a visitor arriving in a few minutes."

"Who is it this time?"

"It's a secret." I kissed the top of his head, ruffling his hair. It was exhausting to keep Jack constantly distracted, but worth it to divert his attention from the pain. "You'll like this one, I promise."

And I was right.

"Look what the cat dragged in, you mangy old fox." Jack's face brightened when Richard Nixon walked in, bearing a potted African violet I'd have bet a hundred dollars his wife, Pat, had picked out. Jack wanted to keep the full extent of his surgery secret, but that didn't mean I couldn't invite a few of his colleagues to visit while he recuperated. He and Nixon had been sworn into Congress on the same day back in 1946, and although they were from opposite sides of the aisle, Jack had told me they'd become friends after discovering a shared centrist platform regarding a more robust policy against the Soviet Union and the extremists in both their parties. "You never miss a good old-fashioned chance to harass a Democrat while he's down, do you, Dick?"

"Never." Nixon offered a lopsided grin before he greeted me. "It's good to see you again, Mrs. Kennedy. This is from Pat—she said to tell you she misses you at the Senate wives' Tuesday bandage-rolling parties." He set down the violet, confirming my hunch before removing an oblong paper packet from his pocket and handing it to Jack. "And from me, the finest Cuban cigars, so you can close your eyes and pretend you're in the Senate library while you puff away."

I liked Nixon, as did all who met the junior-senator-turned-vice president, but I also knew Jack wouldn't appreciate my hovering. So while the men smoked their cigars, I busied myself writing thank-you notes to various dignitaries who had sent well wishes to Jack, starting with a message to Senate majority leader Lyndon Johnson and ending with a heartfelt letter to Mr. Kennedy, who had finally—and begrudgingly—left to take care of necessary business now that Jack was on the mend. I allowed my pen to have free rein to express my emotions to a man I was realizing was almost as dear to me as my own father.

Dearest, dearest, dearest Mr. Kennedy,

You have to be addressed in such a formal way because you have been silly enough not to appreciate the tender nickname of Poppy Doodle which I bestowed upon you this winter. Never mind, it is too late to change back now.

In all the ups and downs this winter, you exuded such force and convic-
tion that no one would dream of getting discouraged. . . . It's just empty and
no fun without you. And what is the fun of doing something you're proud
of—like giving a speech or writing a poem or holding a hearing . . .

My pen paused before I continued that particular train of thought regarding Jack's and my shared hopes, hesitated to commit to paper the next aspiration that instantly came to mind. Wavered, then plunged ahead.

. . . or having a baby—unless there is you to tell about it and hear how
thrilled you are?
So much love and thanks and devotion and EVERYTHING from
someone who will be FURIOUS if she is ever "off the team"!

XXXXX,
Jackie

Having a baby . . .

That had seemed such a simple dream, but with Jack's health, who knew how long it would be before Jack and I could make it a reality? Or if we ever could?

I folded the letter into an envelope in time to hear the men discussing Jack's idea of writing an article about former senators who had exhibited unusual courage—the latest in his string of plans to occupy himself during his recovery. Nixon seemed to heartily approve as he shrugged into his woolen overcoat and said his farewells.

"Thank you for visiting," I murmured softly as I walked him out. "I don't think there is anyone in the world Jack thinks of more highly than you, except maybe his father. That just goes to show how incredible you are."

And it was true, for Jack spoke often of Nixon's resolve against the reactionaries in his party, his ability to reason his way to the center, traits Jack prided in himself. Nixon actually flushed. "You're quite the flatterer, Mrs. Kennedy," he said.

"Sometimes," I said with a smile. "But this time I mean it."

Only after another spinal surgery a few months later did Jack begin the long road to true recovery from our room at Palm Beach. The surgeons had inserted a metal plate into Jack's spine during his latest surgery, so he had an eight-inch suppurating wound that I persuaded the nurse to teach me to clean and tape when he was still unconscious. It was foul, really, and it took everything I had not to shrink from the yellow pus oozing from my husband's flesh.

"You don't have to do this, Mrs. Kennedy," the nurse said kindly. "That's why I'm here."

Part of me wanted to gratefully slink away, until I recalled the way I'd been barred from Jack's room when he slipped into a coma. My husband had needed me then as he needed me now, and I'd never allow anyone to keep me from his side again. "Show me one more time." I nodded to the forest of orange prescription bottles by Jack's bed. "And his medications too."

So the nurse taught me to administer the dizzying schedule of Jack's medications, made me repeat back the Byzantine labyrinth of instructions until I had them memorized. "They'll be scaled back as he heals," she said. "But it's likely that he'll need a steady supply of steroids and painkillers to manage flare-ups."

"For how long?"

She shrugged. "Potentially the rest of his life."

I bit a fingernail, imagining my brawny, larger-than-life husband permanently hamstrung by this injury. It didn't paint a pretty future, for him or me. And that picture only got drearier as his mood grew more turbulent with each passing day.

At least he's still alive and at least he's still walking. . . .

"Get out, Jackie," Jack ordered by way of protest the first time he was coherent and I arrived to change his bandages. "You can't see this."

What he meant was that he didn't want anyone seeing him like this, especially those he thought should look up to him. He'd forbidden everyone from his room except his father, who refused to take no for an answer. Perhaps it was time to take a page from Mr. Kennedy's playbook, one team captain helping the other.

"Fine." I crossed my arms, fingers strumming against my elbow. "Prove to me you can reach your own bandages and that you know which medications manage which symptoms. Then I'll leave."

No need to tell him that I could scarcely keep the medications straight: cortisol for his Addison's, procaine for his back, penicillin to heal an abscess, phenobarbital for his stomach, and Tuinal to help him sleep. I'd had to write out a cheat sheet to keep it straight at first.

Barely able to lift his head from his prone position, Jack's eyes glared like the sun on metal as he glowered first at me and then the mosaic of medication bottles on the bedside table. "That's why I have a nurse."

"The nurse is gone for the day"—because I'd sent her home—"so unless you can change your own bandages, I suggest you let me help you. And she won't always be here to manage your medications."

No answer.

"I want to help you, Jack," I said in a low voice. "I'm your wife."

"Which is exactly why you're the last person who should see me like this."

That again. I crouched down beside him. "For better or worse, sickness and in health, Jack, remember? I swore an oath to you and God, and I'm not going to back out at the first sign of trouble."

Jack groaned, which I took as a good sign. "I'll bet they didn't know you were this obstinate when they named you Debutante of the Year."

"I'm a woman of many hidden talents." I rose, reveling in a rare flush of triumph. "So how are you going to fill all this free time?" It was a meager attempt at distraction as I lifted the edge of the old bandage, grimacing at the terrible wound below, the flesh angry and raw.

"I suppose I'll read a stack of histories like when I was in the Harvard infirmary." He pressed his face into the mattress as I peeled back the entire bandage, but his voice was muffled even as his knuckles went white. "I'm the best-read Kennedy alive because of that football injury."

"Yes, well, that's because your sisters haven't read anything besides the *Social Register* in years, and Ted is still on Dick and Jane books."

Jack's chuckle turned to a hiss of pain as I used quick and efficient swipes to clean the wound with iodine. I could imagine him gnashing his teeth to powder with all the time he'd spend lying in bed. Reading was wonderful, but he needed something more, and painting wasn't going to alleviate the months of recovery that stretched ahead of him. "You mentioned to Nixon the idea of writing about senators who had demonstrated bravery during their time in office. What if you wrote something longer than an article?"

He craned his neck to look at me. "Like a pamphlet? A serial-ization?"

"Like a book, you ninny." I ignored his scoff. "Remember when I told you about my Georgetown professor lecturing on John Adams's hard choices in Boston during the Revolution, how you agreed there was a story there, elected officials who went against popular sentiment to accomplish what they thought was right? You'll never find time to write it once you're healed, so why not now?"

Jack fell so silent that I feared he hated the idea. It wasn't until I'd affixed the surgical tape to the new bandage that he pushed himself onto his forearms. For the first time I saw a sparkle of my old Jack peer out through the pain that had clouded his eyes for so long. "You know, you've got a point."

I kissed his nose. "I'll fetch paper and pen to get you started and see if I can track down a dictating machine."

"So soon?" He gave a mock frown. "I have a nap scheduled for later. And I thought maybe I'd whine some more."

I laughed, and he surprised me by grasping my hand with a firmness I'd forgotten he possessed. Before I knew it, he'd tugged me to my knees and he was pressing dry lips to mine. It was the first true kiss we'd shared in weeks, and I felt myself melting into it, wanting more. Missing him.

Soon, I told myself. *Soon everything will be back to normal.*

"Thank you, Jackie," he whispered.

Something in me unfurled in the warmth of his simple words. It was then that I knew everything was going to be all right. If only because Jack willed it.

Jack might have held me at arm's length since our honeymoon, protected me from knowing his inner thoughts when he was in excruciating pain. *But,* I thought as I swept the old bandages into the wastebasket with sure hands, *now he knows how much he loves me, how much he needs me.*

Because while Jack Kennedy might be more obdurate than a hardheaded mule, I had bested him at his own game.

And it had only taken him almost dying to do it.

Jack's modest article began as a trickle of words that turned into a deluge until he had a full-fledged book: *Profiles in Courage.* Many of those words were captured by Theodore Sorensen, a young senatorial aide who sat by Jack's bedside with a typewriter perched on his knees, but it was Jack's ideas about political courage that made it onto paper.

"I feel like I've birthed something monumental." He was dressed in a freshly pressed suit for his second week back in the Senate, thinner than before but otherwise mostly returned to the rakish man I'd married. Mostly, because it took sporadic Novocain injections to keep him off his crutches while he healed, and because, to my dismay, he'd once again retreated behind his protective barriers since our return from Palm Beach. Once he even accused me of looking at him like he was an invalid, which I denied, of course.

He'd speak to me about his book, but not about how he felt or even how his days went. It was as if my larger-than-life husband couldn't quite reconcile that I'd been allowed to glimpse his secret vulnerabilities, and that I now knew he wasn't the immortal he wanted everyone to think he was.

Jack had fought for his life, and dammit, I would fight for him and for us, for his promise that we were going to soar toward the sun.

"If a person produces one book, they've accomplished something wonderful in this life. You've already written a book, so this second one means you've done something profound." I tidied one of the many haphazard stacks of research volumes from the Library of Congress that filled every surface of our house in Georgetown, including several historical memoranda I'd requested for Jack from my professors at George Washington University. "I'll finish looking over the manuscript this week."

"There's no one else I'd trust with it except you." For I'd offered to edit Jack's book, and to my delight, he'd grudgingly accepted. And if that wasn't enough to bring down his defenses, I had another secret tactic waiting in reserve.

He straightened his tie, then moved stiffly to pick up his briefcase before I reached it first. "Good luck house hunting."

I tapped a finger on my chin as I watched him go, for with Jack mostly recovered and our lease up, it fell to me to find us a new home. Our house here in Georgetown was fine, but I craved a real home of our own, something European with a small sort of courtyard perhaps, maybe even situated on a hill with land for keeping horses. We'd talked of building something on Hughdie's extra land at Merrywood, but yesterday I'd received word that a lovely little nineteenth-century Georgian estate at Hickory Hill was for sale, with sweeping views of the Potomac.

I visited the brick house that afternoon and wandered through its echoing corridors and empty grounds, entranced by the wraparound veranda and sloping lawn with its picturesque giant oaks and maples whose leaves shimmered in the breeze. I sat in an abandoned rocking chair outside and found myself tumbling into storybook images of the future we might share here in this tiny corner of the world: summer parties held on the lawn, crisp autumn walks, snowy Christmas sleigh rides. I waited eagerly at home for Jack that night, setting aside his manuscript pages to jump from the sofa every time a car passed by.

He looked so frayed around the edges when he finally came in that I almost fetched his crutches, but his lips were warm as they pressed distractedly against my temple. "Someone looks like she has good news," he said as I helped him out of his coat.

"I found the perfect home. A rambling white Georgian on six acres, so close to the Potomac that you can hear the river. And it has stables."

I wanted him to enfold me in his arms, to feel him share my excitement, but Jack only thumbed through his briefcase as if he wasn't even listening. "I assume you bought it already?"

Shutters and barriers. Tonight I'd scale every last defense he'd built around himself. Or blow them all to hell.

"Almost," I said. "You're going to love it. And it might have been a Civil War command post for George McClellan."

"That sounds promising." He didn't glance up from his papers.

"Some of its rooms are a little outdated, but nothing I can't redesign." I hesitated, then drew a deep breath and plunged ahead. "Including a darling little room off the main bedroom that we'll need to get started on right away. That one needs to be finished soon . . . by October, according to my calculations."

The papers finally lowered.

"Jackie . . ." he said slowly. "Are you saying what I think you're saying?"

My nod lit his face with the force of an atomic blast.

He swung me around so my felt circle skirt flared out behind me—spine be damned—and I wondered if the arrival of this baby would convince Jack that I didn't see him as somehow less of a man because of his surgeries. Jack stopped mid-turn and set me down with the reverence due a saint. "Jackie, you have no idea how much I love you, how much this means to me. We should celebrate—let's go to Europe!"

I laughed. "I don't know if it's a good idea for me to go gallivanting around the globe right now."

Jack sobered at that, then grinned anew. "I can't wait to tell my father. Bobby too."

Of course, because Joe Kennedy had had nine children and Jack worshipped his father, he couldn't stand to be seen as less than a man in his father's bespectacled eyes. Until now, he'd even stood in the shadow of Bobby, who had already fathered four children.

Gone were the shutters and barriers, reduced to rubble. My moment's triumph was scarcely dampened when I placed a gentle hand on Jack's arm. "I'm not even two months along. Maybe we should wait to tell anyone until I'm a little further?"

"Not a chance." The magnitude of Jack's pride seemed to press on the very walls, expanding until I thought the house might burst. "I'm going to shout this from the top of the Capitol dome."

I chuckled. "Do they let senators do that these days?"

"They do if it's me."

Jack may not have actually climbed the Capitol, but he crowed the good news to everyone he knew and even some he didn't, down to our milkman and postman. All the while, I planned the remodel of the house on Hickory Hill, pondering every minute detail so Jack wouldn't so much as have to bend down for his shoes on their shelves. In his illness, we'd weathered the eye of the storm and now our future looked becalmed.

Until the morning I woke up with the feel of a knife in my belly and a sea of blood on the sheets.

Jack had already risen and gone to the Senate, so I was alone in our new house at Hickory Hill when it started. My hands shook so badly I could scarcely dial the rotary phone while sharp ridges of agony contracted around my belly like shockwaves.

I called Jack next and left an incoherent message with his secretary, then curled into myself as the blood fauceted out of me, knowing it was too late to save this child.

The doctor confirmed my worst suspicions when he arrived, Jack bursting in shortly afterward. "Has she overexerted herself lately?" he asked Jack from the bedroom doorway after he'd examined me. The blinds were drawn, leaving me in a haze of semidarkness, so I wondered if I'd imagined the half-wild look in Jack's eyes. The ruined sheets had been taken away and I was clean again.

Clean, and hollow. So very, very hollow.

I couldn't hear Jack's answer, but the doctor's response broke me still further.

"It may be difficult for Mrs. Kennedy to carry and deliver a child, especially after this," he said in a low voice. My skin rippled with cold gooseflesh and I closed my eyes, hot tears coursing down my cheeks. "You'll have to be very cognizant of that if she conceives again."

If.

Was this how Jack felt before his surgeries, as if the very foundation on which he stood had suddenly turned to quicksand?

If.

There was a chance that I'd never again grow a baby inside me. That I'd fail Jack and myself at this most basic function of womanhood, the one thing guaranteed to make us a real family.

I squeezed my fists under the pillow.

I won't fail. Not at this.

Like Jack, I would find my way through this. And I would do it with Jack, for there was no doubt that he'd be at my side as I'd been at his. The doctor said something more I couldn't—and didn't care—to hear.

Followed by Jack's murmur: "I'm a monster. First, she has to nurse me back to health, and now this. She'd be better off without me."

"Things rarely go as we plan, my boy, but your wife is young and resilient," the physician responded. "There's a reason they say life is hard, you know, but we all get through it."

Then I felt the mattress sink and Jack curled up against my back.

"I'm sorry, Jack," I whispered, equally distraught by the events of the day and what I'd just overheard. "I'm so, so sorry."

"Shhh." His arms wrapped around me, gingerly, as if unsure how to hold me now. "It's not your fault, kid," he said, but he sounded so far away. Too far. "This is on me. I pushed you too hard, made too much of this."

"I won't fail you, not at this," I started, but felt him shake his head.

"Just rest, Jackie. Rest, and we'll try again later."

I didn't want later, and I didn't want another child; I wanted the one that I'd lost. And I wanted Jack to feel the same. "What do you think our baby would have looked like, Jack?"

There was no answer, only the creak of the mattress as he shifted behind me. "That doesn't matter now. The baby's gone, Jackie, and you need to get some sleep."

I felt a flare of anger at his dismissal, but it sputtered and died as my heartbeat drummed his family's motto in my ears, in my head, everywhere I had a pulse.

Kennedys don't fail.

I didn't want to sleep, but exhausted and spent, I drifted into unconsciousness in the warmth of Jack's arms. And when I woke in the middle of the night, I startled to find him gone, his side of the bed empty and cold.

Hickory Hill was so quiet that I felt myself a lonely island with only the servants to converse with when Jack was away at the Senate. The sprawling lawn I'd dreamed of filling with children and horses, the nursery I'd lovingly designed . . . Everything rang hollow and empty, made worse when the condolence bouquets sent by my father and Lee wilted and died. My mother came to visit more than once, but I longed for Jack, felt myself come alive when he came home each night, although it was common that he was so weary we scarcely spoke. I'd thought it would be Jack who would see me through my recovery from my miscarriage, to be my golden lighthouse beacon amid a dark storm of grief and guilt.

So it came as quite a surprise to learn he was leaving the country.

"I'm going to Sweden," he said one night before bed. He hadn't moved back into our bedroom after taking up residence in a guest room to allow me time to recover. I yearned to keep his warmth beside me, but he wore his melancholy like a shroud and always offered some excuse when the lights went out.

"For Senate business?"

Jack's eyes scudded to the ceiling, to the floor, anywhere that wasn't me. "For the summer. I've gone to Europe almost every year since I was young."

"Really?" I set down the leather-bound volume of Proust's *In Search of Lost Time* that I'd been reading, already envisioning the two of us enjoying Sweden's northern vistas. "I'll have my trunk packed."

"I need to get away." This time he stared directly at me, as if daring me to contradict him. The shutters slammed shut again, suddenly reinforced and impenetrable. "Alone. That same look is back in your eyes from after my surgeries—as if I'm broken."

"That's not true—"

"I need to do this, Jackie, to find the man I used to be before everything I touched fell apart. To live. Things will be better for both of us when I come back. I'm sure you can stay with my parents in Hyannis Port if you'd like company."

What he meant was that he needed to get away from me.

Kennedys don't fail.

The words had drummed in my mind that night after the miscarriage; did they now haunt Jack as they had me? My eyes stung from rejection and humiliation as I tried to sift through everything that was happening too fast. Where was the caring husband who had so recently consoled me and who was now this cold stranger that stared at me from across the room? Was this the only way Jack knew how to process his own grief—to put an entire ocean between himself and his sadness?

You need to get away, I almost said but bit my tongue for fear of how this new version of Jack would respond. *But I need you.*

True, Jack had tried to freeze me out while he'd recuperated from his surgeries, but we'd managed that. Was this sudden about-face because my confident and self-assured husband could muster the courage to overcome his own physical limitations, yet didn't know how to face weakness in others, save to run as far from me as he could manage?

Perhaps the Senate's former Gay Young Bachelor didn't fully

understand the meaning of for better or worse, in sickness and in health. How could he think of leaving right now?

"I see. I was thinking of visiting Lee in England, actually." My voice sounded gray and shriveled as I punted, for although Lee had offered, I'd had no intention of accepting the invitation. Until now. "Perhaps you and I can meet somewhere in Europe," I said off-hand, every word killing me. "The French Riviera is lovely this time of year."

Jack scarcely grunted his acknowledgment, only gave my temple a distracted kiss. "That's settled then. Good night, Jackie."

I stared after him, feeling the echoing distance he put between us with every step until the door to the guest bedroom closed firmly behind him. Only then did I let the hot tears course unchecked down my cheeks.

The cold reality of Jack's surgeries and the stark truth of my miscarriage had infused an icy frost into the summertime promise of our marriage. And I was too shocked to know what to do about it.

immediately regretted my hasty trip to Europe. Not because I didn't want to spend time with Lee—the one soul on earth I might confide my troubles to—but because rumors followed me like sharp-beaked crows, nipping to draw blood when I least expected it.

"Claire Baring wants to know if your separation from Jack is permanent." Lee pursed her lips into a perfect moue before dabbing them with a shocking shade of royalty-red lipstick. We were in the plush ladies' room of our hotel, having excused ourselves after high tea with Lee's society friends. "I told her spending the summer apart from your husband doesn't constitute a separation. I also mentioned that she'd give herself a hernia by being such a dreadful boor."

Were Jack and I truly separated? Was that what happened when one spouse fell out of love with the other? For I feared that Jack's love for me had evaporated and might never return, or worse, that the Jack I'd married really was the man who Bobby had tried to warn me about.

"Thank you," I said to Lee. "The next time she asks, you have my permission to gag her with a pair of nylons."

Lee smirked, then fell serious as she tucked the lipstick into her handbag. "But darling, is it?" she asked. "Permanent?"

"Surely not." Yet the words rang hollow to my ears, for with each passing day away from Jack, I felt cast adrift. I tugged the fingers of my glove, a nervous habit I caught myself doing more and more these days. I didn't like this wraith I was becoming, yet I couldn't seem to find my way back to the Jackie I'd been before the miscarriage, perhaps even before I'd married Jack. "I mean, I had been lonely at home, even when Jack was there, but I keep telling myself that he'll come to his senses in Sweden."

Despite our past rivalries, it was a relief to confide in Lee, to resume our childhood Whispering Sisters club again, even if it was me we were whispering about this time. At least I didn't feel so terribly lonely with my sister by my side.

And I refused to waste this trip to Europe, was suddenly determined to convince myself—and Jack—that I didn't need him to be happy. To somehow prove it to him when we met in Cannes in two weeks for a pleasure cruise on Greek shipping magnate Aristotle Onassis's yacht.

It was a visit Lee's husband had arranged when he realized that Onassis was shepherding Jack's all-time hero around Cannes. For while Jack might not have cared to spend five minutes with me, he'd have moved heaven and earth to say two words to the god that was Winston Churchill.

"Jacks." Concern shone in Lee's wide eyes and she clasped my gloved hands, finally stilling them. "You know Jack isn't alone in Sweden, right? He's taken up with some Swedish woman—I can't remember her name—or so Claire claims."

A sudden chill settled over my skin. "There's nothing that says Jack can't associate with other women."

"He's with her." Lee grabbed my shoulders, roughly, almost hissing her whispered next words. "As in *with* her."

My sister's words were a matador's flag that prodded to life the snarling surge of my deepest fears about Jack. Every inch of me went stiff, the thoughts tumbling uncontrollably through my mind.

Jack had been dubbed America's Most Eligible Bachelor before I'd met him. He'd been with Inga-Binga and countless other women before me. And now some Swedish woman.

There was a word for that in French. *Polyamour.*

I could picture that man with her already, her lush and flowing blond hair, blue eyes framed by pale lashes, curves a man could hug and hold on to.

I need to do this, Jackie, to find the man I used to be before everything I touched fell apart.

Another rare string of words surfaced in my mind, this time in English.

Son of a bitch.

I was not my mother, and Jack was not my father, but I wondered if some hidden part of Jack was trying to provoke me into leaving him, all because he doubted his own worth. I realized with horror that some hidden part of me had expected this from the start, had assumed that since most men cheated, it was inevitable that Jack—the Senate's Gay Young Bachelor—eventually would too. What made me think that Jack would be different?

But this could never happen to me. I wouldn't allow it.

Slowly I forced myself to shake my head. "Jack wouldn't do that. He couldn't."

Lee touched my chin so that I had to take in the fierce set of her lips, the angry embers in her eyes. It was how I should have looked, except I felt my heart bleeding out, all my love for Jack becoming black and tainted around the edges. "I hope you're right, but if not, make him look you in the eyes and admit it when we meet him in Cannes. He owes you that at least."

The very idea had me sinking onto the restroom's velvet settee, all the stale air expelled from my lungs in a violent gust. The fantasy I'd built for myself—the silly fairy-tale ending—was imploding around me and I had no idea how to stop it. Except school my features into a rigid mask and face the likes of Claire Baring as if nothing was amiss.

For I'd sooner die than break in public. Or even in front of Lee.

could barely bring myself to look at Jack, much less really talk to him when he arrived for our rendezvous in Cannes a few weeks later. When we met his yacht in the harbor, my tanned and tranquil husband seemed content to discuss mere pleasantries: the size of the swells they'd encountered on the French coast, the party planned for later that evening, and how our parents were faring stateside. No one else caught the way he fiddled nervously with his tie, so it occurred to me that I'd married someone as adept at shape-shifting as I was.

"It's good to see you, Jackie," he said, his voice so detached it might have come from the far side of the moon. He could barely meet my eyes, so I wondered if it was guilt or something else that weighed down his gaze.

"You too" was all I managed to eke out before he retrieved a flat black-velvet box from inside his jacket. "For you," he said.

Inside was a stunning triple-strand pearl necklace, each lustrous bead gleaming in the fading light. A gift? Or an apology?

I gave a hollow laugh and gestured to my white Saint Laurent trapeze summer dress, my long legs bare beneath. "It matches perfectly."

Jack lifted the pearls, clasped them behind my neck so I couldn't see his expression. "I'm glad you like them."

How am I going to confront him about another woman? I thought as he casually greeted Lee and strode alongside the other men up the dock and toward the casinos. Lee gestured with mascara-rimmed eyes and a succinct jerk of her chin for me to follow and make him heel, but I only gave a discreet shake of my head. *Can I bring myself to drop that firebomb on our marriage? What if Lee is wrong and I've been worrying myself over nothing?*

I didn't have time to ponder those questions as we were all whisked aboard the *Christina*, the sinfully appointed 315-foot yacht belonging to Greek millionaire Aristotle Onassis.

Our host was nowhere to be found, but I knew from Lee that Onassis had spent $4 million renovating this former Canadian frigate until the newly christened *Christina* was decadent enough to entertain a panoply of Greek gods, with its spiral staircase that soared three levels above a glittering mosaic floor bearing the image of the Greek letter omega. I passed the Siena marble baths and wended my way around white-jacketed waiters bearing offerings of colorful drinks before I was reminded of why we were really here. Why Jack was here.

With a daiquiri in hand, I leaned against an onyx pillar to watch Jack approach the eighty-year-old leviathan that was Winston Churchill, whom I'd briefly met almost a decade before at a Buckingham Palace garden party during my debutante's tour of the Continent. This Churchill, with his bulbous, pink-veined eyes, looked even more exhausted than the war-weary politician of 1947, although he'd recently retired as Britain's prime minister. Jack might have been mistaken for Apollo that night in his white tuxedo and crisp summer tan, but I could smell his tang of nerves as he neared Churchill.

"Good evening, sir." Jack's head was bowed in reverence to this titan among men, one of Aristotle Onassis's antique leather-bound volumes open on the elder statesman's lap as he sat before the lapis lazuli fireplace.

That very titan glanced up with a pinched scowl as he puffed away on a ubiquitous cigar, several more jammed into his pocket. "It's about time you got here," he chewed out, and I watched as tension melted from Jack's shoulders. Until Churchill picked up his empty Scotch glass and shook it at Jack. "Get me another one of these, will you?"

If I hadn't been so angry at my husband, I'd have gone to soothe Jack's crestfallen expression at being mistaken for one of the tuxedoed waiters. Instead, the despondent and broken part of me wanted to laugh that Jack wasn't the golden immortal he thought he was, especially when he slunk away, dejected by his idol.

"*Bonsoir*, Madame Kennedy." The gravelly voice at my side startled me from my uncharitable reverie. "I hope your husband can one day enjoy the story of the prime minister mistaking him for my staff. I'm surprised Winston didn't ask your husband to spoon-feed him caviar."

In my heels, it was a queer feeling to look down on the man who could only be Aristotle Onassis, who I'd imagined as a giant among men but was actually several inches shorter than myself. *"Je suis certaine qu'il le fera."* I loved the feel of French, the way it rolled off my tongue. *"Bien que ce ne soit pas ce soir."*

I'm sure he will. Although perhaps not tonight.

"You're likely right." Onassis bit the end from a Montecristo cigar and lit it with an efficient flick of his light. "Your French is exquisite. You could pass for a European, blending in amongst the beauty of our continent."

If Jack was Apollo and Churchill played Kronos, then this stocky flatterer with brilliantined hair and hawkish eyes would have to be . . .

Dionysus? I glanced at the murals over the bar, all depicting colorful scenes from Homer's *Odyssey*.

Not Dionysus then, but Odysseus. Wily and with a thirst for glory.

"Merci beaucoup. I haven't had the opportunity to thank you for your hospitality tonight." I gestured to the decadence surrounding us. "You must love your daughter very much to name such a splendid ship after her."

To which Onassis only offered a one-shouldered shrug. "I spoil all the women in my life, but especially my Christina. It's a father's right, you know."

I thought of my own father, who had indulged my every whim, found myself nodding. "Well, I hope she realizes what a wonderful father she has in you." I stepped a little closer to Onassis when I felt Jack's attention settle on us—I might be furious with him, but that hadn't severed the bond that told me exactly where he was or how he was feeling. Inhaling the scent of cigar smoke, I hated myself as I turned up the wattage of the smile I bestowed on Onassis. As I willed Jack to *care*.

Onassis raised his cigar with its artful cloud of smoke to me, as if he knew what I was doing, and perhaps even approved. "Please enjoy yourself tonight, Madame Kennedy."

He had scarcely stepped away when Jack was at my side. "What were you and Onassis talking about?" he asked by way of greeting, his jaw tight.

"You." He waited, but I refused to elaborate, only walked outside onto the aft deck. This portion of the ship was just as decadent as the rest, overlooking the *Christina*'s seawater swimming pool, which was inlaid with a breathtaking mosaic I recognized as copied from the Palace of Knossos on Crete. Yet I didn't care about the view as I held my breath and half hoped that Jack followed me. The other half of me wished he'd walk away and we'd never have to weather the squall to come. Because I knew I could no longer keep the questions bottled up inside.

Tennyson had once written, "Hope smiles from the threshold of the year to come, whispering, 'It will be happier.'" In the moment I heard Jack's footsteps follow me, I wanted desperately to believe we could cross that threshold and be happy again.

"Do you know that Onassis can drain the pool with the push of a button?" I stood at the railing, needing to fill the space between us with words, with something. Anything. "Lee told me the floor rises and becomes a dance floor."

"I don't care two shits about Onassis's pool." Jack's proximity made my heart stutter as he reached out a hand, ran a rope-calloused thumb along my jawline so I had to stop myself from leaning into his palm. He gently turned my face to capture the perfect slant of moonlight, as if he were an artist who wanted to paint me. Or a man who wanted to kiss me.

I shivered as his eyes emptied of their earlier indifference. Replaced by what, I couldn't tell. But God, how I wanted to know.

"I've missed you, kid."

"I've been here, Jack."

I wanted to leave it at that, but my mother's voice echoed in my head.

Weakness isn't something you're born with, Jackie; you learn it.

I wasn't weak. I wasn't.

"I heard you weren't alone." My voice came out low and strangled. "In Sweden."

Jack's hand fell from my cheek, replaced with the chill of night. "What?"

"You said you'd never lie to me. What's her name?"

There. Proof that I'm not weak, Mummy. I couldn't take the words back, but I still waited and hoped and prayed that Jack would tell me I was wrong. God, how I hoped, with every filament of my threadbare soul.

Something within Jack's eyes broke and the light seeped out of them. "Gunilla," he finally answered. "Her name is—was—Gunilla von Post."

That was all it took—one name—and the thing with feathers that perched in my soul died, cut off mid-song.

Why, oh why, couldn't he have lied? In my mind, I screamed and shouted and shoved Jack as far away from me as I possibly could, but my body stayed frozen in place. I wanted to rage as my mother had against my father, to don her costume of the wronged and long-suffering wife, even as I swallowed that scream.

I will not *become my mother.*

Jack gingerly lifted his hand as if to touch me, but I reared back as if slapped, my palms up like ineffective shields. "I had to get away, Jackie," he said, his voice anguished. "Away from everything that was falling apart, that I couldn't control. You, me . . ."

"Us." My voice cracked on the single damaged word, even as he nodded.

"I have so many dreams, Jackie." There was so much torment woven into his words that I felt my unwilling heart fracturing for him. "And it feels like everything was sidelined from the moment I had surgery. Then, with the baby . . ."

Another broken dream.

I hadn't realized how selfish Jack was, how it felt to be the sun everyone else orbited around. As if my dreams of a loving husband and family mattered not at all. My vision blurred and I wrapped my arms around myself. "I could divorce you for this." I hated the taste of the words as the very air between us turned raw. Jack blanched and my words tore away the veil of innocence that had cloaked his vision of me. "Ruin your career forever."

"I know and you'd have every right." His hands fell open at his sides. "It was a mistake, Jackie. A colossal fucking mistake that I wish had never happened. My father told me I should crawl on hands and knees over hot coals and beg you to forgive me."

That explained the pearls, the three exorbitant strands that suddenly seemed to strangle me. Dear God . . . Even Mr. Kennedy knew about this? How could I face him—or anyone—again? And even though I wouldn't expect him to turn against his own son, how could he not warn me?

I realized the answer almost immediately. *Because where do you think Jack learned his cheating ways? Almost certainly from his father, whose affair with Gloria Swanson is the stuff of legends. . . .*

I glared at Jack with hard eyes. "We could have made your dreams come true, Jack. Instead you've humiliated me. Publicly."

"Things will be different when I come home, I swear."

I squared my shoulders, forced open the fists I hadn't realized I'd made. "I don't want to talk about it anymore." Or ever again. "Don't bother coming home if you don't intend to hold up your end of our vows."

Then I walked away, each step of my white kitten heels echoing ever louder in my mind.

CHAPTER

4

December 1955

Jack knew my terms, but he did come home.

He and I briefly parted ways after seeing each other on the *Christina* to finish our respective trips, me to Paris with Lee and him to Capri, before I eventually returned stateside, alone. We'd become two silent icebergs, the depth of our true feelings hidden so far beneath the surface of our lives that I feared they'd never emerge again. I didn't truly believe he was returning to Hickory Hill to stay until I heard the car in the drive and he slunk through the front door, luggage in hand.

"I swear things will be different this time, Jackie. Better." He lifted three fingers, just as he'd done after his surgery. "Scout's honor."

"Okay, Jack." I'd barely been able to scrape the words out of my throat. Had he only returned because I'd threatened to divorce and ruin him? I boxed the thought into the furthest recesses of my mind. Even still, the fog of my threat hung between us.

I recalled a sermon from my youth, a verse from the Book of Luke: *Even if they sin against you seven times in a day and seven times come back to you saying, "I repent," you must forgive them.*

No matter how much it hurt, I'd force myself to forgive him. Even if it almost killed me.

The promise of another chance of happiness hinted at sweetness, like an unexpected epilogue at the end of a classic novel. So I would work every day to forgive him if that meant this sad chapter of our lives was over.

Come the end of that dark year, I was ready for a new beginning, and I believed Jack was too.

Profiles in Courage was to be published on New Year's Day, a new annum rising from the old year's grave amid snow squalls and starless winter nights. The New Year's Eve crush of too-warm bodies and overdone smiles held no appeal to me, so Jack had attended a party alone, yet he arrived home before midnight bearing a brightly wrapped package.

"For me?" I asked softly as he popped the bottle of celebratory Champagne I'd set to chill, holding it over the sink to avoid being splashed by the effervescent froth. I'd taken to speaking more quietly than usual, a reminder that I was nothing like my brash mother, but also a way to maintain an air of lovely inconsequence, so no one—including Jack—knew what I was really thinking.

"For you." He poured two glasses, winking as he drank straight from the bottle, so that for a moment I wondered whether my wish for this New Year might already have been granted.

I tugged the ribbon and paper away to reveal a copy of *Profiles in Courage*, the pages crisp and the binding unbroken. I'd meant what I said when persuading Jack to start writing: that if a person produced one book, they'd have done something wonderful. Not for the first time, I wondered what I was going to accomplish in my own floundering life.

I ran a reverent hand over the dust jacket, wishing for a moment that it was my name on the cover. "My own copy."

"The book isn't the gift." He didn't meet my eyes as he opened to the dedication. I read the words there, so precious that my vision blurred.

THIS BOOK WOULD NOT HAVE BEEN POSSIBLE WITHOUT THE
ENCOURAGEMENT, ASSISTANCE, AND CRITICISM OFFERED FROM THE
VERY BEGINNING BY MY WIFE, JACQUELINE, WHOSE HELP DURING ALL

*MY DAYS OF CONVALESCENCE I CANNOT EVER ADEQUATELY
ACKNOWLEDGE.*

All those words had come from Jack, who kept his feelings closer
hauled than a sailboat in a hurricane. And they were in print, forever
destined to outlive both of us.

He caught me staring at him and cleared his throat. "I mean every
word. I know I'm a pain in the ass sometimes—"

I pushed away the book, needing only him. Things would never be
the same between us, but we could make a fresh start, and we could
do it tonight. My hands were on his cheeks, the golden stubble there,
the back of his neck, my fingers weaving into his hair as I pressed
myself closer until our lips met with a ferocity that made me tremble
at the sudden insanity of my emotions. I'd been fractured these past
months and so terribly alone, but when Jack kissed me I felt almost
whole again.

As if I could conquer the world. As if we could do anything and
everything.

Jack seemed to think the same thing, for he pulled back, the question clear in those quicksilver eyes, our twin glaciers suddenly melting
to their hidden cores.

"Let's go to bed," I whispered.

Jack answered by picking me up and carrying me to our room.
"You don't have to ask twice."

Three weeks later, I discovered I was pregnant.

don't think you're up for it, physically."

My belly had swelled and proclaimed my joyous news to the
world, but now I had to protect Jack from ruining his own fragile
health. Fortunately, I didn't have to fight alone.

Jack glared at me, then rounded on his father. "And you agree with
Jackie, that I shouldn't run for vice president?"

Mr. Kennedy leaned back in the striped armchair of our Conrad

Hilton suite. With Bobby's help, Jack had today impetuously announced his candidacy for vice president at the open Democratic National Convention, leaving only Mr. Kennedy and me to steer Jack onto the correct political course. "With the sentiment, yes," Mr. Kennedy said as he steepled his fingers. "With the reason, no."

Jack threw up his hands. "*Profiles* is a bestseller and I'm exactly the man the Democratic party needs with my youth and war record. Yet you're telling me I shouldn't be vice president? I'm too feeble, and what else?"

I bit my tongue. For while I doubted whether Jack was physically capable of a rigorous campaign schedule, I worried more that those same campaign pressures would act like a magnet, drawing him toward politics while polarizing him away from me, just when we were finally reconciled. And if he lost the election . . .

I'd seen what failure had done to Jack before. I had no intention of reliving it, not until we were on more solid ground.

Mr. Kennedy uncrossed his legs and leaned forward. "Temper tantrums don't become you, son."

I held my breath. Both Kennedy alpha males in one room was a fearsome sight to behold.

"The physical rigors of campaigning will be hell, but if those surgeries didn't kill you, this probably won't either." Mr. Kennedy tapped his pointer fingers against his chin. "No, son, my concern is more philosophical. The vice presidency is a bucket of warm spit. Kennedys don't settle for second best. Never have, and never will."

Second best. Perhaps I'd drunk too much ambrosia from the Kennedy fountain, for second best chafed me now as well. I planned to come first in Jack's life, come hell or high water. And I needed time to ensure that nothing—not even politics—would come between us.

"The vice presidency isn't second best." Jack might have protested, but he was deflating before my eyes. "It's a stepping-stone."

"It's a political coffin and you well know it." His father jabbed two fingers toward Jack, then forced himself to relax. "You lose even if you win."

"It will garner me more name recognition."

"As would campaigning for Adlai Stevenson."

Jack turned to me. "Do you support this? That I should campaign for the Democratic ticket, but not myself?"

Here lay a critical difference between the two of us: while I could inhale all the political gasses around us and never be affected, Jack became instantly immersed imagining how the next step might catapult him into the Oval Office.

"Your father's plan is a good one." I folded my hands in my lap. "And I'll be with you every step of the way. I'll even help you with Adlai's campaign events."

Mr. Kennedy lit a cigarette, took a long drag, and blew a cloud of smoke toward the ceiling. "Think of this as a warm-up, son, for 1960—"

"1960?" Jack muttered under his breath. "At the rate I'm going, who knows if I'll even still be alive in 1960."

His father held up a hand. "The country's not ready for you—yet—but give America time to know you, and in four years a charismatic, youthful presidential candidate who just happens to be Catholic won't seem such a huge jump for those Midwestern bumpkins. Especially with Jackie at your side, awing them with her charm and poise."

Jack's father gave my rounding belly a pointed stare, the insinuation obvious. This baby would make us a real family, which would appeal to undecided voters while also keeping Jack at my side. I could already envision the photos Mr. Kennedy would have splashed in every paper in circulation, of Jack leading his daughter on a Thoroughbred pony, of playing football with his robust son on the sprawling Kennedy lawn.

Of us, together. Happy. But we needed time to build that foundation.

"It's a good plan, Jack," I repeated.

"Fine." He gave a long-suffering sigh. "I'll tell Adlai. But you two damn well better hold up your end of the bargain four years from now. The presidency is the only game that's worth the candle to me."

As I watched him go, I wondered, *Was that an ultimatum?*

fell into the hurly-burly of campaigning despite the scathing Chicago heat that summer, fulfilling my promise to Jack with gusto as I climbed onto a seat to cheer his nominating speech and staying up so late each night that nothing could fully mask the dark half-moons under my eyes. I promised myself it was worth the exhaustion and swollen ankles when the *Boston Herald* proclaimed Jack the real victor of the entire convention, that his was the one new face that actually shone with charisma, dignity, and gracious sportsmanship.

Yet I'd discovered that I detested campaigning. Thankfully, we could put the circuit to rest for a few years at least, until Jack's Senate seat came up for reelection.

Or he ran for president.

I'd think about that later, tomorrow. Never.

Unless he was on a stage, I scarcely saw Jack in Chicago since he stayed with Bobby and their aides at the Stockyard Inn behind the Convention Hall, while I lodged more comfortably with the Shrivers, who were longtime Kennedy friends and also family now that Jack's sister Eunice had married one of their sons. I was looking forward to a few months of peace before the baby arrived, but I'd forgotten about Jack's annual jaunt to Europe.

I'd thought that tradition was over after last year. Apparently, I'd been wrong.

"I'll miss you," I said as I watched Jack fold a white polo shirt, the same he'd once worn to take me sailing. I'd considered dissuading him from this abbreviated trip—at eight months along, I was far too pregnant to safely join him—but I didn't want to push as this year's version was a family jaunt with his father and Ted. There hadn't been the slightest hint of other women since he'd been in Sweden last summer. Everything had changed since then: my husband was a married man with a baby on the way and a plan to run for president in just a few short years.

Yet a voice in the back of my mind whispered that old habits died hard, or not at all, even as I wondered if Jack was leaving because he was scared to face another potential disaster.

But I only had one month to go; surely we were out of danger, which meant Jack's place was at my side.

"Don't go." The words were out of my mouth before I could stop them. "Please don't go."

"It's just a boys' trip." He scarcely looked up as he tossed the shirt into a suitcase. "You said you didn't mind me going."

I lied, Jack, I wanted to shout. *Can't you see that?*

It suddenly didn't matter that Ted was accompanying Jack or that Mr. Kennedy was meeting them. All the doubt and distrust I'd carefully folded away from the prior summer reared its ugly head, then multiplied like a Greek hydra from tales of old.

Perhaps I was a better actress than I thought, for Jack didn't seem to notice my turmoil, even as I had to force myself to stop twisting the hem of my angora cardigan.

I will not be the clinging wife. Smile, flutter your fingers, and let him go.

"I suppose I'd rather have you go so you won't be here to watch me balloon up." I smiled and gestured to my belly. "I'm already the size of a small whale."

He kissed the top of my head. "You've never been more beautiful. I'll be back before the baby. One more month." His hands touched both sides of my belly, framing it worshipfully for a moment, but then his gaze strayed to his suitcases, as if his mind was already skip-skimming across the Atlantic to the sun-kissed shores of the Mediterranean.

And could I blame him? Me, who loved Europe so dearly?

So I let Jack go. And wished very quickly that I'd done everything to keep him by my side.

. . .

I woke before dawn at my mother's house at Hammersmith Farm a few days later, gasping my way out of a dream where I was trying in vain to swim to Jack, who stood—literally stood—on the Mediterranean, the dappled sunlight gleaming on his rumpled copper hair and the cerulean waters in equal measure. All the while, my arms and body ached as he grew farther and farther away.

Jack was godlike even in my dreams, while I remained an earthbound mortal. As I struggled to the surface of consciousness, the remembrance of our phone conversation the day before made me want to let out such a scream of pain and rage that my very marrow was filled with it.

"Where are you?" I'd asked after he'd said hello.

"France." He'd sounded as if he were calling from the far side of the moon. "On our way to Nice, actually."

I'd scowled at the rain outside drizzling down the windowpanes, wishing I was sipping Champagne with my husband on a forty-foot sloop in the French Riviera. But my pleasant imaginings had come to a grinding halt when I heard a woman laughing Jack's name on the other end of the phone line.

I knew then. I'd wanted to tell myself I was being paranoid, but deep in my gut, I knew Jack was up to his old tricks.

Don't upset yourself, I'd thought as my hand strayed to my swollen belly, to the child there almost ready to be born who bound me to Jack more tightly than ever. As I remembered my mother struggling to raise Lee and me on her own until she'd met Hughdie. *Turn a blind eye—at least for now.*

"Listen, I've got to go," Jack had said before I could ask why some mystery woman was tagging along on what had been sold as a boys' trip. "I'll call you again after we rendezvous with my father."

Now, with the afterimage of my dream fresh in my mind, I recalled the crushing wave that had pummeled me with every stroke I took, pushing me farther and farther from my husband.

Only this pain was no dream.

I curled into it, gasping as I cried for my mother, inhuman sounds that seemed to come from some wretched, beleaguered animal. She came, her smocked bed jacket scarcely wrapped around her, eyes bulging with rare fear when she turned on the lights. We saw the dark stain on the duvet cover at the same time. She recovered first, the sort of woman who could ride her horse into a raging hurricane and never bat an eye.

"Hughdie," she commanded in a voice that shook the walls, and my stepfather's footsteps pounded down the hallway. "Call for the medics, now."

"Not again, Mummy," I sobbed as another white-hot flame of pain licked its way across my belly. "I can't do this again."

Not now. Not while Jack was on the other side of the world. *I need him.* . . .

My mother took my chin between her fingers and forced me to look into her becalmed eyes. "You're eight months along." Her voice was that of a field sergeant commanding men into a grim battle. "Fight like hell, Jacqueline. Save yourself and save this baby."

So I fought.

I screamed as the pains crashed into me one after another until my bones threatened to shatter, and only my mother's arms tight around me kept me from flying apart while we waited for the medics. They put me under when they arrived, and when I awoke from the fog of sedatives it was to see the blurry outline of a man in the chair next to my bed at Newport Hospital, his dark suit like gathered shadows.

"Jack?" The lone word was akin to shards of glass dragging across my throat.

It wasn't Jack.

"Hey, Jackie." Bobby's tie was loose and his blue eyes—glacial whereas his brother's were stormy—were so somber that my heart constricted until I feared it would never beat again. He pulled his chair closer to my bedside with an ear-wrenching scrape across the linoleum. "I'm here. And your mother's outside waiting."

I glanced around the room, wildly searching for the bassinet that would tell me everything was all right. Bobby didn't make me ask the question.

"They gave you an emergency Cesarean section." He reached out to clasp my icy hands, his palms firm and cool. Grounding. "I'm sorry." His voice cracked in half. "Your precious little girl didn't make it."

Your precious little girl.

Maybe it was the words that broke me, or perhaps it was the tiny fragment of human contact, my cold fingers entwined with Bobby's when the blood rushed from my head and left me so horribly dizzy. My heart fractured first, tiny fissures that streaked out along every vein, so painful I had to make sure my skin was still whole.

I was still whole, but then again, I'd never be whole again.

"Where's Jack?" My whisper was smothered, as if a garrote limned my throat.

This time Bobby didn't meet my eyes. "I've tried calling everywhere. He must be at sea."

At sea. That's how I felt, having just lost our daughter and hooked to a barrage of IVs while my husband was acting the playboy on a yacht in the Mediterranean.

My heart may have been a bleeding, fractured mess, but in that moment it hardened, ossifying harder than obsidian.

My vision blurred as I lifted my gaze to Bobby. Not to Jack, who should have been here to hold my hand and help me heal, but to his brother instead, who was the only one brave enough to tell me the news not even my mother could bear to break. Bobby, who looked so like Jack and whose wife was expecting their fifth child in only a few weeks, was here beside me because he knew what it was to love a child. What it was to love. "Jack should be here," I said, scalding-hot tears streaking down my cheeks. "And he's not."

"You can bet I'm going to make him feel like a piece of shit for it when I get ahold of him." Bobby tugged his tie completely loose, snapped it helplessly, and gave a ragged exhale. "God, Jacks, I'm so, so damnably sorry. I'll do everything I can to help you, although God knows what use I am."

Of course he would. Because to Bobby, family was everything. And even if Jack didn't act like it, I was family.

"Can I see her?" My hand was still in Bobby's and I clung to it, hanging on for dear life. "Can I see her before they take her away?"

He gave a tight nod, his hand brushing my cheek for the briefest second. "I'll move heaven and earth so you can."

He slipped out and my mother slipped in, her tweed-draped shoulders slumped and half-moon shadows carved deep under her eyes. A well-worn copy of *The Book of Common Prayer* was tucked under her arm, and she silently took up a post on the edge of my bed and pressed my head to her shoulder. "I'm sorry Jack's not here."

I ran a hand under my nose, marveling at the hollowness where my heart had once been. "My daughter is dead, and he's not here to see her because he's cheating on me again. How could I have been so stupid?"

"You're not stupid. You just put your trust in the wrong person." She stroked my hair with a steady hand. "You come from a long line of women with that character flaw. The good news is it's not fatal."

My mother and I sat in silence until Bobby returned with a uniformed nurse carrying a tiny pink-wrapped bundle. I held out my arms and then felt the bittersweet weight of my own child for the first and last time.

"Arabella," I breathed, so quiet that Bobby had to lean down to hear me. My tears were unchecked, as were my mother's across the room. "Her name is Arabella."

It was a fanciful name, a sweet and secret name, for surely if my darling girl had lived she'd have been given a proper Irish name handed down through generations of Kennedys. But Jack wasn't here, which made her mine.

And Bobby, dear wonderful Bobby, touched Arabella's forehead with his lips. "Arabella," he agreed.

I'd always love him for that, even as I'd never forgive Jack that he hadn't been there instead.

I t took three days for Jack to receive the news.

Two miserable, never-ending days, followed by a third when Arabella was buried.

Bobby took care of all the arrangements and finally managed to contact his father, who waited for Jack when they moored in Genoa, the news he carried signaling the end to Jack's sun-swept vacation.

Jack was downcast when my mother let him into my darkened room at Hammersmith, his face drawn. "I'm sorry I wasn't here," he said by way of greeting.

I could barely look at him, all my pent-up grief and rage transforming into a feral, clawing beast at the sight of his Mediterranean tan. To make matters worse, Lee had grudgingly reported the rumor that Jack had returned only after his friend told him, when news of my miscarriage broke, that if he ever wanted to run for president, he'd better haul ass back to me.

"The hospital believes it was a result of all the campaigning I did for you." Hoarfrost tinged my voice even as I buried deep the worry that I was physically incapable of bearing children. I was so damn angry, so tired of pretending. "Or maybe it was the realization that you'd lied, that you were out with some other woman on a pleasure cruise. That you cared more about that than me. Or your child."

There were no protestations, no denials. And there was no longer a baby to urge me to turn a blind eye, although neither was I so bold as to demand details.

Jack paced the tiny room, a wild animal straining against its cage, his right hand snapping against his thigh all the while. "I'm sorry, Jackie, and I swear it won't happen again—"

"Stop lying!" My bellow halted his pacing and he gaped at me with raw shock. "At least have the decency to tell me the truth—you owe me that much."

"I've almost died twice, Jackie." The words tumbled from his mouth, those poisoned lips I'd let kiss me. "I know it's wrong, but I can't help myself. I just want to live—to have it all—because I never know when all this will end."

So that was the naked truth, the real reason why he couldn't stay faithful to me. My breath clotted in my throat. One of the reasons I loved Jack—his unquenchable thirst for life—was the excuse he now turned against me.

Twin icebergs, were we? Well, Jack was about to feel how deeply I could freeze him out, how far we could fall from the sun.

"If you want absolution, you won't find it here." I leveled my most withering glare at him. "I want you to stay away from me. For a long, long time."

My voice was so small then, so hard. So dead.

"What do you mean?" His eyes narrowed. "You want a separation?"

"I don't know exactly what I mean." I shook my head to stop his protestations, slammed shut my eyes to block out the image of his wounded expression. As if he somehow thought he could get away with this, his second round of betrayal and public humiliation. "If I leave you—if I even whispered the word *divorce* for what you've done—it would all be over for your dreams of the White House, Jack."

"We're Catholic, Jackie. Catholics don't get divorced." Yet I could tell the instant he realized he'd walked into a trap.

"My mother and father divorced and lived to tell the tale. You, on the other hand . . ."

It remained to be seen whether I was brave—or stupid—enough to drag Jack across that particular bridge into hell.

"Maybe what's happened to us is my fault, Jackie, but nothing would have changed if I'd been here," he whispered. "Our daughter would still be dead."

Dead.

Would that word ever cease to be a weapon?

I rolled over, gave him the view of my back so he wouldn't witness the fresh tears that flooded my eyes. "I want you to leave. I'm going to Europe with Lee once I'm recovered. Through November."

His only further response was his footsteps toward the door. But I couldn't let him off so easy.

"She's buried in St. Columba's Catholic Cemetery in Middle-town." My voice trembled as I glanced over my shoulder at him. "In case you care."

I waited for him to say anything, to fall to his knees with protestations of how much he cared, or even to rage against my callousness.

Instead, the door only clicked shut behind him.

November 1956

J ack sold our perfect house at Hickory Hill to Bobby under the guise that it was too remote for us and would better accommodate his brother's ever-expanding family. The real reason was because I wasn't returning home, not to the house I'd lovingly decorated with a baby in mind, especially as our marriage shattered into a thousand jagged pieces. No home, no baby, and barely a husband meant the doors of my dreams were slamming shut in my face everywhere I turned.

I ran away to Europe to escape Jack and to make up my mind over what I was going to do, but my troubles only followed me.

Just days into my trip, I read a month-old gossip column interview from the sloop captain who had skippered Jack's recent yacht trip. The captain stated that not one but three young Scandinavian ladies were on the passenger list with the famous Kennedy senator.

Including one named Gunilla *goddamned* von Post.

Lee and I were readying for a four-day stint in Paris when a white-aproned maid entered my sitting room that overlooked the bustling Champs-Élysées. My sister had been a balm to my battered soul during this trip, for her marriage had also turned rocky—her prince of a husband had recently lost his meager position at the American embassy and now spent his days in an alcoholic fog reminiscent of our father's debauches. "Living in a fairy tale can be hell," Lee had said late one night as we commiserated over Picon Citron aperitifs. "Don't people know that?"

It seemed we Bouvier sisters were doomed to repeat our parents' miseries, whether we wished it or not.

The hotel maid now bobbed a curtsy in my direction. "Mr. Kennedy is on the phone for you, madame."

I hesitated. Thanksgiving had come and gone without a word from Jack, so I wondered why he deigned to telephone now.

"Make him beg." My sister preened before a mirror and I pushed aside the irrational flare-up of my old jealousy at her casual elegance. Lee had always been the prettier between us—as Mother had often pointed out—more petite and more fashionable. I supposed it was best that my sister and I suffered our marital tragedies together, lest we find ourselves falling into the habits of our old rivalries. "Make that son of a bitch get down on both knees and promise you every star in the sky," Lee continued. "You could ask for the moon and Jack would have to give it to you."

Jack did promise me the moon once, I wanted to say. *A lifetime ago.*

Lee's words ringing in my ears, I braced myself and walked to the telephone, almost replaced the receiver back in its cradle without saying a word. Instead, I held my breath and perched on the edge of a floral chaise longue, holding the receiver from my ear to ward off the loud crackles as my greeting was carried across the Atlantic.

"Hello?"

"Hey, kiddo."

"Mr. Kennedy." I startled, then slumped with relief that it was only Jack's father and not my husband. "Did Jack ask you to call?"

"No. This is all me, and you have my undivided attention." I could easily imagine the way Mr. Kennedy adjusted his spectacles on the bridge of his nose when he was mulling over something serious. "Isn't it about time you came home?"

"I'll be stateside next week." What Jack's father didn't know was that I'd made arrangements with my mother to return to Hammersmith Farm, not Hyannis Port. If I ever went home to Jack—and that was a big *if*—he was going to have to crawl his way back to me. And things were going to be different. Otherwise, I'd walk away.

I *would*. Even if it killed me to do it.

Mr. Kennedy cleared his throat as I lit a fresh L&M, inhaled a long drag. "You've been gone nearly four months. I can only squelch the rumors about your marriage for so long."

"Why bother?" I bit the edge of my already ragged fingernail, until Lee covered my hand and shook her head. "The rumors are all true. And everyone knows because Jack flaunted that woman under my very nose."

That woman. Because I'd never be able to bring myself to speak Gunilla von Post's name out loud.

There was a longer than usual pause. "I know. And I'd box my son's ears if I thought it would knock some sense into him. Still might, actually."

I wanted to scream with the irony of it all. Much as I loved Mr. Kennedy like a second father, he was a notorious philanderer in his own right and it was from him that Jack had learned to cat around on me. *But it's not Jack's father you're furious at. . . .*

I swallowed several times in a row, another new habit I'd have to break once I crawled out from under this horrible sense of being overwhelmed. "So you think I'm justified in leaving him?"

Across from me, Lee nodded so hard I thought her head might come loose even as she stood to pour our drinks from the afternoon tray. Yet I knew the answer wasn't so simple.

Of course Mr. Kennedy doesn't think that, Jackie. He may love you like a daughter, but he cheated on his own wife for decades and she never left him; instead she gave him nine children and helped run his empire.

Jack's father sighed. "I'll tell you what I think. We had a family conference over Thanksgiving and everyone agreed Jack was in the wrong. However, we also agreed that 1960 is going to be his year. And I'll spend every cent I own to see him elected president and you as First Lady. I want this for both of you, for all of us."

I cared little for castles spun from clouds just then and more for the fact that everyone assumed Jack's dreams were mine as well. "Well, I wish you all luck. Jack's going to have quite the mountain to climb as an Irish Catholic, especially a divorced one."

The silence on the line lengthened until I wondered whether the call had been disconnected. Finally, Mr. Kennedy cleared his throat. "You can't divorce him, kiddo."

"Is he going to stop me?" My voice rose an octave. "Or will you?"

"Money and image will win him the White House. I've got the money, but you, Jacqueline Bouvier Kennedy, you have the image. We Kennedys never settle for second best, and you, Jackie, are the best. You're our winner, and goddammit, we need you."

"Really? Then why isn't Jack telling me this himself?"

"Because he's an idiot. Which you've already figured out." Mr. Kennedy sighed, and I imagined him running a hand over his balding pate. "Truth is, Jack had a piss-poor example of marriage from his mother and me, and he didn't want to mess this up. Think of me as the mediator."

You could ask for the moon and Jack would have to give it to you.

Maybe Lee was right.

"What is Jack going to do to keep me?"

"My son is prepared to make certain sacrifices to see to your happiness." Mr. Kennedy spoke in such a way that I wondered if Jack was standing there with him, arms crossed and glowering. "And to encourage you to give him a chance, I'm prepared to transfer one million dollars to an account in your name."

I held the receiver away from my ear, gaped at it as if it were a writhing rattlesnake. They thought my happiness could be bought, that I could be bought, like one of their tawdry mistresses. Lee offered me a martini and cocked her head in question, but I only shook my head.

"One million dollars is hardly a bribe," I finally said into the receiver, my stomach churning. "Why not ten?"

Jack's father misunderstood me. "Ten it is, if that will make you stay. You're a part of this team, kiddo, whether you like it or not."

"I don't want your money. I only want to come first in his life." My voice was so quiet I wondered whether Mr. Kennedy had heard me at all. Whether any of them had ever heard me. "That's all I've ever wanted."

"You do come first. It may not seem like it, but you're his partner. Those other women . . ." He trailed off. "They're just lollipops."

"But why does he need them? He says he needs to grab everything life has to offer, but there are other men who've almost died and they don't act like this. Why isn't life with me living to the fullest?"

"You're not going to like this answer, but I want you to think about it for a while because it's the honest-to-God truth." Mr. Kennedy paused, so I knew he was choosing his words carefully. "What you have with Jack is special, Jackie—sanctified by God—and no other woman can touch it. You were there for him when he needed it most; the others are just girls du jour—he doesn't feel anything for them. Certainly not what he feels for you."

I shook my head, rejecting his convoluted rationale. "I don't think Jack feels anything for me."

"Now you're wrong there, all wrong, but I can see how it would seem that way. Jack understands now that this needs to be a partnership—that you have to come before anyone else. That he can't humiliate you anymore."

I wondered what it had taken to make my husband realize that. God knew I'd tried to teach him that since the days of our honeymoon.

But Jack's father wasn't done. "I'll buy you two a proper house to give you both a fresh start. All I ask is that you give Jack six months to prove that things will be better this time. If it doesn't work, my offer still stands. But Jackie, you're going to have to show him how it's done. Lead him. Can you do that?"

Could anyone lead John Fitzgerald Kennedy anywhere? I doubted it, even as I imagined moving back into my mother's house, divorced and humiliated. I'd sworn sacred vows before God with Jack; I supposed the least I could do before I found myself excommunicated like my mother was to try this one last time.

After all, Jack had already broken my heart, so I had nothing to lose. And everything still to win.

"I'll give him six months." I ignored my sister's grimace at my promise, realized with a start that I'd lit at least half a pack of L&Ms, all of them unsmoked and stubbed out in the ashtray on the desk. God above, I was a mess. "If things haven't improved by then, I make no guarantees."

Another long pause. "That's more than fair, kiddo. Jack will pick you up at the airport."

"I look forward to it."

As I hung up, I knew that was an egregious lie.

I dreaded seeing Jack again.

I wasn't sure which was brighter when the press's cacophony of flash-bulbs went off: the cameras or Jack's pasted-on million-watt smile. "It's been a long time since you've seen her, Jack," one middle-aged reporter urged with a waggle of his unkempt brows. "Give us a kiss!"

Tugging at the jacket of my black Chanel ribbed wool suit, I felt a sudden wave of revulsion for the entire press corps to whom I'd once belonged and who now dogged my most private moments. I tried to ignore them and focused instead on my husband before me, the way his nervous fingers tapped out some secret message against his thigh.

Six months, Jackie. A lot can happen in six months.

Jack pressed a dry kiss to my temple and I stiffened, knowing the rare display of affection meant he was firmly on the campaign trail. The gesture rang hollow, no matter how the press spun it.

"My wife has had a long trip and I'm sure she'd like to rest at home." Jack gave a jaunty salute to the reporters. "However, I expect to see you all when the Senate is back in session."

I scarcely avoided rolling my eyes as I walked to the waiting car, my heels clicking on the concrete tarmac while Jack hurried after me. We didn't speak until he'd opened the car door and I'd slipped into the passenger seat, keeping close to the door.

Once alone, Jack jumped straight to the heart of the matter. "My father told me you turned down his bribe."

"I did." I tilted my chin in the air, then flicked on the radio to fill the awkward silences that were destined to come. I almost laughed aloud when the final lines of "Why Do Fools Fall in Love" filled the air. "For now."

"For now?"

"Don't think for a minute that I'm a sure thing, Jack." I looked askance and leveled my frostiest glare at him. "You want to be president and I want my husband back."

"I never left."

I opened my mouth to lambaste him about Gunilla von Post, then snapped it shut. After all, this was my chance to chart a bold new course, not to follow in my mother's footsteps.

I crossed one ankle over the other, watching the Potomac pass by. "Hard to leave when you've never truly been here."

"That's not fair. I love you, Jackie."

In his own way, he probably did. But the dregs he'd offered me weren't enough.

"Life isn't fair, Jack. Take it on the chin." I barely tempered my tone. "Your father once said it's not what you are, it's what people think you are, right? And since you want America to believe you're the perfect husband and thus the perfect presidential candidate, I'm sure we can come to some sort of understanding."

I pinched the bridge of my nose, wondering what the hell I was doing. One thing was certain: I was done doing things Jack's way, and Mr. Kennedy had asked that I show Jack how this was done. Well, if Jack wanted the presidency, then he was going to have to play by my rules. And I was playing to win.

"We're a package deal, Jack, the White House and me. So you'd better start acting like it. I come first. Always. And you will never, *ever* humiliate me again."

We approached Georgetown in painful silence, Elvis Presley crooning from the radio and me waiting for Jack to suddenly swerve and speed back to the airport. Instead, he cleared his throat and his thumb tapped nervously on the steering wheel as he drove across Key Bridge. "My father said he wanted to buy you a house. For us." He glanced at me. "I found one I thought you might like. I could take you to see it now, if you want, that is."

As he finished stumbling his way through the invitation, I realized one thing: Jack Kennedy was nervous. All because of me, because I held the key to his happiness, just as he held the key to mine. Apparently, he'd agreed to my terms.

"That would be fine." I reached out and touched his hand briefly, gritting my teeth even as I imagined him touching Gunilla von Post with those same fingers. "I want this to work, Jack. For both our sakes."

"Me too," he said. "Me too."

And in that moment, I'd have given everything to believe him.

The Federal-style redbrick house Jack found on 3307 N Street was delightful, and we moved in one chilly January day. Now, as I directed where the movers should unpack lamps for the little spare bedroom off the master, I wondered how much I was willing to sacrifice to make this marriage—this partnership—work.

This time will be different, I promised myself as the doorbell rang. *It has to be.*

Until now, I'd always seen myself as somehow lesser than Jack. His slip-up with Gunilla had forever tumbled him from his lofty pedestal, had transformed him from demigod to flawed mortal. And I had the high ground, for I wasn't the one who had erred.

I was trying to decide which picture to hang in the dining room when the butler announced an unexpected guest. My mother.

"I've come to share with you my ironclad rules on how to run your own estate," she said when she breezed in with well-organized examples of menus and account books tucked under her arms.

"I already ran Hickory Hill on my own, Mummy."

"Yes, well, you were more focused on the remodel, and then with everything else that happened . . . I thought this was the perfect opportunity for a refresher."

Although our side of the family never really talked, I saw this visit for what it truly was: an opportunity to check up on me. So I let my mother demonstrate the only acceptable way to organize the spice cabinet (alphabetically, of course), and the best schedule for having the windows washed (biannually, in the spring and fall).

"Mummy, you run Hammersmith like a very strict, very mean hotel in a Communist country," I finally said after she'd drilled me on the need for daily fresh floral arrangements. "I'm not sure it's even possible to meet your standards."

My mother looked at me as if I'd suddenly sprouted a second head. "That doesn't mean you shouldn't give it your best effort, Jacqueline. I'd never forgive myself if you made all the same mistakes that I did."

Touché, *Mummy*.

"You have a lovely new home and one day you might raise a family here. Just be certain before you make any significant changes."

While Hughdie was kind and consistent, I'd always known that my father had been the real passion of my mother's life, and now I wondered if she harbored hidden regrets over her divorce with him. While asking would break some unwritten family rule, I felt better knowing that this newest attempt at salvaging my marriage—we both knew my mother wasn't referring to my housekeeping—had her vote of confidence.

That night after my mother, the butler-valet, the cook, and the maid had gone home for the day, Jack came home bearing good news, perhaps the best we'd had in a while.

"*Profiles in Courage* is going to be awarded the Pulitzer Prize," he exclaimed, his chest puffed out with pride. "Can you believe it?"

"Why, that's wonderful." I might have left it at that and continued to freeze him out, but this felt like a door—or perhaps just a window—opening a crack. And it *was* wonderful, that this project we'd worked on together was going to receive such an illustrious award.

So I finished my cigarette and rummaged through myriad unlabeled boxes in pursuit of the Champagne flutes Jack and I had received for our wedding. Unable to find them, I shrugged and settled for two ceramic cereal bowls. (Which broke at least six rules in my mother's exacting formula for good living.)

Jack's eyebrows knit together from where he sat on the couch in his shirtsleeves when I brought him a bowl, then chuckled as he realized what it held inside.

"Now why hadn't I thought of using bowls for Champagne before?" he asked.

Much as I hated to admit it, he was handsome sitting there, those quicksilver eyes focused on me and his head slightly cocked in question. That was the potency of Jack's allure, his ability to make you feel as if you were the only person on earth who mattered to him, even if it was only a façade.

"A toast." I ruthlessly hammered down the misgivings that arose in my mind. "To *Profiles* and the courage to face fresh beginnings."

Because while it would be easier to remain tepid toward Jack, far more difficult was forgiveness, to do the opposite of what my mother had done with my father and embrace Jack as my husband.

If I ended up divorcing him, I wanted to know I had done everything in my power to hold our marriage together. If Jack and I fell apart, it would be his fault, not mine.

Jack set aside his Senate papers and rose with that fluid grace of his, loosening his tie. He stood close enough that I could smell his woodsy cologne—vanilla with a hint of pine and something so decidedly male that I felt my entire core go molten. I hated that my traitorous body responded on a visceral level to Jack's nearness as he clinked his bowl against mine. "To fresh beginnings."

Jack surprised me then by offering me his bowl in an echo of our wedding day. I hesitated, then wrapped my arm around his to offer him my bowl.

And we drank. Together.

. . .

Saffron-hued tulips sunned themselves in the wrought-iron planter outside our N Street home, each petal ablaze with spring sunshine while the open window let in the gentle May breeze, as I frowned into the phone receiver.

"Is this how fathers discover that they're going to be grandfathers now?" Black Jack Bouvier's hoarse voice rumbled on the other end over what sounded like ice cubes clinking in a whiskey glass. "From the newspaper?"

It had been ages since I'd heard from the lovable tramp that was my father—and five months since the move to N Street—so I did feel a deep pang of guilt for not having telephoned him sooner. With the announcement that Jack's *Profiles in Courage* was to be awarded the Pulitzer Prize, we'd been busier than usual, and unlike with the last two pregnancies, Jack and I had tried to keep our news quiet, but somehow word had been leaked to the press.

It was something I knew I should get used to—having no secrets— but I doubted whether I ever would.

"I didn't want to bother you," I said to my father. "Or get your hopes up."

"My hopes for you are already sky high, my girl," he said, which made me smile. My father had that rare gift of making people love him, another trait he shared with Jack.

"I need to visit you soon. Lee told me you're having back pains? And sinus problems?" I should be the one to visit our father since Lee was touring Tuscany with her husband in a last-ditch effort to save her own crumbling marriage from a plague of money troubles.

From the outside, the Bouvier sisters seemed to have twenty-four-karat marriages, but scrape off that top layer of gilding . . .

As my due date neared, I could sense Jack fighting the panic that this pregnancy would end as the others had. Yet he'd controlled himself, placated now that I was under doctor's orders to be a lazy lotus-eater and do as little as possible. My father seemed to read my mind. "Don't you dare make the trip up here. Rest, and let Jack and your mother take care of you."

"Someone needs to pry you out of that apartment of yours with a crowbar and get you a meal of something other than lamb chops and lima beans."

"Lamb chops and lima beans are my favorites." My father coughed, sounding like a far older man. "And I left my apartment just a few weeks ago for a night out with that husband of yours. Made me realize I'm getting old. The doctors claim my liver's shot; they want me to have some tests done."

I frowned, scarcely hearing the last part; Jack hadn't mentioned seeing my father. I envisioned my womanizer of a father out for a night with Jack and winced at the debauchery my imagination immediately concocted. But Jack might have passed for Saint Joseph since I'd told him of this new pregnancy.

"What sort of tests?" I asked, after my father's words penetrated my worries. "Nothing serious, I hope."

"Routine stuff."

"You'll have to visit in November, after the baby's born," I said. *If it's born*, the thought whispered, but I shoved it away before the blow could land.

"I'll camp on your lawn if I have to." I scoffed, for I doubted whether my debonair father had ever camped a day in his life. "How old do you think the little tyke will have to be before I can teach her to play poker?"

I smiled. "At least a few weeks."

He chuckled into the phone, a raspy sound. "You'll likely have her reading Faulkner and Melville by then too."

"I was thinking we'd start with Edna St. Vincent Millay." Jack's car pulled up to the curb just then. "I'll see you soon, Dad."

But I didn't see him. It was Jack who drove me to New York like a bat out of hell after the phone call came over my birthday weekend that Black Jack Bouvier had fallen into a coma.

The doctors claim my liver's shot; they want me to have some tests done.

Apparently, that translated as his having been diagnosed with liver cancer for some time. Anger made my stomach clench, followed by an icy wave of fear. *How dare he not tell me?*

Jack's fingers remained threaded through mine the entire way to Lenox Hill Hospital—that right hand that always had a life of its own: tapping, tugging, snapping, now only squeezed my hand every so often so I might borrow from his silent well of strength. My nerves were stretched taut by a helplessness even stronger than I'd felt after Jack's surgery, for this time I was too far away to do anything.

"Can you drive faster?" I whispered once.

Jack's foot pressed into the pedal was his response. "I'd fly you there if I could," he answered softly. "I wish there was more I could do."

"Just stay with me?" It was the only show of weakness I allowed myself in front of Jack, and I expected him to spin some excuse of flying back tonight for Senate business, but he surprised me by squeezing my knee.

"I'm not going anywhere, kid."

We made it to New York in what must have been a Guinness record, but the intensive-care nurse only shook her head sadly when I asked for my father's room number.

"I'm sorry, Mrs. Kennedy," she said. "But Mr. Bouvier passed an hour ago."

It was Jack's sudden arm tight around me that kept me upright, that gave me the strength to keep my tears inside even as a fissure cracked open my heart when I recalled my father teaching me to climb trees in Central Park and spoiling me—his favorite child—with peppermint candies and stacks of novels when I was a little girl.

An hour . . . How could an hour make such a difference?

I was angry then—so furious that I nearly trembled at its sudden heat—at the father who had broken our family apart and drowned his sorrows until he couldn't even walk me down the aisle at my wedding, at the man who had lied rather than tell me he was sick so I might visit him one last time. That anger quickly crumbled, consumed by my guilt at being so faithless a daughter. My father had loved me, had done the best that he could with what he had. What more could a daughter ask for?

"Is there someone I should contact to make arrangements?" the nurse asked. "Mr. Bouvier listed his housekeeper for emergencies, but since you're here . . ." Her voice trailed off. "Or is there someone else I could call? His wife, perhaps?"

I almost choked at the thought of my mother having to make my father's final arrangements, how she'd rant and rave that he was tormenting her from the grave.

This was my duty, and my duty alone.

"Tell me what needs to be done," I said to the nurse. My emotions roiled with the force of a winter hurricane, but I kept my expression and tone as placid as freshly fallen snow. "I'll take care of it all."

So I painstakingly penned Black Jack's obituary, placed the dozen phone calls to my sister and the Bouvier side of the family—my father had long ago alienated most of his friends—and chose an austere gold tie pin and matching cuff links to accent the dark blue suit he'd be laid out in.

To my surprise, Jack remained by my side through it all, a guardian against my grief and a solid shoulder for me to cry on.

He stood tall next to me the day of the funeral in St. Patrick's Cathedral in New York, the church's damp coolness a welcome respite from the glare of the summer sun outside. The pews were mostly empty, just a light scattering of family and, in the back rows, a handful of women—strangers to all of us save my father—with faces obscured by black veils. Yet, through the blur of my own veil, rare splashes of color made me smile, for I'd foregone the traditional funereal waxen white lilies in favor of a cacophony of yellow daisies and blue cornflowers, my final gift to my carefree father who had so loved the month of August at our seaside retreat in East Hampton.

Even in death, there can be beauty and hope, if only we dare to look hard enough.

When the service finished and everyone else had filed out of the church, I knelt at my father's casket and requested that it be opened so I might tuck the bracelet he'd given me for graduation beneath his stiff hands. "Jack hasn't left my side these past days," I whispered to my father, glancing over my shoulder to where my husband waited for me in an empty alcove. "I have you to thank for that final gift." I clasped my hands as if praying, uncaring of whether what I was about to ask was sacrilegious. "Will you take care of my two angels, and if you can, will you look out for this new baby? Please, Daddy?"

I rose, my vision blurring, and with one final glance back at my father, retreated into the safety of Jack's waiting arms.

And stepped back out into the summer sunshine and into the business of living.

November 1957

Perhaps my father heard my prayer, for Caroline Bouvier Kennedy, christened after my sister and father, made her way into the world one calm autumn night. A single word came to mind as I gazed at her sleeping form in the moonlight.

La douceur.

It was French for gentle sweetness, the perfect word to describe my exquisitely formed daughter. She was my *douceur de vivre*, the sweetness of my life.

When Jack first placed Caroline in my arms—he carried her as if she were a delicate porcelain doll, his face transparent with joy—my heart swelled to realize I'd made the right decision in staying with Jack. I caught the way he blinked and cleared his throat as if trying not to cry when he gazed at our miracle of a daughter.

"She's so perfect," he whispered, his hand hovering over her downy head. "Our forever girl."

"She's our legacy." Jack had given me a precious gift in Caroline, one I knew would count among the greatest accomplishments of our lives. "The one to carry our torches after we're gone."

Jack smiled, ran his thumb down her soft cheeks. "Look at her precious little nose." His voice was full of wonder. "Like a perfect button."

If you bungle raising your children, I'd thought to myself as I'd let her tiny fingers clasp mine that first night, *I don't think whatever else you do well matters very much.*

No matter how many versions of Jacqueline Kennedy might one day exist—daughter, sister, debutante, wife—the one created this day—mother—would always come first.

For the first time since my wedding day, I was finally content.

Like a fairy-tale dragon hoarding its treasure, I might have happily remained home with Caroline for the whole of every day and kept her hidden from the curious gazes of the press, but that was an impossible dream considering our social status and Jack's political aspirations. As my mother swiftly reminded me when I'd broached the idea, it simply wasn't done.

"Is the nursery ready for the photographers?" I asked Caroline's efficient new English nanny one afternoon. Maud Shaw was in her mid-fifties, with a crown of frizzy reddish curls and a strict demeanor that belied her hidden streak of good humor, a veritable Mary Poppins without the magic. Impressive as she was, I was still determined Caroline would spend more time with me than the nanny.

"It is indeed, ma'am." Miss Shaw's impeccable British manners were one of the reasons I'd hired her; I thought it adorable that she steadfastly referred to Jack as Senator Kennedy because she claimed that titles ought to be used. "She took her bottle well, and I've dressed her in a ruffled day dress that will have the entire country wanting to pinch her adorable cheeks."

I smiled and resisted the urge to pick at the itchy gold embroidery on the blue satin dress I'd chosen. It was me who had dug out the long-forgotten *Life* photographer's business card from our engagement shoot and requested that this interview take place, mostly because I sought to parlay with the press on my own terms. Together, in Caroline's pink-and-white nursery with its dado of little bunches of red roses on the wallpaper and frilly white organdy curtains above the pink-bowed bassinet, we'd look the perfect upper-class American family once Jack joined us.

And we were a family now, and so we would forever be. With Caroline's birth, my threat of divorce dissolved. I'd never put my child through the knock-down-drag-out fights or the residual stigma that Lee and I had endured when our parents separated.

Jack had come through on his end of our deal—Caroline, this new house, and my contentment were proof of that—so it was my turn to grit my teeth and showcase for Massachusetts voters that my husband shared their values as a family man while he stumped with a hard stance against Communist Russia.

I'd help Jack win the reelection to his Senate seat, and after that . . .

Nineteen sixty is going to be his year.

The White House seemed a fantasy locked in the tallest tower of a stone castle perched on the highest cloud, but I'd made Jack a promise. I could scarcely imagine the future he dreamed of each night, for surely we were too young and untested to follow the likes of staid Ike and Mamie Eisenhower. Heaven only knew how well I could balance being a wife and mother while managing a household, much less the duties that would come with being First Lady.

One thing at a time, Jackie. There's no need to worry about a future that may never materialize.

"I'll tell you what, you have good taste, kid," Jack said to me when he breezed in, having squeezed the photo shoot between morning and committee meetings. He glanced around our sunny third-floor bedroom while I cinched the striped tie that complemented his sophisticated charcoal suit. "Expensive, but good taste nonetheless."

"It's part of my charm." I stepped back to admire the debonair senator who'd replaced the cocksure congressman who had once dressed for a dinner party wearing scuffed brown shoes. "This interview is going to capture you so many votes it will be a veritable landslide come November."

Jack offered me his arm. "The photographers await. Shall we?"

The sun streamed into Caroline's nursery, where afternoon tea had been laid out with a porcelain plate of *petit beurre* biscuits. This was meant to be a quaint family story—Jack didn't have to work hard to showcase his true affinity for fatherhood as he tickled Caroline until they were both giggling—but while the photographer began the shoot with effusive praise of Caroline's demeanor and my decorating, his questions quickly took an unexpected—and unacceptable—turn.

"So, Mr. Kennedy," came one as a flashbulb was changed. "Do you have any response regarding the claims that one of your speechwriters actually wrote *Profiles in Courage*?"

The reporter didn't pick up on the way Jack's jaw clenched, but I did and prayed this innocent family photo op wouldn't turn into an unfortunate scene. Only I had witnessed Jack's barely restrained rage in our living room when journalist Drew Pearson had recently gone on *The Mike Wallace Interview* and claimed in grainy black and white that Jack was the only man in history who won a Pulitzer Prize for a book that was ghostwritten for him.

"That's my goddamned book being called into question," Jack had growled in such a way that even our new Welsh terrier, Charlie, had whined and hid his head. "The one I wrote when I was half dead, not that this Pearson prick knows anything about that."

The phone had started ringing immediately, for Pearson's claim had set the entire Kennedy family in an uproar. I refrained from reminding them that Jack had used the services of one of his speechwriters, Ted Sorensen, to do the physical typing of his ideas. Still, those ideas had been Jack's, and his alone.

Some journalists really did deserve to have their credentials stripped and fed to them.

Especially the one simpering across from me, I thought, ruing my decision to invite him as I readjusted Caroline on my lap and placed a gentle hand of warning on Jack's thigh.

"Off the record?" Jack recovered to ask with that movie-star smile of his, to which the reporter only leaned forward, obviously held in his thrall. "I'd say I wished a ghostwriter would have lain in that hospital bed with nothing else to do all those months instead of me. And that Pearson's claim must not have been true since ABC dropped the entire story and printed a retraction."

I pretended to be immersed in smoothing Caroline's ruffles. *Only because your father threatened to sue the studio for $50 million.*

After that, there were a few more photographs, and the whole sordid thing was finished. But that photo shoot with its barbed questions was only the beginning.

Next came the whirlwind of whistle-stop trips I took with Jack from Nantucket to Boston. I forced a smile into my eyes and posed for pictures until my cheeks hurt, my arms aching from missing Caroline, and my eyes perpetually blinded from flashbulbs.

Yet Jack fed off every event, drew energy from each crowd until he was a force to be reckoned with.

Whether I liked it or not, the Kennedy machine worked its magic, for Jack won reelection with an astounding 850,000 votes, the largest total vote ever for a Massachusetts politician.

The results were scarcely in before whispers of the Oval Office solidified into murmurs, then into Jack's pledge from the Senate Caucus Room that he would run for president in 1960. I stood beside him then, dressed in a crisp snowy-white suit and a black onyx necklace, my heart juddering in my chest.

Perhaps that castle on a cloud was a little nearer than I'd thought.

Jackie will be useful for hosting press teas in your Georgetown drawing room," drawled Kenny O'Donnell in his Irish brogue as he gestured offhand in my direction while I poured everyone's coffee. One of the members of Jack's intellectual blood bank, the man looked like an overgrown leprechaun, and he sounded like one too. "Otherwise, ma'am, I'm afraid you'll need to stay out of the spotlight."

"Pardon me?" Although this critical planning meeting was taking place in Bobby's house instead of our own, I wasn't about to be excluded, now or ever. Jack was flanked on Ethel's floral chintz couches by a veritable Praetorian Guard, all the way from Bobby to every top-ranking campaign aide who had assisted his successful bid for the Senate. Only his father was missing—to keep it from appearing that the old ambassador was pulling Jack's strings—but I knew father and son would talk on the phone at least three times today. I was the only woman in the room, and while part of me wanted to collapse in relief that I wouldn't have to continue with the ballyhoo of campaigning, it was imperative that I remain useful to Jack, which was why I'd recently braved the crowds and January cold with a copy of *War and Peace* under one arm of a beautifully cut imitation Givenchy red coat, all because Jack wished to add a veneer of elegance to a simple campaign stop in the dairy country of Wisconsin. "Why wouldn't I be at Jack's side as I was during the senatorial campaign?"

Kenny glanced at Jack, who remained entirely impassive, as if testing whether his logic for excluding me would ring true. "I'm afraid, ma'am, that you're not what the American people expect in a future First Lady. You've got a little too much status, and not enough quo."

I cut my eyes at him. "I'm not sure what you mean."

I did, but I wanted the man to have to look me in the face and say it.

"Picture Bess Truman, or even Eleanor Roosevelt." He didn't even have the decency to look abashed as he continued. "Nice, dowdy, with enough wrinkles around the eyes to remind voters of their mothballed grandmothers."

So I was too young? And better dressed?

Perhaps someone should have informed the likes of Dolley Madison and Grace Coolidge that they were too youthful and stylish to be First Ladies. . . .

"Jack is barely forty." I clasped my hands in front of me, the better to keep from using them to wring Kenny's throat. "They can hardly expect him to be married to a grandmother."

"No, but they'll prefer that he's married to an unassuming American girl." Kenny set down his coffee. "To be blunt, Mrs. Kennedy, you're too young, too pretty, and too foreign."

"Foreign?" Now I was horrified. "I'm more American than you are, Mr. O'Donnell. At least the press doesn't refer to me as the Irish Mafia."

"That may be so, but I wasn't educated at the Sorbonne and I'm not fluent in five languages. And I'm not going to be the president's wife."

Red-faced and fuming, I found empty cups to rearrange on the coffee tray so the men couldn't see the steam coming out of my ears. The only way Jack and I worked was when we operated together as a team, which meant I wasn't willing to be sidelined. Ever again.

I pivoted slowly to face them once more, a fresh pot of coffee held in midair. "I'm only fluent in three languages, Mr. O'Donnell," I said sweetly. "I'm merely proficient in Italian and Polish. Considering that America is famous for being a melting pot, I'd think that an asset to Jack's campaign, not a hindrance."

It was Bobby who smothered a smile and crossed lines to join my side, tapping a pen on the table in my direction. "Jackie has a point there."

I gave him a weak nod of gratitude, but O'Donnell and the rest of the Irish Mafia had already moved on. "So we'll have you go alone to most of your speeches, Jack, maybe accompanied by one of your sisters or your mother."

I waited for Jack to argue with them, to insist that it be me at his side, but his gaze held mine for a mere second before he turned his attention to the mountain of schedules strewn over the coffee table. Bobby frowned and shrugged, as if to tell me he'd tried.

Enfoirés. I set down the coffeepot and walked stiffly from the room. Let them pour their own goddamned coffee.

Kenny O'Donnell and the entire Irish Mafia were fools if they thought I was going to spend my husband's presidential campaign sipping tea with the damned press corps.

That night I was already in bed pretending to reread a biography of Madame de Genlis, the French mistress of Philippe d'Orléans, when Jack finally came into our room and nudged off his shoes. No matter how many times I helped him shrug out of his collared shirt and remove his back brace as I did now, I would never grow entirely accustomed to the angry red lines streaking his torso where the brace had pressed into him all day, or the savage scar that ran along his spine. I'd spent the afternoon concocting my argument for why I should remain part of the self-same presidential campaign it would have been far easier to abandon, but Jack didn't give me a chance to explain my reasoning.

"I'm going to Louisiana in a few days to start campaigning." He leaned slowly back on the bed, groaning as he relaxed into the mattress, and I waited for the freshly sharpened guillotine of his next sentence, the words that would cleave me from him. "I want you to come with me."

"What?" I stopped folding his shirt, unable to entirely believe my ears. "Did O'Donnell change his mind?"

"Hardly." Jack laced his fingers behind his head, a smile tugging up the corner of his lips. "I don't need Kenny's—or anyone else's—permission to run my campaign how I want."

"I wish I could have seen his face when you told him."

Moreover, I wished Jack had put Kenny in his place when I was still in the room, although that wasn't Jack's style. I knew he'd continued to ruminate on the matter while they'd plotted out the rest of the campaign, all the while silently analyzing the benefits and drawbacks of having me at his side before making his final decision.

None of that mattered. All that mattered was that he'd sided with me.

I knelt on the floor, my forearms on the bed as I gazed up at him. "You've chosen well, Bunny."

"Have I?" His eyebrows quirked in question, and he tucked a stray curl behind my ear.

I gave an artful shrug. "Can you imagine Kenny in New Orleans trying to answer a constituent in French with that awful Irish brogue of his? It would sound like a bulldog choking on marbles."

Jack gave a chuff of laughter. "That would definitely put voters off."

"I just have one question, Mr. Kennedy." I did my best to affect my old wide-eyed newspaper girl demeanor. "Before I agree to campaign for you."

Jack cocked his head, still grinning. "And what might that be, Mrs. Kennedy?"

"Why do you want to be president?"

Why?

It was a question I'd never asked him before, that I wasn't sure anyone had ever truly asked. Jack seemed to sense what I wanted—not the tired rationale about fulfilling his father's dream after his brother's death or a canned campaign answer about needing fresh vitality in the White House now that Eisenhower had allowed America to fall behind the Soviets. I wanted to know what fueled the furnace of this dream he'd clung to for the past decade.

His expression sobered, his hands turned to fists he clenched and unclenched. "I want to do things, Jackie. I want to wring every second out of each day as if it was my last, and I want America to do the same—to stop this stagnation so she can accomplish great and mighty things simply because we can." He gave a shaky breath, leaned over on a forearm to better pierce me with those storm-tossed eyes of his. Even in stillness, those eyes were never calm, always seeing and always moving. "Because I want to live on after I die. And when I do die, I want to be able to say that I used up everything I had, and I did it for America. For us."

I gave a tiny nod, my throat so tight from his rare and heartfelt words that I couldn't speak. He collapsed back to the pillows as if such an admission had cost him dearly, and my vision blurred as I rose and placed my hands on either side of his face. "Then, to Louisiana we go," I whispered as I kissed him. "And then, the White House."

Louisiana was a Cajun whirlwind spiced with the sound of Zydeco accordions and seasoned with the aromatic flavors of peppery jambalaya. Jack and I flew into the town of Lafayette, where I was presented with two white camellias in full, fragrant bloom before we clambered into one of twelve gleaming white Cadillacs that spirited our entire party to the Oakbourne Country Club for a barbecue prior to the crowning of the Queen of the Rice Festival.

"I don't think I've seen so many people in one place since the queen's coronation," I murmured breathlessly to Jack. His eyes sparkled, for he was in his element at the head of the crowd, but so many voices and the crush of bodies made it impossible for me to draw a full inhale.

"They want to hear from you." Jack inclined his head—still crowned by an uproarious fedora bedecked in rice that marked the festival's guest of honor—toward the podium he'd just vacated. "Give them a speech."

"Never." I gave a tight shake of my head, my hand fluttering to the pearls at my neck. It was one thing to smile and wave from Jack's side, quite another to give a speech I wasn't prepared for.

"Do it, Jacks." He gave my lower back a nudge, causing a tremble down my spine. "For me."

I want America to do the same . . . to accomplish great and mighty things simply because we can.

Jack's words and his heady, guiding presence made me want to find the courage to spread my wings and soar into the unknown, no matter how much it frightened me.

I stepped up to the podium, clasping my white-gloved hands to keep them from trembling while suddenly feeling overheated in my white wool jacket. A hush of anticipation fell over the crowd. In that moment, every word I'd ever learned evaporated from my mind and the silence held several beats too long.

There are so many of them. . . .

Then, as I looked at the women holding their babies, the husbands with their wives, I realized what I could say that would speak to them.

"*Bonjour, mes amis,*" I began, so softly I worried the microphone hadn't picked up the words. But the French-speaking Cajuns went wild at the sound of me speaking their native tongue. All these people had contributed so much to our country's culture; it seemed a proper courtesy to address them in their own language. I glanced behind me, buoyed by their raucous applause and Jack's encouraging nod.

He believed in me, so I would believe in myself.

I might have been the pope come to bless a crowd of Catholics for how loud the crowd cheered as I continued speaking in French. It was a short speech, but Jack embraced me when I finished. "Good Lord." His expression was tinged with awe. "What did you say to them?"

"I told them how happy I am to be in southern Louisiana," I answered with a grin. "That my father, Black Jack Bouvier, told me when I was a little girl that Louisiana was a little corner carved out of France, and that of course, as a Bouvier, I love everything French and I'm so happy to see everything my father said is true."

"Well done, kid," was all he had a chance to say before women streamed forward to hug me and shake my hand, all jabbering over one another in French so that I caught only snippets of their words. But I smiled and answered, accepting their congratulations and collecting their promises to vote for my husband.

"*Tu es l'une de nous!*" one exclaimed, while another kissed both my cheeks as if we were in France. *You are one of us!*

A hidden part of me recoiled at so much attention, but I affixed my most brilliant smile to my face, for their adoration was precisely what Jack needed to win this election.

It's only another costume, Jackie. The happy politician's wife. . . .

Afterward, in the backseat of the hired car that would drive us to the airport, I felt a thrill at my success, at having been actively helpful to Jack's campaign and not just the sort of wife who waved from the sidelines. I opened a mason jar of homemade pralines one woman had pressed into my hands and offered them to Jack, but he had eyes only for me.

"You were amazing." He said each word slowly, as if he still couldn't believe it. "With you at my side, there's no way I can lose."

He surprised me then by kissing me, a hungry, possessive sort of branding that I could have lost myself in. I almost did, were it not for the campaign worker sitting in the front seat next to the driver, both of their eyes flicking to the rearview mirror and quickly away.

"Reggie," Jack finally said to the campaign worker. "Mrs. Kennedy and I need the evening alone in the French Quarter tonight. Please make the arrangements and let the other staffers know."

"Sure thing, Mr. Kennedy."

Jack might need the White House to be happy, but I could have stayed in New Orleans forever, just him and me.

Sadly, all good things come to an end. Louisiana was just one state, and there were many more to go. . . .

G iven the vast sum of money Jack's father spent on politics, one would have thought he could have gotten Andy Warhol elected president. Yet there was no guarantee that any amount of money would win Jack the Democratic primary, much less the general election, especially as Lyndon B. Johnson—whom we all called Senator Cornpone due to his Texan roots—surged forward in the polls. Mr. Kennedy's wire before our first campaign stop in West Virginia reminded us of that.

Jack,

Forget West Virginia—there's no way a Catholic Irishman can win in that backwoods state. Don't buy a single vote more than is necessary. I'll be damned if I'm going to pay for a landslide.

Good luck to you, Boy, and I hope to see you soon.

Still, every vote counted, so while Jack was off giving a speech to West Virginia local unions, I stood by the cash register of the run-down neighborhood Big Bear supermarket to greet the hardscrabble coal miners waiting in line. As at home as I'd felt in New Orleans, the gruesome reality of Appalachia coal country's grinding poverty had me at a complete and utter loss. Black coal dust was pervasive in this county: caked into the corners of the store's peeling linoleum, limning the deep crevices of the men's gaunt faces, and ground beneath the ragged fingernails of women grown old far before their time.

I offered them what little I could: soft smiles and gentle handshakes while I listened to their quiet stories. Many averted their eyes and went to great lengths to avoid me, but others were relieved to have a sympathetic ear.

"My husband works at the glass factory and I take in laundry." A worn Negro woman stood with a baby on one hip and two boys in line behind her, all in their pressed Sunday best. "West Virginia makes the best glass in the country, not that you'd know it in this economy. We set aside every penny so our eldest can go to Bluefield when he gets older." She glanced at my belly, a sly smile on her wide lips. "When is your little one due?"

I let my fingers flutter over my French black-and-white-houndstooth tweed jacket, where my latest pregnancy was just beginning to show beneath its black braided hem. "Right before the New Year."

Only three weeks before Jack might potentially be sworn in as the thirty-fifth president of the United States. Because when life changed, it did so in the blink of an eye.

She pressed my hand into her own. "Remember us when your husband wins, won't you? And do what you can to help us?"

"I will."

And I would, for I recognized now what Jack had already seen, how much good we could do from the White House. Not just with Jack as president, but with me as First Lady . . .

The White House was not just a prize to be achieved, but the start of things to be done. Worthy things.

I was exhausted that night when I returned to the hotel, although I perked up a bit to see Joan Kennedy, Teddy's newly wedded wife, waiting for me in the lobby.

Bright-eyed and convent-educated, I liked Joan more than all the other Kennedy women combined, especially because she wasn't a toothy girl who liked to play football with the boys. Instead, she preferred the piano and secretly bemoaned the fact that she and Teddy had been living in his parents' compound in Hyannis Port since their honeymoon a year and a half ago. I recalled almost falling into that trap, so I had helped her find a house in Georgetown to rent, much to Rose's chagrin.

"The boys are at the bar." Joan linked her arm through mine, her blond hair cloaking us like a confessional curtain. "Jack's fighting mad after the unions gave him the religious treatment to the nth degree today for being Catholic." I sank gratefully into a plush leather chair at the table Joan had reserved for us, acknowledging Bobby's salute to me while Jack laughed at something Teddy had said, before all three brothers eyeballed a passing waitress with back-seam stockings that drew elegant lines up her shapely calves. I'd once thought that Kennedy men had only politics on their minds, but that was only half of it. They did think of politics. And sex.

The two go hand in hand. For women are drawn to powerful men . . .

To my dismay, I'd learned that Bobby and Teddy possessed the same wandering eyes as their older brother—probably all inherited from their father—but when Bobby and Teddy strayed at least they were discreet about it, which was more than I could say for the other Kennedy men.

"Long day?" Joan asked as she passed me a club soda.

"Very." I longed to kick off my pumps and stretch my throbbing feet, but instead crossed my ankles and sipped demurely at the club soda. "You know, it absolutely kills me to try and keep up with Jack. Even I don't know how he keeps going day after day."

"Says the woman who's been matching him event for event."

"For now. I'm not sure how much longer I can do this."

Given my history, I worried constantly of overexerting myself as the doctor said I'd done with my first pregnancy. Even with Caroline born healthy and sound, some unswept corner of my mind always feared that I'd wake up to the familiar cramping and the loss of my hopes and dreams.

I had a little time left, but I was concerned about leaving Jack's side when this pregnancy became too cumbersome, especially as I glanced over to find him laughing with not one but two brunette waitresses. Jealousy and insecurity reared their ugly heads, but I tamped them down.

Jack was running for president, which meant he couldn't afford any public indiscretions. While suspicions sometimes cast dark shadows, I had no proof of further roundering on his part, nor was I willing to jeopardize our fragile rapprochement, especially when I'd come to the cold realization that with Caroline at home and another baby on the way, there wasn't much I could do if Jack decided he preferred a French model to our marriage.

Instead, I reminded myself that I was Jack's wife, a position no other woman could threaten, certainly not if Jack wished to be president.

Still, that didn't mean I was going to give him *carte blanche* to do as he wished.

Joan—who had already come to me in tears over Teddy's infidelity—seemed to know what I was thinking. "What will happen when you retire from the campaign?"

"I've arranged to write a syndicated column: 'The Campaign Wife.'" I pursed my lips, gathered my courage. If anyone could help me with my main worry concerning leaving the campaign trail, it was Joan. "Still, I think it's a good idea that Jack should have a Kennedy woman at his side at all times," I added, thinking of the parade of smiling women at today's campaign rally, their red-and-white-striped dresses with blue sashes that read *Kennedy* at the waist, all paid for by Jack's father. If my husband was going to be constantly surrounded by temptation, it wouldn't hurt to remind him to resist such prettily packaged bait. "Don't you think?"

Joan followed my gaze and gave a sage nod. "You know, I'd be happy to tag along."

As I watched Jack toast one of those brunette waitresses, I found myself accepting Joan's offer. As if on cue, Joan stood and situated herself between Jack and Teddy at the bar, just as a reporter closed in and snapped a whole ream of photographs. Joan caught my eye and I nodded approvingly over the rim of my club soda.

My husband couldn't help that he burned all the oxygen from the very air, and nor could he help that women were forever flocking to him. But I'd do my damnedest to ensure that if Jack was photographed with a pretty woman, that woman would be a Kennedy.

Even when it couldn't be me.

With Joan on guard duty, I hosted teas at our N Street town house so women from all over Washington could sip from my Wedgwood china and let me convince them to vote for my husband. Managing the teas was a yawn-worthy matter of keeping the cookie plates filled and guiding the conversation back to Jack's planks of American exceptionalism and a durable peace while my perplexed mother looked blithely on. "It is a new world, isn't it," she nattered under her breath at one of the afternoon soirees, wrinkling her nose at my guests from the kitchen. "You're letting perfect strangers into your house to sit on your antique furniture. I'll bet you didn't expect this humdrum sort of divertissement when you signed on to marry Jack."

"Not exactly, Mummy." I gestured for her to hand me the sugar pot. "But every vote counts when you're pursuing the Golden Fleece. We can't let Senator Cornpone win."

Then came the night—morning, really, since it was almost two a.m.—when I sat rapt before my mother's television and witnessed my husband accept the Democratic presidential nomination from thousands of miles away in the Los Angeles Coliseum. I wished I could be there, by his side, celebrating this moment. But there would be many more moments for us to celebrate. Together.

Snug on my lap in a frilly pink nightgown, Caroline sucked her thumb and clutched her Raggedy Ann doll while Jack announced Lyndon Johnson—the same senator who had fought us tooth and nail through the primaries—as his running mate. LBJ looked none too thrilled, but Jack was only getting warmed up as he launched into the pitfalls of a Nixon presidency—his old friend had run essentially un-opposed on the Republican ticket, much to Jack's chagrin—and America's stagnation before arriving at the speech's denouement, lines I'd urged him to include because they were honest and echoed the real reasons why Jack so desperately wanted to be president.

"We stand today on the edge of a New Frontier—the frontier of the 1960s, the frontier of unknown opportunities and perils, the frontier of unfilled hopes and unfilled threats."

I whispered the next bits in Caroline's ear, my heart thudding a steady pulse at the words I'd helped Jack rehearse over the phone.

"I believe that the times require imagination and courage and perseverance. I'm asking each of you to be pioneers toward that New Frontier."

Jack was asking each and every American exactly what he asked of himself. The crowd loved him for it, and I did too.

My mother turned the seventeen-inch set off as soon as Jack finished his speech. "Well, Caroline," she said to my daughter. "You should be very proud of your father. And your mother too."

Caroline nodded slowly; at nearly three years old she seemed such an old soul in such a little body. "Yes, *Grand-mère*."

Maud Shaw swept up Caroline and her doll, pausing only to let my daughter plant a kiss on my lips. The night was over for them, but for me it had just begun.

I checked my reflection in the hall mirror before pausing to trace the figure in the surprise birthday present I'd painted for Jack earlier that afternoon, a watercolor titled *El Senadore*, of him striking a Napoleonic pose while sporting a three-cornered hat, a mob of adoring Kennedys behind him.

El Senadore indeed. It's more and more *El Presidente* with each passing day.

That meant I was no longer merely Jackie Kennedy, wife and mother. Now I was Jackie Kennedy, potential future First Lady.

I braced myself for the publicity onslaught before stepping outside into the cacophony of glaring floodlights and flashbulbs that exploded from Hammersmith's front lawn. It was an impromptu press conference that was far from impromptu considering Mr. Kennedy had arranged it all, but I reminded myself that I preferred this to the alternative of being ambushed on my way to the dress shop in the morning.

Not for the first time, I wondered as I covered a flinch with a demure smile whether this was the life I wanted, constantly on stage and scrutinized for America's entertainment. Since my retirement from the campaign, it had fallen to me to shield Caroline from the view of some of these same photographers intent on turning her into a ghastly little Shirley Temple, with her face plastered on every magazine under the sun. But Jack had asked for courage and perseverance as we headed into this New Frontier. If he could do it, so could I.

I suppose now is as good a time to start as any.

A rumpled reporter shone a floodlight more directly in my face. "Mrs. Kennedy, how did you feel watching your husband accept the nomination?"

My gloved hand fluttered to my pearls. "Why, I thought I was all alone in the country," I said softly, dropping my gaze so as not to be blinded by the lights. "I'm so excited."

"Any thoughts on how your husband will conduct his campaign against Nixon?"

A gentle smile. "None at this time."

"Will they really face off in the country's first televised presidential debates?"

"I'm afraid I can't say for sure."

After that, I excused myself to catch a few hours of sleep before I had to relive the experience again and again with fresh rounds of reporters. I was already exhausted but also thankful that Lady Bird Johnson had promised that she'd carry Texas for us and appear for all the photo ops I didn't care to do.

"Well, I've just been to your house," my mother reported once I'd finished my breakfast in bed—it was strange to be back in my old childhood room at Hammersmith while so many monumental changes churned underfoot. "The rambler roses have been stripped from your front fence."

"What?" I'd loved those roses, their cheerful blossoms and the heady fragrance that accompanied lazy summer days. "How did that happen?"

My mother shrugged. "Souvenir seekers, I expect. There were a number of airplanes flying overhead too." She clucked her tongue at my distraught expression and wrapped a tweed arm around me. "You're going to have to manage the publicity, Jacqueline. Otherwise, it's going to chew you up and spit you out."

can't talk now, Lee." I glanced from the bustling kitchen into the Kennedy living room at Hyannis Port, the sound of the live television broadcast mingled with the spirited conversations of my dinner party guests. "The debates are starting and I have guests over to watch."

For tonight's debates were the election's final main event, and they were televised, the first in the history of America. Jack wasn't even president yet and he was already making history. I worried the rest of us were going to have a difficult time keeping up.

I'd acquiesced to Jack's request that I host this one final event, invited a slew of newspapermen and well-heeled society ladies to view the Great Debates—as tonight's entertainment had been dubbed by the television stations—and my mother had come to help me play hostess since Rose was out of town. I'd wanted to invite Lee as well, but my gorgeous, fashionable, and recently rich sister (following her divorce and subsequent marriage to a dashing Polish prince named Stanislaw Radziwill) was still recovering from the premature birth of her daughter. I'd been meaning to visit her, but kept putting it off as I entered the final months of my own pregnancy. What Lee was going through as a mother terrified me, especially given my own history.

Somehow, she'd managed to call just when the timing couldn't have been more inconvenient.

"All anyone can talk about is you and Jack," Lee said over the crackling line. "I was there for you when your marriage was unraveling at the seams and now that I need help, you don't care."

"That's not at all how things are, Lee," I said. "It's just that we're a little busy. Jack is running for president, you know."

"As if I could ever forget. I married a prince—a real one this time—and became a goddamned princess, but no one batted an eye. Now your husband runs for president and everyone acts as if you're more popular than Grace Kelly, Sophia Loren, and Elizabeth Taylor all rolled into one. If you become First Lady," Lee sniped, "it will be all over for me. You know that, don't you?"

I held the phone away from my ear, barely keeping my jaw from dropping before the cook caught me gaping through the steam from the beef bourguignon. My relationship with Lee had always relied on a healthy dose of competition, and my mother had warned that my sister was sifting her way through a determined case of the blues following a difficult birth, but that didn't countenance this guerrilla attack. "What are you talking about?"

"I just had a baby—who is still fighting for her life—but no one gives a shit because all anyone cares about is you. I've always been Jackie's little sister, and I'll never escape from under that cloud if Jack gets elected. Hell, you were always Daddy's favorite, and probably Mummy's too."

This is why I have so few female friends, I thought as my vision went spotty with anger. *Men are less petty than women. Women hold grudges, men don't.*

Yet it seemed Lee wasn't done. "What exactly have you done to deserve everyone's adoration, Jackie? Aside from speaking French and making sure that Jack's dinners are served on time?"

In that moment, I didn't have an answer for her.

I pinched the bridge of my nose and reminded myself that Lee's infant daughter was still hooked to an incubator in the hospital, that any mother might lash out in such a situation. Still, my voice was curt. Her words had wounded me more than I'd ever let her know. "I'm sorry you feel this way, Lee, but I really have to go. I'll keep you and little Christina in my prayers."

In all honesty, I had no idea what else to say to Lee. She was right that I hadn't been there for her these past weeks, had been too scared to muster my courage and support my sister. It was easier to make excuses about why I couldn't make it to New York to visit and instead focus on the task at hand—getting Jack elected.

"Was that Lee?" My mother entered the Kennedy kitchen so I wondered if she'd been eavesdropping the entire time. "She'll get over her misgivings about your becoming First Lady, you know."

"So Lee complained to you too?" I wanted to throw my hands up in exasperation, but instead nodded to the maid to take out the tray of pre-dinner aperitifs. "I hadn't realized Lee's life was going to end if we moved into the White House."

My mother *tsk*ed under her breath. "Don't be dramatic. Keep your eyes on the prize and Lee will fall into line."

"I hope you're right, Mummy. Because I really can't add Lee's histrionics to my plate right now."

"I almost feel sorry for Nixon." My mother's upper lip curled in distaste as she led me to the living room, where the debates were already in full swing and everyone sat clustered around the wooden television cabinet. "Did they embalm Tricky Dick before the poor man even had a chance to die?"

I placed a silent finger before my lips, studied the grainy black-and-white image from the doorway. Poor Dick had obviously made the mistake of succumbing to the studio's Lazy Shave pancake makeup to disguise his perpetual five o'clock shadow, which only resulted in the makeup dripping off his face from the dual assault of the studio lights and his nervous sweating. Still, I couldn't help whispering over my gleeful smile. "This is good for Jack, Mummy. So, so good."

I knew I should have felt more remorse over our lost friendship with Richard Nixon—and perhaps my squabble with Lee as well—

but I still resented his wife Pat's recent barbed campaign comments that my hair looked like a floor mop and that I preferred French couture to American designs. *So much for our being pals at the Senate wives' bandage-rolling parties,* I thought as I scowled down at the shapeless sack of a maternity dress I now wore as a result of her sniping, for Pat had agreed with the media hounds who touted that I spent thirty thousand dollars a year on Paris couture.

"Honestly," I'd scoffed to Jack the morning of her accusation before he left for Chicago. "I couldn't spend that much unless I wore sable underwear."

To which Jack had waggled his eyebrows suggestively before handing me a glossy Bloomingdale's catalog. "Order whatever you want, including sable underwear," he'd said. "Only make sure it's made in America."

Worse, Jack had been sweating in recent weeks as Nixon's poll numbers surpassed his own following the vice president's state visit with Russian premier Nikita Khrushchev, which had cast Jack's own youth in the unbecoming light of inexperience.

Now I waved a hand to hush my guests' twittering so I could sift through every word being broadcast from Chicago. This decisive moment could make or break Jack's campaign.

Like me, Jack possessed a dozen faces, and I watched with a private grin as he transformed into the familiar guise of an enigmatic young professor, his skin bronzed dark from all his outdoor campaigning. I waited for the tick of his nervous necktie adjustments or the snap of his right fingers against the lectern, but he instead solidified into the vice president's equal, then surpassed Nixon to grasp the attention of 115 million American viewers while he discussed national security and the threat of communism.

"He seems so relaxed," one of the reporters murmured. "Like he was born for this."

"More like bred for it," my mother muttered under her breath as Nixon stumbled his way through an answer, mopping his forehead as if he were traversing the Sahara at high noon. I did feel a tepid pang

of pity for him then; Jack had called earlier to tell me Nixon was bat-
tling the flu after being released from the hospital following a knee
injury, which didn't make this seem entirely fair.

"Jack looks like a movie star," the wife of one of Massachusetts'
congressmen mused as the beef bourguignon was served and Jack and
Dick took turns giving their summations on every topic from Social
Security to the Soviet Union. Jack spoke straight into the cameras and
thus into every living room in America, while Nixon spoke to the off-
screen moderator, making him seem positively shifty-eyed.

"Dick, on the other hand, looks like he's ready to rob a bank," said
another, prompting a ripple of feminine giggles. "I wouldn't be surprised if Tricky Dick's own mother called him today to see if she
needed to post his bail."

One of the newspapermen finished scratching on his notepad,
likely a slew of comments on everything from the Kennedys' floral
couch upholstery to the quality of Merlot I'd served with dinner.
"What did you think of the debates, Mrs. Kennedy?"

You're on, Jackie.

I smiled, not having to search for any words outside of the truth. "I
think my husband was brilliant."

Later, after I'd seen off all the reporters and guests, I murmured to
my mother, "This might do it for him. Jack might actually win now."

"Honestly, Jackie." My mother cocked her head, her perfectly penciled brows drawn together. "Did you ever doubt it?"

I had, until now. But when I'd watched the cameras pan away from
the podiums where Jack and Dick remained standing, I'd started
thinking of which boxes I should pack first for the White House.

Election Day was barely a month away.

CHAPTER

7

November 1960

rose early on Election Day so I could meet Jack in Boston.

"You must love me to be up before eight o'clock," Jack joked as he adjusted his striped tie, then readjusted it again. The man would end up choking himself if someone didn't stop him.

No press was allowed inside the polling place, but there were plenty of precinct workers and curious bystanders scrutinizing Jack's every move. I stilled his hands with my own, then, despite the vastness of my pregnancy, buttoned his jacket over the tie so he wouldn't fidget with it. He may have been able to fool the debate audience with his poise, but this morning his face was puffy from fatigue and his every movement was a loud jangle of nerves strung too tight.

"I must love you to cast my very first vote for you," I said loud enough for everyone to hear, for I'd never voted in any election before, had always interviewed politicians without getting swept up in their battles. Until I'd met Jack.

"I love you." I smoothed the whispers of new lines around his eyes. "And I'm proud of you. We all are."

He gave a halfhearted smile, turning so only I could see his tortured expression. "Kennedys don't settle for second place."

"Well, I still haven't decided which box I'm going to check on my ballot." I tapped my chin absentmindedly as I signed in and received my ballot. "Shall it be the shifty-eyed vice president from California or the handsome young senator from Massachusetts?"

Jack let out a bark of laughter, then escorted me to the striped voting booths. My pencil hesitated over the tiny little quadrants that were being filled out all over America, boxes that would change the course of my life and perhaps the entire country.

DECKER and MUNN ....Prohibition
HASS and COZZINI ....Socialist Labor
KENNEDY and JOHNSON..............................Democrat
NIXON and LODGE ....Republican

I startled when I heard Jack's laughing whisper from next to me. "You better vote for the right man, Mrs. Kennedy."

To which I chuckled, checked Jack's name, and swept out of the voting booth to deposit my ballot in the waiting box. It was done, and in a few hours, this would all be over. The exhaustion and irritation of all the time spent campaigning was suddenly swept away, and now I could only hold my breath alongside the entire country and wait to see if Jack would be our next president.

Come what may, Jack had soared toward the sun these past months, and I'd loved sharing that vista of the White House, not just for him but also for Americans like those I'd met in Appalachia.

For all of us . . .

We sojourned to the Kennedy compound at Hyannis Port, where together we took positions in the unlikely command communications center set up in one of the pink-and-white children's bedrooms in Bobby's house. The precincts wouldn't close for hours, so it was all speculation as Teddy directed the phone center and teletypes began to trickle in.

A trickle that quickly became a deluge.

"Favorable results from Connecticut," Teddy announced to cheers just after the caterers had laid out a spread of the Kennedy clan's favorite foods: chicken, tuna, lobster, and egg salad sandwiches. (Apparently, hard work required copious amounts of mayonnaise.)

A jubilant hour passed until a dispatch from CBS came through. Teddy's face went pale as he read it, and Bobby grabbed the message from him. He, too, looked as if he'd come down with a fever when he dropped it into the wastebasket.

"What does it say?" I asked him quietly.

"It's the latest CBS computer analysis." He ran a hand through his thick hair. "They predict a Nixon sweep with four hundred fifty electoral votes."

I hoped Jack hadn't heard from his place at the window seat, but he only stared at the plate I handed him, his eyes so vacant that I worried what would happen if he did lose. "Eat," I commanded. "You have a long night ahead of you and there's no sense starving yourself."

I'd never seen him look so haggard, and I almost cheered aloud when a new dispatch came in after twilight had fallen.

"Fifty-one percent of the electoral vote." Bobby shook the paper for emphasis, his grin a beacon of hope. "CBS has switched sides. It's going to be close, but they predict you'll win, Jack!"

This time my husband lit an Upmann cigar and sat back, puffing it like a self-satisfied Cheshire cat. It wasn't until the cigar had burned down to ashes that he stood up, suddenly energized. "I need to tell Caroline good night."

So we walked back to our rented house together and I watched from the bedroom door as Caroline scrambled into bed, an illustrated copy of *Black Beauty* gripped tight in one hand. "How's your race going, Daddy?"

Jack tucked her in as he did every night he was home, a dazed expression he would never let slip to the press—or even to his own father—on his face. "Well, Buttons, your daddy might be president when you wake up."

Caroline clapped her hands, then frowned as she arranged her Raggedy Ann dolls—the first named Raggedy Annie and the second, a gift from some Canadian well-wishers, dubbed Mother Annie—along the pillows. Her feet twitched beneath the down comforter. "In the morning, will you take me to look for seashells on the beach?"

I opened my mouth to remind Caroline that her father was a very busy man, perhaps about to become the busiest man on earth, but Jack just tucked her in tighter.

"Of course." He dropped a kiss on her forehead. "We'll race the waves too."

I smiled then, my heart overfull as I clasped my hands over my swollen belly. Jack might compartmentalize people—even me—but he never did so to our daughter; instead he poured her imaginary tea while seated at her doll-sized nursery table and tucked her into bed each night. I only prayed that wouldn't change if he woke up as the new president-elect of the United States in the morning.

We walked downstairs together, but I stopped him outside the formal white dining room and drew him inside where a surprise awaited. "I've ordered you lamb chops and mashed potatoes. And daiquiris," I said before he could argue. "We're going to lock ourselves inside for one hour: no TV, no dispatches, and no updates."

Jack relented, some of the tension loosening from his shoulders. "One hour might do me good."

Those sixty minutes passed too quickly, but I'd enlisted Bobby to stand outside with a dire warning to keep everyone away. Finally, voices buzzed outside as the hour ended; someone pounded on the door and Jack fairly twitched out of his chair.

In front of the television again, the broadcasters all had the same news.

"A Kennedy landslide!" Teddy grasped his brother's arm and almost shook it out of its socket, so it was easy to imagine him as a child on Christmas morning.

"Oh, Bunny," I exclaimed to Jack, hearing the awe in my own voice. This was the sort of moment when history was made, the no-turning-back point. "You're president now."

But Jack only shook his head. "No. It's too early yet."

I only smiled. Jack had lost so much, had to fight for so many things, so it didn't surprise me that he wasn't willing to celebrate until the results were certified. Still, I squeezed his hand, and was relieved when he squeezed it back.

We sat side by side for the next hour as more results came in, all telling the same story. The clock on the mantel chimed eleven thirty when I finally excused myself, my mind awhirl. "I'm going to check on Caroline. Don't stay up all night."

In truth, I needed to gather my thoughts. Unfortunately, I'd forgotten about the members of the press, who doggedly followed me as I strode back across the lawn, the damp grass soaking through my thin shoes.

"What do you think of the results so far, Jackie?"

"What sort of concessions will you be making in your new role as First Lady?"

I paused, pretended to consider the last question, then gave what I hoped was a calm and dignified smile. "I will wear hats."

Once the door closed firmly behind me, I looked in on Caroline, so peaceful and angelic in sleep. How would her life change now that Jack was poised to become president? How would all our lives change?

I didn't know the answer to those questions, only that they would change. Permanently and irrevocably.

My mother surprised me by calling just before I slipped into bed. "You are America's First Lady." She spoke with so much pride in her voice that I didn't dare correct her that nothing was set in stone yet. "I just can't believe it, Jacqueline! I am just . . . I am just . . ."

This really was a whole new world if my own mother was at a loss for words.

"Thank you, Mummy. Do you think Lee has heard the news?"

"You'll have your hands full; I'll call." A hesitant pause. "You really do need to talk to her though."

"I will, Mummy," I promised, but made no guarantees on when. My mother was right; my hands were about to be too full to listen to Lee's recurring complaints that I'd eclipsed her.

As a distraction from both the bitter and the sweet after I hung up on that conversation, I skimmed a few pages of the Duc de Saint-Simon's memoirs about life at Versailles, then tossed in and out of sleep until Jack came to bed at four thirty that morning, his face gray in the moonlight. "It's no landslide." He fairly swayed with exhaustion as he shed his clothes and back brace, recited his brief nightly prayers, which were a little longer than usual. "The Midwest and Far West have gone for Nixon. I might lose this, Jackie. I still need seven electoral votes."

"What you need is some sleep," I said. "Do you have your speech ready for tomorrow?"

He nodded, pulled two envelopes from his jacket. "Both of them."

Regardless of how this went, he'd have a speech to give in the morning. And no matter my own exhaustion, this time I wouldn't be across the country when the time came. Victory or concession, I'd be by his side.

Where I belonged.

I curled up next to Jack, relieved to hear his breath finally relax into the gentle cadence that heralded sleep, my thoughts swirling like a Shakespearean tempest. In the predawn light of six o'clock, sharp headlights swung into our driveway. I waited for a knock on the door that never came, then rose and padded to the window to investigate.

Black cars had joined the police cordon at the end of the drive, and joining the officers were men in dark suits and white shirts.

The Secret Service.

I drew a trembling breath. That meant only one thing: that my husband had been elected the thirty-fifth president of the United States.

The Secret Service took up silent posts outside the dining room while the entire Kennedy family crowded into our dining room to breakfast on poached eggs on toast and Jack's favorite home-made waffles I'd prepared from scratch. When Caroline had come in to greet her father that morning, she'd shot across the bedroom and pulled the blankets from Jack's tousled head with a squeal. "Good morning, Mr. President!"

The results hadn't yet been certified, but every network prediction said Jack was going to win, although with one of the slimmest margins in history. Now I watched from the window as those same Secret Service agents followed Jack and Caroline to the beach, everyone's hair and jackets flapping wildly in the wind. I'd already warned the agents to keep as well out of the way as possible—while still being on guard—because I didn't want Caroline to feel crowded. No matter the blustery weather or the fact that he was almost president, Jack still kept his promise of a walk on the beach with his daughter, and I melted to see him do it.

It was while he was out enjoying the briny sea air that word came that he'd taken Minnesota, clinching the final electoral votes needed.

When Jack came in, everyone stood, even Bobby.

The man who entered was no longer simply a brother, husband, or father.

He was the president-elect and would soon be the most powerful man in the nation, if not the world.

"You did it, my boy," Mr. Kennedy said, his eyes wide with awe and reverence.

"We need a family photograph to save this moment for posterity." Rose snapped to attention and, in a daze, I scarcely heard her order her grown children to straighten their ties and meet in the library in ten minutes.

No one noticed when I tied a silk head scarf around my hair and shrugged into a red raincoat that no longer buttoned around my vast belly, then slipped silently outside.

Alone.

Despite the biting wind and spitting rain, I savored every breath of crisp fresh air, walking until I lost sight of the house, listening to the crash of waves on the shore and the lonely howl of the wind. Moments like this were precious, for with those final votes, my life was no longer my own.

Another sacrifice for Jack. For us. For America.

I was excited—who wouldn't be to learn they were about to become First Lady—but overlaying my trembling sense of pride was an overwhelming sense of being frightfully out of my league. I was determined to do justice to all the expectations that loomed, but there were so many and they were so much larger than managing an estate. What sort of Ozymandias was this that I now faced?

It was Jack who finally came to fetch me.

"You disappeared." He wrapped a strong arm around my shoulders, enveloping me in his warmth and the clean, woodsy scent of his signature Eight & Bob cologne made especially by a French perfumer for him, a few of his closest friends, and Bobby, resulting in its name.

I breathed in the reassuring scent and smiled, reached up to touch his cheek. "I needed a minute to myself."

He answered in kind, the same beaming image of vitality and energy that had intrigued me at Charley Bartlett's dinner party all those years ago. Jack—my Jack—was going to rebuild the country, maybe even the world. He would seek peace through fresh new alliances and transform America into a golden beacon of art and learning. And I—his young, sophisticated, and foreign-educated wife—was going to help him do it.

He gestured to the path that led back up to the house. "To Washington?" he asked as he offered me his arm, as if he needed my permission.

As if he needed me.

I nodded and threaded my arm through his. "To Washington."

Thus, into the hands of fate we went.

PART TWO

. . . . .

November 22, 1963

*A*ir Force One touched down in Love Field with a teeth-jarring thump, and minutes later, the cabin door swung open to admit such a blast of scorching sunlight that the First Lady instinctively shielded her eyes against the unusual November brightness. In this, the first scene of an act she and her husband had replayed during each stop during this show-the-flag trip to Texas, she sniffed at the warm, oil-smelling Texas breeze and smoothed the skirt of her watermelon suit as the president stepped alongside her.

"Last stop." The president's unstaged line was murmured so only she could hear. "We've made quite a team this trip."

Her smile made her almond-brown eyes sparkle as they stepped onto the tarmac. "Always."

Then they were in character again, waving their way down the metal ramp to greet Lyndon and Lady Bird Johnson in the same silly masquerade that had been staged for each crowd of waiting Texans. Aides pressed local papers into the president's waiting hands while the First Lady accepted the ubiquitous welcome bouquet from the Dallas mayor's wife. The unseasonable heat made their fragrance almost cloying.

She had been greeted with Texan yellow roses—meant to convey welcome—in every other city, but Dallas's bouquet was a shocking shade of ruby red. Everyone knew red roses symbolized love, but the White House floral staff had taught her they also represented regret. And sorrow.

She didn't have time to ponder that, for the president's expression went gray as he skimmed the headlines. "Have I mentioned how much I loathe this state?" he muttered.

"What now?"

He passed her that day's edition of the Dallas Morning News, folded open to the headline of "Storm of Political Controversy Swirls Around Kennedy on Visit." She tried—and failed—to mask her shock when she skimmed paragraphs about leaflets that had been spread by the state's Republicans—those same rabble-rousers who claimed America had been sliding into paganism since 1960—about her husband's stances on racial integration and Russia. This, after their speculation that he planned to replace LBJ as his running mate and their accusations that her husband was making secret deals with the Communist party.

"What is it you always tell me when I read something upsetting in the newspaper?" She pretended to think hard, then dropped her voice an octave. "'Be more tolerant, like a horse flicking flies away in the summer'?"

"These Texan flies need swatting," he grumbled. "We're heading into nut country today."

She turned up the wattage of her smile to distract him from several hostile misspelled placards and a cluster of hissing students who must have taken the day off from school, used her body to block the sight of Confederate flags flying right side up next to American flags flapping upside down in the meager breeze. They passed the Secret Service follow-up cars and lines of police escort motorcycles, each step taking them closer to where the midnight-blue Lincoln Continental convertible awaited. With the warm sunshine, the protective bubble top had been removed.

The president's lips quirked into the briefest of smiles when he helped her into the car, using his free hand to wave to the crowd. His voice dropped, turning conspiratorial so she might have been the only person in their private little world. "What do you say I return Texas to Mexico during my second term?"

"I'd say you should make that your top priority." She settled the red roses on the floor between them. "Right up there with jettisoning Nikita Khrushchev and Fidel Castro into orbit just like Sputnik."

The president gave a chuff of laughter and the Continental's engine rumbled to life. "We're so glad you're here, Mr. President," Governor John Connally exclaimed as he and his wife were seated up front, garish Texan smiles plastered on their faces. "It's an honor to show you the best the Lone Star State has to offer."

"Don't forget to smile, Bunny," the First Lady whispered to her husband when the driver eased the convertible onto West Mockingbird Lane. Their destination was the Dallas Business and Trade Mart, where the president was scheduled to give a canned speech about the importance of Texan elbow grease in the machine of the nation's economy, before sharing a steak luncheon with a smattering of local civic leaders and their spouses.

Dallas today, then back to Washington.

But first they turned onto Houston Street, bound for Dealey Plaza.

CHAPTER

8

November 1960

A week after Jack's election, my well-laid plans for scheduling a mid-December birth followed by an easy recovery were scrapped when I went into premature labor. An ambulance had been called and Jack had rushed back from Florida, arriving too late to hand out cigars in the waiting room following the birth of the precious dark-haired mite that we'd agreed would be Jack's namesake.

John Fitzgerald Kennedy Jr.

John's delivery via emergency Cesarean left me battered and exhausted, too weak to shuffle my way to the restroom unassisted. Now with a pang of empathy I understood Jack's frustration and mortification when he'd struggled white-faced with his crutches after his surgeries.

There were moments of great elation when I held my tiny, red-faced son in my arms, but those were too often chased away by clanging headaches, a bone-deep lethargy, and an overwhelming crescendo of sadness I just couldn't shake. I recalled my sister's melancholy after her daughter's difficult birth and might have reached out to ask her advice, but given our last conversation, I didn't know how Lee would react. Better not to ask and wind up regretting it as I was too exhausted to take care of anyone else's feelings right now.

So I rowed alone against that riptide of sadness, and thus far had managed to keep my head above the waves. Barely.

The sketches of the inaugural ball gowns before me on the metal bedside table blurred, multiplying from ten to a hundred—maybe more—so that I had to close my eyes to block out the oversized tucks of tulle and hideous puffs of bunched lace. I swayed on my feet while pinching the bridge of my nose, feeling the pain of a fresh headache competing with the morphine-dulled ache at my incision site.

"Perhaps you'd be more comfortable in bed, Mrs. Kennedy?"

I recalled the steady stream of family and friends that had visited after I'd had Caroline, but after the election, aside from an occasional visit by Jack, Mr. Kennedy, or my mother, my new social secretary was my only bedside companion. A fellow Vassar scholar, Tish Baldrige was older than me and recommended by my Auchincloss family, yet I hadn't decided whether I liked the tall and energetic woman, especially after she'd announced that morning that I'd be giving regular press conferences once I began my tenure as First Lady, the third youngest of the twenty-nine wives to live in the White House. Of course, Julia Tyler and Frances Cleveland didn't have to face the press juggernaut that I did, so I couldn't look to their examples for guidance.

"I will not be giving regular press conferences." I hadn't looked up as I struggled to tuck tiny white socks over John's wiggly little feet. "I'd rather have my fingernails pulled off and fed to me."

When she realized I wouldn't budge, Tish had acquiesced about the press conferences, although her pursed lips told me she wasn't pleased about it. "The doctors would prefer you stay in bed, ma'am." The reprimand now in her Julia Child–like voice grated on my last nerve before she went to fetch a hot cup of tea.

The leaden weight in my head lurched to the back of my skull and set off a fresh pounding as I eased myself onto the bed and pulled the wheeled bedside table into place so I might focus on the design sketches abandoned there, gowns by American designers Norell, Sarmi, and Andreas of Bergdorf Goodman.

Stiff satin dresses in amaranthine and mauve, accompanied by heavy winter furs of mink and sable. They were dark and severe, dowdy and traditional.

They were wrong, each and every one of them.

I blamed the effects of childbirth for the wave of futility that crashed over me and the tears that stung my eyes, even as I knew I couldn't succumb to this dangerous malaise. So I reached for one of my ubiquitous yellow foolscap legal pads and began jotting down what I wanted—what I needed—in this, the most important gown I'd ever wear. (Most women believed their wedding gown to be their penultimate dress, but I'd hated the frilly lampshade Mother had chosen for me. I'd pick my own inauguration gown. *Je m'en fiche.*) I started filling each page with sketches as I once had in the margins of notebooks of French verbs while a student at the Sorbonne. This was the dress that would break from the old to the new frontier of Jack's presidency, which meant that it had to be perfect.

Timeless. Elegant.

Clean lines. White gloves.

White or off-white, to stand out.

I was still sketching when Tish returned with her thick black notebook, which held my social obligations. "Mrs. Kennedy, I brought your forthcoming itineraries, including the invitation from Mrs. Eisenhower for your traditional tour of the White House." She handed me the vellum envelope. "It's still set for December ninth."

Only a few days from now.

The invitation—more like a command—should have come right after the election but instead arrived late, as if Mamie Eisenhower hoped I might not be able to attend because of my pregnancy. I winced at the idea of having to endure hours on my feet with the woman who had derisively called me "college girl" throughout the campaign.

I looked to Tish. "Can we reschedule?"

Tish looked dubious. "With the First Lady of the United States?"

"Right." I bit my lip, found myself biting my nails, and stopped myself. God, I was a wreck.

Somehow, I'd manage the tour. I'd have to.

"Make the necessary plans and see what the doctors recommend." I rubbed my eyes, growing even wearier as I remembered my other upcoming project. There were too many acts to juggle; I wasn't sure I could manage them all. "Oh, and Tish, please write to my decorator, Sister Parish, to see if she might be interested in helping me on the house with columns."

"Ma'am?"

"I have hopes that she'll help me make the White House a showcase for great American artists and creative talent. I'll need schematics on the entire building before we can start the necessary remodel."

Because I'd heard from Jack—and everyone who had ever set foot in the executive mansion—what a sad, worn-out relic it had become. Since I'd remodeled every home Jack and I had ever lived in, I saw no reason why the White House shouldn't join that list.

"Of course. Also, a Mr. Oleg Cassini is here to see you." Some vague recollection tickled the back of my mind as Tish spoke the name, but I didn't care if the Queen of England was in the waiting room. Tish's next words stopped my protest that I didn't wish for visitors. "I tried to send him away, but he said to tell you he's a gift from your father-in-law."

From Mr. Kennedy?

I frowned. "You'd better help me with my hair and lipstick then."

Two minutes later—after I'd arranged myself to give the impression of rapid recovery—Tish ushered Cassini into my hospital room. I recalled seeing him at social events over the years; today he looked natty in a gray suit with a shocking maroon tie and matching silk pocket square ironed into a presidential fold, a black jacket folded over one arm. But what I liked most was the ebullient smile beneath his pencil-thin black mustache as he reached out to take my hand.

"Mrs. Kennedy," he said in a voice rounded with the most delicious and unique accent. *"Enchanté."*

I quickly learned the source of his unique accent, for Cassini had been born in Paris to an aristocratic Russian family and studied political science in Florence before turning to fine art and finally fashion under the tutelage of couturier Jean Patou. Which meant that although he now lived in America—and qualified as a thoroughly American designer—his style sense was more European than Coco Chanel's little black dress. "I design for Hollywood," he added with a little bow. "Now Mr. Kennedy has asked that I design for you."

That was when I recalled Cassini's name, for outside of his Hollywood connections, he'd once been engaged to Grace Kelly, and had dressed the likes of Rita Hayworth and Audrey Hepburn.

"Kennedys only deal in winners." I smiled as I echoed the clan motto, remembering my initial introduction to the family. "Are you a winner, Mr. Cassini?"

"Better than most." He folded his jacket over the back of a chair, squared his fists on his hips. "Second to none."

I laughed. I liked this Oleg Cassini. In fact, I liked him very much.

"Then perhaps you can rescue me from inaugural hell. I need a gown that is simple and elegant," I said, gesturing to the detritus of eye-numbing dress sketches. "And it has to match the earrings and necklace Jack gave me."

I gestured toward a black velvet box on the windowsill. Oleg whistled in approval when he opened it, the emeralds and diamonds within catching fire in the light. They were the most stunning jewels I owned, but I treasured them even more because of what Jack had said when he'd clasped them around my neck.

"I can never thank you enough for all your help on the campaign." He'd kissed the words into my temple as he stood behind me. "But I hoped this might be a start."

Gratitude from a man who had everything. That was more precious than the gems themselves.

"The president-elect knows his jewels." Oleg closed the box. "They certainly make a statement."

"I need a gown that makes a statement too."

"Then you've come to the right man. My mother once attended a Washington ball wearing a saber strung to her hip." Cassini chuckled over the fond memory. "Simplicity is the key to perfection, but it's in my blood to make a statement."

I held up two of the most offensive dress sketches. "Hopefully not this sort of statement."

His upper lip curled and he reared back, one dramatic hand over his heart. "Pass me a tissue. My eyes are bleeding."

To which I laughed and pushed them aside, relieved. "I'll also need another gown for the gala the evening before, plus an outfit for the inauguration itself. Unfortunately, I'm on a budget." The word tasted dirty in my mouth, but it was a political necessity as Jack couldn't be seen as a man with a silver spoon in his mouth. Or married to a woman who wore sable underwear.

Oleg waved a hand, his delicate fingers fluttering as he glanced at the list I'd created. "Mr. Kennedy has instructed me to send him an account at the end of the year." He studied me in the way Leonardo da Vinci might have before sizing up Lisa Gherardini del Giocondo for the *Mona Lisa*. "There are sacrifices you'll have to make as First Lady that you wouldn't have made as plain old Mrs. Kennedy of New York, London, and the Riviera. While I would enjoy dressing you for all of the inaugural events, perhaps we should allow Bergdorf to dress you for one."

A creative genius, and one with political savvy too. I'd have to thank Mr. Kennedy when I next saw him.

"Perhaps we should create the inaugural design together before we send it to Bergdorf's," I mused. "A sort of peace offering before you become my official designer."

His mustache twitched over his smile. "That's a grand idea, Mrs. Kennedy."

I reached for the legal pad to show Cassini what I had in mind, but my new designer produced his own sketch book with a flourish, along with a sharpened charcoal pencil. "Like an ancient Egyptian princess, with the sphinx-like quality of your eyes, your long neck, and the sweep of your shoulders," he said under his breath when he glanced up at me. "One can never underestimate the importance of good shoulders." He stopped, lowered the pencil. "I want you to be the most elegant woman in the world. For you, Jackie Kennedy, I will create a look that will set trends, not follow them."

I blushed, but with a few fluid lines I could already see our shared vision coming to life.

I grinned, feeling like a child on Christmas morning. While my children gave me great joy—nature had cunningly designed it that way—this visit with Oleg Cassini was the first time I'd smiled in a while. "I think, Mr. Cassini, that you and I are going to get along just fine."

The doctors released me for the White House tour on the non-negotiable condition that a wheelchair would be available during the entirety of the afternoon. I only gave in to the stipulation because the idea of hours on my feet combined with the social niceties required of me during this, my first formal duty as future First Lady, made me want to crawl back into bed.

"You're going to be perfect, Jacks."

This time it was Jack taking care of me, wheeling me into the hospital elevator while the Secret Service agents crowded in behind us. I tried to ignore them as I cradled John to my chest, our son bundled in a frothy nest of white blankets to shield him from December's biting cold.

"My first official visit to the White House, and I'm going to have to be pushed everywhere." I grimaced and touched John's nose to mine, breathing in his newborn scent. "It's humiliating."

"I know it seems that way, but you're tougher than you know. In fact, I often tell people that of all the women I've ever met, there was only one with the strength for me to marry—and I married her." Jack pushed the button for the lobby. "Think of the speeches I had to give on crutches. Act as if you don't mind and all anyone will see is your grace and strength. The chair is just an accessory, like your hat."

I laughed and touched my dark red wool beret. "The hat is much more fashionable, I'm afraid."

Jack wheeled me out of the elevator, and I allowed a Massachusetts nurse who had cared for sixteen of Rose Kennedy's seventeen grandchildren to carry John the rest of the way, for I wasn't allowed to lift his weight yet and my hands already trembled from nerves and weariness. All I wanted was some quiet and perhaps a warm cup of tea, but Jack halted on a black X taped to the floor and reporters with 16 mm news cameras rushed at us.

"The press told me to stop here for a picture," he said under his breath.

Since when does the press dictate the actions of the future president?

"Oh, Jack," I growled through clenched teeth. "Please keep going."

"Just one picture," he answered. "I already agreed."

I'd once foreseen my future as the circus queen who married the daring young man on the flying trapeze, and now I was entering the big top yet again. Flashbulbs exploded, but I only smiled wider, presenting to the world the sequined costume of the radiant new mother and future First Lady that the country expected, and not the nervous, exhausted young woman I was beneath my tweed suit.

Secret Service agents following our every step. The press infiltrating our most intimate moments. Any privacy I might have had?

Gone.

I bit the insides of my cheeks, so hard the taste of copper pennies flooded my mouth.

"Are you sure you'll be all right to go alone?" Jack asked once he'd guided me beyond the police cordon to the waiting white sedan. The agenda Tish had given me this morning showed we'd spend the next two hours allowing the media to photograph my homecoming, then I'd change and drive myself to Pennsylvania Avenue while Jack met with potential cabinet members.

"I won't break," I reassured Jack, although I wasn't sure I believed it. The transfer to the backseat left my legs so wobbly that I found myself missing the white-walled sanctuary of the hospital room.

"I've instructed J. B. West, the head usher over at the White House, to have a wheelchair waiting," Jack said. "And Mamie knows you've just had a baby, so I'm sure she'll keep things short."

Not short enough.

I bit my tongue, saving my energy.

I was going to need it.

I felt very young when I arrived alone at the White House and paused at the North Portico to inhale the crisp scent of a winter forest from the evergreen wreaths that had been hung in preparation for Christmas.

It's just a house, I told myself. *And Mamie Eisenhower is just a woman.*

But the White House was more than just a house, it was entering the idea of this house, this monument to American history. And Mamie Eisenhower was both more—and less—than the archetype of the First Lady I'd imagined.

I was ushered upstairs, where Mamie met me in the drafty center hall on the second floor. My first impression was that she was a grand old dame, her tiny frame dwarfed by a gray brushed-velvet broadtail jacket with a lurid swirled satin hat perched awkwardly on her head. In contrast, I'd chosen my outfit carefully with Oleg Cassini's help: a simple aubergine wool jacket and black dress that was loose enough not to aggravate the incision site from my surgery, black satin gloves, and a black fur pillbox hat.

"Mrs. Eisenhower, meet Mrs. Kennedy." J. B. West, the chief usher, introduced us. I waited for Mamie to move, but she only extended a gloved hand, forcing me to walk toward her, past mismatched chairs and tables placed piecemeal against the yellow-wallpapered walls.

Which I did, slowly, so light-headed I worried I might topple over at any moment.

"How good of you to come." Mamie's clipped voice made it apparent she didn't think it good at all. "You look quite pale, dear."

I ignored her comment. *Of course I look pale. I just had a baby, for Christ's sake.*

"Thank you so much for inviting me," I said softly. "I'm honored to be able to partake in this long-standing tradition."

"I understand from your press secretary's recent comments that you intend to make the White House a platform for artists and the like." Mamie gave such a dramatic sniff that I was glad I was almost a head taller so she had to look up to meet my eyes. "One shudders to think of these historical walls covered with modern art."

I silently cursed Tish for making that announcement, yet the flush of anger only left me more unsteady as I realized the one accessory I sought was entirely absent.

Quel bordel. Had Mamie forgotten the request for a wheelchair? Was this a test of some sort? Either way, I didn't dare ask for the chair and expose my soft underbelly for her to strike.

Instead, I followed while Mamie pointed out historical memorabilia in a monotone that would have made the dullest of college professors pea green with envy. With each step, I shivered from sheer exhaustion and the cold drafts that seemed to kick up in each room.

And with each step, I grew more and more appalled.

I knew that the White House hadn't been remodeled since 1901 under Theodore Roosevelt's tenure, but nothing could have prepared me for the $2.98 heavy white porcelain jardinière (the price tag was still attached) housing three ailing ivy plants on the State Dining Room's great marble mantelpiece or the brass spittoons better suited to a Wild West saloon that lined the reception rooms. There weren't proper linens or flowers anywhere to be seen, and I grew dizzy upon my first glimpse of the shades of vomit green and rose pink that Mrs. Eisenhower had chosen for the presidential bedroom and bathroom.

"I don't allow the maids to walk on my carpets," she informed me, looking rather pleased with herself. "No careless footprints allowed."

What about careless faux plants? Or the stained burgundy rugs? Or just the general hideousness and air of utter neglect?

This was meant to be the greatest house in all of America—something for the entire country to take pride in—but its rooms were decorated helter-skelter with several decades of furnishings better suited to a wholesale furniture store in a January clearance. Or a bonfire.

I felt like a moth banging against the pane of a window that hadn't been opened in years. Every room in the house needed to be redone. And that was going to cost several kings' ransoms.

Twin daggers of pain knifed at my temples by the time we finished an hour and ten minutes later—Mamie never once even offered to let me sit—and it was all I could to do to stay upright and put one foot in front of the other as we exited the White House.

"Good-bye, Mrs. Kennedy." The First Lady didn't wait for a response to her Spartan good-bye before she disappeared into the back of the Chrysler limousine that whisked her away to her daily card game. I waited until the car was out of sight before allowing my shoulders to slump. I made it only a few steps toward my blue Buick station wagon when a voice sounded behind me.

"Mrs. Kennedy! Please wait a moment!"

It was J. B. West, carrying a small paper-wrapped package. "Photographs and schematics of each of the White House's rooms," he said. "So you can plan ahead for where you'd like things to go."

I gave a wan smile. "There are going to be a few changes."

As in Mamie Eisenhower won't even recognize the place when I'm done with it.

I turned to leave, but his hesitant touch on my shoulder stopped me. "Are you all right?" he asked.

"Just a little tired." In truth, I was on the verge of collapse but couldn't resist one more question. "Did you know my doctor ordered that I have a wheelchair for the tour today?"

Mr. West actually looked abashed at that. "There *was* a wheelchair. Mrs. Eisenhower had it hiding out of sight. She wanted you to have to ask for it."

I just stared at him, barely swallowing the vulgarity before I cursed the First Lady aloud.

Mamie Eisenhower, *vous êtes vraiment une vache.*

J. B. West gave a kind smile. "I'll walk you the rest of the way." He even closed the Buick's door behind me, his hand raised in farewell as I eased my way toward the airport where I'd meet Jack for our flight to the Kennedy estate on Palm Beach.

One thing was certain as I glanced back in the rearview mirror, the White House fading from view. Things were going to be different when I was First Lady.

Very different indeed.

CHAPTER

9

January 1961

I dabbed my wrists with a demure spritz of Joy—some things might change, but I'd always love the French *parfum* that required ten thousand jasmine blossoms and three hundred May roses to create a single precious ounce—before dismissing the maid and leaving my dressing room in search of Jack. I found him in the hall, breathtaking in his tuxedo but pacing so frenetically he didn't notice me.

I slipped on my fresh white gloves one at a time, tilted my chin ever so slightly. "How do I look?"

Jack paused his pacing and ran a hand over his pomaded hair, then whistled a single languorous note, long and low. "No one's going to pay me any attention when they see you, kid."

I smiled, for this was a gown worthy of being buried in, a symphony of sumptuous swan-white Swiss double satin with a nod to my French Bouvier heritage in the cockade at the waist, all designed by Oleg Cassini for tonight's pre-inaugural gala. My Bergdorf dress for the ball tomorrow was lovely, but in this A-line with borrowed Tiffany diamonds and emeralds glittering at my neck, I felt like the First Lady.

In fact, I felt every inch a queen.

The falling snow sparkled like diamond dust and a cape of star-strewn night sky arched over all of Washington as we stepped outside for the gala, greeted by the ravenous flashes of cameras and barking shouts of the newspapermen. Secret Service agents held umbrellas for us to duck under before we slid into the quiet cavern of the waiting limousine's backseat. I relaxed into the cold leather when the door closed behind us, but Jack had other ideas before we'd even pulled away from our house on N Street.

"Turn the lights on," he said to the chauffeur. "So they can see Jackie."

My life is now a spectacle, I thought as I forced a smile and waved through the window, ignoring the throbbing headache gathering at my temples. *I'll be forever on display, from this day forward.*

I'd known this before Jack had started campaigning, of course, but this media circus was nothing the likes of which staid Ike and Mamie Eisenhower would have encountered. This frenzy was something new to the presidency, more akin to that of Hollywood stars than the commander in chief.

Fortunately, the celebrity-spangled guest list Mr. Kennedy had arranged for the night's fund-raiser meant that their glittering fame overshadowed mine, allowing me the rare opportunity to sit alone with a glass of Champagne after Frank Sinatra had escorted me to my box. Whereas the inauguration tomorrow would be a jubilee for America, this gala was a victory party for all of us Kennedys.

And what a party it was!

Nat King Cole. Laurence Olivier. Harry Belafonte. Bette Davis.

They all performed, and Jack and I laughed until our ribs ached when Frank Sinatra transformed the lyrics of "That Old Black Magic" into "That Old Jack Magic." Afterward, I made the rounds alongside Jack, watching him grow ever more energized as I became wearier from the continuous string of introductions, ending with film star Angie Dickinson, who had recently starred in *Rio Bravo* with John Wayne. It didn't escape me that Jack's gaze constantly tangled with Angie Dickinson's California tan and perfectly coiffed blond hair. From a distance, she could have been Inga-Binga, or worse, Gunilla von Post.

Jack and I had a deal, and now, two children and the presidency later, that deal was complete. The ship of self-doubt had long since sailed.

Thus, I pushed my suspicions as far from my mind as I could manage. *If I don't think about it, maybe it won't happen.*

Exhaustion made my head swim by the time Harry Belafonte finished his last song, heralding the conclusion of the first part of the evening. Tomorrow was Inauguration Day and I still wasn't fully myself yet.

"I'm heading home," I told Jack once the gala ended, infusing my voice with borrowed gaiety. "Enjoy yourself at the dinner your parents are hosting and try not to stay out past dawn."

I couldn't tell if Jack even heard me as he waved to Sinatra across the room. For the sake of harmony, I refused to say anything else. Instead, I cornered Mr. Kennedy near the coat room and nodded in the direction of his son, feigning nonchalance as I adjusted my white satin gloves.

"One team captain to the other?" At Mr. Kennedy's nod, I plunged ahead, deputizing him as I once had Ted's wife, Joan. "Keep him out of trouble tonight."

"We got him this far, kiddo." Mr. Kennedy nudged his spectacles higher onto the bridge of his nose, dropped his voice to a conspiratorial level. "I sure as hell won't let him stumble at the finish line."

I certainly hoped not. Still, I couldn't be too sure.

I stepped out into the snow and tugged my white satin cape closer, casting a final glance over my shoulder in time to glimpse Jack laughing with Angie Dickinson. Yet it wasn't Angie who had campaigned at Jack's side and won over America to get him elected, meaning I was the only woman on earth who was irreplaceable to Jack. Tomorrow, when my husband took the oath of office, his words would transform us into the president and First Lady. And just as I'd once seen Queen Elizabeth wed to her nation, tomorrow meant that the good of my country came before my own wishes as Jack's wife.

Which means you can no longer countenance any sort of scandal. You may have to learn to turn a blind eye, Jacqueline Kennedy.

Even if it killed me.

. . .

Standing erect behind the podium on the steps of the Capitol, Jack looked every bit the assured captain at the helm of his ship, the youngest U.S. president ever elected and the first ever Roman Catholic. He was a vivid Technicolor image of youth and vitality on this frigid winter day, having purposefully foregone his coat and hat at my suggestion, the better to stand out in his stiff winged-collar shirt and black suit among a sea of aged statesmen who now sat huddled and shivering in their woolen jackets.

"Let the word go forth from this time and place, to friend and foe alike, that the torch has been passed to a new generation of Americans."

The rest of us mortals were merely dust motes on the filament of history while loudspeakers broadcast Jack's Bostonian voice to the massive crowd gathered, even as his immortal words rippled out across the country via radio and television, sounding just as strong as the recorded speeches of Winston Churchill he'd pored over all week. "Let every nation know, whether it wishes us well or ill, that we shall pay any price, bear any burden, meet any hardship, support any friend, oppose any foe to assure the survival and the success of liberty."

That was when I realized that my mother and Hughdie weren't near the main box, but instead tiny—and glowering, in the case of my mother—faces in the peanut gallery far behind us. Lee was still recovering in England and unable to attend today's events, but I'd left clear instructions that my mother and stepfather should be seated in the stand facing the presidential box.

How had I managed to bungle the seating of my own family at the most important event in our history? And how many decades would it take before my mother forgave me for that failure?

I tried to focus on Jack's speech, on the words I'd helped him rehearse these past weeks.

"And so, my fellow Americans: ask not what your country can do for you—ask what you can do for your country." There seemed to be a collective inhale as Jack held us in his thrall, his words coming in puffs of frost in the bitterly cold air. "My fellow citizens of the world: ask not what America will do for you, but what together we can do for the freedom of man."

As Jack finished his address, the crowd broke into raucous rounds of applause. I rose, passing Eisenhower, and laid my finger upon my husband's cheek. "Jack," I whispered. "You were so wonderful."

"Thanks, kid. This is only the warm-up." Jack's grin was full of pride as I took up my muff (sable this time, although my underwear wasn't), which Oleg Cassini had hastily fitted with a warmer due to the biting cold. Oleg had agreed that I should wear a simple fawn wool dress and coat with a circlet of Russian sable at the neck, both in a shade so pale that, like Jack, I was bound to stand out among all the other wives who were loaded down like bears in their bleak and mothballed furs.

Let there be no doubt that if we had to play this game, we were going to win.

Jack and I were siphoned toward the parade reviewing stand, but not before the rest of our families rejoined us. Including one very upset Auchincloss matriarch who looked like she'd had a fifty-pound dumbbell dropped on her foot.

"I don't know what happened to the seating arrangement, Mummy," I said by way of apology as my mother took me by the arm. "I don't understand what happened, and I promise to get to the bottom of it."

My mother's lips were tight with hurt, but she surprised me with her concern. For *me*. "Jackie," she said as we walked. "If such a terrible situation can occur to your own mother, then anything could happen during your time as First Lady. Despite the efforts of the people who work here, in the end, it all falls upon you."

I suddenly realized that she was right, that every protocol mishap during Jack's presidency would inevitably land in my lap. I had just turned into a piece of public property, one that would be under constant scrutiny. "Thank you, Mummy," I said, dazed at this new reality I'd mistakenly hoped I'd prepared for. "I'll remember that."

Knees wobbling, I found my place in the reviewing stand beside Mr. Kennedy and the rest of Jack's family. "Are you all right, Jackie?" Bobby asked, but I only gave a distracted nod, feeling my mother's eyes boring into the back of my head.

Focus, Jackie. Don't worry about what your mother said.

Instead, I watched with surprise as Jack's father doffed his top hat to his son—now the President of the United States—in the only time I'd ever seen him defer to any of his children. Beside me, Bobby stiffened so I wondered what it was like for him growing up in the long shadows of these two men, whether his talents were ever overlooked simply because he wasn't the older brother. I wondered, too, how things might have been different had the eldest Kennedy brother, Joe, not died in a fiery plane crash during the war.

Whether Jack and I might have wound up leading quiet, mundane sorts of lives.

As if reading my thoughts, Mr. Kennedy leaned toward me.

"Are you ready for this, kiddo?"

I suspected he didn't mean just the parade.

I managed a sanguine smile, but a steady pounding started behind my eyes when the marching bands blasted by with thumping drums and honking tubas, followed by endless and perfectly synchronized lines of cadets from the United States Military Academy and the white-capped midshipmen from the United States Naval Academy. It was only six weeks since my Cesarean section and my body was screaming that I'd already overtaxed myself today, to say nothing of the five inaugural balls I was expected to attend tonight.

I stared at the back of Jack's head, imagining his hale and hearty smile, willing him to turn and reassure me with a silent exchange only he and I could understand. Instead, a passing U.S. Navy float complete with a model Polaris ballistic missile kept him eagerly absorbed.

How will I ever manage to catch his attention, or worse, keep up with him over the next four years? I bit my lip, willing that dull pain to keep me tethered. I couldn't even arrange decent seats for my own mother at Jack's inauguration. How on earth did I think I could manage being First Lady?

Jack's dream of the presidency had seemed distant when we'd first met, but now the weighty responsibilities I'd assumed as wife, mother, and First Lady hung themselves all at once like malevolent albatrosses around my neck.

Support Jack as he runs the entire country.

Raise Caroline and John with some semblance of a normal childhood.

Greet lofty heads of state at Jack's side.

Plan and execute flawless diplomatic receptions.

Restore the White House.

Never, *ever* make one single mistake.

"I need to rest." It was suddenly impossible to breathe and I was barely able to gasp the words. Something was crushing my chest, brutally flattening my lungs.

"Are you sure you want to miss the state floats?" Mr. Kennedy joked. "Texas has a hideous buckskinned cowboy riding a bison, all made of god-awful papier-mâché." He glanced sideways at my blood-less expression, then snapped to get Bobby's attention. "To bed with you, kiddo," he murmured. "Now. I'll send a doctor."

Jack finally turned my way. "Is everything all right?" he asked as Bobby and I passed behind him. Was it dismay that I saw flicker on his face? Or disappointment?

I can't burden Jack, won't let him see me as weak. We saw how that turned out after my miscarriage.

"I just want to be rested for tonight," I lied.

Bobby guided me back to the White House. "Which bedroom?" he asked once we were inside, his hand under my elbow.

I could scarcely breathe, much less answer as I focused on placing one foot on each stair, ignoring the curious looks from the White House staff. This was not how I'd planned to make my initial en-trance as First Lady, but the more I thought about breathing, and what was expected of me now for the rest of my life, the more impossible it was to draw air.

"The Rose," I managed to gasp out, garnering a reassuring smile from him.

"Fitting." He chuckled. "That's where all the queens stay, isn't it?"

I homed in on the much-needed distraction he provided, let the facts I'd dusted off and memorized these past weeks crowd out some of my panic. "The queens of the Netherlands, Greece, Norway. And many others. So far."

"Well, we're almost there, Your Majesty."

I thought Bobby spoke in mockery, but his blue eyes softened as he glanced my way. He was so like Jack, only smoother around the edges, as if he didn't expect life to try to thwart him at every turn. "My mother would disagree, but to my eyes you're the uncrowned queen of this family," he said when he opened the door to the dark and dreary Rose Room. Even in this anxious state, I cringed at the mismatched floral chairs and the worn cornflower-hued carpet. "Things are going to change after today, Jackie, but that never will."

I'd have put my hand in fire for Bobby then, who of all of the Kennedys I found the most levelheaded and calm. I wanted to feel like the queen he spoke of as I stretched out on the four-poster bed's pink satin duvet, but instead I could only cling to each fragile thread of my composure as Bobby rang for one of Jack's physicians. During the examination, I grew ever angrier at myself for this weakness. What sort of First Lady had to flee the inaugural reviewing stand out of sheer exhaustion?

The worst kind, Jackie. The sort who needs to pull herself together.

"One Dexedrine tablet to ease your anxiety and this bed," white-haired Dr. Janet Travell commanded as she dropped the orange pill into a glass and closed up her bag. "Don't even think about getting up until you absolutely have to. This exhaustion is to be expected after your third C-section."

To which Bobby waggled a finger. "You hear that, Your Majesty? Doctor's orders."

Which might have been possible for a regular woman to obey. But I was no longer a regular woman, and likely never would be again.

I boxed up the thought and shelved it on the furthest shelf of my mind as I swallowed the blessed orange pill. Then Bobby closed the curtains, bathing the room in calming darkness. It might have been a dream, but I thought I felt Bobby stoop over me to whisper in my ear. "Choose one thing, Jackie, and do it well. The rest will take care of itself."

Then he slipped out into the hall on silent feet.

And I allowed myself the luxury of fading into sleep.

After attending three inaugural balls, I woke the next morning in the queen's bed. Alone.

I refused to entertain ideas of where Jack had spent the night. Or with whom.

Instead, determined that this would be the day I recovered my energy, I threw on a pair of jodhpurs and boots to walk laps around the White House grounds—I was going to have to find a way to go riding or else lose my mind—while ignoring the silent Secret Service agents who followed me like dark shadows.

Now that I was First Lady, it wasn't only Jack who had a security detail. I cringed to realize that both Caroline and John would wake up at Glen Ora—a four-hundred-acre horse farm Jack and I had leased in Virginia—to find they, too, were being guarded, although I was grateful for the extra protection. I realized then how much I missed hearing Caroline's laughter, and longed for her and John, who would arrive with Miss Shaw once their rooms were ready.

I knew then that my first crusade now that Jack was president was to fight for a sane life for my babies and their father.

It took at least a dozen laps before my walk calmed me well enough that I could return to the Rose Room, only to find Tish waiting with my crisp daily schedule tucked under her arm. "Good morning, Mrs.

Kennedy," she said. "You have a meeting with Mr. West in five minutes to tour the White House again and meet all the staff."

"Tish." My honeyed voice might have put Scarlett O'Hara to shame as I combed my fingers through my exercise-tousled hair. "Do you know if Jack made it to all of the inaugural balls last night?"

For I'd only managed three of the five balls on Jack's arm the night before, armored in an off-white sleeveless crepe chiffon gown over *peau d'ange*, its strapless bodice covered with diamond-hard brilliants anchored by silver thread. A full-length matching cape and the emerald drop earrings Jack had gifted me after the election completed my ensemble.

It had been surreal when "Hail to the Chief" had played as it had for Ike and Mamie Eisenhower eight years prior, only this time for Jack and me, like a page borrowed from someone else's life story.

This is your life now, Jackie. Find a way to revel in it.

There was dancing, of course, and the announcements of Jack's new cabinet members as they paraded with their satin-swathed wives down the center aisle of the DC Armory. My favorite moment had come when Jack raised a glass of Champagne to me from our place in the presidential balcony as the Marine Corps band struck up a Celtic folk song called "Black Velvet Band." I'd expected Jack to toast his presidency or our future, but instead he'd looked as he had from across the booth at Martin's Tavern. Only this time, instead of proposing, he serenaded me.

> *Her eyes they shone like diamonds,*
> *I thought her the queen of the land,*
> *And her hair, it hung over her shoulder,*
> *Tied up with a black velvet band.*

The hum of the crowd died away so I could have fallen into the pools of his eyes. "To you, Jackie: my wife, my partner, my friend." He ran a finger along my jaw in the most delicious way. "My queen."

This is why I do it, I thought to myself as our glasses kissed and my cheeks flushed with pleasure. *This is why I love him.*

Tish cleared her throat and brought me back to the present moment. "The president attended all five balls, Mrs. Kennedy; his stamina is the talk of the town." A glance over my shoulder couldn't answer what sort of stamina Tish was referring to, but I hoped to God—for her sake—that she wasn't mocking me. "Apparently, Angie Dickinson and Kim Novak both tried to cajole President Kennedy into escorting them to a party after the last ball. Can you imagine? Not one but two actresses?"

You'd be surprised what I can imagine, Tish.

Bile rose in my mouth. "And did the president go with them?" I kept my tone normal, but time seemed to tick more slowly as I held my breath. "To the party, I mean?"

Tish tapped a pencil against the day's schedule I suspected she'd already memorized. "He returned to the White House. The Secret Service told me it was pretty humorous when he couldn't find anyone to make him anything to eat, so he ended up with a bowl of Wheaties they scrounged up. Ate them in the Lincoln Bedroom, I believe."

Thank God. The tension between my brows eased. *Who knew Jack could resist the temptation of not one but two stunning blond actresses?*

Still dressed in my jodhpurs, I motioned for Tish to match my brisk pace as I headed back downstairs. "Have the workmen for the redesign of the upstairs family rooms arrived yet?"

"I believe they have—"

"Good. I want the four-poster bed taken from the downstairs guest bedroom to replace the one in the room the Eisenhowers shared." I ticked off items on my fingers. "Put those terrible straight-backed host and hostess chairs from the dining room into storage, along with that tacky mirrored screen. I'll also need to order a special cattle-tail hair mattress for Jack's back—he's allergic to horsehair so double-check it's cattle hair only. In fact, order two, so he has one when he travels. Make sure that Air Force One can accommodate it."

Tish glanced at my social calendar, and started writing in a frenetic manner, but not fast enough. It wasn't just Jack who could maintain a feverish pace.

You'll have to keep up with me, Tish. I can't fall apart if I never stop moving.

"Also," I said, "contact Stéphane Boudin of Jansen in Paris. He renovated a portion of Versailles, and I'd like to take him up on his offer to do work on the White House for free."

J. B. West, the White House chief usher whom I'd met during the tour of misery with Mamie Eisenhower, awaited us in the dreadful eyesore that was the Red Room. West was a nondescript sort of man with a receding hairline whose most memorable characteristic was the pair of thick-rimmed black glasses often perched on his nose. However, I soon learned he preferred to fade into the background, to perform his duties as chief usher with tact and utter anonymity.

With the recent loss of my own privacy, I found much to admire in that trait.

"I want to make this—America's *Maison Blanche*—a great house," I said to him as Tish scampered off to order the mattresses, doing my best not to cringe as I inspected the White House anew. I'd spent the past weeks scrutinizing schematics of the mansion and had requested every piece of print material on its history from the Library of Congress. Yet I was still shocked as I perused each floor with West, dismayed anew at the forlorn palms that drooped dejectedly in corners and the furniture that looked like it was ordered from a Sears catalog. I repressed a shudder as we passed the drinking fountain installed on the wall of the third-floor hall, the level that was supposed to be our family's private floor. "That," I said, pointing to it, "is the first thing to go."

J. B. West almost smiled. "Of course, Mrs. Kennedy."

I nodded and introduced myself to the barrage of plumbers, electricians, and carpenters already at work. I recalled the coaching my mother had given me for running an efficient estate; her formula for good living would serve me well now that I was in charge of the most famous home in America. "We're going to need proper family rooms up here. With a school for Caroline down the hall. I'm sure other members of the administration have children who can join her."

You're a mother first, Jackie, then a wife. Then, and only then, are you the First Lady. That always comes a distant third.

"Do you have children, Mr. West?" I asked in an attempt to draw him out. He reminded me of Miss Shaw, very much of the stuff-and-nonsense school of thought.

"Two daughters, Mrs. Kennedy," he responded, his eyes alight. "Although I'm afraid I don't see them as often as I'd like."

"I suspect not, given that you're the miracle worker of the White House. You'll have to bring them to meet Caroline one day." I frowned, wondering what my daughter would think upon seeing her new home for the first time. "Mr. West, may I meet the gardeners? I have a special request for them."

J. B. West was like my own personal genie, for all I had to do was ask, and my wish was granted. Two uniformed gardeners were escorted upstairs moments later, and both removed their gloves to shake my hand.

"I was wondering if I might ask a favor of you gentlemen," I said in a soft voice. "You see, I'd like this to feel like home when the children arrive. Would it be possible for you to build a snowman in the yard for them? Perhaps a silly one with a floppy Panama hat, with carrots for eyes and an apple for its nose, to amuse and distract them—especially Caroline—from the strangeness of their big, new house?"

"Of course, ma'am," the first said with a slow smile. "We'd be happy to."

Simple things. These were things I could manage that might make a big difference.

There was a pleasant surprise waiting when J. B. West brought me downstairs to the White House cellars. Instead of walls stacked with dusty vintages or strings of garlic hanging from the ceiling, the entire cavernous room contained rows of silent people bent over desks, their pens busily scratching, so that if I closed my eyes I could imagine myself in some medieval monastery with monks illuminating precious sheets of vellum with priceless inks and tiny flakes of gold leaf.

"What in heaven's name are you doing?" I whispered to one of them as if we were in the holiest of cloisters, entirely intrigued and unwilling to fully break the spell of silence. My heart fell when the pens ceased their scratching and all heads swiveled in my direction so that the intimate moment evaporated. Chairs scraped across the floor as everyone rose, but I waved away the formality.

"We're the White House calligraphers." The man closest to me gestured to stacks of thick parchment, which I now realized were blank invitations and place cards. "Whenever you organize an event, we're the ones who write it all out."

My face lit with pleasure and I clapped my hands. "How magical," I said, and I meant it.

Sometime later, my head swam with names as West had introduced me to squads of staff who paraded by while I sat perched on the edge of a desk, some of whom had blinked in surprise at the sight of a First Lady in pants. "Is that everyone?" I whispered to West after two Filipino navy stewards who acted as the upstairs housemen had shaken my hand.

"Well," he answered, "there are three men in the flower shop, two women in the laundry, five downstairs housemen, three plumbers, three painters. . . ."

I hardly heard the rest, glad I was sitting down as I realized the magnitude of the operation I was now in charge of running. Even my mother would have been in awe. "How much is our operating budget?"

"Five hundred thousand dollars a year, not including your personal expenditure."

"Well, I want you to run this place just like you'd run it for the chintziest president who ever got elected." I gave him a wink. "We don't have nearly as much money as you read in the papers."

Mr. West chuckled so I wasn't sure he believed me, but quickly grew serious. "On that subject, Mrs. Kennedy, you were appropriated fifty thousand dollars for the renovation." He glanced at the notes he'd been taking, pausing as if doing the math in his head, although I suspected he'd been tabulating each room down to the penny along the way. "And you will have exceeded that just in the family rooms."

"Damn." I made a point never to curse in public, and certainly never in English, but this poor broken house was worth an epithet or two. I was still appalled that the only antiques in the entire house that West had been able to show me were a pair of card tables in the Green Room. The White House sagged under the weight of its neglect, its hodgepodge of dusty B. Altman furniture and cheap repairs almost worse than if it had simply been abandoned. These were the hallowed halls that Jefferson and Madison had walked and the rooms where Lincoln and the Roosevelts had slept, and they deserved more than bargain basement furnishings.

"Perhaps the project will need scaling back?" West asked. "Something smaller, with fewer antiques?"

I've never done anything small in my life, Mr. West, and I'm not about to start now.

I quickly brightened. "We may be out of money, Mr. West," I said, already envisioning the heavy green silk damask wallpaper of the Green Room replaced with a delicate green watered silk fabric. "But never mind. We're going to find a brilliant way to get real antiques into this house. And fully restore the White House into something America can truly be proud of."

Everyone claimed that Jack and I were fast becoming celebrities. Surely that meant I could leverage that fame to my benefit just this once?

I breathed a deep sigh as J. B. West closed the doors to the Green Room behind us. Rather than feel overwhelmed, a bit of the pressure in my chest lifted as I imagined filling the rooms with Cézanne paintings and fresh silk upholstery, tracking down Monroe's silver French flatware and Theodore Roosevelt's area rugs.

These were small problems I was good at solving, a ship I knew I could steer.

Like any president's wife, I would only reside in the White House for a brief time. Before time slipped away, before every link with the past was gone, I wanted to restore the White House.

So I would. One day at a time.

CHAPTER

10

April 1961

Y ou must be joking. People really want to know what shampoo I use?" I glanced up from my editing on the White House guidebook to answer Tish's question. The book was only a small facet of my plan to finance the restoration now that I'd established the fine arts committee for the White House and enticed several wealthy donors in order to alleviate the need to petition Congress to appropriate more funds. (I'd had to promise to have tea with several donors, for even the rich aspired to share a pot of Earl Grey with me. It honestly boggled the mind.) The guidebook temporarily forgotten, I stared incredulously at Tish as she placed the day's already opened mail on a desk in the Red Room.

Well, part of the mail, since it was difficult for her to carry hundreds of letters at once.

"That, how you stay so slim, and how many foam rollers you wear in your hair each night." Tish scanned the letter in her hand. "And whether the president minds them or not."

I turned so Tish couldn't see my expression, for the truth was Jack and I saw each other less and less these days. Craving solitude, I often escaped the White House for the tranquility of Glen Ora, which was the most private place I could think of to balance life in the White House. We might have gone to the presidential retreat at Camp David—which Jack preferred—but I cringed at the compound's motel shacks with their bomb shelters churning underneath. Jack came to Glen Ora most weekends, where he played blocks on the floor with John—who the press dubbed John-John after hearing Jack call to him twice in a row, although no one in the family used the nickname— and cheered Caroline's recitation of Edna St. Vincent Millay's poem "First Fig," which I'd taught her to memorize. When Jack was with me, he was a doting and caring husband, both in the day and in the night. Yet there were whispers about when he wasn't with me, of willing girls tucked into elevators and smuggled into the White House.

I told myself they were only rumors, for the very thought of Jack with other women . . .

Well, that didn't bear thinking about. Most of all because I'd never put my children through what Lee and I had endured when my mother divorced my father. Worse, I could guarantee the headlines if Jack and I had so much as a disagreement over which color tie he should wear to a cabinet meeting, much less anything more serious.

No, it was now my mission to maintain the image of our storybook marriage, at least on the outside. The cost of my pride wasn't worth the cost of my children's happiness. I would bring up the issue with Jack when we were alone. Except nowadays we were never alone.

And yet, even surrounded, I often felt as if I were alone on some windswept island. I worried constantly about letting anyone see the real Jackie, for fear they might leak some unsavory tidbit to the press: my imperfections, my anxiety, or my inability to juggle all my new roles. Worse still, that someone might feign friendship and somehow betray us with a sordid tell-all.

"Tell them I use five rollers," I told Tish as I rubbed my temples. In truth, my beauty regime was a legion of horrors, but there was no need to mention that or the fact that I weighed myself every morning and adjusted my meals to ensure I remained the same size as before my pregnancies. "Give them minimum information with maximum politeness—no need to tell all my secrets. How are plans for the trip to Europe?"

The trip would be our first across the Atlantic together since Jack had become president, and I wanted everything to be perfect. *Needed* everything to be perfect.

Now that he was president, I suspected no matter what I did or how faultless I was, Jack might appreciate me, but I doubted I would ever be the center of his universe as he was mine.

Still, that didn't mean I wasn't going to try.

"In France, you'll be staying at the French foreign ministry's mansion on the Quai d'Orsay." Tish sorted envelopes into piles. "Charles de Gaulle himself will guide you around Paris."

I scarcely restrained a squeal of girlish delight; Charles de Gaulle was to me what Winston Churchill was to Jack, so much so that as a girl I'd named my poodle Gaullie in honor of his leadership of the French resistance during World War II. Of course, I didn't plan to inform the French president of his canine namesake; instead I'd been rereading Charles de Gaulle's memoirs in their original French to prepare for my return to France.

I glanced at the gilded bronze and marble mantel clock, a truly hideous gift to President Truman from France that featured two golden cherubs riding horned goats. "I trust you to answer those letters for me, Tish. Else I'll be late to welcome the Greek prime minster and his wife to lunch."

I made a note to move the eyesore of a mantel clock—hopefully to the basement—and found Jack waiting outside the Diplomatic Reception Room for the Greek entourage to arrive. He gave a nervous slap of his leg when I greeted him, as if he hadn't even heard my hello. "Is everything all right?" I asked.

"I may need you to take the lead on this lunch. The invasion in Cuba isn't going as we expected." Jack's furious growl sent a shiver up my spine. "The damn CIA knew of a leak to the Soviets a week ago, but they still pressed for my approval. Fifty bucks says the Bay of Pigs becomes synonymous with unmitigated disaster."

Now I understood the tension evident in his shoulders and the stiff set of his jaw. While Jack didn't apprise me of all his presidential decisions, I'd have been deaf and dumb to be unaware that he'd authorized a risky plan to send an invasion force of Cuban exiles to topple the new Russian-allied Communist dictatorship established on our island neighbor to the south.

Jack had promised during his presidential campaign that he would be the new leader to propel America ahead of the USSR, that with him at the helm we would have the will and the strength to resist and overcome communism. Only three months after taking the oath of office, the outcome of this critical mission in Cuba would determine whether he would be the hero of the free world or a reviled failure. "I'd be happy to take point on lunch," I assured him.

We made it through the lunch, but barely, Jack compartmentalizing the potential calamity in Cuba so he could turn on his charm to impress the Greek prime minister. As the soup tureens were brought into the State Dining Room and a successive train of stone-faced aides came to whisper in Jack's ear, I kept up a steady stream of airy conversation while the prime minister's wife invited me to see the Parthenon in Athens, as if Castro and Cuba and the rebels had ceased to exist.

If only it were that easy.

It wasn't until the next night during a congressional reception that we received definitive word on just how bad things were.

Still in his tuxedo, Jack slipped out to attend a classified meeting in the Cabinet Room, and I waited in my Cassini-designed sheath gown of pink-and-white straw lace until after midnight for the meeting to adjourn. In his new role as Jack's freshly minted and fairly controversial attorney general, Bobby emerged first, a hangdog expression turning down his handsome features. I rarely bothered Jack for political details—it felt criminal to badger my weary husband over how things were in Borneo when I knew all he wanted was to change into a happy evening mood and forget his worries following a long day— but I wasn't going to walk about uninformed, not when the stakes were this high.

"What happened?" I asked.

"I warned Jack, but he didn't listen to me." Bobby loosened his tie with an angry jerk of his hand, then shoved his fists into his pockets. This was an entirely different Bobby from the self-assured lawyer who had dared take on the mob as counsel for the U.S. Senate, who had made boss Sam Giancana plead the Fifth a whopping forty times. "The entire damn thing was botched from start to finish and now we're trying to rescue almost twelve hundred men we set up to fail. Jack's going to take a shitload of heat for this, both here and with the rest of the world. And unfortunately, it's justified."

I cringed, then startled as Jack burst from the Cabinet Room, each muscle in his body taut as if straining to contain a supernova. He scowled in our direction before storming away, every atom of oxygen in the West Wing corridor condensing after him. I glanced at Bobby and we fell into step behind Jack, but Bobby's hand on my wrist made me pause as we approached the stairway, and he shook his head. "Give him a second."

A door upstairs slammed and I forced myself to count the overhead fluorescent lights in the corridor before following after my husband, Bobby close on my heels. I stopped outside the door to the Yellow Oval Room, the muffled sound from within giving me pause. When I finally opened the door, it revealed a scene I'd never witnessed before, one that tore my beating heart from my chest and set the very blood in my veins to blackening.

Jack cowered on the overstuffed sofa with his back to me, his lovely, tousled head in his hands and his broad shoulders shaking with the force of a thousand earthquakes. I almost crumpled to the floor with the realization of what I was witnessing.

Jack was weeping, sucking in brutal gasps of air as if he were drowning.

A great man, failing in earnest for the first time in his life and being overwhelmed by an ocean of his own mistakes.

"Shit," Bobby whispered behind me. "Shit, shit, *shit.*"

Jack lifted his head then and peered at Bobby and me through puffy and bloodshot eyes. His voice cleaved in two when he spoke. "Close the door."

He scrubbed a fist over his eyes, doing nothing to erase the fact that the man before me was more vulnerable than when he'd been on the cusp of dying after his spinal surgeries. This time I could only sit beside him, a steady presence.

Jack didn't respond when I placed a hand on his knee, but nor did he push me away as he spoke to Bobby, his words coming in fits and starts. "Those sons of bitches just sat there nodding over their fruit salad, saying Eisenhower's plan would work. They promised it would work." He ran both hands through his hair, making it stand out at odd angles before drawing ragged breaths to steady himself. "I want Allen Dulles and Richard Bissell removed. Quietly, but immediately." Somewhat recovered, he stood and stormed toward his bedroom before calling over his shoulder. "From now on, I want to know everything about Castro: every time he so much as calls Russia, who he sleeps with and whether he takes his boots off when he does. It's just you and me, Bobby."

Which was exactly what Mr. Kennedy had wanted when he pushed Jack to appoint Bobby as his attorney general. We'd been betrayed—not quite in the manner I'd feared but all the same—and now the Kennedys were closing ranks.

And I was a Kennedy, too, *bon Dieu*. Which meant that I, too, needed to look out for Jack, lest we find ourselves engulfed by flames and quicksand.

"Dammit," Bobby muttered under his breath. "I knew I should have been more forceful, that I should have told him in no uncertain terms to call off the whole invasion. Instead I let him listen to his goddamned war hawks."

"Jack can make his own decisions," I reminded Bobby. "You deal with firing Dulles and Bissell. I'll take care of Jack."

Bobby sighed, his jacket open with one hand fisted on his hip while the other gripped his forehead as if to ward off an ache there. Poor Bobby, who had gladly played the bad guy since the campaign so people wouldn't get mad at Jack. "You sure? That leaves me the easier job by far."

I gave a wan smile, knowing Bobby was always willing to be the bad cop, so long as it was for Jack. "We're on the same team, Bobby. You can owe me one."

"Deal."

Tonight I'd comfort Jack as best I could. Tomorrow we'd face a bleak world ruined by this failure in the Bay of Pigs.

And we'd do it together.

Wind from the jet engines whipped my hair as our two truck-loads of baggage were transported onto the planes surrounding Air Force One. We were about to take off for what now promised to be a disastrous goodwill trip to Europe, for there was no escaping the sour fog of failure that was the Bay of Pigs. Jack couldn't run from the image that he was inept and inexperienced, that he'd authorized a slapdash mission and then lacked the nerve to send in U.S. forces after the Cuban exiles were surrounded and taken prisoner.

It was like the plot of some terrible Russian novel, one bleak catastrophe after another, and I was forced to keep turning the pages as he grappled with this failure that would forever blacken his presidency.

Something had to be done, for my cowed, anxious husband now suffered from insomnia and groaned with pain after wrenching his back at a recent tree planting ceremony. It was obvious as I helped him board Air Force One that he was not ready to joust with Europe's heads of state. For my part, I felt my anxiety from Jack's inauguration lurking in the shadows, threatening to ambush me at any moment.

Maybe we were wrong. Perhaps Jack and I can't manage all this after all. . . .

Although it felt like weeks since I'd slept, I wasn't so far gone as to fully believe that, so I waved to a disheveled Dr. Max Jacobson—known to his vast list of celebrity clients as Dr. Feelgood—who would be accompanying us as we country hopped around the Continent for the next few weeks. I hadn't realized until after the fact that Jack had first seen Jacobson before his debates against Nixon. "Jacobson's joy juice did the trick," he had told me after I'd congratulated his stellar performance. "But the injections had side effects I didn't like."

The medicine could turn us both blue in the face or make us dance a polka on the steps of the White House, so long as they made us happy again. Otherwise, we were both too fragile to make it through this trip unscathed.

"My juice isn't for kicks, only for people who have work to do," Jacobson reassured me as he flicked the syringe with an expert hand, his fingernails stained soot black. His hooked nose, thick-rimmed glasses, and guttural German accent made him a caricature of Sigmund Freud. "And you two have serious work to do."

"What exactly is in these injections?" We were airborne and I distracted myself from the wickedly long needle by staring out the cabin window at the Washington Monument. The rest of DC sprawled on the horizon: the National Mall with its bevy of monuments, and beyond that, the Capitol and Arlington National Cemetery.

"Oh, you know." An efficient swipe of a cool alcohol pad on my arm, followed by the sharp sting of a needle. "Methamphetamine, steroid, calcium, and monkey placenta."

I gave him a startled glance, but he only winked. Was he serious?

"One for me, too, Doctor." Jack rolled up his sleeve and offered his arm, not even wincing as he received his dose of joy juice. "Dr. Travell claims I need to use crutches this whole trip. We all know those bastards de Gaulle and Khrushchev will eat me alive if I do that."

"Everything will be fine," Jacobson assured both of us. "They don't call me Miracle Max for nothing. This little cocktail will give you wings, erase your pain, and give you both the energy to cheerfully attend all your social engagements. There's a different miracle syringe before bed each night so you'll sleep like babies."

"It sounds like heaven," I said to Jacobson, but Jack was still mired in the mud of his presidential worries.

"De Gaulle fought Nazis, for God's sake," he muttered. "I can't even deal with Castro, and Khrushchev is rabble-rousing in Berlin."

"You fought in the same war de Gaulle did, so you're just as much a hero as he is," I reminded him as I moved to rub his shoulders, giving Jacobson a discreet nod so he could retire.

Maybe it was Dr. Feelgood's joy juice, or perhaps the realization that I was about to meet my idol during the European tour of a lifetime, but I was suddenly so energized that I rocked on my toes, feeling as if I could have run faster than the plane that was now winging us across the Atlantic.

There were benefits to this fishbowl sort of life, if Jack and I chose to seek them out. This goodwill tour was one of those benefits, despite us having to navigate around the political shambles created by the Bay of Pigs. No matter what, I was going to enjoy—not just enjoy, *revel*—in this trip, just as I was somehow going to transform Charles de Gaulle into one of our staunchest allies.

Sometimes men forget there's more than one way to fight a war.

If Charles de Gaulle and Nikita Khrushchev wished to slander my husband, they'd soon find themselves fighting an altogether different sort of battle, one they were ill prepared for. After all, who expected Jack's general to come not clad in camouflage or decorated with gleaming medals, but instead decked out in Givenchy and pearls?

After a smooth landing, a snowy-haired and distinguished General de Gaulle welcomed us in a *salon d'honneur* at the Orly Airport, and I almost exploded with happiness when the towering leader bent over my hand. "*La gracieuse* Madame Kennedy," he murmured with a soft smile through a translator after he'd snubbed Jack with an abbreviated greeting that bordered on rudeness. I knew he spoke many languages—including English—but thought them all inferior to French. "Or do you prefer *la belle Jacqui*?"

"Either will do nicely." The bull-chested French president could have called me anything he liked as he escorted us outside to the waiting motorcade, where a cavalry of plumed Republican guards flanked the cars. A holiday had been declared in our honor, and the streets were jammed with thousands of people waving tiny American flags and chanting at the top of their lungs, *"Vive le président! Vive Jacqueline!"*

This promised to be a far different trip from my carefree college days when I could stay out until three in the morning at a café along the Rive Gauche without worrying about a gaggle of photographers snapping a jungle of photos. Those days were long gone, replaced by something altogether new and exciting.

"The French sure do know how to make a fuss, don't they?" Jack muttered under his breath. He and I both jolted when the city was shaken by the start of a 101-gun salute, but it was as if I were at one end of a live wire, suddenly electrified by this city I had always loved.

"They do indeed," I said, waving to as many people as I could as we drove through the Place de la Concorde. And I loved them all the more for it.

La Ville Lumiére!

As an American, I could never truly be a queen, but in Paris I felt like the uncrowned queen of the world, just as Bobby had once said.

It was a whirlwind tour; in a single afternoon I enjoyed an intimate five-course luncheon of *langouste à la Parisienne* and *foie gras en gelée* before decamping to the Élysée Palace to visit an infant-care nursing school. There I gifted the children with American candies and the facility itself with a set of brightly colored modern furniture to cheer up their drab waiting room (for I remembered all the cheerless waiting rooms I'd sat in while Jack was in surgery). The most moving event was witnessing my somber husband lay a wreath at the Arc de Triomphe—the limestone memorial commemorating Napoleon's many victories—before performing the ritual rekindling of the eternal flame at the Tomb of the Unknown Soldier.

My very blood thrummed with the sheer pleasure of it all; I never wanted to leave Paris.

Upon arriving at the French Foreign Ministry's mansion on the Quai d'Orsay, Jack and I were happily ensconced in a five-salon suite that overlooked magnificently restored gardens from the time of Louis-Philippe, the room's Napoleonic ceilings spangled with soaring cherubs and the walls hung with celebrated paintings loaned from the Louvre just for our pleasure. My bedroom had last been occupied by Belgium's Queen Fabiola, and the silver mosaic bathtub I soaked in before dinner had been designed for Britain's Queen Elizabeth II.

"Well, there's no doubt de Gaulle likes you," Jack groused that night as I brushed my hair—fifty strokes with a spritz of Joy for good measure. "He's hardly said two words to me."

"We're a team, Jack," I reminded him, although I knew it grated on him to take the passenger's seat. Worse still, he'd have been flat on his back had it not been for Miracle Max's ethyl chloride spray and the dose of cortisone keeping him upright. "Just try to enjoy yourself."

And let me do the talking.

It took the famous French stylist Alexandre two hours to transform my hair into a Gothic Madonna coiffure, complete with false topknot and a diamond rose, making me glad that I'd sent him a lock of my hair from Washington in preparation. Once my hair was complete, Tish zipped me into a floor-length Givenchy gown—a goodwill gesture toward French couture that Oleg Cassini approved and I thoroughly enjoyed—that honored the tricolor French flag with its pale red-and-blue appliquéd bodice over a slim white satin skirt.

"Ce soir, Madame Kennedy, vous ressemblez à un Watteau." General de Gaulle's compliment made me blush as he kissed my hand in a grand display of pageantry. The man renowned for being a severe judge of character now raised a glass in my honor at the presidential Élysée Palace.

The translator next to him cleared his throat. "The general says that this evening, Mrs. Kennedy, you are looking like a Watteau."

I bit my lip, for while I'd allowed the translator this afternoon for Jack's sake, I couldn't countenance the stop-and-go necessary to continue having our conversation translated sentence by sentence.

"Merci beaucoup," I said to de Gaulle in low, melodic French. *"Le gala est tellement spectaculaire."*

The general's face lit with pleasure, and on de Gaulle's other side, Jack finally relaxed, his smile warm with pride as I translated anything he didn't understand while the former general and I continued conversing in rapid-fire French, the frowning translator dismissed with a wave of de Gaulle's hand.

Keep going, Jack's eyes seemed to say to me. *Make me a gift of de Gaulle.*

You need me, Jack, I wanted to say aloud. *Just as I need you. I only hope you realize how much we can accomplish together.*

"I am afraid that Boulevard Saint-Michel from your student days here was not available to host the gala." De Gaulle winked as we abandoned the banquet in the stunning Hall of Mirrors to the palace's restored Louis XV jewel-box theater, Jack and Madame de Gaulle trailing behind. "I hope you don't mind making do with our little palace here in Versailles."

"Making do?" I asked, incredulous. "There is nothing about making do in Paris."

In fact, it was as if the entire goodwill tour had been lifted straight from the pages of some precious illuminated manuscript, painted in swirls of priceless azure and cerulean before being gilded with gleaming gold leaf.

"I'm enjoying this trip terribly," I breathed now as we approached the jewel-box theater. "One can feel the history in the very air."

"You are quite the student of history, much like your husband," de Gaulle said, a compliment I'd be sure to share with Jack later. "Did you know this ballet was first performed for Louis XV?"

"Not France's best ruler." I recalled that Louis's draining of the treasury had paved the way for the governmental collapse of the French Revolution and the guillotines that followed. "Still, I suspect he had exquisite taste in ballets."

De Gaulle let out a ribald guffaw and patted my hand. "*Le belle Jacqui,* you are about to find out."

A hush fell over the theater, and as the ballet began, I could imagine a near identical moment reenacted hundreds of years ago, the only changes the perfumed courtiers in their elaborate curled wigs and rustling silks, the flutter of lace fans and flaming spotlight torches blazing to life as the beribboned French king took his seat in the royal box.

It was moments like this that made every drop of pain, every pounding heartache of pursuing the White House worth the sacrifice, especially when Jack reached over and wove his fingers through mine in a rare public display of tenderness.

I wiped tears of rapture from my eyes when it was all over, wishing I might crystallize into amber that precious hour with Jack on one side and de Gaulle on the other, romantic Parisian ballerinas in arabesque before me while history sparkled in the air like dust motes.

It would forever be one of the most perfect moments of my life.

"I know the palace here at Versailles shall serve as inspiration as I undertake the restoration of the White House," I said to de Gaulle as we lingered at the entrance to the theater that I never wished to leave. This was a golden opportunity, and one I wasn't going to let slip by. "In fact, I hope for stronger relations between our two countries during my husband's presidency, an exchange of cultures if you will. After all, there would be no America without your Lafayette."

"And there would have been no revolution here if not for America leading the way." De Gaulle handed me into the backseat of the lead car of the waiting motorcade, but his fingers lingered on mine. "Jacqueline, you play this game very intelligently. Without mixing politics, you give your husband the prestige of a Maecenas."

I flushed with pleasure, for Gaius Maecenas had been the friend and adviser of culture to Caesar Augustus, and his name had become synonymous with a generous and enlightened patron of the arts.

Choose one thing, Jackie, and do it well. The rest will take care of itself.

I smiled to hear Bobby's advice in my head, wishing that he was here to witness firsthand de Gaulle's full about-face. I imagined him winking, blue eyes sparkling. *Well done, Jacks.*

The general turned to Jack after our motorcade stopped in the gardens of Versailles and we'd spilled back out into the magic of the warm night air. "You are much superior to everything that has been said or written about you," he said to my husband before giving me a pointed glance as he waited for me to translate. Which I did, with pride. "I can safely say that French-American relations have just made a new start."

And Jack, who earlier in the day had introduced himself to the French press as the man who accompanied Jacqueline Kennedy to Paris, only smiled at me, genuine warmth and love lighting his eyes. "Oh, I agree with you wholeheartedly, General."

I had the heady realization then that here, dressed like a queen and surrounded by art and beauty and politics, I was capable of shaping history. I suddenly understood the allure of power and politics, the way both beckoned Jack like the finest ambrosia.

How I wished we could linger in those final moments, beauty multiplying in the air and the scent of flowers wafting in the mist-filled breeze, especially when de Gaulle and the rest of the motorcade lingered behind as Jack led me toward the Neptune fountain, its splashing waters sparkling from the light of a moon in full blossom overhead.

"This trip has been your triumph," he murmured to me. "You are truly the apotheosis at Versailles."

It was flattery, and I knew it, but that didn't mean my heart didn't ache as if the moon overhead had entered my chest and filled it up.

He cocked his head to one side. "When did you become so beautiful?"

When you started looking at me like I was beautiful, Jack.

"Are you only just noticing?" I asked from under my lashes. "Or is the evening's smashing success coloring your judgment?"

"I assure you, my judgment is sound." Jack's laugh rumbled deep in his chest, but a touch of awe softened his handsome features as he glanced around. "You know, this is your gift from the gods, Jackie, to inspire beauty in everything you touch."

I dared stand on tiptoes to brush a rare kiss against his lips. "I'm just getting started."

How I wished we could have stayed in that heaven of grace and beauty; instead, we headed straight for a hell made of Soviet bravado and test ban treaties.

• • •

He savaged me. He absolutely fucking savaged me." Jack paced our room in the U.S. embassy in Vienna, his back brace recently discarded so that I worried he'd do irrevocable damage to his spine. Either that or wear the priceless Turkish carpet to threads. Perhaps both.

I'd watched earlier in the day as Jack, buoyed by our success in Paris and a fresh dose of Dr. Feelgood's joy juice, burst from the front door of the embassy like a bronco-buster sprung from his chute and bounded down the steps to shake bald and boxy Khrushchev's hand.

Khrushchev had ignored him. Utterly and totally ignored him.

Things had only gotten worse from there.

Now Jack barely ground out his next words. "Khrushchev is hell-bent on pushing me into starting a war over Berlin. Negotiating with him is like dealing with my father, all give and no take."

I winced to think of what Mr. Kennedy would have said to that. I'd just gotten off the telephone with him, and my ears were still ringing with lengthy admonitions.

Jack can't appear weak. Do whatever you have to do—I don't care if you have to bribe the KGB or kidnap Khrushchev himself—to get that Russian fool to acknowledge that Jack is a worthy adversary. Otherwise, it's all over, kiddo, and we may as well pack our bags and board the first train back to the land of obscurity.

This trip to Europe had been full of tiny triumphs—I'd even managed a final afternoon of stolen Parisian pleasures spent perusing the Impressionist paintings of Degas, Manet, and Monet at the small Jeu de Paume museum—but this stop had been a cataclysm from the moment our feet had touched the Viennese tarmac. Now all my good work in France wobbled on its axis and threatened to topple at any moment.

"It's this damn test ban treaty and Berlin," Jack said, so I wondered whether he was really talking to me or simply sorting his own thoughts. I continued brushing my hair in silence, my rumpled pink-beaded white evening gown still draped over a chair where I'd discarded it. I'd wait until after Jack went to bed to apply my nightly Erno Laszlo face cream and rinse my teeth with peroxide, a necessary evil given the number of cigarettes I smoked each day. "Khrushchev won't back down and neither will I, and in the meantime, he may well seize West Berlin. All the while Washington's bombarding me with memos about the buildup in Vietnam and how we need to commit our forces there. I can't fight wars on two fronts."

All his angst finally spent, Jack deflated and gingerly knelt at the foot of the bed, wincing so I wished I'd sent ahead one of his oak rocking chairs from the White House. The Bay of Pigs debacle and this European tour had forced Jack for the first time to calculate the real dimensions of the burden of being president. Not even a dose of Miracle Max's joy juice had been able to lift his morose mood, nor did Jack's recitation now of three Hail Marys, one Our Father, and a Glory Be. He peered at me through weary eyes. "How did you fare with the Russian juggernaut?"

Distract him, Jackie, and do it with good news.

I shrugged, adjusting the bow on the shoulder of my canary-yellow peignoir. "I had a lovely tour with Mrs. Khrushchev. By the end the crowd was shouting at the top of their lungs." I cupped my hands around my mouth, doing my best toned-down impression of the raucous crowd. "Jack-ee! Ni-na!"

In fact, dowdy Nina Khrushchev had grabbed my white-gloved hand in hers and held it high in a salute to the people, which only drove the Austrian throng near to ecstasy. Further proof that women were able to finesse politics just as well as any man.

"And at the banquet?" Jack asked. "I noticed you and the Soviet premier were quite friendly."

To which I gave a sly smile. "Jealous?"

"Of you and the pug-nosed buffoon? Not in a million years."

Now it was my turn to deflate a little. I rather liked the idea of Jack's jealousy over my being deep in conversation with another man, even if it was the paunchy and combative Soviet premier.

Jack closed his eyes. "So what did you and the Soviet clown discuss?"

I set down my brush, as if trying to remember. In fact, Khrushchev had started the conversation by commenting that the recent events in Cuba were a crime that had revolted the whole world, and then extolled Ukraine under communism after I'd tried to switch the topic to Ukrainian history. I'd recognized the test, had smirked that the Russian premier believed I might storm off in high dudgeon and cause an international incident. Instead, I'd laughed and asked him not to bore me with statistics. "He expressed his admiration for my dress." Only after I reminded him that we were in the cultured city of Vienna and not his Moscow war room. "Then we chatted about horses and Ukrainian folk dances, in that order."

Jack opened one eye to peer at me. "Anything else? You didn't end the crisis in Berlin, did you? Because I'll nominate you for a Nobel Peace Prize if you did."

"No, but I did ask him about Strelka, the dog the Russians sent into space."

"You what?"

I shrugged. That dinner next to Khrushchev had been one gag after another, akin to sitting next to Abbott and Costello. And that was just to get through the appetizer course. "I ran out of things to talk about. The man isn't a de Gaulle, you know."

Jack groaned. "So you two talked about mutts, and in the meantime, I'm trying to avert World War Three. I'm going to have to increase our intercontinental ballistic missile forces just to counter this summit."

I set down my brush, turned to face Jack. "So what if Khrushchev isn't going to commission a statue to you in Red Square? You didn't let him have the whole of Berlin, which proves that you can play his little game. Not every presidential success can be a Gettysburg Address or V-E Day, you know."

"Maybe, but that doesn't mean I wouldn't mind my own Emancipation Proclamation." Jack managed a ghost of a smile before settling back into glowering at the ceiling. "I need a chapter in the history books, not just a footnote."

There it was, that glimmer of greatness. I wished Jack could see himself the way I saw him, the surety of a sadder and wiser young president who was going to do great things, even if they weren't happening as quickly as he hoped.

"Bunny, those chapters take a long time to write. Rome wasn't built in a day, and neither was your presidency."

I believe in you, Jack, I silently added as I turned off the lights and laid next to him, my hand over his beating heart. *Don't you dare let me down.*

CHAPTER

11

July 1961

'd been inspired by the splendor that was Versailles, and although it was unfair to hope the White House of America's democratically elected president could ever compare with the former palace of France's anointed Sun King, at least Versailles could play muse to my *Maison Blanche.* Of course, I had no intention of draining America's treasury as France had done, for I was no Marie Antoinette, willing to squander her country's goodwill and wind up with her head in a basket.

Instead, I'd remodel the White House and win America's appreciation in the process.

And while this project—for better or worse—would inevitably reflect back on Jack, selfishly, I wanted the White House restoration for myself. To prove that I was capable of all that was expected of me.

To leave my mark on history.

"These are all wrong." I shook my head at Tish before gesturing to the silk eagle pattern destined for a set of Monroe-era gilt chairs. The sample upholstery had been painstakingly re-created from a portrait James Monroe had commissioned of himself with the set in the background. "The weaving is coarse and the poor eagle looks like a plucked chicken. We need another manufacturer."

I wrinkled my nose before turning my back on the chicken-eagle and strode to the one room whose partial transformation was so far to my liking. I felt my shoulders relax as I glanced around the Oval Office, letting my hands trail over the warm wood of a Hayes-era desk I'd discovered abandoned and forgotten on the ground floor of the White House. Jack had claimed the piece with an assortment of his own holy relics: a framed photograph of our family, the coconut shell he'd scratched with a rescue message after his PT boat accident, and a bronze plaque inscribed with the Breton Fisherman's Prayer that I especially loved: "O, God, Thy sea is so great and my boat is so small."

"You were right. She's a beauty."

I smiled to see Jack in the doorway, his hair still damp and curling at the ends from his swimming lesson with Caroline, who he'd been teaching to back float in the warm waters of the indoor pool I'd had freshly repainted with Nantucket boating scenes. No matter how busy he was, or what catastrophes crossed this desk, Jack carved out time each day to play with our children and tuck them into bed each night. While he hadn't always been the perfect husband, he was the best father Caroline and John could have asked for. In that, I'd chosen well.

"It was a gift from Queen Victoria, made from the timbers of the HMS *Resolute*." I'd done some research on its provenance and knew Jack would appreciate the history. "She was an Arctic discovery vessel, you know."

"Fitting, as I've already made sure she's well provisioned." He opened a top drawer to display a stash of Lemonheads and Double Lollies, Caroline's and John's favorite candies.

I smiled. "You spoil them."

"You're raising them right. That means I can afford to sneak them candy in the Oval Office once in a while." He shut the drawer, tapped the top of the desk with a knuckle. "Which reminds me, I need you to get me some books, or something. I'm running out of children's stories at bedtime."

"But the children love your stories, especially Bobo the Lobo. Maybelle too."

The latter was Caroline's favorite, about a girl who raced a horse and hid in the woods with all the forest animals. Jack didn't read books to the children, instead he spun from his imagination fantastical stories that featured characters like their nanny, Maud Shaw, and a fictional Mrs. Throcklebottom.

Jack scratched his head, offered a sheepish grin. "Yeah, but yesterday, I told Caroline how she and I shot down three Jap fighter planes."

I laughed as he picked up a newly appointed silver candlestick from the mantel, tested its heft. "Let me guess," he said. "Madison era. A gift from Napoleon before Waterloo?"

"Close." I smiled, then pointed to the Tiffany stamp on the base before returning the candlestick to its rightful home, turning it ever so slightly to align it with the mantel. "Kennedy era. A gift from your loving wife before she goes public with her plans for the White House remodel. *Life* is going to do a special spread."

Jack scrutinized the heavy candlestick. "Tiffany? Do I even want to know how much that cost? How much any of this is going to cost?"

I'd prepared for this, had prepped and rehearsed my response. "Only the best for the Kennedys, remember? Plus, between the donors and the guidebook for the White House Historical Association, we should have plenty of revenue."

I'd made sure of that. No heads in baskets.

"So long as we don't end up bankrupting ourselves. Or the country." Jack riffled through a stack of papers already piled atop the Resolute Desk. Outside, a high-pitched giggle caught my attention; beyond the curtains Caroline threw a tennis ball and John toddled after the furry white streak that was Pushinka, a puppy of Strelka's that Khrushchev had surprised us with by sending to the children. I'd never forget the afternoon two sweating, ashen-faced Russians staggered into the Oval Office carrying the poor, terrified puppy who'd obviously never been out of a laboratory, with needles in her every vein. "Are you staying in DC this weekend?"

I scarcely heard his question, for something on the collar of his shirt—just inside and hardly noticeable until he'd bent down—caught my attention.

Lipstick. In a flagrant Valentine-red shade that was decidedly not my own.

An icy trickle of unease rilled its way down my spine. Upon my return last weekend, our upstairs apartments had smelled of a woman's perfume, decidedly *not* my Joy by Patou, and I'd overheard two staffers giggling about women skinny-dipping in the White House pool.

I wasn't naïve or dumb—as some people in the White House must have thought—but I had to survive somehow, which had meant turning a blind eye, at least until I was confronted with more than rumors.

Lipstick on a collar seemed terribly cliché, but there it was. Something I—or anyone else who saw it—could hardly ignore.

"Jackie?" The moment passed as Jack straightened, and I shook my head to clear it.

"The children and I will be at Glen Ora this weekend." Despite my wariness, I longed to soak up our estate's pine-scented breeze and the musty aroma of its stables. Lyndon Johnson had recently gifted Caroline with a ten-year-old roan Shetland pony with four white stockings and a star, and I'd looked forward all week to teaching her to use a hackamore while riding Macaroni. In the meantime, Jack was scheduled to speak at the Hollywood Palladium on Saturday and would stay with his brother-in-law Peter Lawford, who was famous for his alcohol-drenched pool parties and all-night card games.

Still, I mustered a confident smile when Jack joined me at the window. "You know, you could come with us. Enjoy horse rides through the woods and mugs of apple cider before cozy warm fires."

Except Jack hates horses and can't sit still long enough to finish a mug of cider.

I straightened Jack's slate-toned tie and together we smiled as Caroline and John taught Pushinka to go down the slide on the newly installed playground. "Or you could come with me," Jack said. "Sinatra will be in Los Angeles, and he even had Lawford install a heliport for Air Force One."

The very idea of spending a weekend smiling and downing martinis, not to mention playing nice with reptilian Frank Sinatra (who still referred to my husband as Chicky Boy when he thought I wasn't listening), repelled me. Much more appealing were the thoughts of my jodhpurs and a pell-mell ride on my frisky bay gelding I'd named Bit of Irish, while Caroline learned to trot on Macaroni and John played with Pushinka.

So I only smiled at Jack. "We'll see you back here on Monday."

Yet there was something I needed to see to, for my own peace of mind.

Tell me," I demanded of Joan several weeks after I'd returned from Glen Ora, for I'd asked Teddy's wife to manage the reconnaissance I couldn't do myself. Now Joan and I were sharing a bench in the White House's unkempt East Garden, which I planned to redesign with a central lawn and flower beds planted in the French style. But right now I cared little for visions of rambler roses and wisteria, and far more about the reality of what my husband had been up to. I readied myself to receive a blow. Any blow. Every blow. "Spare no details."

"Brace yourself." Joan crossed one ankle over the other. "This isn't going to be easy."

Joan was right; I felt as if I was going to be ill when the floodgates opened. I didn't want to hear, but nor could I stop listening as the names poured forth.

A woman named Judith Exner with connections to the Mafia.

Divorced Washington, DC, artist Mary Pinchot Meyer.

White House intern Mimi Alford.

Two West Wing staffers who happened to be best friends, aptly nicknamed Fiddle and Faddle.

And more. So many more.

"Ted claims Jack's been discreet, but Jackie"—Joan leaned forward—"he also says Marilyn Monroe was with Jack at Peter Lawford's house in California. If that's true . . ."

I shook my head to clear it and held up a hand, my pulse pounding in my ears. "Give me a moment."

Trying to tame my thoughts at these revelations was a vain attempt to bottle a winter wind. *To love is a bitter task . . .*

I always knew Jack couldn't be faithful forever. I knew he couldn't change.

I recalled what he had once said of this weakness in the early days of our marriage: *I know it's wrong, but I can't help myself. I just want to live—to have it all—because I never know when all this will end.*

Jack might have married any woman in the world, but he'd chosen me, and we built a kingdom together. Those other women were fools if they believed they were more to Jack than a dose of Miracle Max's joy juice.

I am the mother of Jack's children, his queen and equal, I reminded myself. *I am the only woman in his life who will forever be more than any of his lollipop girls.*

It would be enough. It *had* to be enough.

Still . . .

"I need to talk to him," I muttered under my breath.

"Why?" Joan asked. "What do you want to get out of it? Will you ask him to stop?"

I shook my head. "No. Because he can't change and he won't stop."

"Then what do you want? Think about it first, Jackie. I get one of these"—Joan held up a wrist, shook the diamond tennis bracelet there—"whenever Teddy strays. Make him give you something expensive."

I recoiled at the thought—I refused to be one of those bitter women who extracted jewelry from their husbands for bad behavior. This was one of the subtle differences between us that made up the reason why Joan and I might be collaborators, yet we'd never gossip and scheme as Lee and I once had. Still, she was right. I couldn't start that conversation without a goal and neither could I ask him to stop. Nor could I threaten to leave him—the children and the presidency prevented that. So what did I want?

"I'm afraid I can't stay—I have to get home to the children. Will you be all right?" Joan finally asked, to which I nodded. Only then did I realize I'd shredded a late-blooming chrysanthemum while she'd spoken; its sunset-hued petals now lay ruined in my lap.

"Better to know the truth," I said softly. "Don't you think?"

Joan cocked her head, a mildly poleaxed expression on her face. "Actually, I think there's a reason they say ignorance is bliss."

Perhaps that was how Joan dealt with her relationship with Teddy, but as First Lady I didn't have that luxury.

"I needed to know, Joan." I folded my trembling hands over the corpse of the chrysanthemum. "Now I do."

Only one question remained . . .

What am I going to do about it?

As a necessary distraction, I immersed myself in planning the final details of a White House concert dinner for Puerto Rico's governor. The star of the evening was Spain's virtuoso cellist Pablo Casals, who had just concluded his second hour-long performance in the White House, the first having taken place almost sixty years prior in 1904 during Theodore Roosevelt's tenure as president. Jack had nearly fallen asleep during Casals's rendition of the traditional Spanish folk melody "Song of the Birds"—my husband indulged my love of music and dance although his interest in the arts ran more toward history books and biographies—until I'd prodded him in the ribs, albeit harder than was necessary.

"Cello music is a bit stuffy," he mumbled under his breath.

My tart response: "I suppose we could just have Casals play your favorite piece—'Hail to the Chief.'"

Jack sat up straighter after that, while I stared placidly at Casals's bow flying over his cello strings, the tempestuous music mirroring my own thoughts.

To confront or not to confront?

To act Jack's queen? Or be his wife?

I tried to set the questions aside for I still had another role to play: that of America's First Lady.

To all those who have heard about the grace and charm of the Kennedy White House and wondered, was it really that extraordinary? I'd made sure that night that the answer was decidedly yes.

The wine was superior and there were ashtrays on every surface that would hold them. After the concert, men in crisp tuxedos and women in sparkling gowns puffed away in the East Room like the glittering Hollywood starlets they wished they were as they waited for the *mousse de sole amiral* and *filet de boeuf Montfermeil* to be served. I merely picked at my food and it was a relief to finally sneak into an alcove so I could light a cigarette in a vain attempt to calm the riot of thoughts that demanded my attention now that there were no guest lists or seating charts to distract them.

"Jacqueline Bouvier Kennedy, your head is in the clouds." My mother was suddenly there, snatching the fragrant L&M from my fingers. "There's a photographer around the corner looking to get a good shot of you. I'm sure he'd love to break the story that America's First Lady smokes like a freight train."

Because heaven forbid that I should ever be less than perfect. While Jack, on the other hand . . .

I knew my mother meant well, although I cringed when she snuffed out that wonderful cigarette in a Waterford ashtray etched with the Kennedy coat of arms. "Thank you, Mummy. It's difficult to be on stage all the time. . . ."

I almost confided to her, but I couldn't bring up the words in my throat to tell her that I'd failed. We Bouviers didn't discuss things as mundane as feelings, and somehow, even though my mother and I were often at loggerheads, I couldn't bear to be reduced in her eyes.

To be *lesser* . . .

Although that wasn't quite fair. No matter what, I was still the First Lady of the United States of America.

Yet I ached to unburden myself to someone, anyone. Isolated within the walls of the White House and confronted with the undeniable evidence that my husband was catting around on me, I desperately missed my sister then, wished Lee and I had mended our relationship so we could stay up all night while she gave me advice. Instead, surrounded by all these people, I was suddenly so lonely that my eyes stung and I barely managed to blink my mask back into place before my mother whisked away the ashtray, as if a negative press photo was the worst that could happen to me.

Never let them see you bleed, Jackie. And above all, never let Jack see you bleed.

I rejoined the party in time to see balding General Douglas MacArthur pound a fist on the polished Honduran mahogany top of a Steinway grand piano that dated from Franklin Roosevelt's administration. He was telling a story about leading the United Nations forces during the Korean War, one which of course cast him as a hero worthy of a bronze statue in the Capitol.

"You know, that one reminds me of blustery Joseph McCarthy." One of our more ancient guests had sidled up next to me, tiny and wraithlike in a shimmering black gown with a sable fur slung over her bony shoulders, her pinned twist of white hair in startling contrast. She rummaged in her handbag and jutted her sharp chin toward MacArthur. "Here's some life advice for you, Jackie: never trust a man who combs his hair straight from his left armpit."

I nearly choked on my laugh, for MacArthur did wear what little hair he had left extremely long so he could sweep it over his otherwise empty pate. Yet I doubted whether anyone other than Alice Roosevelt Longworth could have gotten away with pointing that out.

The eldest wild-child daughter of Theodore Roosevelt, I'd invited Mrs. L tonight to hear Pablo Casals since her father had last hosted him at the White House so many decades ago. Known by the moniker the Other Washington Monument, the widow's once-lovely face was now an explosion of wrinkles, each of which surely told its own outrageous story. Alice knew everything about everyone in this town and had entertained me with her caustic bon mots during historical lectures I'd hosted.

Thanks to her comment about MacArthur, I now relished the feel of actually laughing for the first time in ages. Jack glanced in my direction just as I recovered my aplomb, but I pretended not to notice. "I think the devil may have rocked your cradle, Mrs. Longworth."

Alice chuckled, her blue-gray eyes flashing with glee. "Don't I know it."

We watched Jack move through the room and Alice's keen eyes darted to me. "No one has a drier, more delightful, humorous, and ironic view of life than that husband of yours," she said thoughtfully. "That one needs no window dressing, does he?"

Well, Mrs. Longworth, I thought to myself, *without all that window dressing, he's just another politician who sleeps around on his wife.* Likely with Marilyn-I'm-a-Tramp-Monroe, no less.

I only smiled. "Don't let Jack hear all those compliments. You'll puff up his head until he gets lodged in the doorway."

"Nothing unusual about that. Every president I've ever met—and this old fossil has known them all back to McKinley—is already full of himself as it is." Her raspy chuckle as she lit a Lucky Strike made my fingers itch for my own pack of L&Ms. She leaned closer, as if we were sharing some sort of girlhood bosom secret. "Still, I hope you're able to seize every scrap of happiness with that husband of yours while you can. You don't realize how short a time you have together until it's over. Then you wish he was still around to exasperate the hell out of you."

"Jack doesn't exasperate me."

No, he only infuriates, maddens, and vexes me until I can hardly think straight.

"Pish-posh." Alice waved the cigarette in its slim plastic holder with an idle and age-spotted hand, scattering smoke to all four corners of the room before offering me a tantalizing taste. I glanced around for any reporters—or my mother—before accepting a clandestine drag, luxuriating in the warm smoke as it rolled down my throat. "You Kennedys have an epic quality, the sort that legends are made of. To everyone else you two shimmer like the king and queen of some bedtime fairy tale."

"And to you?"

She took back the cigarette, blew a perfect set of smoke rings toward the ceiling. "My husband possessed far less hair than Jack, but he had a laugh like caramel and the same gift of making everyone—

especially the fairer sex—love him. It can be irritating for a wife, which I think you understand far too well."

I did understand, and somehow, although she wasn't Lee, I felt I could confide in this tiny wisp of a woman who had seen everything there was to see in this town. "Indeed," I agreed. "And how did you cope with that particular irritation?"

"Hold the wolf by his ears." Alice gave what could only be called a smile of detached malevolence, so I pitied whoever found themselves at the end of her sword. "Sometimes powerful men need reminding that they're not all-powerful, don't you think?"

I nodded slowly, mulling that over as I noticed that Jack was missing from the party. "I hope you'll consider joining us for the unveiling of the bison mantel in the State Dining Room next summer." I watched her stub out our shared Lucky Strike, regretting that it was only half burned down. I could have smoked a whole pack tonight and still not had enough. "It's from your father's era, one of the authentic antiques my team tracked down for the White House restoration."

Alice grinned so I could almost imagine her as a younger woman causing all sorts of trouble. "I wouldn't miss it. That mantel almost ended up with lions until my father reminded the designers that the lion wasn't American enough."

I filed that tidbit away before excusing myself with a promise to see her at the next International Horse Show, then made the rest of the necessary social rounds, smiling and chatting with artists. Until . . .

"Lawford said he can meet you next weekend," I overheard Frank Sinatra say to Jack from where they loitered in the cavernous Cross Hall outside, the singer's voice slurred as if he'd had at least two drinks too many. "There's a certain voluptuous blonde with a beauty mark who wants to see you again."

If Jack responded, I couldn't hear it through the roaring in my ears. To stray in private was one thing, for Frank Sinatra to air those episodes in public was quite another. *That's my cue.*

And suddenly, I knew what it was I wanted from this conversation with Jack.

"Gentlemen." My gaze as I entered the crimson-carpeted hall needled Sinatra, who tipped his hat and slunk away with his tail between his legs. I tilted my chin to Jack, daring him.

Yet my husband seemed suddenly entranced by the crystal chandelier overhead. "I'm ready to call it a night soon; we have the breakfast for the foreign ambassadors in the morning." His fingers drummed along his thigh. "How about you?"

Sometimes powerful men need reminding that they're not all-powerful. . . .

I smoothed the crystal beading along the waist of my gown, a sleeveless pale Venetian yellow with a bodice of gold embroidery on silk crepe de chine, another of Oleg Cassini's fanciful creations. I took a deep, slow breath. "I forgot to mention, I won't be able to make the breakfast."

"No?" Jack frowned, finally met my gaze. "But everyone is expecting you."

"Yes, but sometimes our expectations of someone else don't quite measure up, now do they? I want out of some of the more tiresome and unimportant duties as First Lady." For while I enjoyed my work on the White House restoration, the press teas and various meet-and-greet events set my teeth on edge. My stare was bold beneath my raised eyebrows, and to his credit, Jack had the decency to drop his gaze, one hand at the back of his neck.

A tiny victory, I told myself. *Hold this wolf by his ear and remind him that I have my own version of strength.* Thank you, Mrs. L.

And I wasn't quite done. I wasn't quite sure of everything else I wanted, but I knew I wasn't going to find it in tiny Washington. I remembered how much I felt like myself in France, suddenly yearned to bottle up the incandescence of that feeling even as I knew I'd never recapture it while standing in Jack's shadow. "After you're done with breakfast, I'll meet you in the Oval. We need to discuss my trip to India and Pakistan."

Jack groaned. "You mean the trip that's going to cost us a small fortune? I'd have thought our upcoming visit to Venezuela and Colombia would have been enough."

I smiled sweetly. After hosting the president of Pakistan for a spectacular dinner at Mount Vernon, I'd eagerly accepted the request to visit his country. Not to be shown up, India had quickly extended its own invitation. "I think I'm due a trip on my own, considering your recent jaunt to California. And your upcoming visit with Peter Lawford?"

My meaning was crystal clear, and we both knew it.

When Jack answered, he spoke more slowly than usual, so I knew he was processing the full import of my words. "Then I'll see you in the Oval after breakfast, won't I?"

Suddenly, I wanted nothing more than to get away, from both Washington and Jack, to find my own footing in this strange new world I no longer recognized.

To rediscover my confidence, my purpose. To hit my own bedrock.

Jack's other women—including certain blond airheaded actresses— might satisfy his mighty physical desires, but I was far more than that. Which meant I deserved something more, even as I turned a blind eye to his engagements with lesser women.

Jack has everything he's ever wanted—the picture-perfect family, the presidency, and apparently any woman he crooks a finger at. I want—I need— something of my own.

And I was willing to fly halfway around the world to find it.

W hy do you and Daddy argue?" Caroline asked as we swam in the bathwater-warm pool of the Palm Beach house loaned to us for Christmas. I was teaching her the backstroke, but it was obvious her mind was elsewhere. As was mine, for I'd hoped to ask Mr. Kennedy's advice about his son, but Jack's father had left early for a round of golf, leaving me to stew in an uncomfortable mire of my own worries.

"Well, Buttons, your daddy and I don't always agree on everything." While we'd come to a tentative agreement on the dates for my trip to India and Pakistan—this coming March, just one month after my unveiling of the fully renovated White House—this morning we'd argued over our budget before Jack returned to Washington for a few days. According to Jack, liquor was flowing out of the White House as though it were the last days of the Roman Empire and my clothing bill for the year was outrageous (I countered that four thousand dollars to Givenchy was money well spent for de Gaulle's reaction and subsequent friendship). I'd learned that Jack was donating his presidential salary to the United Negro College Fund, the National Association for Retarded Children, and the Boy Scouts of America—all worthy charities—but I'd responded that perhaps we should refill unfinished glasses at banquets and serve them again, unless they had obvious lipstick marks on the rim.

"You can't be serious." Exasperated, Jack retrieved the indulgence of an Upmann cigar from his walnut humidor and lit up, filling the room with a thick fug of smoke and discontent.

To which I'd only crossed my arms. "It'll save you a few precious dollars, even if some people do get hepatitis from a White House function."

No, things were not at all smooth in the Kennedy household these days.

I'll admit, while I was learning to navigate this new French-style marriage and turn a blind eye to my husband's weaknesses, I wasn't above making him pay for them with tiny jabs here and there. Not just Jack, but also his lollipops. A few days ago, when my usual game of morning tennis on the White House court was threatened with cancellation for lack of a partner, I'd conscripted staffer Jill Cowan—also known as Faddle, who was inclined to smirk at me when she thought I wasn't looking—to play against me. It just so happened that poor Faddle didn't have tennis shoes and had to play in her bare feet. The poor, poor dear.

Sometimes I felt as if I was being smothered, as if everything I did was somehow tied to Jack, and that I was losing—perhaps had already lost—a critical part of myself.

Now I brushed Caroline's wet hair out of her eyes, glad Jack had returned to Washington that morning and wasn't around to witness this poolside conversation. "Occasional arguments are normal when you're married. But your daddy and I love each other, and that's all that matters."

Caroline didn't have a chance to respond, for Mr. Kennedy's car turned up the drive and he shambled toward us, still wearing his eye-numbing green golf shirt and cap. Caroline waved and splashed toward him, but I only narrowed my eyes. Unlike Jack, whose return meant he was lucky to have menaced the field mice with nine holes, Mr. Kennedy never played less than eighteen. His early return meant either the Apocalypse was upon us or some other dire situation was at hand.

"Are you all right, Poppy Doodle?" I asked.

"Fine," he said, but he appeared haggard and pale to my eye. "I just felt a bit wonky teeing off on the eighth green. I'll lie down and be fit as a fiddle in no time." He winked at Caroline, but even that movement seemed to cost him. "You'll save me a game of charades, won't you?"

I still wasn't convinced. "Are you sure you don't want me to call someone?"

He waved a hand over his shoulder. "Don't call any doctors!"

I watched him go, then helped Caroline into a towel warm from the dryer for a lunch of watercress sandwiches and fresh-squeezed lemonade. After several hours, we were joined in the reading room by Rose, who sent the maid, Anna, to check on Jack's father.

Anna came rushing back, her face blanched the color of curdled milk. "Mr. Kennedy can neither move nor speak, ma'am," she said.

Rose stood as if she'd just been informed someone was at the door, the white-knuckled hand on the arm of her chair the only tell that she wasn't as steady as she appeared. "Please summon an ambulance, Anna."

I wasn't so calm and took the stairs two at a time only to find Jack's father trapped in bed, dressed in his blue flannel pajamas. He moaned and his eyes were unfocused as Caroline hovered in the doorway and I tried unsuccessfully to move him.

"Help me get you up, Poppy Doodle," I said, but to no avail. "Help me, Caroline."

Sounds came out of his mouth but no words, only incoherent groans as the left side of his lips struggled to work. The effort was ruined by the right side of his face, which hung slack as if formed not of flesh but warmed candle wax.

I straightened his glasses and cradled him in my arms. "Your grandpa is going to be all right," I crooned to Caroline as I wiped away a silent tear that slid down her cheek, but not even I truly believed my words.

It wasn't until after they'd loaded him into the ambulance with Rose and I'd scrambled to pack his overnight bag that I came across a stack of letters in his sock drawer. The one on top caught my eyes, for I recognized it as the one I'd sent to him during Jack's stay in the hospital following his final back surgery.

In all the ups and downs this winter, you exuded such force and conviction that no one would dream of getting discouraged . . .

I touched the final line with my finger, feeling a shiver as I wondered what was happening in the hospital across town, if Mr. Kennedy would survive what I surmised to be a massive stroke of some kind.

It's just empty and no fun without you.

Mr. Kennedy had drafted his family into politics, had demanded Jack's success just as he'd demanded that I be a part of the Kennedy team. My squabbles with Jack seemed very small when faced with the thought that we might forever lose the captain of our team.

Mr. Kennedy survived, but only just. After several days in the balance, doctors warned us he would never be the same again.

The stroke had destroyed his right side so it was impossible for him to move his arm or leg. "It's inoperable and irreversible," the physician announced somberly when we were all allowed into the hospital room. The Kennedy siblings kept their eyes downcast from where they stood at the farthest reaches of the room; only I had the where-withal to sit on the bed next to their father. "I'm afraid Mr. Kennedy will never walk or speak properly again."

I watched Jack's stoic face crumple when the surgeon made the terrible pronouncement and the undeniable shock that flickered deep in Bobby's eyes, for neither brother had ever believed their father to be less than invincible. The remainder of the gathered Kennedy siblings covered their mouths in horror to realize that tragedy had struck this family once again.

Was there any crueler fate than being imprisoned in one's own body, especially for a man who had once been considered an all-powerful ambassador? Caroline would never again laugh her way through a round of charades with her grandfather. Jack could never again call for advice at three a.m. and hear his father bark, "Holy cow, fella, call me in the daylight!" My young son—who would never remember a time when his grandfather could talk—would never catch a football thrown by Mr. Kennedy on the sprawling lawn of his Hyannis Port kingdom.

And me? I'd never again hear Mr. Kennedy call me "kiddo" or feel the warmth of his smile. I'd lost one of my only confidants in this sprawling family and shivered at the encroaching emptiness I knew would only grow with time. Yet I couldn't let him see how deeply I felt the blow.

Mr. Kennedy's children seemed frozen in place, their gazes flicking everywhere in the room except to their father, as if unsure how to deal with a man who was suddenly shrunken and broken in their eyes. It galled me to see the Kennedy children—whose ranks included America's president and attorney general—transform into such untried fledglings in the face of their father's unexpected weakness.

Mon dieu. Their father wasn't gone yet. And I'd never let anyone forget it.

"It's all right." I reached for a towel to wipe the saliva from Mr. Kennedy's chin. "Mr. Kennedy is the man who made everything happen for us, and now it's our turn to make things happen for him."

I looked Jack's father square in the eye and held his gaze, lending him strength to shore up the overwhelming depths of sadness and helplessness and tears welling there. "We're here for you, Poppy Doodle. Always and forever."

As I straightened the lapel on his bathrobe, a single tear slipped from the corner of his eye, wobbling over the creases there. I wiped it away with a stern shake of my head. "No tears."

Instead, I placed my hand over his, lifting my expectant gaze to Jack and Bobby and Ted and the girls. One by one, they placed hesitant hands over mine.

"We're a team," I whispered to Mr. Kennedy. "And you're still our captain."

We were a team, and I was no longer content to sit on the bench while cheering on everyone else. However, team sports were never really my style.

The time had come for the Kennedys' uncrowned queen to assume her position on the board. And I was going to do it on my terms.

CHAPTER

12

February 1962

My footfalls echoed along the marble-lined corridor of the White House as I strode toward the rolling movie camera, black-and-white frames spooling away with each of my nervous steps. It was Valentine's Day—I'd dressed in a triple strand of pearls and a Cassini two-piece claret bouclé day dress in a trompe l'oeil design for the occasion—and it was also the day that I would take my place front and center to unveil to the American public my grand restoration of the White House. This was no longer the public shabby house it had been known as in the 1800s. I'd returned the entire mansion to its former grandeur so it could hold its head high among visiting peers from the likes of Versailles and Buckingham Palace.

This was my magnum opus as First Lady, and everything had to be faultless.

Although Jack's father would never fully recover from his stroke and my marriage to Jack was rocky, this renovation and tour was something I could control. Something I could perfect.

Something that was all mine.

Yet my heart felt so terribly hollow as I strode down the corridor. I knew it seemed to everyone as if I had the perfect life—a powerful husband, beautiful children, designer clothes, plenty of money, and now this stunning house—but, inside, I was as desperately lonely as I'd been in the early days of my marriage.

Lonelier now, perhaps, for while I might dine with the likes of Charles de Gaulle and Pablo Casals, I was always on display, the main attraction in the parade of perfection the country expected, even when I felt like I was falling apart on the inside.

I reminded myself that when this tour was over, I'd fly away on a magic carpet, bound for a whirlwind trip to India and Pakistan. Perhaps I'd invite Lee and attempt to mend our relationship, although I wasn't sure I could stomach her picture-perfect marriage with her Polish prince. However, living under Jack's presidential shadow meant I now understood Lee's chilliness toward me; she would forever be the First Lady's sister just as I would always be John F. Kennedy's wife.

Still, I needed someone I could confide in, someone to ease the weight of loneliness off my shoulders. Since that person couldn't be Jack, or even his father now, I hoped it might be Lee.

"Mrs. Kennedy, I want to thank you for letting us visit your official home." Debonair reporter Charles Collingwood approached as we'd rehearsed when I entered my cluttered office, an antique dealer's dream with its jumble of desks, gilt picture frames, and paper-wrapped paintings piled helter-skelter now that this room served as both attic and cellar for all the items sent for us to evaluate. A chest belonging to President Van Buren balanced on a sofa, and I'd arranged a rare nineteenth-century American-made pottery ewer with the eagle and shield atop the main table.

"Mrs. Kennedy, every First Lady and every administration since President Madison's time has made changes—greater or smaller—in the White House." Collingwood was the by-the-book reporter I'd chosen to cover today's tour for the special that would be broadcast on both CBS and NBC. "Before we take a look at any of the changes you've made, what's your basic plan?"

I clasped my hands before me, culling the last of my nerves. "Well, I really don't have one, because I think this house will always grow and should." My restoration wasn't as massive a project as the full-scale rebuild during Truman's administration, when the entire crumbling interior was scooped out to the exterior walls and reassembled like a jigsaw puzzle, but it would certainly go down as one of the most personal. I was finally bringing history back home to this great house, where it belonged. "It just seemed such a shame when we came here to find hardly anything of the past in the house, hardly anything before 1902. I know when we went to Colombia the Presidential Palace there has all the history of that country in it, where Simón Bolívar was, every piece of furniture in it has some link to the past. I thought the White House should be like that."

That seemed to satisfy Collingwood, and from there we traveled with the cameras through the Diplomatic Reception Room, freshly enhanced with New England wing chairs and early nineteenth-century wallpaper from France that depicted vividly colored scenes of Niagara Falls, New York Harbor, and West Point. Smiling softly and feeling entirely in my element, I displayed to Collingwood the famed Gilbert Stuart painting of George Washington that was the oldest item in the White House, followed by the Eisenhower gold china service in the State Dining Room. Next to all that grandeur was the glassware I'd ordered from West Virginia, fulfilling my campaign trail promise to stimulate their economy. The factory had already sent me a thank-you note and ramped up production to fill the many orders that would flood in after this broadcast.

Hands still clasped like a supplicant to mask my nerves, I might have passed for a walking encyclopedia of American history as I recited facts I'd memorized about Rutherford Hayes's oath of office in the Red Room, Mary Todd Lincoln's estate sale after her husband's death, and how President Andrew Johnson had moved his cabinet office because he believed it was bad luck to use Lincoln's after his assassination. The interesting minutiae I'd committed to memory made me wonder if one day someone would point out a fountain pen I'd used or trace my steps through this house. (*And here we have the closet where Jacqueline Kennedy stored all those pillbox hats.*)

Finally, after seven hours of rehearsing and shooting various takes—and smoking at least a pack of cigarettes to brace myself—my time in the limelight was winding down. One last stop, informing Collingwood about the still-unfinished Treaty Room.

"I'm afraid this work-in-progress is a chamber of horrors," I said with a rueful smile. "Eventually it will be a comfortable place for the men who now wait in the hall with the baby carriages going by them. They'll be able to sit in here and have a conference around the table while waiting for the president."

"Mr. President." I could hear the reverence in Collingwood's voice as Jack—whom *Time* had just named their Man of the Year, writing that he showed qualities that made him a promising leader—entered at precisely the moment we'd rehearsed. (Jack had derided the nomination as it came on the heels of the Bay of Pigs fiasco. Difficult to argue when *Time* had also chosen Adolf Hitler and Joseph Stalin as previous winners.) I myself breathed a silent sigh of relief to see my husband now, for I hadn't been entirely sure Jack would show on time, given that this simple home tour was far less important than so many of the other gears that were constantly churning in the running of this great country. (That, and the fact that I'd skipped several more state events in my own form of silent protest regarding Jack's sleeping arrangements.) Part of me loathed relinquishing my spotlight to Jack even for a few minutes, as if somehow his appearance put the official stamp of approval on my project.

Still, I supposed it couldn't be helped. So I smiled for the cameras, knowing I'd soon be on the other side of the world, and likely missing Jack more than I cared to admit. . . .

Collingwood withdrew my chair from the Ulysses S. Grant table that had once served his entire presidential cabinet and was currently strewn with wallpaper samples. "Mrs. Kennedy has been showing us the White House and telling us about the changes she's made," he said to Jack. "What do you think of the updates?"

Jack remained solemn, his sandy hair swept from his forehead as we assumed our assigned seats. I could tell he was choosing his words carefully. "History is a source of strength to us in the White House, and I think the great effort that she's made has been to bring us more intimately in contact with all the men who lived here. After all, history is made by people and, particularly in great moments of our history, presidents. So when we have as we do today Grant's table or Lincoln's bed or Monroe's gold set, it makes these men much more alive. I think it makes the White House a stronger panorama of our great story."

My heart grew at least three sizes as Jack praised me and then the guidebook I'd established, and spoke of his hope that we'd soon top the more than 1.3 million visitors who had toured our house last year, that some of the schoolboys—and even girls—might dream of one day living here.

How could I help loving you, Jack? I thought as I listened to him. *Every dream you have, every thought in that brilliant head of yours is on such a grand scale.*

In that moment I almost felt guilty for wanting my own space to breathe, to accomplish my own dreams separate from my husband's, especially as Jack's words recalled to mind an inscription from John Adams in the State Dining Room that I'd shown to Collingwood earlier in the tour.

I pray Heaven to bestow the best of Blessings on this House. . . . May none but honest and wise Men ever rule under this roof.

Jack was not always honest, and perhaps not always wise. But he could deepen in both, that I knew, and there was no doubt that some of the best of blessings had in many ways fallen upon us both.

Oleg Cassini planned my light and airy wardrobe for my entire trip to India after his ebullient praise following the smashing success of my White House tour. Matching the public's enthusiastic response to the televised special, he telegrammed a note right after Valentine's Day that had made my heart sing.

YOUR PERFORMANCE LAST NIGHT ABSOLUTELY FIRST RATE. THE
ONLY LOGICAL DESTINATION FOR YOU IS HOLLYWOOD. YOU
LOOKED MORE BEAUTIFUL THAN ANY STAR. CONGRATULATIONS
AGAIN.

—OLEG

I was no queen, or Hollywood star, but my success made me feel
like both.

My designer wasn't the only one singing my praises—I even won
an unexpected Emmy for the program, and more fan mail poured
into the White House than ever before. I scoffed at the *New York Times*
assertion that I'd made the world safe for brunettes and transmitted
upper-crust habits to the common woman, but suddenly everything
that had been a liability about me before—my hair, that I spoke
French, that I didn't adore campaigning, and that I didn't bake bread
with flour up to my elbows—was an asset. Now, after three years, Jack
had every reason to be proud of me.

With that single broadcast, I had found my rightful place in the
Kennedy administration.

"I was wrong," Jack said to me one night over a family dinner of
lamb chops and corn muffins. "You don't just turn everything beautiful; you turn it to gold." He glanced at Caroline, who was keenly
following the conversation while John devoured a hot dog Miss Shaw
had ordered especially for him. "Buttons, your mother is a veritable
Rumpelstiltskin, did you know that?"

"Daddy." Caroline pursed her lips. "Rumpelstiltskin was a boy."

Jack laughed and leaned across the table to rumple her hair.
"You're right. But your mother is still the most accomplished and
impressive woman I know. We're going to miss her while she's in India, aren't we?"

Caroline nodded sagely, her eyes so wide that I almost wanted to
cancel the trip. Instead, I blinked hard and leaned over to cut John's

hot dog into still smaller pieces. "I'll miss you all too. And I promise I'll write and call every day."

As I looked around the table at Jack and my children, I knew that I would miss them, even Jack. It would be difficult to leave, but harder still to have never done this for myself.

So I gave myself permission to be selfish, just this once.

Like a fairy tale, I felt as though a foreign djinni had swept me away to a land of enchantments. Lee and I had made peace enough that she'd deigned to join me, and we stopped for a Roman holiday on the way, where I showed off my Somali leopard skin coat and black mink pillbox hat before changing into a full-length black silk dress and lace mantilla required by protocol for a private audience with Pope John XXIII. The audience was so private, in fact, that Lee hadn't been allowed to join us due to the unsanctioned divorce that had ended her first marriage. I gifted the Holy Father with a signed collection of Jack's speeches in a velvet-lined vermeil letter case, and he recited a Mass for me, which touched the Catholic in me deeply. Yet my papal audience was also a secret mission known only to Mother and me, for while in the Vatican I'd also hinted to the pope that my family would be grateful if he granted my sister the annulment that would authorize her marriage to Stas in the eyes of the church.

It might be some weeks—or even months—before we learned if my request had been granted, but I hoped I could make a gift of happiness to my sister.

Still, all that paled in comparison with the scent of exotic spices that laced India's warm spring breeze and greeted Lee and me as the cabin doors opened to reveal the most beautiful blue sky at the New Delhi airport.

"My God, Jacks," Lee breathed next to me. "There must be one hundred thousand people here."

My sister's estimate was spot-on as I glanced at the seething mass of people, including women in brilliantly hued fuchsia and turquoise saris with their bullock carts parked wheel to wheel so they might catch a glimpse of us.

"They are here for you," Prime Minister Jawaharlal Nehru—a compatriot of Mohandas Gandhi—announced in his accented English after he'd applied a smear of vermillion powder to my forehead during our official introductions. He and his hawk-nosed daughter, Indira Gandhi, would be my guides for the entire trip, although Indira had a bitter purse to her lips every time she glanced my way. "Listen."

I did, and although I was fluent in several languages, my confusion must have shown on my face as we were ushered toward the motorcade that would whisk us into the city. *"Amriki Rani."* Indira was resplendent in an orange sari that made my white wool suit appear plain in comparison; I realized I'd have to adjust the wardrobe Oleg had created for me while I was here. "They are calling you Queen of America."

"I'm no queen," I said softly, but the truth was I felt the same surge of pride that I had upon greeting Charles de Gaulle in France. Yet, this time, all the festivities were for me, not Jack.

I told myself that shouldn't matter as I waved to the crowd, but it did.

With my restoration of the White House, I'd proven that I was worthy of the title of First Lady, that I could stand outside of Jack's shadow. That I was worth more than any of Jack's other women. This trip was further proof of that accomplishment.

But I had one more Everest to climb.

"I want us to be friends again," I said to Lee that night after we'd attended a polo match and a dinner reception, finally exchanging our stiff traveling clothes for airy linen nightgowns. "I miss my whispering sister."

Lee gave a small smile as she removed her earrings, tucked her feet beneath her on my satin settee. "I'd like that."

I took a deep breath, broached the topic that had so weighed me down. "Jack's up to his old tricks again, you know. There's been so many times I've wanted to call you. Just to talk."

"We could have drowned our sorrows together. Stas and I haven't been the same since Christina was born."

Now that was a surprise.

"I thought you two were so happy." I sat next to my sister so we were knee to knee. "What happened?"

She shrugged. "He wanted more children after Christina. I refused. We fought. I slept around, he slept around."

I gaped. Lee had always excelled at shocking me, but this was a new level even for her. "You had an affair?"

I wish I'd known about all this before I asked the pope to annul your first marriage, I thought. *I'll be damned if I ask him to annul your second one too.*

A sly smile tugged at the corners of her carmine-red lips. "Several. In fact, I'm having one now."

"What? With whom?"

Lee winked. "I don't kiss-and-tell. But Jacks, he makes me feel like no man ever has before." She dropped her voice. "Both in and out of bed."

I shook my head, shocked and awed at this new, more daring version of my sister. Part of me was appalled at the scandal, but another bit was jealous that she was free enough—and possessed the confidence—to seize her own happiness, husband be damned.

Why was it that Lee and I only seemed to get along when our marriages were in trouble? Still, I was glad to have my sister—my confidante—at my side again, especially as I planned to revel in every foreign pleasure India had to offer.

So together we threw Holi chalk powder, ate wild boar and candies wrapped in pounded silver, and watched endless folk dancing and singing. Knowing I was an animal lover, Air India gifted me with twin Bengal tiger cubs, whom I promptly named Ken and Kitty, after two old family friends. "We'll keep them at the White House with Caroline's dogs, Charlie and Pushinka, at least until they reach the scratchy age," I said to Nehru as Lee and I peered wide-eyed into their cage. "Then perhaps a zoo where we can visit them."

To which Nehru had an unexpected response. "I hope they can be friends with my own gift to you."

Suddenly I wished I had both Caroline and John with me so I could experience rather than imagine their shrieks of glee when a trainer emerged into the garden with a baby elephant in tow. "Here." Nehru offered me a bouquet of sugar cane fronds and a milk-filled bottle. "Like all babies, Urvashi loves these. And bananas."

So I fed a baby elephant—something I'd never in a million years have imagined doing—all the while thinking of the letter I'd pen to my own children about the day's fantastical escapades.

"Urvashi!" Indira Gandhi scolded when the tiny pachyderm dribbled milk down the white silk of my dress. "Mind your table manners!"

To which I only laughed and petted her hairy head—Urvashi's, not Indira's—and found myself surprised at its smoothness. "Oh, no. She's being very good."

A dress could be replaced. Experiences like this were once in a lifetime.

That same day I sent the first in my daily string of picture post-cards addressed to both Caroline and John, covering them with *X*'s that they could recognize as kisses from me.

Thirteen days until I saw them again and could cover them with real kisses.

As much as I missed them (and I missed them so!), I needed my children to look back on photographs of this trip one day and be proud of their mother's adventures and accomplishments. I wanted to soak up everything this goodwill tour had to offer, to show Caroline and John what it was to really live.

India was the land of spices, sandalwood, and snake charmers, but so too was it a place of infinite beauty. Yet nothing could have prepared me for the wonder that was the Taj Mahal.

Built over the course of seventeen years at the behest of Shah Jahan for his beloved wife, the shimmering white mausoleum felt like walking through a living painting. I was spellbound when I first beheld it in the pale glow of the setting sun, the sky behind it ablaze with all the robust colors of a summer peach. The site had been cleared of spectators for my visit, and my official entourage lingered at a respectable distance so if I closed my eyes I might pretend I was alone. The twisted cypresses that lined the path cast ethereal shadows in reflecting pools that replicated the four white minarets, and the warm spring breeze made the waters ripple in a subtle dance.

It was a flawless moment. Utterly beautiful and unspoiled.

I missed Jack so much then that it caused a palpable ache in my heart, wished he was at my side as my throat grew tight. Loneliness and longing pierced me afresh, even as I realized how silly it was that a woman like me, in a moment like this, could want for anything.

Not anything. *Anyone.*

What was the point of moments like this if I couldn't share them with those I loved?

For I realized now that no matter what he did, for better or worse, I would always love Jack. My love for him was Shakespeare's ever-fixed mark that looked on tempests and was never shaken.

Lee bumped my shoulder with hers, interrupting me from my somber reverie. "Are you all right, Jacks? You look like you're about to cry."

I was glad Lee was here beside me, although I wondered what other adventures we'd missed since Jack's election had cooled our relationship. But that was in the past and all I wanted to do now was look to the future. Lee had helped simply by sharing her life with me again, for I couldn't countenance being unfaithful to Jack as she was to Stas.

I knew what needed to be done when I returned home, was suddenly eager to see my husband again.

"I've seen pictures of the Taj, but for the first time I am struck with a sense of its mass and symmetry." I spoke slowly around the knot in my throat, finding that words simply failed me, so I was thankful that my sister was there to steady me by holding my hand. "I'm overwhelmed. Awed."

"Good." Lee wrapped an arm around my shoulder. "Being overwhelmed means you're still living. And I suspect we're going to be thoroughly overwhelmed when we leave civilization tomorrow to visit Benares."

I knew Benares was a holy city, one of the oldest inhabited in the world, with its location on the Ganges, and that morning I dressed to fit in with the city's riot of bright and lively jewel tones.

"That orange is positively shocking," Lee said of my skirt, dropping her sunglasses to the tip of her nose for emphasis. I bit my lip in a moment of uncertainty; while I had Oleg Cassini and a whole host of hairdressers and stylists making sure I was always classically turned out, Lee had always been a natural at fashion. She could put on a coat and know how to turn her shoulder and her head and wear the coat so that it was perfection. My sister laughed and gave an appreciative nod. "You should wear that color more often."

I almost wished I could twirl like a little girl in my vivid Veronese orange silk skirt—inspired by the colors of Moghul miniatures—as we waited to board the boat that would take us downriver, dragonflies darting back and forth as if they were stitching up the air. Was it my imagination, or did each of our steps down the petal-strewn path release a heady floral fragrance into the warm air? I was sans hat and sans stockings, and not even the wall of oppressive heat could dampen my spirits. Scarlet-liveried bearers sheltered my sister and me from the worst of the sun's glare while the crowds ashore blew blasts on conch shells that were so loud they might have shaken the heavens loose. "Isn't it marvelous?"

The crowd continued cheering and added a mix of tinny triangle notes after we'd boarded a boat garlanded with festive orange marigolds. Yet I sobered as we continued our slow procession downriver to view the city's traditional bathing spots. Alongside those areas where laughing children and happy families splashed in the muddy waters was a reminder that together with this vivid, unapologetic life, there was death.

"Cremation platforms," I said, pointing them out to my sister.

Lee wrinkled her pert nose but didn't avert her gaze. "Life and death are close neighbors in this country."

"So they are." A shudder worked its way up my spine as I watched a flame set to a bier, the body cocooned there seeming to writhe within its linens. Suddenly, the air smelled of ash and sadness to me, and despite the sunshine I suppressed a shiver. It was difficult to re-capture the convivial spirit from earlier as the flame took and the smoke carried a lost spirit heavenward. Although we were in a Hindu country, I recited a silent prayer from my childhood, knowing I'd want someone to do the same for me one day.

"Your visit to my country has added greatly to the psychological pull of friendship between India and the United States," Jawaharlal Nehru proclaimed after he spent one morning teaching me how to stand on my head to meditate, which I planned to demonstrate for Caroline and John. "We are happy to count you as an ally, *Amriki Rani*."

Adventure and accomplishment in the form of a new ally for America. Well done, Jackie.

If I'd ever doubted it, there was no denying I was fully in my ele-ment when traveling abroad, that I had reached my pinnacle as First Lady. And the trip wasn't over yet, for then Lee and I were whisked off to Pakistan, where we were draped with traditional welcoming tinsel among the sound of drums and a shower of flower petals and bursting balloons.

It was there that I received the best gift of all, more touching even than tiger cubs or Khrushchev's space puppy.

"His name is Sardar. It means Chief in our language," said Presi-dent Ayub Khan of the ten-year-old gelding with a velvet muzzle that begged to be stroked. "When I learned of your love of horses, I knew he would make the best ambassador from our country to yours."

"May I?" I asked, and President Khan only gestured for stunning Sardar to be saddled.

After a get-acquainted canter, I was in love. Truly, madly, and ever so deeply in love.

"I don't think I've seen you look at any man or beast like that," Lee said with a laugh when I returned to the paddock. "Don't worry, I promise not to tell Jack."

Flush with happiness, I declared as I dismounted in one swift movement, "No one at home will be allowed to ride him but me."

I knew Jack and the children would have chortled with laughter when Lee and I clambered aboard a camel on our final day, sitting sidesaddle because of our knee-length skirts. (One of the few times I've wished to be a little less fashionable!) I practically had to hog-tie Lee—who fretted about ruining her pristine white leather gloves—to the poor creature, and I couldn't help a mischievous grin at the stricken expressions of my Secret Service detail as the camel hoisted us jerkily aloft, imagining every agent visualizing the misfortune of a runaway camel, or us being thrown and breaking our necks. Lee seemed to feel the same way, groaning while she clutched the reins in white gloves I was sure matched the color of her knuckles underneath.

Fortunately for my Secret Service detail, our biggest mishap came when Lee lost a shoe while I drove from the perch behind my sister as we were jerked helter-skelter.

"Well," I said for the benefit of the inevitable gaggle of reporters after we found ourselves on solid ground again, laughing and hugging each other like we'd done when we were girls. If press interviews were the cost I had to pay for a goodwill tour, oh, it was a price I'd gladly pay. "Riding a camel makes an elephant feel like a jet plane."

I was sad to bid a fond adieu to Lee when our magic carpet trip finally ended, but we had already made plans to see each other soon. I'd mended my relationship with my sister; now I needed to do the same with my husband.

My heart swelled to see Jack bound up the metal ramp after my plane landed in Washington, his tie coming loose as he ducked inside, scarcely sparing a nod to the pilot as his eyes sought me out. Suddenly the cabin seemed too small, as if nothing so mundane as an airplane could possibly contain my husband.

"You're back." His face lit with barely contained enthusiasm. This was more than I'd expected for my welcome home, yet I could tell

Jack was trying not to overdo it when he cleared his throat, one hand snapping against his leg. "How was it?"

"It was absolutely magical. . . . I've never had such an enchanted time."

"I'm glad, Jackie. Really, truly glad."

I didn't need a monument like the Taj Mahal when Jack was staring at me with such naked pleasure. All I needed was him and his excitement that I was finally home.

"The children can't wait to see you," he said. "Well, you and the baby tigers. And the elephant."

Suddenly I couldn't stand it anymore, and I launched myself into his arms, breathing in the pine-and-power scent of him as he hugged me back until I thought my lungs might burst. "Don't forget the horse."

I smiled to imagine four-year-old Caroline and sixteen-month-old John tumbling with—or in the tigers' case, petting from a safe distance—the veritable zoo I'd brought home, and felt a visceral need to hold them. I smiled as Jack wrapped an uncharacteristic arm around my shoulders, settling into the warm scent of him and realizing the full force of how much I'd missed all of them in only two weeks.

And how much Jack had missed me.

"So, Madame Ambassador." Jack's words were warm in my hair as we disembarked the plane together. "Does this life of globetrotting suit you? Shall we expect further solo world tours in the near future? Perhaps this time to Timbuktu?"

Was that worry I heard in his voice? Had he truly missed me that much?

"No solo tours," I assured him. "For a little while, at least."

"Are you sure you don't want to come to New York with me for my birthday celebration?"

"We both know that so-called birthday celebration is really just another Democratic fund-raiser, Bunny. It isn't even on your birthday. Plus, Caroline would be crestfallen to miss the Loudoun County Horse Show." I almost laughed at Jack's earnestness but tempered my reaction to a gentle smile worthy of any Southern belle. "You know, she aspires to enter Macaroni one day."

Jack planted a kiss on my forehead. "With a horsewoman like you as her mother, I expect no less than a wall of blue ribbons from her one day."

So we parted ways only a couple weeks later, me pausing only to glance over my shoulder as Jack boarded the helicopter that would whisk him away to New York while the children and I packed ourselves into the car that would take us to Glen Ora.

I'd told Jack I wouldn't go to New York with him, but that didn't mean I wasn't going to watch his televised pseudo-birthday bash alongside forty million Americans, even if it was ten days before his real birthday.

I was still flush with pleasure from placing third in one of the Loudoun County Horse Show classes after entering as a surprise participant, but that joy dissipated as if it had never existed when I settled in alone in front of our television screen. One glance at the grainy black-and-white live broadcast and my fists balled in my lap. "What fresh hell is this?" I muttered under my breath.

Who on God's green earth thought it would be a good idea to have her *perform for Jack's birthday? Mr. Kennedy would be beside himself to see this. . . .*

It took three introductions for Marilyn Monroe to finally take the stage, and when she did, it was with the swaying, prancing steps of someone who'd already tippled a few too many drinks, or worse, backstage. The boozy starlet clutched a snowy ermine wrap around her shoulders as she teetered her way to the podium, then shrugged it off into the announcer's waiting arms. I gasped, thinking she was naked before realizing the blond doxy was only mostly nude, barely dressed in a scandalous skintight flesh-toned sheath glistening with rhinestones borrowed from the she-demon Lilith herself. Marilyn shielded her eyes and scanned the audience.

There was only one man she was looking for.

Jack.

She sang out the four lines of "Happy Birthday" in a breathless, off-key voice before snapping her fingers and launching into a new verse, her diamond teardrop earrings glittering like tiny stars.

"And, Mr. President, for all the things that you've done, the battles that you've won . . ."

I stopped listening as a haze of crimson clouded my vision at this *crétine* making love to my husband in direct view of forty million Americans. I was still seeing red as a massive multitiered cake was carried out on the shoulders of two chefs and Jack was announced.

Bordel de merde.

"Don't you dare," I growled as he jogged up the stairs, seemingly unfazed at this scandalous turn of events. Thank God and all the saints that Marilyn had already been escorted off the stage or I'd have found a way to drag her down the steps myself. And all the way to the deepest depths of hell.

Jack waved to the crowd and band as if taking a moment to collect his thoughts. I wondered what was going on in his head then, whether he was as repulsed by Marilyn's showy—and tasteless—exhibition, or whether it excited him.

I fiddled with my pearls. *Do I really want to know?*

Absolutely not.

Finally, Jack sheepishly addressed the audience, including most of America, who now watched him from their living rooms. "Thank you." He didn't look into the cameras, could barely drag his glance up from the podium. "I can now retire from politics after having had 'Happy Birthday' sung to me in such a sweet and wholesome way."

Sweet and wholesome?

I laughed aloud, a furious yip that probably woke the children upstairs. If there was one thing Jack knew, it was how to play a part so he didn't seem party to Marilyn's tawdry act.

Now all that remained to be seen was how true to life the act really was.

I decided not to meet Jack upon his return to the White House, because I couldn't bear to add further fuel to the fire by transforming into the harridan wife—reminiscent of my own mother—who stormed across the South Lawn to lambaste her husband for his errant ways. Instead, I let him come to me. The stage was set, the sweet sounds of Caroline and her friends reciting "The Owl and the Pussy Cat" in her upstairs private preschool floated down the hallway of our family apartments, while I painted at my new easel, my feet bare and my hair pulled back in a ponytail. I'd written this scene between Jack and me at least a dozen different ways in my head, yet I remained unsure how our lines would unfurl when he entered the room.

"That was quite the birthday song, Jack."

Yes, I jumped straight to the heart of the matter, because honestly, what point was there in pontificating and avoiding the elephant in the room?

"I know." At least he had the decency to give me a hangdog look. "Marilyn is . . . unbalanced, I think."

What was your first sign?

"And . . . ?"

I refused to make demands. Instead, I allowed the question to expand in the air between us, full of all the accusations about his other lollipops that I'd never made.

"Don't worry. It's been taken care of." Jack stood shoulder to shoulder with me, stilled my paintbrush with one hand and waited for me to look him in the eyes. "I'd never have gone if I'd known what Marilyn was up to. Truly. And I sure as hell wouldn't have let it be filmed."

Did I believe him? To this day, I can't say. I supposed the latter part was closest to the truth, for Jack wasn't one for a public exposé, especially now that he was in the Oval Office.

He must have read the doubt in my eyes. "You know me, Jackie. Any woman who makes an exhibition like that?" His scowl, although not directed at me, made me shiver as if a storm cloud had passed over the sun. "Marilyn has no class. And class goes a long way."

He knows he overstepped this time, I told myself as his eyes beseeched mine. *Let him have his lollipops and come home to his First Lady. After all, he'll never need them, not the way he needs me.*

So I set down the paints and turned to face him. "I know it's almost your birthday, Jack, but there's something I want from you. Two things, actually."

His eyes started to shutter, and I knew he was imagining what demands I might make about this indiscretion. Instead, I softened my voice, made my expression pliant as I remembered the decision I'd made in India.

Was it an act? Just one of a dozen different versions of myself, I supposed.

"First, I'd like to take Caroline with me to Italy to visit Lee."

Jack seemed to relax at my innocuous request. "It's not an election year, so I suppose I can spare you girls. And your second demand?"

"I'd like another child, Jack."

That truth had exactly the effect I desired. Jack's eyes turned to liquid fire, his lips tilting into the edge of a smile. "Well, far be it from me to deny you such a humble request."

Because no matter what those lollipops might offer Jack, there were some things that only I could give him.

must admit, Mrs. Kennedy, that I'm surprised to be seated next to you." I was hosting yet another spectacular White House dinner— the first after Marilyn's scandalous birthday spectacle—this time in honor of Charles de Gaulle's minister of cultural affairs, André Malraux, whom I was trying to convince to allow the *Mona Lisa* out of France and into America for the first time. Arthur Miller, illustrious playwright and ex-husband of Marilyn Monroe, was seated next to me, and he pushed his spectacles higher on the bridge of his nose, the deep grooves of the smile lines around his mouth delving ever deeper. "I'd have thought you'd have seated me with Pushinka out in the dog-house rather than in the place of honor."

I traced the rim of my wineglass with one manicured finger, for I'd maneuvered the bespectacled playwright's seating card directly to my left only this morning. "And why is that, Mr. Miller? Because you were once suspected of being a Communist? Or because of your ex-wife's performance for my husband?"

Miller patted the tobacco pipe in his breast pocket, then let his hand fall. I wondered if that was a nervous habit, just as I idly mused whether anyone tonight would pick up on the way my voice slowed when my nerves jangled too loud. Probably not, for I'd honed the image of quiet refinement for so long that it was difficult to tell where the act ended and the real Jackie began.

"I had to abandon Marilyn for her own good," Miller confided, even as a multitude of conversations continued unabated around us. "That girl's a mess, addicted to sleeping pills, all because of her goddamned doctors."

"Don't worry." I placed a gentle hand on Miller's forearm. "I won't hold Marilyn's infatuation with Jack against you. I simply like to surround myself with interesting people."

Even when it exhausted the hell out of me.

So it was that my feet felt like boulders in their kitten-heel pumps later that night, when I finally closed behind me the doors to the private rooms upstairs in the White House. I was almost to the children's rooms to kiss them good night when the telephone rang in the darkened sitting room, only one Tiffany lamp still lit for the night. Normally, I'd have allowed the staff to answer, but this was our private line and Jack wasn't yet upstairs.

So I answered. And immediately wished I hadn't.

"Jack?" The feminine voice on the other end was slurred and woozy. "S'it's Marilyn."

Woozy with alcohol, and if Arthur Miller was to be believed, drugs too.

Don't worry. It's been taken care of.

Except it obviously hadn't been.

I should have slammed down the receiver. I should have told Marilyn she had the wrong number, even though she'd called the White

House's private line and there was only one way she could have gotten that number. I should have done at least a dozen different things.

But I didn't do any of them.

Instead, I threw back my shoulders. "This isn't Jack, Marilyn. It's Jackie. We've never met, but perhaps you've heard of me? I'm the First Lady of the United States. And Jack's wife."

I swore there was a hiccup of surprise from the other coast, or wherever she was calling from. "Oh," she said. "I wasn't s'posed to call tonight, was I?"

I imagined her in some teenaged pose somewhere in California just then, on her back with those long legs up the wall, eyes half lidded with that bottle-blond hair spread like a halo on her pillow. Marilyn Monroe might have made a fascinating psychological study or perhaps the subject of a lurid novel, had it not been my life she was ruining. I breathed a sigh, deep enough so she could hear it. "Is there something I can help you with, Ms. Monroe?"

Because I wouldn't give her the satisfaction of my issuing an ultimatum and letting her know she'd gotten under my skin—*if you call here again, if you so much as look at my husband again*—no matter how much I wanted to give her one. Oh, no . . .

"I'm gonna marry him, you know. Jack-ie." She enunciated my name like the ecstatic crowds sometimes did. "I mean it. I'm gonna marry Jack one day."

I hadn't thought the peroxide *putain* capable of surprising me, but her declaration of marriage caught me off guard. But only for a moment.

Then I forced myself to laugh at her, drawing deep into my own skills as an actress to create a full-bodied chortle that mixed with the tears welling in my throat before bursting free. "That will prove difficult, Marilyn." I leveled out my tone. "Given that he's married, Catholic, and president of the United States. Jack and I are a team, Marilyn, as president and First Lady. In case you haven't noticed, you can't have one without the other."

I infused ice into every next word. "Good night, Marilyn. Please don't call here again."

I slammed the receiver into the cradle, confident that Marilyn would only hear a calm click wherever it was that she was sprawled in her alcoholic fog.

That was the last time I heard from Marilyn Monroe. Yet I somehow doubted whether the peroxide *putain* was finished firing shots at me.

It was during the sweltering heat of July that Mr. Kennedy was finally released from New York University hospital, bound for the residential Horizon House. Jack's schedule was a beast, but I'd made sure both he and I could attend, for this was a family matter.

And I'd come to realize that family was *tout le monde*, the most important thing in this life.

"Watch out," Ethel warned us when we arrived. "The emperor is in a right foul temper, banging his feet on the ground at all the noise."

Which I could believe and even empathize with, given that this was a monumental change for a man accustomed to ruling his own small empire, and whose entire life was now restricted to one small room. The rest of the family seemed nonplussed, what with Bobby and Ethel's menagerie of children running helter-skelter like ill-behaved little pirates while Jack's sisters nattered in the background.

"I'll take care of this," I said to Jack, who seemed relieved to let me take charge. He acquiesced to me more easily these days, perhaps as a result of the Marilyn debacle and our renewed quest for another child. I gave a soft smile, then pulled the stillness around me as I walked quietly into Mr. Kennedy's new room. It was less sterile than his prior space, yet it still wasn't home.

His eyes softened as he saw it was me, and I knelt on a footstool in front of him, placed my head in his lap. "I'm doing my best to help Jack make all the right decisions," I said after a little while. "And I'm praying for you every day, Grandpa, so you work hard while you're here."

Everyone always pretended not to notice the side of his body affected by paralysis, but I kissed his gnarled right hand and the broken side of his face, glad that he looked more peaceful than he had in the early days after his stroke. "I have a present for you too." I gestured to Mr. Hill, my Secret Service agent, who had obligingly carried and kept hidden the striking hand-carved walking stick that I now presented to Jack's father. "Remember our deal?"

For I'd kept up correspondence with Mr. Kennedy now that he could write again, albeit his truncated letters were written in a stilted, childlike hand. Still, we'd made weighty promises to each other in those letters, about Jack and the future.

Stay with my son, Jackie. He needs you.

Learn to walk again, Poppy Doodle. Your family needs you.

Jack and his siblings filed in, and we all watched as Mr. Kennedy claimed the walking stick with a determined gleam I recognized from his son's eyes. The family patriarch struggled to rise from his chair, but he'd kept his end of the bargain in the weeks since I'd seen him last, for once he was upright, he struggled with Herculean effort to place one foot in front of him.

One step. Then two.

Just as Jack and I were doing as we pieced our relationship together. It should be a simple act to learn to walk again, just as it should be simple to learn to love again, yet each act was fraught with complications and pitfalls.

Jack and Bobby helped their father back to his chair, and when he was seated again, trembling from the effort, I took both his age-spotted hands in mine and kissed them. "Remember when you told us that you didn't believe in coming in second place? You came out first today, Grandpa. You had yourself a victory."

Afterward, Bobby nudged me as we waited for the Secret Service to bring the car around to the front of the hospital. "I wanted to let you know that things with a certain blond actress have finally been taken care of." His voice dropped even lower. "Marilyn's unhinged these days. I made it very clear to her not to so much as speak Jack's name out loud ever again."

"Thank you."

Bobby looked askance at me, finally just shook his head. "I don't know how you do it."

"Do what?"

"Work your magic. On my father, on Jack . . ." He ran a hand through his sandy hair. "No one else can take the Kennedy men in hand like you can, Jackie."

To which I only laughed. "It's one of my special talents, Bobby."

Yet that talent was like walking a tightrope over a pit of fire. I never knew if I was going to survive the act unscathed.

'd thought Marilyn Monroe wasn't done taking shots at me, and I was right.

The peroxide *putain* showed up on the pages of *Vogue* in June dressed in a brunette wig, a white silk shirt, and black palazzo pants, strings of trademark pearls around her neck.

Dressed as me.

I saw matador red even as every sign pointed to the fact that Jack had had no contact with Marilyn since her phone call to the White House. Then I picked up the newspaper one August morning to discover Marilyn's final headline splashed across the pages.

MARILYN MONROE FOUND DEAD: Sleeping Pill Overdose Blamed

I recalled my conversation with Arthur Miller, even as I worried that Jack's refusal to so much as answer her calls or perhaps even Bobby's ultimatum had pushed her over the edge, that the shattering of her dream to steal away my husband had been too much for her to bear.

And I felt bad for her, even though the woman with her effervescent, Champagne giggles had been a thorn in my side for so long. But there was nothing to be done that might rewrite her final chapter to give her a happy ending.

We all had our own tragedies to live. And, in the end, death would claim us all.

. . .

couldn't rest from travel; I wanted to drink life to its very lees. I'd promised Jack I wouldn't journey alone again, but he had given me carte blanche to travel after Marilyn's *Vogue* spread, so this time when I packed for a summer jaunt to Europe and Jack planned his summer's presidential itinerary, I took wide-eyed Caroline with me for an unforgettable mother-daughter trip aboard the Agnellis' private yacht.

Brilliantly flamboyant Gianni Agnelli was the Italian czar of Fiat and an unabashed lover of all things American, who had offered to shepherd us around for the prestige of hosting the American president's wife and daughter. He also had a secret motive, for Fiat was working on technology to save Egypt's awe-inspiring ancient temples at Abu Simbel, which was going to be submerged by the impending construction of the Aswan Dam. However, the project was short on funds and that meant Agnelli wanted my help.

"I know you are a lover of all things historical," he said to me one day aboard his yacht. "And that you hold sway over your husband. It would be a crime against humanity to let such a treasure be lost forever, especially if we had the means to save it."

It would be a crime, and I *did* want to help. After all, I'd sat through enough dull teas and interviews with the East Wing press hens to allow myself the indulgence of choosing a few pet projects. With the White House renovation complete, I supposed it was time to choose a new one.

"I think I could persuade my husband to lend his support to the cause, although I doubt whether Congress will open the United States' pocketbook to the tune of thirty million dollars."

"Fiat does not need one cent of your country's money, Mrs. Kennedy." Agnelli gave a flamboyant wave of his hand. "Only your influence and that of your husband's. If the handsome and energetic American president says he wants Abu Simbel saved, then donors from around the world will eagerly hemorrhage millions to make it happen."

I liked the sound of Agnelli's plan and told him I'd consider his proposition as I helped Caroline buckle her orange life jacket. The exquisite coastline of Capri bobbed in the background, the picturesque little village favored by the jet set beckoning with its evening promise of shopping for silk palazzo pants and dancing the Twist in the famed Number Two nightclub. Yet its afternoon sunshine was reserved for Caroline and me to revel in like two heathens of old. "Are we really going to ski on water, Mommy?"

"You better believe it." I tweaked her nose, making both of us laugh as Lee's mustachioed Polish prince of a husband, Stas, set the jet engine to rumbling. Their relationship was still strained—Lee had confided her affair hadn't ended, although she'd received and thanked me for the annulment to her first marriage that I'd requested from the Vatican—but I secretly hoped they would patch things up and find the same sort of fragile harmony that Jack and I had reached. I wasn't pregnant—yet—but I was sure that final piece would fall into place upon my return stateside. In the meantime, I'd revel like a pig in summer mud during this precious time with Caroline. "Let's go kiss the wind!"

Caroline and I zipped around on water skis, laughing each time we dunked ourselves face first in the Amalfi's turquoise surf and hooting in celebratory laughter when we stayed afloat for more than five seconds. In that sun-drenched afternoon it was almost easy to forget the extra speedboat of Secret Service agents assigned to Caroline and me, or the other armada of boats stuffed with foreign press photographers that hovered at a distance like pesky gnats. Mr. Hill and the rest of the Secret Service detail deserved a special award for speeding around to foil the press's battalion of zoom lenses, which Caroline thought was all in good fun and which I fully appreciated.

"Mommy." Caroline laid her wet head on my lap when we were finished, her cheeks pink from sun and exertion. "That was fun. I wish Daddy and John were here so they could water ski too."

"Me too, honey. Maybe next time."

We spent the next days making real Italian spaghetti for dinner, buying sandals in Capri, and taking reams of photographs like gawking tourists. They were all memories that would last a lifetime—as was the fact that the Ravello town council renamed the Conca dei Marini beach the Jacqueline Kennedy beach in my honor—but Middle America was shocked by my Italian antics. (Worse still, that I'd had the nerve to be photographed in my bathing suit. No one cared that I'd never asked to be photographed, that the Secret Service had in fact gone out of their way to ensure I not be photographed.) The *New York Daily News* headlined their story about me as "Jackie's Night in the Pirate's Den." I'd have found it all humorous, had it only stopped there.

"'How can a man handle the problems of a nation when he can't handle his wife?'" I'd ceased outlining a three-page letter to Jack about why we should support saving Abu Simbel when the morning papers had been delivered and reluctantly set aside my yellow legal pad to read Drew Pearson's latest column. I glanced up at Lee over our breakfast of buttery croissants and blushing apricots, but my sister only snorted as I continued reading. "'Wife off dancing with red blouse, red slacks, red shoes with some aristocrat at four in the morning. Doesn't she have enough respect for her husband to be a good wife?'" I pursed my lips. "'Some aristocrat' must mean Agnelli. I suppose I should have chosen someone more grandfatherly as our host."

"You've given them this notion that you are a good wife." Lee shook her croissant at me. "That's your problem, Jacks. Better to be a hedonist like me and prevent them from toiling under these ridiculous, antiquated notions."

I rolled my eyes, but honestly, I did want to be a good wife, and an even better mother. With over 180 million Americans, I supposed it was inevitable that someone should take issue with a woman having a little fun.

Still, I pursed my lips when Jack's telegram arrived.

LESS AGNELLI, MORE CAROLINE. COME HOME BY THE END OF THE MONTH.

Jack had never been one to give me orders, and this one made me want to frown and laugh at the same time. Was Jack jealous of me being photographed with mercurial and flamboyant Gianni Agnelli? Was he honestly worried about my fidelity?

Oh, Jack, I thought as I rubbed the corners of my eyes, enjoying the idea of his discomfiture. *How the tables have turned.*

I didn't bother to keep Lee from reading the message over my shoulder; she'd have dug it out of the trash later anyway. "Oh," she said, with a malicious gleam in her eyes. "I say wear a flaming scarlet *A* on your breast tonight and stay out until five in the morning if it means making that Jack of yours jealous."

"I'm sure it's only political expediency." I set aside the offending papers. "It's not good for Jack to have his perfect First Lady off gallivanting in Europe, looking like a sybarite."

"Formerly perfect." Lee tapped the stack of gossip rags that had headlined me. "I thought he told you he didn't mind this trip because it's not an election year."

"There's midterms," I reminded her. "If Jack was up for reelection this November, you could bet I'd be summering in Iowa instead of Italy."

Lee wrinkled her nose. "Remind me not to accept any invitations from you two years from now. There's no yachts or Chanel ateliers in Iowa."

I laughed, then sobered at the thought of having to endure the rigors of a campaign season again. "Right. Instead I'll be begging you to rescue me."

Still, a reputation was a loud thing, and I had no desire to undo all the hard work I'd done as First Lady. I was home by the end of the month.

Jack didn't ask any questions about Agnelli—it was as if the negative press coverage had never happened—and he agreed to my request to lend his support to saving Abu Simbel. *Now we're even*, I imagined him saying to me when President Gamal Abdel Nasser of Egypt sent us a three-foot-tall Old Kingdom burial statue in gratitude.

Which meant life in the White House during the first week of October 1962 was back to business as usual.

"Everything is ready for the ambassador's visit, Mrs. Kennedy," J. B. West announced when I entered the Lincoln Bedroom late one afternoon. I'd dressed carefully today in what I suspected would soon become one of my favorite outfits: a brand-new watermelon pink wool suit that masqueraded as a French classic when every stitch was really American. The Chanel-inspired outfit came with a pink pillbox hat to complete the ensemble, but today I'd foregone that accessory in favor of a more casual look.

"You're right, Mr. West. Everything is perfect." I took in the newly installed hospital bed with its crisp sheets, the specially lifted suitcase rack so a person didn't have to bend over, and a drink tray at the bedside carefully arranged with gin, tonic, Coke, rum, lemon juice, and sugar syrup in a jar. "You know," I added with a smile as I removed the gin and rum from the tray, "Mr. Kennedy only takes make-believe cocktails. He paid each of his sons one thousand dollars not to indulge in what he calls the Irish vice before they turned twenty-one."

I was looking forward to this overnight visit from Jack's father— the first since his stroke, and in fact, the first since Jack's inauguration as Mr. Kennedy had never wanted to be seen as pulling Jack's strings. "Tell the ambassador I'll see him as soon as my meeting is finished."

With my part to save Abu Simbel complete, I'd turned my eye to a project far closer to home and called a meeting to examine its new plans. The pillared six-story Executive Office Building and the historical nineteenth-century town homes along Lafayette Square— which I could see from the windows of the White House and had once been occupied by the likes of Dolley Madison—were all due to be razed and replaced with colorless modern office buildings.

Jack didn't want to see them destroyed, but he'd resigned himself to their impending doom as he had neither the time nor the fund-raising capabilities to stop the project.

Fortunately, his First Lady wasn't so restricted.

"You off to save Lafayette Square?" Jack scarcely looked up from the memo he was reading when I entered the Oval Office. With the paper upside down on his desk, I could only make out the first words: *Soviet Ilyushin Il-28,* which I knew to be Russian bombers.

"The wreckers haven't started yet," I said. "Until they do, it can be saved."

When Jack finally glanced my way, the tension in his eyes was magnified by the reading glasses he only ever wore in private. I almost asked what was wrong, but the frenetic tapping of the pencil in his right hand told me now wasn't a good time.

"I'll see you tonight for dinner with my father," he said. "Seven o'clock?"

"Of course," I said, and went about my day, greeting architect John Warnecke and heaping praise on his compromise design for Lafayette Square that preserved the historical town houses while also making way for much-needed new government buildings.

Everything seemed so normal. Little did I—or the country know—that dark thunderclouds of war were gathering on the horizon.

A few days later, I took the children and Mr. Kennedy to Glen Ora to relax and enjoy the beginnings of the fall colors. Jack had seemed preoccupied in the days before we'd left, but he had a full schedule, including a midterm campaign tour, meetings with the crown prince of Libya, and a service at the Cathedral of St. Matthew for the National Day of Prayer. After a brisk ride on Sardar one morning, I came inside and read with consternation the newspaper reports that Jack had cut short his congressional campaign stop in Chicago because of a cold, and reached Bobby when I called the White House.

"Jack would never let something as mundane as a cold stop him," I told Bobby. "What's going on? Is it his back again?"

Or is it something—perhaps someone—else?

"Jack's planning to call you in a little bit," Bobby said, not un-kindly. I waited for him to tell me not to worry, but the words never came. "I have to go, Jackie. Off-the-record meetings."

Which meant something was afoot. Something big.

Bobby had warned me to expect a call, but still, the urgency in Jack's tone came as a shock.

"Why don't you come back to Washington?" His voice was pulled taut as a fuse and sounded infinitely more explosive. I worried that it was something I'd done—although I couldn't fathom what—until Jack breathed into the line. "It's that goddamned Khrushchev again. This time he's planted nukes in Cuba."

Cuba, which was in America's backyard. And Khrushchev, whom we'd wined and dined in Austria, and whom had sent my children their beloved puppy, Pushinka.

"We'll be there as soon as we can" was all I said.

"Today, Jackie. I need you."

How I'd waited and prayed to hear those words from Jack's lips. All it had taken was the Soviet premier threatening the entire country—perhaps the world—with nuclear annihilation to prod Jack into utter-ing them.

From that moment on, it seemed there was no waking or sleeping.

I issued succinct orders to my staff before the receiver landed in its cradle. The children were woken from their naps and we were back at the White House at half past one. If there was a crisis, I wanted our family together.

"He's in another off-the-record cabinet meeting with his ExComm team," Tish informed me the moment we arrived. She, too, looked harried, which didn't bode well.

"ExComm?"

"The Executive Committee of the National Security Council, plus a few others the president handpicked who have expertise pertinent to the crisis in Cuba. Of course, none of this is public yet." Tish's of-ficiousness grated on my nerves as she glanced at the calendar in her hands. "Tonight you have a dinner for the Duchess of Devonshire."

"Can't it be canceled?" But I knew the answer before the question was out of my mouth. "Never mind. We continue as if nothing untoward is happening."

As if World War III isn't brewing on the horizon.

During dinner, neither Jack nor I mentioned the crisis, even when we heard that Khrushchev was using this opportunity to publicize the greeting of American guest singers at the Moscow opera, as if Russia was suddenly so open to the West and not at all complicit in trying to destroy our hemisphere. (A fact that made me both appreciate and loathe the clownish Soviet premier on a whole new level.) Anyone who didn't know would have thought this was just another day, another meal. To his credit, Jack scarcely fidgeted as he asked a battery of questions of the Duchess of Devonshire with his usual aplomb, all the tiny facts about people that he fitted into the jigsaw of his mind. The only clue that anything was amiss was the number of times he was called away to the telephone.

It seemed that only I could feel the tension humming around Jack, as if the very air were electrified. Only me, that is, and Bobby.

"He's going to reveal everything tonight on prime time." Bobby had asked me to find him in his attorney general's office after dinner, and I'd distracted myself while waiting by perusing his children's artwork taped to the back of the wooden doors, picking up and setting down the black-and-white family photograph he kept on his desk. Jack had already been called away, and I'd watched, powerless, as he was swallowed once again by his Situation Room. "No one knows how Khrushchev is going to react to the naval quarantine we've set up around Cuba."

"What naval quarantine?" God, how I hated receiving information secondhand, even as I understood the pressure Jack was under.

"That's the option Jack chose," Bobby answered in that New England drawl that was so like his brother's. "Some of those blowhards want him to authorize air strikes in Cuba or do the unthinkable and pretend we don't know about the nukes."

"And you counseled a middle ground? This quarantine?"

I recalled the Bay of Pigs, Jack's wrath after his first failure in office.

From now on, it's just you and me, Bobby.

"Of course. A sneak attack isn't our tradition, and an air strike would mean thousands of Cubans would be killed without warning," Bobby absentmindedly picked up the white U.S. Marshal's helmet displayed behind his desk, dented from where a rioter had wielded a lead pipe after Bobby had recently demanded that the U.S. Department of Justice enforce the integration law allowing James Meredith to attend the University of Mississippi. I knew that had been a clear-cut decision for Bobby, but this crisis with Cuba felt like every possible shade of gray. "Of course, Cuba could retaliate by equipping their submarines with underwater nukes and taking out our destroyers. On the other hand, we sure as hell shouldn't be sticking our heads in the sand. I favor action, to make known unmistakably the seriousness of the United States' determination to get the missiles out of Cuba."

So Bobby had counseled and so Jack would do. It was sometimes difficult to tell where one brother ended and the other began.

"I think it's the right course of action." I clasped Bobby's hand tight. "Thank you for telling me. No one lets me know a damn thing around here, except you."

Bobby smiled. "I know. Here's a copy of the letter he's having the Russian ambassador deliver to Khrushchev tonight before he addresses the nation."

It was short, only two pages. I scanned the front page and found myself nodding at one line—a definitive line drawn in the sands of Cuba, Russia, America, perhaps the entire world—especially.

I have not assumed that you or any other sane man would, in this nuclear age, deliberately plunge the world into war which it is crystal clear no country could win and which could only result in catastrophic consequences to the whole world, including the aggressor.

I glanced up at Bobby after I'd finished the entire letter. "This is good. Really, really good."

And it was. Gone was the unsure president freshly bruised from the Bay of Pigs and kowtowing to the Russian premier in Austria. This new Jack was forceful, authoritative, and self-possessed.

He was everything I had known he could be.

In that moment, in the midst of a perfectly fraught day, I believed Jack could save the world. That he would.

"I have to go." Bobby's jaw clenched as he glanced at his watch. "Another off-the-record meeting."

With nothing else to do save drive myself insane with nerves, I wandered the halls of the White House until it was time to watch Jack's ultimatum to Khrushchev.

I call upon Chairman Khrushchev to halt and eliminate this clandestine, reckless, and provocative threat to world peace and to stable relations between our two nations. I call upon him further to abandon this course of world domination and to join in an historic effort to end the perilous arms race and transform the history of man."

All that remained now was to wait for Khrushchev's answer.

Days passed slowly, as if time found a way to halt each falling grain of sand in its hourglass as America—and the world—held our collective breath and turned our eyes to Cuba.

While Americans prepared their backyard bomb shelters and together we stood on the precipice of assured annihilation, John fell ill with a 104-degree fever. So while Jack labored to save the world, I struggled over our child.

"Cancel the dinner for the maharaja of Jaipur," I told Tish from where Maud Shaw and I sat vigil at my son's bedside. Caroline was down the hall carving jack-o'-lanterns for next week's Halloween parties while her brother's poor little body burned hotter than a raging furnace. "They can still dine here, of course, but it's ridiculous to host a showy dinner with everything that's happening."

For once, Tish didn't argue.

Interminable hours ticked by while I was secluded in the darkened sickroom, and no one thought to bring us any news. The world might have fallen down upon our ears and Maud Shaw and I wouldn't have known until it was too late.

"You need to eat," the nanny finally said after taking John's temperature again. Still high, but no longer 104.

I pushed the stray hair out of my eyes. Food seemed unimportant at a time like this. "I'll have a tray sent up."

Except I'd forgotten that I'd sent the chefs home along with all but a skeleton household staff, wanting them to be with their families in this time of crisis.

"You're not one of my charges, Mrs. Kennedy, but this time you'll do as I say." She crossed meaty arms over her formidable chest. "Take a shower and eat a proper meal, something with a decent cup of tea. I'll send for you if anything changes."

I replaced the cloth on John's forehead. It was constant work to keep the compresses cool. "Maybe just for a few minutes."

"Good girl."

I was so exhausted that I didn't care when one of the guests—thank God it wasn't the maharaja or his wife—made scrambled eggs for all of us. Jack joined us at my request for a quick bite, his face puffy and every bit of him looking ragged around the edges.

My candle burns at both ends. I recalled Caroline reciting to Jack the words of Edna St. Vincent Millay's poem. *It will not last the night. . . .*

"Any word?" I whispered.

He shook his head. "Still waiting for Khrushchev's response." He clasped my hand so our fingers automatically locked together, as if he needed something to anchor him. "This time tomorrow we may be at war."

I glanced around our newly redecorated rooms, trying to imagine the red glare of bombs and chaos falling amid this refined world of austere beauty. The very idea seemed utterly surreal and entirely unimaginable.

"'Things fall apart,'" he muttered, more to himself than me. "'The centre cannot hold; mere anarchy is loosed upon the world . . .'"

I took up Yeats's poem—one of Jack's many favorites—where he left off, whispering so no one else could hear: "'The blood-dimmed tide is loosed, and everywhere the ceremony of innocence is drowned.'" I pressed a kiss onto the back of his hand, hard. "It won't come to that, Jack. You won't allow it."

Jack gave a weak smile, then he was gone again. But the threat remained.

We received Khrushchev's response at two o'clock in the morning, rejecting Jack's ultimatum and stating in no uncertain terms that the Soviet ships carrying military supplies were moving into Cuba, regardless of the U.S. naval blockade.

It was time to prepare for war.

"Ma'am." Clint Hill appeared at John's door, his eyes downcast. My fevered son was sleeping fitfully, and I'd fallen into a light doze at his sickbed, Maud Shaw in the chair opposite. "I'm sorry to interrupt."

"It's all right, Mr. Hill." I rose and rolled my shoulders in a vain attempt to work out the tension there, as if I was a windup doll wound far too tight. "What do you need?"

"The president asked me to discuss the plan with you."

I shivered at his tone. "The plan?"

"In case of attack." Mr. Hill remained stone-faced, but that façade cracked for a moment as he glanced beyond me to where John lay, twisted in his sweat-stained coverlet. "In the event of an imminent emergency, the Secret Service will take you and the children into the bunker beneath the White House."

"And then?"

"And then you'll wait out the emergency."

I scoffed, for I was not the sort of captain to abandon my ship. "That's where you're wrong, Mr. Hill. If that situation develops, I will take Caroline and John, and we will walk hand in hand out onto the southern grounds. We will stand there like brave soldiers and face the fate of every other American."

I tipped my chin, waiting for Mr. Hill to argue. He only gazed at me as if he'd never truly seen me before. "Yes, ma'am," he said. "You may want to speak with the president about this, ma'am."

There was no doubt in my mind that should it come to it, I'd have to fight for the right to die the way I wished, courageous at my husband's side, with our children beside us. I was raising our children to be model citizens, not to shirk their duties or flee in the face of disaster.

To sacrifice for their country.

I found Jack in the wood-paneled Situation Room surrounded by the flotsam of crumpled notes from all his off-the-record meetings, his tie undone and his eyes rimmed an ugly red. Bobby was there, too, a look of warning in his eyes that I pretended not to notice while Jack absentmindedly petted Charlie, our Welsh terrier, whom I guessed he'd asked to have brought down, ostensibly to soothe his nerves.

A floor-to-ceiling map of the world had been tacked to the wall behind them, and for a moment I found it almost laughable that Cuba—such a tiny island—could have brought the entire world to this terrifying precipice.

"Mr. Hill just spoke with me, Jack." My tone caught his attention and he raised those bleary eyes to mine. "If anything happens, I want you to know we're all going to stay right here with you." I held up a hand as he opened his mouth to argue. "Don't even think of sending us away. I'd rather be with you and die with you, and the children, too—than live without any of you. This is one decision you're not allowed to make."

I let the pause lengthen to give him the opportunity to argue, which I was prepared to shoot down. Instead, his shoulders only slumped, whether from relief or the extra weight of my decision, I couldn't tell.

"All right," he said, his eyes blank.

Then I sat in the empty seat, prepared to wait out the night alongside him and Bobby.

And a long night it was.

The world heaved a sigh of relief when Jack received a rambling letter from Khrushchev complete with an offer to withdraw the Soviet missiles in Cuba in exchange for a promise from the United States to never again invade the island nation and to secretly remove the now-obsolete Jupiter missiles from Turkey. After several tense days and countless arguments with his ExComm staff, Jack accepted their offer, and Radio Moscow announced that Khrushchev had accepted our terms.

It was a gift to the world, but then it turned out Jack had a gift for me as well.

"This is for you." He handed me a robin's egg–blue box tied with a white ribbon. On the table behind him were a host of similar boxes.

Hesitant, I unwrapped the package to discover a sterling-silver Tiffany calendar for October 1962 nestled inside, the fateful thirteen days we'd just lived through highlighted in bold. The question must have been writ on my face, for Jack gestured to the companion boxes. "One for every member of the ExComm team, in gratitude for helping me save the world. Victory has a hundred fathers, you know."

"But I'm not part of the ExComm team."

"You're part of my team." He tapped the top of the calendar. "And only yours has these."

There in the silver were six letters. Six perfect, wonderful letters.

JBK + JFK.

I blinked back the tears that welled in my eyes. "Do you mean to tell me that you didn't engrave your initials with Bobby's? Or Robert McNamara's?"

"I almost did for Lyndon's." Jack bumped his shoulder into mine. "But I think I'll get him a locket instead."

"Only if it's heart shaped."

Jack actually bent with laughter, the tension of the past weeks released in one great guffaw that had him holding his knees. "I'd love to see his face if I did. Oh, God, can you ever imagine what would happen to the country if Lyndon was president?"

"Let's not worry about that for another few years, shall we?" I clasped the calendar to my chest, never wanting to let it go. "Thank you for this, Jack. Truly."

"You're welcome. And I mean it, Jackie." He tilted my chin so I had to look him in the eyes. "You showed real courage during all of this. There will always be a place for you on my team."

His promise was like warmed wine coursing through my veins, recalling his father's words to me so long ago.

I was indeed part of the Kennedy team, for now and for always.

It had only taken the threat of nuclear annihilation to prove it.

May 1963

Those halcyon summer months of 1963 tasted even sweeter after the fraught days of the prior autumn. The end of May meant Jack's forty-sixth birthday, and this year I'd planned a Potomac river cruise—without the help of overbearing social secretary Tish Baldridge, whom I'd replaced with my old school friend Nancy Tuckerman—to wipe out remembrances of last year's scandalous celebration.

No dozy starlets hopped up on Jack Daniels and sleeping pills. Only family and as little publicity as I could get away with.

"Down, Clipper," I ordered the gangly German shepherd who loped alongside me. Rain from a sudden squall lashed down on both of us as we hurried our way to the dock where the 104-foot presidential yacht *Sequoia* bobbed in the inky river.

Jack's father—who had been flourishing after those first wobbly steps he'd made with me—had gifted me the German shepherd puppy for my birthday last November. A Cold War romance had blossomed between Pushinka and Charlie, so now we had puppies— Jack fondly called them pupniks—underfoot, but Clipper was all mine. The first time reporters had spotted me walking him on the West Lawn, they had demanded to know what I'd planned to feed my new dog.

Reporters, I'd answered with a sly grin.

Those selfsame reporters now snapped our pictures like ravenous beasts, nudging Clipper ever closer to my side as Jack waved us onboard. I'd asked everyone to wear yachting clothes and Jack was dressed in his blue nautical blazer, and everyone from Teddy to Robert McNamara had followed suit.

"Nothing for me," I said when the bartender offered me a New Frontier daiquiri—medium, light, and dark rums mixed with sugar, lemon, and lime—once we were safely on deck, the entire party driven inside to avoid the rain. "Just water."

In a rare moment of tenderness, Jack's hand strayed to the telltale bump of my belly. I was due in September and the nation was ecstatic, since the last time a sitting First Lady had been pregnant was Mrs. Grover Cleveland back in 1893. As such, I'd been given carte blanche to take the veil in regard to my responsibilities as First Lady and instead focus on our family.

The only exception had been when I'd worn a Cassini strapless mauve chiffon dress in the French Empire style to see the *Mona Lisa* unveiled in the National Gallery, the culmination of my discussions with Charles de Gaulle and André Malraux, his minister of cultural affairs. The trip to America was the first time Leonardo da Vinci's sixteenth-century objet d'art had been loaned abroad, and thus, its exhibition opening to 1,200 eager ticketholders was my most recent pièce de résistance.

Now it was time for both Jack—who since the Cuban Missile Crisis had dealt with escalating tensions in Vietnam and riots in Birmingham, where fire hydrants were turned on peaceful protesters and police dogs were loosed onto a teenage boy—and me to unpack our schedules and relax.

After the Cuban Missile Crisis, I found I no longer minded that Jack never really confided in me about the events of his presidency that wound up on the evening news. He had always compartmentalized everything—his relationships, his work, his emotions—but I'd proven my worth and Jack knew he could rely on me when the unthinkable happened.

Damp guests packed shoulder to shoulder inside the *Sequoia*'s low-ceilinged cabin, which was festooned with red, white, and blue streamers. The record player blasted Jack's favorite songs—especially Chubby Checker's "Twist"—between tunes from the red-jacketed three-piece band going to town on their accordion and guitars. Toasts to Jack's health and raucous Irish drinking songs punctuated the crabmeat ravigote and asparagus hollandaise. All the while, Jack laughed and joked, a more precious gift than the rare War of 1812 engraving I presented to him.

"Oh, that's all right." I gave Jack a tight smile when a veteran—and quite inebriated—Boston politician smashed his foot into the piece when the boat tilted precariously in the storm. *It's time to tell the bartender to lay off serving the daiquiris.* "I can get it fixed."

"That's a lie," I whispered to Clipper as I placed the ruined engraving next to a pair of boxing gloves gifted to Jack to assist in his battles against Congress. Clipper sniffed the piece of art, decided it wasn't a threat, and sat at attention at my feet. "But tonight's not for me. It's for Jack."

There would be many more birthdays we could spend together, just Jack and me.

My favorite gift was a large envelope I hand delivered to Jack while he sat in the midst of all his friends. "From your father."

Jack sobered at that, for while his father would have loved to celebrate with us, Mr. Kennedy didn't venture into public these days. Jack had torn into his gifts with the speed and attention of a four-year-old child, but he gingerly opened this plain envelope, scanned the contents, and laughed uproariously.

Inside was a facsimile of a lease document. The property listed was the White House, for the term of four more years, signed by three witnesses: Ambassador Joe Kennedy, U. R. Nutz, and I. M. Krazy.

"That's why we love your father." I couldn't have kept the smile from my face if I'd tried, even as Jack and all our guests raised their glasses of 1955 Dom Pérignon in a silent salute to Jack's father. De-

spite Mr. Kennedy's stroke and his continued inability to speak, he
had kept his humor.

Even as I placed the faux lease atop the pile of opened gifts, I worried to watch Jack feasting on the *Bombe Président Sauce chocolat* I'd had
special-ordered just for him. Fresh lines had chiseled themselves
around my husband's eyes and his face was puffy from his Addison's
more often than not, plus his persistent back problems required an
ever more intricate cocktail of medications, even as I tried to steer
clear of Miracle Max's joy juice. If two and a half years of the presidency could wreak this much havoc on him, what might the end of
this term—and perhaps another four years—do?

Worse still, what would Jack do if the unthinkable happened and
he lost next year's election? There were preliminary plans we'd discussed for his presidential library and he'd scouted possible sites via
helicopter, but beyond that . . .

I crated away my worries, packed them on the darkest shelf
in the furthest recesses of my mind as my fingers strummed across
my belly.

This is a time for new beginnings, not endings.

After all, Jack was only forty-six; there was still time to think of all
that was yet to come.

Plenty of time.

Jack was gone again—in Washington while I took the children on
pony rides in Hyannis Port—when my labor began.

And once again, this baby was premature. By three weeks.

I reminded myself not to worry—John had been early and, aside
from his asthma, he was now a healthy, robust boy—as I was flown to
Otis Air Force Base, where a suite had been prepared in advance.

"The president has been called out of a meeting about the Nuclear
Test Ban Treaty," Clint Hill informed me. "He'll be arriving by chop-
per right behind us."

I wanted to wait for Jack, to have him reassure me, but time truly was a fickle thing, for there wasn't enough of it before they put me under.

"Just think," said the nurse as she administered my IV. "When you wake up, there will be a brand-new baby in the nursery with the name *Kennedy* on its bassinet."

I wanted to make her swear that was exactly what was going to happen, but the anesthesia lured me into oblivion before I could form the words.

When I did wake, still groggy with sedative and a double blood transfusion, it was to discover Jack finally at my bedside, a sterile white incubator next to him.

An incubator, not a bassinet. And a somber physician and equally solemn nurse who stood sentinel at the door, where I could see through the window the Secret Service agents posted outside. Fear gripped me and I struggled to sit.

"Is that . . . ?"

"Our son." Jack maneuvered the Isolette so I could slip my arms—still bruised and threaded with IVs—through its portholes. I couldn't hold my tiny baby in my bare hands, but I could adjust the pale blue blanket over his fragile limbs that were no sturdier than a newborn sparrow's wings, stroke his downy brown hair I imagined one day would curl over his forehead just like Jack's.

But deep down in the marrow of my bones I could feel that something wasn't right.

"Your son has been having trouble breathing, Mrs. Kennedy." The pediatrician confirmed my fears as he gestured to the waiting nurse. "We've arranged to transfer him to Boston Children's Hospital for more specialized care."

My alarmed gaze made Jack step closer. "It's just a precaution," my husband reassured me. "Remember how John had to be incubated too? And Lee's daughter spent six months in an Isolette. Look at them now."

That was true, yet his reassurance did little to calm my nerves, especially as the doctor kept looking at the clock.

Time, I thought to myself. *There's never enough of it when you really need it.*

I reached for Jack's hand, even as I kept my gaze on our tiny son. "He needs a name."

"Still Patrick, for my grandfather?"

I nodded. "And Bouvier, for my father."

Jack chuckled, but the sound felt forced. "Patrick Bouvier Kennedy. Caroline will be disappointed to not have the baby Susan that she wished for."

The pediatrician cleared his throat. "Mr. President, Mrs. Kennedy, the ambulance is here for the transfer."

I steeled myself as the nurse wheeled the sterile Isolette from my room at a brisk pace, and my fingers fluttered to my lips as I realized I hadn't even been given a chance to say good-bye. Jack caught the gesture, turned back to press a brief kiss into my temple. "He's going to be fine. I promise."

Then Jack hustled after our son, his suit jacket unbuttoned and flapping behind him. His Secret Service detail closed around him like grim shadows and together their footsteps faded down the corridor, leaving a roaring silence in their wake.

Then I was alone, with only the black crows of my fears to keep me company.

I woke to darkened windows that gave no hint of the coming dawn, while the cold machines inside my room glowed and hummed. Dr. Walsh, my obstetrician, pulled up a plastic chair and sat beside me, clasped my hand. My tongue felt wrapped in cotton swaddling so it was nearly impossible to speak. "Where's Jack?"

"He's on his way back to you from Boston, Mrs. Kennedy." The flicker of Dr. Walsh's gaze away from mine cast a layer of frost around my beating heart. "I'm afraid your son had hyaline membrane disease, which made it impossible for his lungs to work properly."

Your son had . . . *Not has.*

I shook my hands free and held them up, as if that might somehow stop time and keep the roof of my hope from crashing down on me. The air felt suddenly thick and charged, too heavy to breathe.

"Patrick passed just a little bit ago," Dr. Walsh continued, his voice so kind despite the raw cruelty of his words. "Your mother was there with the president and his brother."

Impossible for his lungs to work properly . . . Patrick passed . . .

A moan built at the back of my throat and snapped free in a sudden shockwave of pain, my clenched fist at my lips doing nothing to muffle the animal bellow of agony. Five precious babies I'd carried in this body of mine. Two were already buried in the cold, dark ground, and now Patrick. . . .

Dr. Walsh didn't waver. "Would you like to rest, Mrs. Kennedy?" In one efficient movement, he pressed into my hand a paper cup with an orange pill inside. "The president will be here soon and you need to heal."

You promised, Jack . . . You promised . . .

I took the pill, longing to escape the grief and despair of that starched white hospital room.

Willingly, into darkness I sank.

awoke to a world darker still.

This time it was Jack sitting at my side, his head in his hands. Crying.

No, not crying. Sobbing.

I had only ever seen Jack cry one other time—during the Bay of Pigs—but this was so much worse. Gut-wrenching, silent sobs wracked his entire body. I wanted to rage at him for his broken promise, but the sight of him threatened to shatter what was left of me into a million jagged pieces.

Now, more than ever, we needed each other.

I reached out a heavy hand for him as scalding tears spilled onto my cheeks. I didn't care that he would see them and think me weak; I just let them fall.

"Jack."

His head snapped up at my whisper. A quickly dashed sleeve across his eyes did nothing to smooth his mottled face. "I'm sorry." His voice trembled and he cleared his throat. "I was just thinking . . . of Patrick."

He struggled to bring his features under control. It was a fight he wasn't going to win as his expression fractured anew.

I wondered briefly what it was that had changed for Jack this time, whether he understood what he'd lost because we had Caroline and John now, whereas with my first two pregnancies the idea of a child had been abstract and far off. Or whether it hurt more because Patrick had lived, however briefly.

"You don't have to be brave, not for me." Still attached to an IV and a vast array of monitors, I gingerly shifted until my side was against the cold metal railing of the hospital bed. "Lie next to me."

Jack moved stiffly to accommodate his back brace until he lay beside me, he in his rumpled gray suit and me in my thin cotton hospital gown. Once we were settled, I pressed my head against Jack's chest. The beating of his heart there assured me that life would go on, no matter how shattered we might be now.

"Thirty-nine hours and twelve minutes." His voice cracked on every syllable. "That's all the time our son had, and the whole time he was fighting for every breath he took. Thirty-nine hours and twelve minutes."

I wanted to die then. Part of me *did* die.

With my tears staining Jack's expensive suit, I finally managed to draw a ragged sigh. "Tell me about him. About Patrick."

Jack's chest trembled with his inhale, as if he were gathering much-needed strength to forge ahead. "I held him, Jackie. In my arms. When they knew there was no hope." His free hand clutched the metal railing of the hospital bed so hard his knuckles turned white. "He put up such a fight, but I was holding him when that precious little soul slipped through my fingers. He was a piece of me and of you, and then they took him—our son—away in that tiny white coffin, and I tried to hold on to it, but they wouldn't let me, they had to pry me off. . . ."

He broke off with a jagged sob. The monsoon of our shared grief nearly swept us away then, but we clung to the safe harbor of each other while nurses averted their eyes as they passed outside.

"I'm sorry I wasn't here for you before." He whispered the hot, guilt-laden words into my ear when he could finally speak again. "I should have been here and I wasn't."

"It's all right." I held him as the sharp winds of our anguish continued to howl and tear at us. "I forgive you, Jack. I'll always forgive you."

And I did. I forgave him everything: the years of loneliness, the pain of abandonment, the humiliation of his other women. Inside that stark hospital room, amid the smells of antiseptic and despair, our two broken, freshly scrubbed souls twined together until it was impossible to tell where one ended and the other began. We would be strong, for each other.

So that we might honor our precious son.

The scar from Patrick's death strengthened my relationship with Jack, but every other part of me felt fractured and rubbed raw from the onslaught of my grief. Lee interrupted a vacation with Aristotle Onassis—whom my mother and all the gossip rags believed was the paramour she'd been sleeping with—to be with me in the hospital, but I was so lethargic that most days I could scarcely rise from bed, and my moods swung from a blue-flamed rage to the stygian gloom of utter hopelessness.

"I know it doesn't seem like you'll ever be happy again," Lee said from where she'd curled up next to me in bed like when we were girls. A nurse had tried to insist that she use a guest room, but Lee had proclaimed that I was her sister and she wasn't going anywhere. "You just go ahead and be sad and lean on everyone that's here for you. And know that one day, you'll find a reason to smile again."

I wanted to believe her, but her daughter had lived while my son had been given scarcely two days, had struggled for every breath he took. It was as if my mind knew that the jigsaw pieces of me should fit back together after my son's death, yet I was unable to see the puzzle's picture, much less match the fragments together again.

Thus, I was understandably reluctant when Lee suggested I join her for the second portion of her European cruise with Aristotle Onassis on his richly appointed yacht, the *Christina*.

"It would do you good," Lee proclaimed one dreary morning over my breakfast tray of toast with honey and coffee with skim milk. I wanted to believe her, my own sister, who had almost lost a daughter and taken months to recover from her own dark melancholy. It gave me hope that she *had* recovered. "To breathe that fresh Mediterranean air, to have a change of scenery. To remember that life can be sweet."

I wasn't yet well enough to resume my duties as First Lady, but part of me wanted to stay with Jack. The other part of me—the part that was so inexplicably sad—ached to jump at Lee's offer, to see if sunshine and time away might help me unfurl a bit from the thick loam of anguish I couldn't seem to shake.

"I'll speak to Jack" was all I said, but that wasn't enough for my sister.

"Jack has lived his own life his own way for as long as you've been married. Trust me." She banged the metal breakfast spoon on the plastic tray for emphasis. "He should let you have this one goddamn thing. And if he doesn't, you should seize it for yourself."

"I said I'd speak to him." My iron tone made my sister throw her hands up in surrender. For me to go off gallivanting in Europe with the crooked businessman that was Aristotle Onassis would likely be construed in a negative light, especially when the gossip columns speculated Onassis had designs on becoming brother-in-law to the president of the United States. And I wouldn't have put it past

Odysseus—Onassis—to have just those exact designs. I might have asked Lee about her relationship with Onassis then, but I was so incredibly tired.

Yet travel had always been healing for me. And I wanted to be whole again.

For Jack. For Caroline and John. And for myself.

Lee left, and Jack brought Caroline and John to visit to rouse me from my bed so we could leave the hospital together as a family, bound for Squaw Island and then Hammersmith Farm. Caroline had brought me a bouquet of freshly picked larkspur, black-eyed Susans, and pink trumpet flowers, which I suspected had been filched from the newly renovated White House gardens. Jack, who rarely touched me in public, now held my hand as we walked out the double doors and into the subdued sunshine, his fingers tightly entwined with mine.

As if he needed me.

He continued to hold my hand, to embrace me even—real embraces—in the weeks that followed, as we quietly acknowledged our tenth wedding anniversary. It was a sedate celebration with golf in the afternoon and a few friends enjoying New Frontier daiquiris that evening in Hammersmith's Deck Room, which had been built to resemble an upside-down ship with the beams of the ceiling like the ribs of an ocean vessel. Everyone had gone home and the children were in bed, so the house had fallen quiet when Jack presented me with my gift.

I looked down at the sage-green Van Cleef & Arpels box, at the sparkling emeralds nestled within. "I had it specially commissioned for you. It's an eternity ring," Jack said as he removed the sparkling ring from the box and slipped it over my left finger to join my wedding band. "One emerald for every year of our marriage, with eternity still before us. Because there's no one I'd rather spend forever with than you, Jackie."

Jack had given me a king's ransom in jewels over the years, but already I knew that this ring would be special, that it bound together our history and our future. "I love it," I said. "Almost as much as I love you."

I startled to see two-year-old John suddenly appear at the doorway in his blue pajamas, his dark hair tousled and cheeks rosy from sleep. He glanced around the room and broke into a toothy grin, then pointed at his father and yelled, "Poo-poo head!"

Jack and I stared at each other; my husband's gray-green eyes twinkled with barely restrained mirth. "I don't think I've ever heard anybody call the president of the United States a poo-poo head before."

Our son let out a chortle of glee, then turned and pounded back up the stairs as we burst into laughter.

Jack's face mirrored my simple joy in that moment.

We'll get through this, his eyes seemed to say. *You and me. Together.*

Jack's helicopter continued to arrive every weekend in a chaotic, windswept scene that was half space-age pomp and half *Wuthering Heights* and together we'd watch from the porch as the children tumbled on Hammersmith's lawn with Clipper and Shannon, the new cocker spaniel Jack had received as a gift from the people of Ireland. Our more exotic animals had found their way into zoos, but Jack always had something in hand when he flew up from Washington, which he did every spare moment he had. Last week it was this cocker spaniel puppy; yesterday it had been fragrant rose blossoms freshly cut from the White House gardens. Yet I still felt broken, imagining how things should have been, the baby boy I should have been rocking in my lap.

That was when I finally dared broach the subject of a trip to Greece.

"I don't have to go." My empty hands fluttered in my lap when I finished explaining Lee's plan. "It's up to you."

I knew what the old Jack would have said, that politics came first, but this new Jack only stared out at our children before flicking his gaze to me. This new husband of mine was so quiet, so different. "I think you should go," he finally said.

"Really?"

"Really. I need you by my side from here on out, Jackie, and that means all of you, healthy and whole. If it takes a trip with your sister to do that, so be it."

I reached out and touched his arm, surprised at the effort it took as I let my fingers linger there. "Thank you, Jack."

He still didn't look in my direction, but his voice was gruff when he spoke. "I'm going to miss you like hell, you know."

I threaded my fingers through his, pressed a kiss to his knuckles. Perhaps Lee was right, that this trip would help me find a reason to smile again. And when I did, Jack would be here waiting for me.

did fly to Greece, although I was still weak enough to require oxygen onboard the plane. Still, I felt stronger when I disembarked, as if the briny Aegean air alone was enough to refresh my spirit.

The isles of Greece, where burning Sappho loved and sung . . .

"I'm glad you came," Lee said as she and I boarded the *Christina* alongside a handful of other well-heeled guests, ready to be hosted by Aristotle Onassis once again.

Onassis, whom I'd already met onboard that vulgar boat of his, and whom I'd learned that Jack had ordered Clint Hill to keep me away from during my tour of Greece only two years ago. Jack's belief that the self-styled playboy had an appetite for Kennedy women appeared well founded, for the rivers of sludge in every major tabloid crowed to everyone that Onassis was having an affair with my sister. Publicly, Jack pretended to be above noticing such crass behavior, but Bobby and my mother were fit to be tied now that the gossip was public—Bobby because as attorney general, he'd indicted Onassis for using a front company in America to illegally purchase surplus U.S. oil tankers, and my mother because of the fact that my sister was Catholic, married, and the mother of two children.

For this trip, I had to avoid even the slightest whiff of scandal, something I doubted was possible as Stas walked up the gangplank behind us, one of Lee's hatboxes in his hand.

Surely not even my sister would have invited me on a trip with both her husband and her lover. Would she?

"What is going on here, Pekes?" I whispered to my sister as we stepped onto *Christina*'s main deck, its railings festooned for the occasion with gladioli and colorful roses. Ari was clapping Stas on the back as if they were old friends, but Lee caught my meaning.

"It's complicated, Jacks."

"I'm a smart woman," I responded. "Explain it to me."

"Ari is my own private indulgence," she answered with a shrug, admitting that the rumors were true with that lone sentence. "Stas being here will dispel the rumors."

I scoffed. "Or his presence will cause even more of them to sprout."

"Don't worry." Lee's lips tightened. "It's nothing the First Lady needs to fret about; I swear I won't do anything to embarrass you."

I frowned at Lee's frosty tone, last heard when Jack was running for president, and scarcely kept myself from demanding to know whether this was lust, revenge, or something deeper. Well, I supposed my sister was entitled to some secrets. "The First Lady sounds so dreary," I groused aloud, mostly to defuse the tension. "Why, it should be the name of a horse, not the title of a woman."

My sister's attention had already wandered from me as she approached Onassis, the heat between them so palpable during their prolonged embrace that Stas's eyes narrowed at the way Ari's hand lingered on my sister's back. I almost felt sorry for my brother-in-law, who obviously still loved my sister, until I remembered he had also cheated on Lee while she recovered from their daughter's premature birth.

Still, I wasn't sure this excused infidelity on her part. After all, by that logic, I might have been absolved for sleeping with half the men in Washington by now.

I couldn't understand as we cast off anchor what Lee might see in Onassis, especially after I heard the *Christina*'s staff whispering that Ari had been in Paris with his longtime mistress Maria Callas while Lee was at my bedside in the hospital.

Merde. Were there no faithful men left in the entire world?

Despite his rangy looks, I soon recognized that Aristotle Onassis was an international pirate in Black Jack Bouvier's mold, a multimillionaire with more power and riches than even Blackbeard could have imagined. The *Christina* alone had been stocked with twenty-six vintage wines and eight varieties of caviar, and two chefs—one Greek, one French—were waiting to serve foie gras and steamed lobsters. I'd heard it said that his tanker *Tina Onassis*—named after his ex-wife—was built in Germany, mortgaged in the United States, insured in London, financially controlled from Monaco, and manned by Greeks, all while flying the flag of Liberia.

Despite my misgivings, I was intrigued by the welcome distraction of how this one man juggled such an empire.

"So this is how kings live," I said to him one day as we strolled slowly through the sun-drenched streets of Smyrna—Onassis's birthplace—with Lee and a stone-faced Stas behind us, my silent sister eavesdropping on our every word.

To which Onassis only threw back his head and roared—truly roared—with laughter. "I suppose so," he finally answered.

"Where exactly do all these riches of yours come from, if you don't mind my asking?"

"A little of this, a little of that. Shipping and oil transports, whaling and investments." Onassis gave a one-shouldered shrug. He moved like a potentate through the crowd, as if he owned the very island itself. "I made my first million by the age of twenty-five by purchasing ocean freighters at bargain prices and then charging colossal fees to use them as supply ships during the war."

I arched an eyebrow, doing my best to ignore the small throng of photographers that had sidled next to us. "Isn't that illegal?"

"That depends on how you look at it, my dear. I founded Olympic Airways too. That was entirely legal."

"Founded it in your spare time, I imagine."

Laughter gleamed in Onassis's beady eyes as we approached an atelier with a tasteful display of delicate Greek textiles. "Naturally."

It was an innocent conversation during a blameless stroll meant to help me recover my stamina, but tabloid pictures of me walking through the streets of Smyrna with Onassis at my side were published worldwide.

This at the same time that American papers lamented the fact that I wasn't at my husband's side following the shared loss of our son, that instead I was being entertained halfway around the world by a self-styled playboy renowned as a great lover—an image I suspected Onassis had curated himself.

I wasn't surprised when Jack called.

"It seems like you're enjoying yourself," he said from far away after I congratulated him on signing the Limited Nuclear Test Ban Treaty. Too far away, for I found myself longing for him.

"It's difficult not to enjoy oneself in Greece," I said quietly.

Another pause, as if Jack were choosing his words wisely. But then, Jack always spoke carefully. "I'm jealous, Jackie, and it's a damned uncomfortable feeling. I'm over here trying to secure a lasting peace with the Russians while the gossip columns are chock-full of stories of a brilliantly lit Greek luxury yacht gay with guests, lavish shipboard dinners, and a dance band. I now know how you must have felt before . . . before Arabella died."

A tsunami of guilt pummeled me, for I'd been enjoying myself—or rather, drowning myself in enjoyment to forget my grief—but always there was a niggling voice in the back of my mind, reminding me that this trip was at Jack's political expense, even though he'd said that he wanted me to go, that his mother could help him greet foreign dignitaries at the White House.

That Jack now felt as I had after the stillbirth of our daughter.

I caught a glance in the mirror of the ruby choker at my throat, a token Onassis had gifted me during the trip. He'd given all us women extravagant presents: a gold minaudière purse for Suzanne Roosevelt, diamond-studded bracelets for Lee, and rubies for me. I supposed such luxury was a pittance for the man the press had dubbed "the Golden Greek," but I unclasped it with one hand and dropped it into an open hatbox as if burned.

Suddenly, this trip seemed like a colossal mistake. "I'll be home soon, Bunny," I said to Jack.

"Are you still coming to Texas to help me campaign?"

Jack knew how much I loathed campaigning, yet the staunchly Republican Lone Star state despised my husband with the heat of a thousand midsummer Texan suns. Thus, I'd promised to accompany him in an attempt to deflect some of that animosity. "Of course. I'm counting down the days."

He laughed. "Right. The same way you'd be counting down to a double root canal."

I smiled, hoping he could hear it in my voice. "I love you and I want to help you. That's all that matters."

"Remember how much I love you, Jackie."

Click.

For the first time ever, I couldn't wait to put Europe behind me.

14

November 1963

Both Caroline and John clapped their hands and rocked on their heels as the *Honey Fitz* bobbed over the cerulean waves. We'd taken advantage of the gorgeous fall afternoon by staying on the water all day with the children and their menagerie of dogs. "Throw in another one, Daddy!" cheered Caroline.

Jack peeled from his foot the match to the unfortunate sock he'd already lobbed overboard and dangled it above the Nantucket waters. "Do you see? That white blur over there?" He pulled John onto his lap and pointed east. "Over there . . . It's the elusive Nantucket purple shark!"

His wink in my direction sent me into a torrent of giggles, especially when both Caroline and John peered over the railing to watch their father fling the unlikely bait into the sea. Clipper and Pushinka barked happily, as if they were also in on the joke. "They love to eat socks!" Jack proclaimed before waggling his eyebrows at my feet.

I laughed and unlaced my shoes, tugging free one bobby sock for Caroline and the second for John. "All right, Ahab," I said once Jack had folded me into his arms and our children were using their own pint-sized socks to continue the hunt for the elusive sharks only their father could see. "Just what exactly do you have planned for your next trick?"

He rested his chin on my shoulder, his voice assuming a somber and formal air. "This is Walter Cronkite announcing the winner of the 1964 presidential election. . . ." His palms spread open in front of me. "It's a landslide for Jack Kennedy!"

There he was again, the daring trapeze artist I'd tumbled into love with, hurtling his way through life for the chance at glory.

Jack cleared his throat, suddenly serious. "Of course, for that to happen, first I have to win over Texas."

I leaned against him, loving the solidness of his chest behind me. "I'll be with you every step of the way, Bunny."

Jack turned me in his arms, then shocked the hell out of me with his next question. "What are you planning to wear?"

I stared at him, my eyes wide. In all our years together, not once had Jack ever asked about my fashion choices.

"What?" Jack ran a hand through his hair so it stuck up in all directions. "Have I sprouted horns?"

"Clothes," I finally said. "I think I'll wear clothes."

Jack laughed, an explosive, booming sound so infectious that I couldn't help grin back, especially when the children and dogs joined in. I leaned against the deck railing and lifted our sleepy-eyed son into my arms. "Do you have any requests?"

"There are going to be all these rich, Republican women in Texas, wearing overstuffed mink coats and gaudy diamond bracelets." Jack sat on the hatch, his face tanned and carefree, strong legs stretched out in front of him. "You've got to look as marvelous as any of them. Be simple—show these Texans what good taste really is."

So that night after we'd tucked the children into bed, I stood with pursed lips before my dressing room's tromp l'oeil wardrobe. Its pale blue handpainted doors had been commissioned in Paris to depict *mes objets adorés*—a photograph of me as a six-year-old girl with my father at a horse show, a first edition copy of Jack's *Profiles in Courage*, a portrait of Caroline as an infant, a volume of Baudelaire's poetry, and the watercolor I'd made of the White House. Those doors were open now as I perused the closet's contents before plucking an armful of outfits still on their hangers and parading into Jack's room.

"What's this?" Jack asked, his eyebrows lifted when I dropped the clothing onto his bed.

"An impromptu fashion show."

I held up one dress after another in front of me for his inspection. Our laughter wove together when he'd give a thumbs-up like a Roman emperor from long ago, or occasionally a grimace when I purposely mismatched pieces like some sort of Fashion Week harlequin clown. Our final choices were all tried-and-true veterans of my travel wardrobe: subdued white and beige dresses, suits in blue or yellow, and the Chanel-inspired pink suit with a navy collar and matching pillbox hat that I'd worn for the Lafayette Square meeting and to at least six other events over the years.

"That's one of my favorites," Jack said from where he'd bivouacked in his rocking chair for the show, an Upmann cigar wreathing him in smoke.

Into the pile for Texas it went.

"No other First Lady will ever compare to you," Jack finally said when we turned off the lights, and I could tell he meant it from the way his voice softened. "No matter how hard she tries."

I blushed in the dark, marveling at the power he still held over me, even after all these years and all we'd been through. He reached for me, his hand at the back of my neck, fingers caressing my cheek. "I mean it, Jackie. You're one hell of a woman."

"Show-off," I whispered as I kissed his cheek.

As Jack kissed me, I knew one thing.

I was willing to sacrifice much for this man.

don't like Texas."

I made this announcement from our hotel suite in Fort Worth, a serviceable set of rooms that had been redecorated with Picasso and van Gogh paintings temporarily donated from local Democrats. The bedroom's double mattress had been removed by Jack's aides and replaced with the special one woven from cattle-tail hair that I'd ordered when he'd first won the presidency. I worried that he might need more cortisol tonight to make it through the rest of this trip, for if I was exhausted—which I was, bone weary and scarcely able to prop open my eyes—I suspected he must be doubly so. Yet Jack had the stamina of a small sun, so perhaps he'd surge with fresh flares of energy tomorrow in time to woo more crowds.

Crowds, crowds, and more crowds. All of them gobbling up the sight of us like ravenous beasts.

Jack winced as he shifted over the hot pad I'd placed on the bed for his back, then offered a meager smile as he picked up his reading glasses and the preview copy of an upcoming issue of *Look* magazine, not his usual reading material. "Texas is no Paris, that's for sure," he said as he slipped on his glasses, the ones he never, ever wore in public, lest he lose all his women voters. I liked the look of them on him, the air of studiousness they lent my already bookish husband. "But it could be worse."

I sighed. "Well, no one's booed you so far, and no one's hit you over the head with a protest sign as they did poor Adlai Stevenson."

I still would have been happier if we'd had the added security of the protective bubbletop on the limousine, but Jack had decreed that the top only be used if it was raining, and so far, Texas had given us sunny skies. Fortunately, there had been no posters with Jack's face, damning him for turning America's sovereignty over to Communist nations. Or American flags turned upside down, derided as the Democrats' flag. I wondered if Clint Hill and the rest of the Secret Service had scouted ahead and removed any of those offenses. If so, I'd have to thank them personally.

Jack gave a secret smile as he perused the issue of *Look*. God, he had a great smile.

"What are you thinking?"

He hesitated before handing me the open magazine. "I suppose you may as well see it before it hits the stands."

I didn't know what to expect as I took it, certainly not the black-and-white image of John in his bathrobe peeking out from the secret door of the Resolute Desk while Jack smiled from behind his type-writer. The cover was a color image of Jack with our son. "'The President and His Son: An Exclusive Picture Story,'" I said, reading the title. "When did you have this taken?"

"While you were in Greece." Jack's expression reminded me of our son when he was caught catapulting himself off the veritable cathedral that was the Lincoln bed. "I know you're against having the children photographed, but I invited Stanley Tretick over for the story. I hope you don't mind."

"Not at all." I ran a finger over the glossy photo of my husband and son. "It's precious. I'm surprised John sat still long enough to get the photo."

I loved the sound of Jack's chuckle. "I ran out of planes in my drawer for him that day. So we turned the Resolute Desk into a cave."

"One of the perks of having a presidential father." I closed the magazine and smoothed its cover. "May I keep it?"

Jack arched an eyebrow. "Sure."

"You were great today at the rallies," I added. My husband was accustomed to being revered wherever he went; I knew this trip was a personal sort of hell for him as the Texas crowds were less than ecstatic. "How do you feel?"

"Oh, gosh. I'm exhausted," he said. "But the crowds love you; you should come on these political trips with me more often."

"I'll go anywhere with you, Jack. Even to the moon and back."

Jack took off his reading glasses. "It's not the moon, but how about California? Two weeks from now?"

"I'll be there." I'd go to my grave preferring the quiet tranquility of our own home to any mob chanting my name, but this was for Jack. For us.

One more year of campaigning, five if Jack was reelected next November. Then we'd have peace again.

I bent over him, read the pain in his eyes like a well-read book. It was like old times, when I'd nursed him back to health after his surgeries. We were a team again, Jack and me.

"Do you want me to stay with you?"

He shook his head. "You go on to the other room so I don't keep you up. And don't worry about breakfast tomorrow; stay in bed so you can rest before we head to Dallas."

I pressed a kiss to his forehead, brushed away a lock of the sandy hair I'd always adored. "Good night, Jack."

"Good night, kid."

Back in my room, I perused tomorrow's route map and the frenetic schedule that had both been published in Dallas's newspapers before unpacking my outfit for the next day, running my hands over the freshly pressed pink Chanel-inspired suit Jack had chosen.

Then I climbed into my solitary bed, staring into the all-consuming darkness long after the lights were out.

One more day of campaigning in Texas, and then I swear we'll never set foot in this state again. . . .

PART THREE

· · · · ·

PART THREE

November 22, 1963

I t was hellishly hot that morning in Dallas, the November sun so bright as to be
blinding.

"Be sure to look to your left, away from the president," Dave Powers, the
president's special assistant, instructed the First Lady as the motorcade turned
onto Elm Street on its way toward Dealey Plaza. "Wave only to the people on
your side. If you both wave to the same voter, it's a waste."

The throngs on either side of the street were screaming, and the shouts of her
name were especially loud as they passed the Hispanic areas of the city, following
the First Lady's successful speech in Spanish to the League of United Latin American Citizens the night before. Some held signs that read We Love You Jackie
and several mothers lifted their children's hands to make them wave to the motorcade so they might one day tell their own children they'd greeted the First Lady.
The president laughed when his wife snuck on her sunglasses during empty sections where billboards were the only witnesses.

"They want to see you more than me." He had to raise his voice above all the
usual noise of the motorcade, the engines and motorcycles backfiring. To the First
Lady's eyes, he looked coolly handsome in his blue-gray two-button suit, the dark
blue tie and white shirt with narrow gray stripes she'd ordered for him from Pierre
Cardin in Paris. "Take off the glasses, Jackie."

She did, though it was so bright she wanted to squint and instead dropped her
gaze to her watermelon-pink skirt and the scarlet roses between them as the Lin-

coln Continental crawled past a seven-story brick book depository and emerged into the full sun of Dealey Plaza. The crowd was thinner there.

Nellie Connally saw the First Lady wince and pointed to the blessed darkness of the overpass that beckoned on the plaza's far end. "We're almost through. It's just beyond that." She gave the First Couple a cheery smile. "You certainly can't say that the people of Dallas haven't given you a nice welcome!"

"No, you certainly can't." The president's raised eyebrows—lifted so quickly the governor's wife thought she imagined it—were a coded jest intended only for the First Lady. Then the president waved to a small brown-haired boy dressed in short pants and knee-high white socks. The First Lady blinked, for she almost mistook the child for their son, John Jr., waving from the green.

She turned to the left, with her back to the president, as Dave Powers had instructed her.

It started with a sound she might have recognized, had it not been for the backfiring engines and roaring motorcycles.

If she had, perhaps she could have saved him.

CHAPTER

15

*C*rack.

I thought the sound was a motorcycle backfiring, even as our driver hesitated and the Lincoln slowed to a crawl.

Crack.

Then came Governor Connally's mangled shout. "Oh, no, no, no . . . My God. They're going to kill us all!"

If only I hadn't looked his way in the melee. If I'd looked right—toward Jack—I might have pulled him down.

Crack.

Then came a moment of silence, as if time was taking a deep breath. I swiveled in slow motion toward Jack, confused by the strange and diaphanous pink cloud that haloed around him, his left arm still raised to wave at the child who might have been our son. I recognized the quizzical expression frozen on Jack's face—as if he had a slight headache or was puzzling over a difficult press conference question. He raised his right hand in a gesture of infinite grace, as if to brush back his tousled sandy brown hair, but the motion faltered and his hand fell back limply, revealing something flesh toned.

His skull.

Time folded in on itself, ricocheted forward. At first there was no blood, then, in the next instant, there was nothing but blood.

My husband's bright blood fauceting in a ruby-bright sheet over his suit, spattering the roses between us.

Jack collapsed into my lap and a shard of something that same flesh color rose over his shoulders and tumbled to the rear of the Lincoln, toward the pavement.

I screamed.

Someone heavy and solid crashed into me, sent me spiraling backward. Clint Hill shoved me into the rear seat over Jack, my Secret Service agent blanketing both of us with the heavy weight of his body. Suffocating, I curled around Jack, cradled his ruined head in my lap as the Lincoln's engine roared to life. I was yelling something, I didn't know what. I was shouting and then I was just screaming his name.

The only answer was the squeal of tires on the pavement, Clint Hill yelling in a hoarse voice for me to stay down.

Please, God, please. I was too terrified to think of a more coherent prayer.

"Jack, Jack, can you hear me?" His hair still smelled of November sunshine, now mottled with the pungent copper smell of blood. I crouched over him for an eternity, futilely trying to hold his head together, his blood and gray matter caking my white leather kid gloves. "I love you, Jack."

I love you.

I love you.

I love you.

Unblinking and unable to move with Clint Hill shielding me, I screwed shut my eyes but couldn't unsee the scalding image of the robin's egg–blue interior of the limousine transformed into a charnel house, couldn't block the cloying scent of the Texas red roses now drenched in blood that clung to the inside of my nostrils. I gripped Jack as sirens wailed and the car radio crackled to life. "Jack." I clutched at his ruined head, sobbing. "What have they done to you?"

Our bodies lurched as one when the brakes slammed and Clint Hill vaulted off the top of the Lincoln. It was just Jack and me in that fragile, crystalline moment. Brilliant autumn sunshine transformed the back seat of the limousine into a quiet cocoon; Jack's face was so beautiful illuminated from the forehead down as if he were merely sleeping, as I touched the red rose petals clinging to his body.

It had always been just Jack and me.

Time shattered as people shouted and ran toward the Lincoln and a second Secret Service agent tried to pull me to my feet. "Mrs. Kennedy, you have to let the doctors treat the president."

I shook my head, hard, the rest of my body numb as if suddenly made of stone. "I won't let him go." I ignored the wild-eyed agents, the crush of physicians, and even the frantic Parkland Hospital attendant who arrived with a gurney. "You know he's dead. Leave me alone. I want to stay with him."

I couldn't let them move him, not like this. This would never be Jack.

It was Clint Hill who finally understood my dilemma, who shrugged his wide shoulders out of his black suit jacket and wrapped it gently—as if he were swaddling a newborn—around Jack's head and chest.

Promise you'll stay with my boy. Always.

I recalled the solemn oath I'd sworn to Mr. Kennedy when Jack had lapsed into a coma. I shook off the nurse who made to move Jack's shrouded head as a team prepared to lift him onto a gurney. "I'll do it," I murmured.

I had to run to keep pace as the hospital staff raced to the trauma room. I wanted to scream, to cry, to *hope*.

Until Clint Hill's suit jacket fell from Jack's head and exposed his still-open eyes that no longer saw, that jagged and gaping head wound. I staggered and almost fell.

There was no hope there.

"Mrs. Kennedy, you need to wait in the hallway," the nurse demanded. "The physicians need to be able to work on your husband."

Dazed, I found myself somehow alone in a narrow corridor. A haggard Lady Bird Johnson saw me and embraced me in a fog of musky perfume and fear. "God help us."

I didn't answer, my body still frozen as my gaze strayed to the closed door of the trauma room. And my mind . . .

My mind drifted along somewhere outside my body like a dawdling balloon, unable to comprehend all I'd seen.

Jack was alive this morning.

We made plans to go to California.

Three sharp, shattering cracks.

After some time—thirty seconds, thirty minutes, thirty years—Lady Bird squeezed my hands. "Jackie," she said gently, "do you want a change of clothing?"

I glanced down at my ruined pink suit, seeing for the first time the full magnitude of Jack's dark blood and brain matter that covered my shoes and stockings, my suit and even the gold bracelet I'd clasped on this morning. The gore had stained me to the marrow of my bones, so I'd never be able to scrub myself clean. "No," I murmured softly. "I want them to see what they've done."

They? Who are they? Does it even matter?

I turned my attention back to the trauma room, realizing my mistake in allowing myself to be parted even temporarily from Jack, when a surgeon announced from inside that Jack was still breathing.

It's not possible. No one could survive what I saw. . . .

But if it was possible, I should be by Jack's side.

The door was barred by two stern orderlies who refused me admittance. "Hospital staff only."

"Mrs. Kennedy, would you like a sedative?" Dr. Burkley, Jack's personal physician asked from behind me. He'd been in the Dallas motorcade as well, must have followed us to Parkland.

I shook my head, my thoughts narrowing to one single-minded purpose. "I don't want a sedative—I want to be with my husband when he dies."

Dr. Burkley gestured to the orderlies, who promptly protested when he held the door open for me. "I insist that you allow Mrs. Kennedy to enter."

I pushed past to see a doctor pumping Jack's chest, each push causing a fresh cascade of crimson to spray from his skull onto the floor covered with sheets already sluiced with blood. My legs wobbled so I knelt before they could give out from under me.

I stayed and recited a tumbled litany of prayers without thinking, every forgotten and overlooked prayer from my childhood.

Our Father, who art in heaven, hallowed be thy name . . .

I prayed. I wished. I dared to hope.

I was there, at Jack's side until the emergency room chief finally stopped his work on Jack and approached me, the sharp lines of his face drawn and his eyes dark tunnels of sadness. "Mrs. Kennedy." With his words, that tiny, impossible flare of hope finally guttered and died within me. One look at everyone else's stricken faces told me they felt the same. "I'm afraid your husband sustained a fatal wound."

"May I sit with him?" The words ached in my chest, and my broken voice came out scarcely more than a whisper. "Just for a bit?"

The doctor motioned to everyone and the room emptied, their eyes downcast as if they couldn't bear to look at me.

I sat on a metal folding chair with my husband, alone with Jack for what I suspected would be the last time. I couldn't bring myself to speak, could only sit with my mind and body trapped in that horrible, awful moment, hearing my own fractured heart beat out three echoing words.

Jack is dead.

Jack is dead.

Jack is dead.

No matter how I wracked my mind, I couldn't make sense of this horrific, impossible reality.

Finally, I stood and walked into the hallway, where the team of white-faced nurses and doctors were waiting. I closed my eyes, my tiny nod granting them permission.

"Mrs. Kennedy," a doctor said. "I think you may want to sit in the other room now."

I caught a glimpse over his shoulder of a dark red bronze casket waiting on a rubber-tired dolly, but it disappeared when the physician shifted to block my view. "Do you think seeing the coffin can upset me, Doctor?" I shrugged, my arms out and hands open in surrender.

"His blood is all over me. How can I see anything worse than what I've seen?"

The doctor relented as a nurse used a mattress cover to line the coffin's interior—ostensibly because Jack's head was still bleeding— and winced when she saw me watching. Yet I had eyes only for Jack as a trauma room attendant pulled a fresh white sheet over my husband's face and body.

The fabric was too short; his bare foot stuck out from the bottom, paler than the sheet itself.

I bent down, tucking my hair behind my ears as I kissed his toe, his stomach, then pulled back the sheet to kiss his lips and close his still-open eyes that no longer saw. Only then did they place him inside the casket. A hospital attendant moved to close the lid, but I held up a hand. "Wait."

I tried to tug off the leather glove on my left hand, both it and its mate now black instead of white.

Black, matted with Jack's blood.

Suddenly, I could feel the flecks of Jack's dried blood on my face, forced myself not to wipe them off. Instead, I looked up with wide eyes, unable to put my question into words. A policeman stepped forward.

Funny, I hadn't noticed any police before.

Of course there are policemen. Because Jack is dead.

Assassinated . . .

"I'll help you, Mrs. Kennedy," he said.

And he did, gently coaxing the glove off my hand. Only then could I wrest the gold and diamond wedding ring—so recently joined by the emerald infinity ring of our anniversary—from where I had worn it these past ten years. It, too, was caked with blood, its brilliant facets dulled by Jack's death as I slipped it onto his pinky finger. I wanted to give him something meaningful, and in that moment, it was all I had.

Someone in a naval uniform stepped forward and handed me two dying red roses I recognized from my welcome bouquet. The remainder had been laid to rest in a wastebasket in the trauma room, but now he offered these to me. I recoiled, then remembered my two children at home.

Caroline and John. Dear God, how am I going to tell them about this?

I wanted to collapse then, but I was numb, so very numb. And I needed to be here, for Jack, and for my children.

It would be my job to carry this moment—this entire day—for the rest of my life.

So I accepted the ruined blossoms, tucked them with icy fingers into my pocket.

Still, I refused to leave Jack's side, walked with my empty left hand on his casket as the attendants wheeled him down the silent corridor. An air force aide ran up alongside and offered me a handkerchief. I knew I looked a fright, covered in gore, but I refused the pristine handkerchief, only removed my pillbox hat and handed it to him.

I was ravaged on the inside, but on the outside . . . I meant what I'd said to Lady Bird.

I want them to see what they've done.

"Mrs. Kennedy, you can ride in the follow-up car," someone said as they loaded Jack's coffin into a waiting black hearse.

Again, I shook my head. "No, thank you."

When will they understand? I'm not leaving him.

No one protested when I sat alone next to Jack's coffin as we sped to Air Force One, the November sunlight sneaking through the windows to fall upon that red-gold casket.

Jack was alive this morning and now he's dead. How is that possible?

In the commotion on the tarmac, someone hustled me up the metal stairs. "The president needs you."

I blinked, thinking they meant Jack, only to realize my mistake—and the aide's, for America had no commander until the oath of office was taken—when I stepped inside and saw a gray-faced Lyndon at the far end of the private compartment.

President Johnson.

Jack is dead.

Jack is dead.

Jack is dead.

I swayed on my feet and retreated to the rear compartment, assuming my place again next to the casket. Everything was happening too fast; my beleaguered mind couldn't keep up as the axis of my world spun out of control.

"Jackie." Lady Bird's face slowly came into focus. "Lyndon asked that you make yourself comfortable in the bedroom."

Johnson had seen me then, my hasty retreat. I only shook my head. "I don't want to be a bother."

"You're braver than all of us, my dear," she said kindly. "Come sit where it's quiet for a bit."

I followed her, finding one of my white dresses laid out as Lady Bird closed the door behind her to give me some privacy. I ignored the dress, dared instead to face myself in the mirror for the first time.

Oh, God . . .

I instinctively wiped away the now-blackened blood that spattered my cheeks before I could stop myself, my hands itching to scrub away the nightmare of this day.

Why did I do that? Why did I wipe away Jack? Why did I give away my wedding ring?

Now I have nothing left.

I folded my shaking hands before me, clasped them tight. I hadn't changed when Lady Bird had first suggested it at the hospital, and I wasn't going to now either. Not until Jack was home in Washington.

Whoever had done this would pay. I was proof of the horrors that had occurred, and I wouldn't wipe away the evidence until this day was done.

Another aide knocked hesitantly. "President Johnson would like you to be with him when he takes the oath of office." He stood halfway through the doorway, as if he feared coming too close might somehow fracture me further. "Are you up for that?"

I drew a deep inhale that did little to steady my nerves that jangled loudly in my ears. "At least I owe that much to my country."

The country that murdered my husband.

I shook my head to dislodge the thought. America hadn't killed

Jack. Texas hadn't killed Jack. I didn't know who had, but I had no doubt we'd soon have those answers.

Dry-eyed and hollow with shock, I followed the aide to the gold-carpeted midsection of the plane. "I'm so sorry, Jackie." Lyndon looked like a bronze statue as someone pressed a prayer missal into his hand; apparently a proper Bible couldn't be found on so godless a day. "Bobby suggested I be sworn in before we leave Dallas. In case there's a larger conspiracy . . ."

I only nodded and stood at Johnson's left when he raised his right hand and repeated the oath of office, thereby assuming the presidency of the United States.

"The whole nation mourns your husband," Lady Bird said to me when it was over.

This morning I was First Lady. Now I'm a thirty-four-year-old widow with two small children.

I waited for the storm of grief to break overhead, instead could only marvel at the cold blanket of numbness that had settled over me on this blackest of winter nights. I knew Jack was gone, but it was as if an iron wall had fallen between me and that knowledge so I couldn't touch it, so it wasn't real.

The image of Jack raising his arm to wave to that little boy who looked so like John played over and over in my mind, that quizzical expression on his face as he'd looked at me for the last time.

What could I have done differently? How could I have saved him?

I didn't know. In fact, there was only one thing I did know with any certainty.

Life has no meaning for me anymore.

A world without Jack was shades of gray, and I had no desire to be a part of it.

We landed at Andrews Air Force Base in the gathering dark, the cloudy sky swathed with black streaks like mourning ribbons. As we taxied, I watched from the rear of the cabin as a ground crew wheeled into place the yellow exit ramp. A figure barreled up the still-moving stairs and, like a man possessed, Bobby pushed his way inside the moment the aircraft door opened. He darted down the aisle, paying no heed to Lyndon or Lady Bird, not stopping until he reached me.

"Hey, Jackie." He spoke softly, wrapped a strong arm around my shoulder. "I'm here."

They were the same words he'd said when I'd emerged from a haze of sedatives after Arabella's stillbirth. Because Bobby was always there when I needed him.

"Oh, Bobby." I leaned into his strength as we emerged into the lights and cameras on the tarmac, where grief-stricken onlookers burst into tears at the sight of me. I averted my gaze, stared instead at the military ambulance I knew was bound for Bethesda Naval Hospital in Maryland for the autopsy.

"I have a helicopter waiting for you," Bobby murmured. "To take you straight to the White House." He peered at me, then gave a slow shake of his head, intuiting what no one else had understood that day. "But you're not leaving him, are you?"

"Never."

I continued leaning on Bobby as we sat side by side in the back of the military ambulance, its lights flashing but without sound, a processional for the dead. I'd tried to deny an autopsy, but it was required when a president was slain.

Jack no longer belonged to me, if he ever had. He belonged to the country. To history.

Two hospitals in one day. I was amazed that I was still standing, ached for my bed.

That meant returning to the White House and the fresh round of horrors I would face confronting his closet of suits that would still smell of his Eight & Bob cologne, the horse figurines and toy planes he'd kept stuffed inside the Resolute Desk for Caroline and John. . . .

I swayed in my seat as sunspots exploded around me, the sudden vise around my lungs making it impossible to breathe.

It was Bobby who saved me from the vicious eddies of anxiety that threatened to consume me. "Jackie." His calm voice cut through my panic. "Tell me about LBJ's oath of office. They told me you were there."

I drew in a few sweet gasps of oxygen. I was still carrying this day; my role wasn't over.

Focus on this moment, not the future and certainly not the past.

I managed a wooden nod. "He told me you advised him to take the oath before the plane left Dallas."

To which Bobby gave a sharp bark of laughter, perhaps because he actually saw humor in the situation or perhaps because he'd succeeded in distracting me. "Lyndon's a goddamned liar."

That might have been the case, but the Johnsons had always been kind to me, although Lyndon often referred to Bobby as "that little shitass." But that didn't matter right now.

"Mrs. Kennedy." Dr. Walsh, my obstetrician, who had driven to meet us at Bethesda, approached and pulled out a chair across from us in the waiting area. "You need to rest."

"I can't." I gestured with my hand, a rolling motion. "My mind won't stop."

I nearly sagged with relief when Dr. Walsh riffled through his bag and produced a hypodermic needle. "A dose of Vistaril will help you relax." He waited until I nodded, administered me the injection with practiced ease.

I waited for the drug to drag me into a state of oblivion, but instead I felt a surge of energy, wondered if this was what Jack had felt on the campaign trail and as president, so dog weary but infused with new energy so he might tackle the impossible.

So I found myself sitting with Bobby and Robert McNamara and others who drifted into the hospital's seventeenth-floor presidential suite, telling and retelling the story of the day as if it had happened to someone else. The words came in a terrible torrent, a destructive mudslide intent on destroying everything in its path. Tears were always just a breath away, but no matter how I welcomed them, they never came, could never break through the shield of numbness that still surrounded my mind. Bobby listened to the first telling, his grim face radiating pain. I knew he stayed only for me, but when I finished, he turned and stormed away, as if he couldn't stand to hear another word.

When he returned—and he did return, for that was always Bobby's way—he stood by me with one hand on my shoulder, his back to the rest of the men. "They think they've found the man who did it," he said under his breath. "He's a small-time Communist sympathizer. Lee Harvey Oswald."

I stared up at Bobby. "Jack didn't even have the satisfaction of being killed for civil rights. . . ." The floor rippled beneath me, but Bobby steadied me. "It had to be some silly little Communist."

The rest of the family began to arrive then, save Mr. Kennedy, whom Bobby said they'd decided not to tell just yet. They all looked like shipwreck survivors, and Ethel was stone-faced when she approached, reminding me of my own mother, who alternated between holding me and staring wide-eyed and silent at the bloodstains on my suit. Ethel offered me a tepid embrace, as if she didn't quite know what to do with her arms. "Jack went right to heaven, no stopovers," she said. "At least you have the comfort of knowing he has found eternal happiness."

I reared back as if slapped. No trite offerings would ever bring me solace or comfort about Jack's death, and I found myself suddenly ravaged with jealousy that this was a burden I would have to carry alone. "I would have hoped for more," I snapped to Ethel. "You're lucky to have Bobby. He's here for you."

She patted my shoulder, tears shining in her eyes. "He's here for you, too, Jackie. I'll share him with you."

I glanced to Bobby, found his blue eyes drawn to mine at the same moment. He looked like the strongest thing I'd ever seen, save for those eyes, which were now storm tossed and tortured.

Of all the people in this world, only Bobby's love and adoration for his big brother came close to touching my love for Jack.

Perhaps Ethel was right. Maybe I wasn't entirely alone.

It was Bobby who wordlessly returned my wedding ring, freshly polished and shined. "How did you know?" I asked as I clasped it tight. "I wanted him to have something, but then I had nothing left of him. . . ."

Bobby shrugged. "I just knew."

It was Bobby who remained by my side when I finally accompanied Jack's body—now cradled in a second coffin of African mahogany—back to the White House.

Four thirty a.m., I thought dazedly as I glanced at my watch, then up at the broken piece of moon overhead and the stars, the blinking satellites mixed in. Too early to wake the children.

At this time yesterday, Jack was still alive, his heart still beating.

I retreated to my bedroom after I'd seen Jack's closed coffin installed in the East Room and given instructions for the days to come, slowly removed the corpses of two red roses from my jacket pocket and peeled away the stained pink suit, my ruined gloves, and nylons. Now would be the time to cry, for by morning—true morning—I could scrub away the evidence of tears. But the tears still wouldn't come, somehow encased inside this cold body of mine. Instead, I listened as Bobby's footsteps retreated toward the Lincoln Bedroom, probably still holding the sleeping pill that Dr. Walsh had pressed into his hand. Ethel had left to be with their children at Hickory Hill, but Bobby had wanted to stay with me and with his brother, which I was grateful for.

"Why now, God?" I heard his voice echo as he walked down the corridor. "Why now?"

The door shut, but it wasn't much longer before a new sound replaced the roaring silence. It took me a moment to identify the low moan punctuated by wild, howling sobs that built until finally breaking into a mournful wail.

It would have been easier to turn away, to allow Jack's brother space by pretending I didn't hear. But Bobby's grief gave voice to everything I wanted to feel, everything some invisible steel wall was holding at bay.

So I wrapped a bathrobe around me and padded on silent feet down the hallway. I didn't knock, just nudged open the door to find Bobby sitting on the edge of the Lincoln bed, head in his hands as his entire body shook with the magnitude of his grief.

For a moment, he might have been Jack, trapped in the throes of the Cuban Missile Crisis or having just lost his infant son.

Wordlessly, I sat beside him, wrapped my arms around him, and pressed his head to my shoulder.

In the dark of those early morning hours, the first full day without Jack, together we grieved.

I spent much of that sleepless night writing a letter to Jack, recounting my love for him and the life we'd built together and promising that I'd safeguard his legacy, and his children. Each painful word on the light blue page of stationery had wrung something critical from me, and afterward, I lay alone in my cold bed and willed sleep to come. Instead, I watched with sightless eyes as a pale dawn streaked the sky outside.

Jack had been my raison d'être, my reason for being. Now he was gone and I was cast adrift as surely as an autumn leaf in a sudden storm.

I rose to find a starched black dress had been laid out for me. The watermelon-pink suit had disappeared, ostensibly whisked away by Nancy Tuckerman so I'd never again have to face the brutal reminders that clung to its every thread.

I dressed mechanically and gathered my letter to Jack and every ounce of strength I possessed before walking to the children's nursery. The entire White House seemed to droop with the weight of its grief, every voice silenced, every bit of happiness leached from its walls. There was only a hollow and echoing silence outside the children's rooms where the gaiety of laughter and singing usually greeted me.

The nursery door opened and I startled when Bobby slipped out, scrubbed a hand over his haggard face before he saw me. His features smoothed, but I could still see the fissures of pain that streaked beneath the surface, his normally glacial eyes now the color of a washed-out sky. "I told John," he said. "I told him that his father had gone to be in heaven with Patrick. I'm not sure he understood."

"Of course he didn't." I sighed, heartsick to my very core. "John is only two, three in a few days."

Not a few days . . . in two days.

My eyes burned to realize that my sweet little boy, who loved to smile and play with airplanes, was going to spend his third birthday at his father's funeral.

I'm living someone else's life, I thought as I swayed on my feet. Someone else's horrible, tragic life.

It was Bobby's hand under my elbow that steadied me.

"And Caroline?" I asked.

"Maud Shaw already told her. Last night."

Never before had I been so grateful to Maud Shaw, and to Bobby. I'd been agonizing over how to phrase each word to tell my children that their father was gone forever, but these two kind souls had found a way to lighten my burden.

"I'll do anything you need, Jackie. Just say the word and it's done."

"Stay with me?" I asked. "While I see them?"

"Of course."

So Bobby stood at the doorway while I entered the nursery to find the black-clad and somber shadows of my children seated at their child-sized table, a spread of paper and an abandoned rainbow of crayons on its surface. Six-year-old Caroline glanced up with red-rimmed eyes and ran to wrap her arms around my legs. I knelt, drawing her into an embrace and beckoning for John to join us.

For the first time, the tears came. Finally, the dam within me opened and there was no calling back the water.

"Miss Shaw said God is making Father a guardian angel to watch over me and you and John, and that his light is shining down on us now," Caroline said as she snuffled into her sleeve. "Is that true?"

I hesitated, wishing I could imagine any sort of light or warmth shining down on us. I really believed in God and I believed in heaven, but where was God now? All I felt was the bleak pit of despair that I was tumbling through, no end in sight. Yet I nodded for Caroline. I would be strong for her and John, only because I had no other choice.

"I'm going downstairs to your father's coffin, to pray for him," I said as I used Bobby's handkerchief to wipe the tears from all our cheeks. "Would you like to come?"

Caroline nodded, but first I gave the children a task with their crayons and paper. Only the chirping of their pet canaries broke the oppressive silence while Maud Shaw assisted them and I stepped outside to give further instructions for the funeral. When the children finished, I held Caroline's hand and Bobby took John's, and we all proceeded silently downstairs with precious packages clutched to our chests. The chandelier overhead in the East Room had been draped with black crepe interspersed with branches cut from Andrew Jackson's magnolia tree outside on the South Lawn. Beneath it, Jack's casket remained closed, because although I'd been informed that it was customary to leave open the casket of a head of state, I'd demanded in an iron voice that things be done differently.

No one, *no one* was going to gawk or photograph Jack as he was now.

Caroline knelt next to me in front of the black-draped funeral bier that I'd ordered to be modeled after Abraham Lincoln's catafalque following his assassination.

History is a source of strength to us.

I remembered Jack's statement during my White House special and was determined to use that sacred history to cement this final chapter of his legacy. That was why I'd chosen to oversee nearly every detail of Jack's memorial and funeral, just as I'd done for my father so many years ago, this time also needing something to keep me tethered to this world. Caroline leaned over and patted my hand once during the private Mass, gazed up with such an expression of compassion and intelligence and love, as if she had to be strong for me.

"Is Father really gone?" Caroline managed to ask when we approached the four-man honor guard. I pretended not to see the tears welling in the eyes of those grown men as they overheard my daughter's question. "Forever?"

I wanted to lie, to tell her that she'd see her father soon, that this was all a horrible mistake. Instead, I pressed a kiss onto her temple and said the only word I could say. "Yes."

I watched my little girl grow old in that moment as she straightened her spine and bit her lip, forcing herself to be brave.

It was with my two children in mind that I approached Miss Shaw, who had taken up a post nearby in case Caroline or John needed her.

"I'm so sorry, Mrs. Kennedy." Her eyes were bloodshot but clear, and her British accent fortified me with its stiff-upper-lip cadence. "I wish there was something I could do for you."

I tried to smile. "Just keep the children happy," I managed. "That's all you can do for me. As long as I know they are happy, it will be a great help."

For these two children were my future. Everything I did from this day forward, I would do for them.

Now I gave a terse nod to Bobby, who moved with the head of the honor guard to open Jack's casket. While I didn't want the public or the press to see Jack this way, I couldn't deny my children's right to see their father one final time.

Yet the figure that laid inside bore resemblance to something in Madame Tussauds. A wax dummy of my husband, his face pale and doused with powder. With trembling hands, I unpacked my package of treasures and arranged them around him. My letter to him, a pair of extravagantly expensive cufflinks I'd picked on a whim for our first anniversary, and a piece of scrimshaw carved with the presidential seal I'd given him last Christmas that was one of his prized possessions. Next, I laid two letters next to him, which the children had finished writing with their crayons before we came downstairs. John—too little to know the alphabet—had scribbled with a crayon on a blank sheet of white paper, but with Maud Shaw's help Caroline had painstakingly written a letter with a blue ballpoint pen.

Dear Daddy,

We are all going to miss you, Daddy. I love you very much.

Caroline

I stifled a sob as I tucked the children's letters in around their father, then stepped back so Bobby could place his own keepsakes next to his brother. He'd shown them to me while the children had finished their letters: a silver rosary and a PT-109 tie clasp commemorating Jack's heroic service in the Pacific.

Then I moved forward, caressed Jack's sandy hair one final time. I lingered until Bobby touched my arm, offered a pair of scissors a White House aide had magically procured. So I snipped a lock of Jack's hair, the last piece of him I'd be able to keep as aides waited to carry his coffin to sit in state beneath the Capitol dome.

To the Capitol, and then to Arlington. And then he'd be gone from my life forever.

After Bobby closed the coffin lid, I sagged under the weight of it all and let him lead me from the East Room by the arm. I focused with each step on not falling apart, breathing to keep my body from shattering into pieces, detesting every moment that took me farther and farther from my husband, from those days and hours when he was alive and at my side.

It was then, as Jack's body was being moved, that we learned that a nightclub owner in Dallas named Jack Ruby had shot Lee Harvey Oswald while he was being transferred from local to federal authorities. The story Ruby gave was that he'd shot my husband's murderer in order to spare me the anguish of having to testify at Oswald's trial. With those moments in the motorcade constantly on replay in my mind, I didn't know whether to curse or thank Jack Ruby.

Two hours later, Oswald died. And with him, the answers to why he had killed my husband.

Was it any wonder that later in the night, after Bobby and I had visited the Rotunda where Jack's coffin laid in state and where

250,000 mourners had lined up for three miles to pay their respects, I called for Dr. Jacobson?

"I don't think you should see him." Bobby ran an angry hand through his old-gold hair in a gesture that was so poignant—so like Jack—that I almost crumpled.

"I asked him down from New York this morning. He's the only one who can help me." One glance at Bobby and I knew I'd misspoken. "Please, Bobby. Jack trusted him and so do I."

Bobby rolled his shoulders, as if shrugging off an annoyance.

And so Dr. Jacobson—still known as Dr. Feelgood among his cadre of celebrity clients and who had helped both Jack and me on our way to Europe—was ushered into my bedroom in the White House. He uttered some benign condolences I scarcely heard, then retrieved from his leather medical bag that treasure I so desperately sought.

"This will help me sleep?" I asked. So far, none of the sedatives had done any good, had only keyed me up, and I was at the end of my reserves.

Dr. Jacobson displayed the medical cocktail like a preening peacock. "Guaranteed, or my name isn't Max Jacobson."

That was enough for me. I bared my arm, let him inject the full syringe into my vein.

Bobby had been silent during the entire exchange but leveled a black glare at the closed door after the doctor had left with promises to return the following night. "I tried to get my brother to stop seeing the infamous Dr. Feelgood," he said. "Especially after Jack told me he used crap like monkey glands in his concoctions. And do you know what Jack said?"

I raised an eyebrow, wondering whether it was my imagination that my limbs already felt heavier, or whether the injection was already working its magic. *Please God, let me sleep tonight. . . .*

Bobby scoffed. "He said he didn't care if it was porcupine piss, that it was the only thing that relieved his back pain."

"That sounds like Jack." I smiled and closed my eyes, leaned back into the cloud of pillows on my bed. "I have no idea what was in that shot. All I know is that my nerves have finally begun to settle."

Was it my imagination or did Bobby press a gentle kiss into my hair then?

"That's good enough for me," he whispered as he turned out the lights. "I wish you a dreamless sleep, Jacks."

So did I, for the nightmare of Jack's funeral was soon to follow.

The day of Jack's funeral passed in a blur, like a strip of film run through a projector too fast.

"You can't walk behind the coffin." Dean Rusk crossed his arms in front of his chest and stared me down as I prepared to leave the Rotunda. I clasped my black-gloved hands and gave my husband's secretary of state a steel-lanced glare through the black gauze of my widow's veil as I waited for him to finish. "We've received death threats this morning for both Charles de Gaulle and Khrushchev's emissary for the funeral. Lee Harvey Oswald spent thirty-two months in the Soviet Union so this could be part of a larger conspiracy. There's concern among the FBI, the CIA, the Secret Service—everyone—that all the other dignitaries and heads of state will follow your lead if you walk behind the coffin."

We had just finished the round of somber and official eulogies in the Rotunda, where Caroline and I had kissed Jack's coffin for the last time before my daughter was transported by car from the Capitol to meet me at St. Matthew's cathedral. John had been led away by Maud Shaw long before then, following his bouncing over the laps of the Johnsons in the solemn limousine ride from the White House. Only Bobby had been able to calm him, for I couldn't bring myself to rebuke him on this, his third birthday, which he had to spend attending his slain father's funeral. "They can ride or do whatever they want to," I said when Rusk finished his tirade. "I'm walking behind the president to St. Matthew's."

The former president, I should have said but stopped short of correcting myself.

As I took my place behind the casket to walk the eight blocks to the cathedral, I heard Rusk speaking to Charles de Gaulle, only for the commanding French president to silence him. "President Kennedy died like a soldier under fire," he said in accented English that brooked no argument before he turned and offered me a stiff military salute so full of reverence that I almost lost my composure. "I shall be honored to walk with Mrs. Kennedy."

And de Gaulle did walk, along with representatives from ninety-two other nations. Jack's life—and death—had touched the world.

Thus, the world had come to pay their respects.

A hush fell when the funeral cortege began to move, Jack's coffin lifted by the caisson that had carried Franklin D. Roosevelt's body in 1945 and drawn by six eerily identical white horses. The only sounds that accompanied our footsteps came from the muffled cadence of four drums I'd had modeled after those used in the American Revolution and occasional outbursts of weeping from the hundreds of thousands of spectators gathered along the route. With Bobby and Ted behind me, I narrowed my focus to the riderless horse—a sweating black gelding I later learned was named Black Jack as in some strange sign from above. The animal walked behind the caisson, carrying a sheathed sword and boots reversed in their stirrups to signify a fallen hero.

A fallen hero and president. A brother, father, husband, friend.

John looked up at me with wide eyes once I reached St. Matthew's and was reunited with my children. "Where's my daddy?" he asked. I'd walked each of those eight blocks stone-faced and with as much majesty as I could muster, but my son's simple question caused me to shake with uncontrollable sobs.

As before, it was Caroline who comforted me. "You'll be all right, Mommy," she whispered. "Don't cry. I'll take care of you."

My children are a source of strength to me. . . .

I repeated this new mantra while Cardinal Cushing, who had married Jack and me ten years prior, led the funeral Mass, yet I heard scarcely a word. Afterward, I led Caroline and John out onto the steps of the cathedral, all of us squinting into the somber November sunshine.

As Jack's coffin rolled past strapped to the gun carriage for its final journey, I recalled how John had loved to play soldiers with his father, how his natural exuberance had disrupted a Veterans Day commemoration at Arlington earlier in the month.

I leaned down to whisper in my son's ear. "John, you can salute Daddy now and say good-bye to him."

My sweet little boy who had turned three years old that morning relinquished my hand, then stepped forward and stood at attention in his blue suit before lifting his tiny hand in a perfect salute.

Click.

I didn't have to hear the cameras to know that unlike all of us, that brutal, precious image would withstand the cruel ravages of time.

No matter what catastrophe had befallen us or how bone weary I felt, Jack would have insisted that we laugh and celebrate the birthday of his three-year-old son, funeral be damned.

So despite the bleak atmosphere, a small group of friends and family helped me hang colorful balloons and crepe streamers upstairs in the White House. Together, we mustered convincing smiles for John before he blew out the three candles on his ice cream cake. It was a small blessing that my son was oblivious to the atmosphere of forced frivolity and also untroubled that his black-clad mother was overwrought about how long she might impose on Lyndon and Lady Bird Johnson now that the White House was their home, not ours.

"I'm glad they're happy," I murmured to Miss Shaw as John tore away the paper on his gifts. I meant every word, for some sliver of my heart rested easier knowing my children were taken care of. "Thank you for all you've done."

"Of course, Mrs. Kennedy," Miss Shaw said as Bobby helped John unwrap his final gift. "We're all here for you, you know."

"Mommy, look!" John ran up with his model of Air Force One, Bobby close behind. "It's Daddy's plane!"

My heart fractured anew as I recalled the times Jack had taken our son to the Marine One helicopter hangar, how they'd both donned pilots' hats in the cockpit, John pushing the control stick with his pudgy hands and making all the right noises for taking off while Jack took orders from Flight Captain John.

"It certainly is." I touched my nose to his, just as one of the guests entered and called John's name.

I didn't have to wait long for the inevitable response.

Three, two, one . . .

"Who the hell invited him?" Bobby scowled as he jutted his chin at the short, olive-skinned man asking John to explain how the plane flew. Aristotle Onassis chose that moment to let out a great belly laugh, the sound of which seemed to surprise him and everyone else.

"I did." I crossed my arms over my chest, daring Bobby to counter. "He called after Dallas and offered to help however he could. Ari was a comfort during my recuperation after Patrick's death and I thought Lee might appreciate having him here."

I suspected Bobby would take umbrage over my facilitating Lee's reunion with her married lover—although she had discreetly slipped out of the room a few minutes ago—but he locked on to a different target.

"Ari?" Bobby's visage darkened further. "You're awfully comfortable with the man I indicted for using a front company in America to illegally purchase surplus U.S. oil tankers. That slimeball was a snake then, and he's still a snake."

"I know he's not a Kennedy family favorite. . . ."

Bobby snorted, then turned his back to Onassis. "Yeah, and the pope's just a little bit Catholic. If it was up to me, I'd sink Onassis's fucking yacht, and the damn Greek with it. Aside from his bankroll, I don't see what you or your sister see in him."

Decidedly *not* a Kennedy family favorite.

"Play nice, Bobby." I glanced to where Onassis approached Caroline. Unlike John, my daughter was old enough to understand the magnitude of the day and had set herself apart in the far corner of the room, ignoring her brother and cousins. She was the more reserved of my two children, always preferring solitude and her horses to the attention John craved. I moved to join her and overheard Onassis's advice from where he was crouched beside her.

"Miss Kennedy, it's a Greek custom that there should be a few tears at every wedding and a little laughter at every funeral," he said. "So if you find anything funny tonight, don't be afraid to laugh. I suspect your father would love to hear the sound."

He stood and patted my shoulder as we passed before resuming his place on the floor next to John. I fished for my daughter's hand and squeezed it.

We'll weather this storm, I hoped that brief connection said, and Caroline seemed to understand as she laid her head in my lap.

Perhaps I could persuade Bobby to mind his manners, but it was impossible for one lone woman to wrangle all the Kennedy men.

"Onassis," Teddy piped up from his spot on the couch, a glass of bourbon in hand. "What are you discussing with my nephew?"

"The finer points of Greek shipping," the filthy-rich magnate responded. "Also, how to become a pirate."

I smiled when Caroline lifted her head and gave what might have been a muffled giggle, thankful for the playful spark that lit my daughter's eyes, no matter how briefly. But like a territorial dog, Teddy wasn't standing for this interloper making inroads into his family.

"Piracy is illegal in America." Teddy suddenly removed a ballpoint pen from his pocket and scratched something on his napkin before presenting it to Onassis with a flourish. I noticed then that Ted wasn't too stable as he strode across the room, and reminded myself to cap his drinks at future White House events.

Except Lady Bird Johnson was now America's First Lady. Which meant I would no longer plan any White House events. When life changes, it does so in the blink of an eye.

Onassis's overexuberant laugh knocked aside the grief that waited to ambush me. "An ersatz contract?"

Ted only shook the paper in Ari's face. "Stating that you'll give up half your material assets to the poor in South America."

To my surprise, Onassis accepted the napkin and signed it, the pen cap pinned between his lips as he then kept writing. "What are you doing?" Teddy demanded, as if this were a real business deal.

"Just adding a few codicils in Greek." Onassis winked at me as he spoke around the cap. I couldn't help but smile back, despite Bobby's and Teddy's combined glares.

"What do they say?" Teddy demanded.

"That's for you to figure out." Onassis looked downright smug as he pushed the napkin back to Teddy.

Odysseus indeed, always dancing one step ahead of everyone else in the room.

Bobby rolled his eyes, but fortunately Maud Shaw interrupted to escort the children to bed. I knelt before them and kissed their foreheads as Jack had always done. "Thank you for being brave today," I whispered to Caroline. And to John, who still clutched his model of Air Force One, "Happy birthday, my little pilot."

I watched as they trundled away to the comfort of their warm beds, where I prayed that pleasant dreams awaited them. Behind me, Bobby murmured to the rest of the party, who filed out as well.

All save one.

"I have something for you. A gift." Aristotle Onassis reached inside his suit pocket and retrieved a small rectangular package. There were no jaunty bows, just a black ribbon around the silk-wrapped package. I was surprised when I opened it to find a simple book.

"*The Greek Way* by Edith Hamilton," I read, then arched an eyebrow at Onassis in question.

"It is a collection of essays, like your husband's *Profiles in Courage*, but about preeminent figures of Athenian literature and history. Heroes in a world of suffering where men struggled on in the face of tragedy and fickle gods." He gently flipped the book's pages so I could see some sections had been underlined by a meticulous hand. "There is wisdom in these pages, words to help you heal, if you take the time to read them."

"I will." One passage caught my eye and I stopped to skim it.

"'When the world is storm-driven and bad things happen,'" I recited, "'then we need to know all the strong fortresses of the spirit which men have built through the ages.'"

It sounded like something Jack might have written, or at least agreed with.

"I'll read it," I promised Onassis. "Perhaps not today, but one day."

"You have to mourn, Mrs. Kennedy, but soon, you must live." Aristotle Onassis clasped my hand between his so I felt the strength there, wished I could draw upon its silent well. "I meant what I said on the telephone. I am always only a phone call away."

I watched Onassis go, then returned to the couch in silence until Bobby joined me, both of us sitting in companionable silence fraught with our own grief.

Finally, Jack's brother leaned forward, elbows balanced on his knees. "Shall we go visit our friend?"

I knew who he meant, and offered a silent nod before stopping upstairs to take a coat from my room. A small slip of paper waited on the bed, and curious, I unfolded the note.

Good night, my darling Jacks, the bravest and noblest of them all.

—L

I gave a soft smile at my sister's sweet note. I might have invited her to join us, but somehow that felt like an intrusion. Instead, I gathered a small bouquet of lilies of the valley from the eighteenth-century vase in the second-floor hall. Together, Bobby and I climbed into the waiting black Mercury that he had arranged in advance, my Secret Service detail following at a discreet distance when we parked on Hatfield Drive and entered Arlington's main gate.

This was the second time Bobby and I had visited Arlington that day, for earlier that afternoon we'd laid Jack to rest.

Dressed in my widow's black, I had stood beside Bobby to light the eternal flame I'd asked to be built at Jack's gravesite, inspired by the flame at the Tomb of the Unknown Soldier Jack had rekindled during our trip to Paris. For now, it was a makeshift Hawaiian torch under a wire dome, covered with dirt and evergreen bows and fed by a propane tank hidden several hundred feet away. *That will need to be replaced*, I thought distractedly. *One day.*

Together, we had watched as Air Force One flew overhead, the pilot dipping the plane's wings in tribute. I might have had Jack laid to rest anywhere, but I requested that he be buried at Arlington after I recalled him telling me he could have stayed at Arlington House forever, that the view from the lawn in front of old Bobby Lee's plantation house was downright spectacular.

I stood there seeing the same vista Jack had seen, and somehow, I imagined him standing beneath one of the towering trees and nodding his approval.

You're right, Jack, I thought to myself. *It is spectacular.*

"Mrs. Kennedy." The official at my elbow interrupted my macabre reverie. "There's about to be a twenty-one-gun salute."

I was grateful for the warning, for each explosion had brought hurtling back with crystal clarity those terrible moments in Dallas. I couldn't help flinching, clutching the crisply folded flag that had draped Jack's coffin and gritting my teeth as I struggled to maintain my composure.

Bobby—my Rock of Gibraltar—stepped closer, offering me his silent strength until the barrage ended.

With the final shot, Jack's funeral—and his short forty-six-year life—was consigned to the past. Only one question had remained in my mind as we'd walked in stillness back to the White House and my children.

Where do we go from here?

Later that evening, I still didn't have an answer to that question as

Bobby and I stood gazing out at Washington's night-filled skyline. As I looked at the stars, I recalled the lines Bobby had borrowed from Shakespeare for his eulogy to Jack earlier that day.

> *When he shall die,*
> *Take him out and cut him out in little stars,*
> *And he will make the face of heaven so fine*
> *That all the world will be in love with the night*
> *And pay no worship to the garish sun.*

Jack had always been my sun, my day . . . I wasn't ready to face this endless night.

"I'm sorry," Bobby said.

"For what?"

"For all of this." He swept an angry hand toward his brother's grave. "I should have stopped him from going to Dallas. We knew the political climate was shit in Texas. . . ."

"Stop." I gripped his forearm, gave a single, violent shake of my head. I took Bobby's hand in my gloved one, forced him to look at me—really look at me—in the darkness. "None of this is your fault."

Me, on the other hand . . .

If only I'd looked right. If only I'd pushed Jack down . . .

I didn't realize I'd spoken aloud until Bobby made me face him, one hand on each of my shoulders. "If I can't blame myself, neither can you." He touched my cheek. "Deal?"

In that moment, I was so thankful to have Bobby, to not be so terribly, horribly alone. Of all the Kennedy brothers, Bobby was the one who was most like his father. He was also the most like me. "I'll try."

With Bobby watching at a discreet distance, I added the bouquet of lilies I'd taken from the White House as my silent contribution to the flowers, military brassards, and cockades left at my husband's grave. A streak of orange pollen from the lilies marred my sleeve, but I left it there, a reminder of this moment.

Was what we had worth this moment? All this pain?

I already knew the answer to that: without Jack as my husband, my life would have been a wasteland, and I'd have known it every single day. Just these few days without him had taught me that.

"I'd do it all again," I whispered to Jack, my hands digging into the freshly turned earth. "All of it—the tears and heartache, those one thousand and thirty-six days of magic."

Because that's how many days Jack and I had lived in the White House. I'd counted them as I'd wandered the empty rooms I'd redecorated—including the newly completed full renovation of the Oval Office I'd planned to surprise him with after our return from Dallas— rooms we'd never again share together.

One thousand and thirty-six. And now how many days must I face without you, Jack?

I didn't know the answer to that. I only knew that he was free. . . . But I had to continue to live.

And I would, one desolate and colorless day at a time.

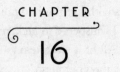
December 1963

was a living wound.

A beating, bleeding wound.

The media claimed I both broke the nation's heart and held the country together after Jack's assassination, yet I wanted to rage when I heard people say that I was poised and maintaining a good appearance, for I wasn't a movie actress. The truth was I was alone: cold all the time as if trapped in some personal winter while wandering a landscape as black and white and stark as a printed page.

Only days after the funeral, I'd arrived at Hyannis Port for Thanksgiving, had ignored the Rah-Rah Girls and gone straight to Mr. Kennedy's room. The shipwreck that was old age was apparent in the tufts of white hair like cotton on Mr. Kennedy's head and in the sagging crevices carved ever deeper around his eyes and mouth. I felt a guilty twinge of relief that Jack at least hadn't suffered in death, that he hadn't been confined to a wheelchair like his father, mute and paralyzed. That had been Jack's greatest fear before his spinal surgery, that he'd be forced to live a half-life.

He had, but a half-life in years instead of actions. I wasn't sure which was worse.

I pulled a wooden stool next to Mr. Kennedy's bed, sank onto it gratefully. "Hello, Poppy Doodle," I said. "It's been a long time."

In reality it had been only weeks since I'd seen him last, but the world had transformed—*I* had transformed since then.

Now I dared to look into Mr. Kennedy's blue eyes and nearly wept at the lightning streaks of raw grief there. I knew how my three dead children had passed, knew every detail of their brief stories. Mr. Kennedy was trapped here, unable even to attend his own son's funeral, but I suspected he would want to know Jack's story.

"Would you like to hear?" I asked him. "How it happened?"

He'd blinked once, so definitive an answer that I hadn't needed to move his chalkboard into his age-speckled hands. Instead, I recounted those horrific events once again, how my lap had become Jack's blood-stained pietà, how they'd finally wheeled him away from me in the hospital.

When I finished, I wiped away the tears that had slipped down Mr. Kennedy's cheek. "When this is over," I said with a ragged sigh, "I'm going to crawl into the deepest retirement there is."

I meant it too. The only question was whether anything could ever extinguish the hell I now bore within me.

I had a duty to safeguard Jack's legacy, which meant reliving his final moments in Dallas to forever commit them to history. That was my burden to carry.

Later that same day, I drew a long drag on my cigarette and knocked its ashes into the Waterford crystal ashtray, my gaze skittering away from William Manchester's penetrating stare. I knew I'd eventually be interviewed by the federal Warren Commission investigating Jack's death, but I'd asked to meet with Mr. Manchester, a writer whom I trusted, in order to immediately record the events of Jack's assassination for posterity and preempt other salacious retellings.

And to try once again to purge myself.

He topped off both our daiquiri glasses before asking me his next question. "Do you think the president's assassination was the result of a conspiracy or even of governmental involvement?"

I'd given myself a set of simple commands to follow this morning when I'd woken up, to ensure that I made it through the day. *Brush your teeth, Jackie. Sit with the children during breakfast, Jackie. Answer Manchester's questions and be done with it, Jackie.*

Now I was regretting not staying in bed.

"What difference does it make whether he was killed by the CIA, the FBI, the Mafia, or simply some half-crazed misanthrope?" I lit a fresh cigarette, ignoring the already overflowing ashtray. "It won't change anything. It won't bring him back. What matters now is that Jack's death be placed in some kind of lasting historical context."

Each time I recalled the shooting, I hoped it would ease this oppressive weight I'd been carrying since that awful day. Instead, the weight only shifted and settled more firmly upon my shoulders, so each detail remained more vivid than a full-length Technicolor feature. I wondered if time would change my recollection, whether the nightmares from the backseat of a midnight-blue Lincoln Continental limousine that woke me screaming in my sleep would change my memories.

Now that I was speaking to William Manchester, that day in Dallas would be recorded for posterity. History would know what had been done to Jack, what the nation and I had endured. Perhaps then I could rest.

In the meantime, the grief inside me was a living animal, clawing in rage and trying to escape.

But it couldn't escape. I couldn't escape.

Everywhere I looked were reminders of Jack.

I twisted the pink diamond ring on my right hand, mulling over the new memory that went with this gift from beyond the grave. Evelyn Lincoln had delivered the ring with tearstained eyes after it was sent to the White House, a forty-seven-carat pink kunzite surrounded by twenty diamonds that Jack had picked out from Van Cleef & Arpels when he was in New York City after Patrick's death.

Jack and I were closer than ever in those days. . . .

"It was meant to be your Christmas present," Evelyn had blinked back tears when she'd placed the velvet box in my trembling hands. I'd taken off my wedding band and the infinity emeralds Jack had given me for our anniversary, but I couldn't bring myself to put this ring away. Not yet.

I stared at Mr. Manchester's kindly face, willed my own tears not to fall. I'd anticipated this question and given its answer much thought since agreeing to this interview, having searched for a fitting epitaph for Jack's presidency, a way to solidify his place in history. And in the wee hours of dawn, I thought I'd finally found one.

There was a reprise from the musical *Camelot* that captured how I wanted those one thousand and thirty-six days to be remembered, in a shining city upon a hill where valiant men danced with beautiful women, when hope reigned and great deeds were done.

I took another drag on my cigarette to steady my nerves, to recite the words I'd practiced this morning. "When Jack quoted anything," I said to Mr. Manchester, "it was usually classical, but I'm ashamed of myself because all I keep thinking of are these lyrics from the *Camelot* musical. At night, I'd get out of bed and play *Camelot* on a ten-year-old Victrola. Jack especially liked that last bit of the last song: 'For one brief shining moment there was Camelot.'"

It was a white lie, for Jack couldn't stand Broadway musicals. Yet I imagined him standing now in the corner of the kitchen in Hyannis Port, arms crossed as he leaned against the counter, a cigarette in his hand.

Good work, kid, his voice echoed in my mind. *They'll never forget me now.*

Manchester jotted something in his notebook. "And that's how you want your husband's presidency to be remembered? As a sort of Camelot?"

I waved my cigarette in the air, imagining Jack egging me on. "Bitter old men write history. Jack's life had more to do with myth and magic than political theory or political science. History belongs to heroes, and heroes must not be forgotten. If only for my children, I want Jack to be remembered as a hero. There will be great presidents again, but there will never be another Camelot."

There was more scratching in Manchester's notebook as the Jack of my imagination raised an eyebrow, lifted a daiquiri to me in salute.

Well done, kid. Now get on with the act of living.

I'd soon find out if such a feat was even possible.

H oney, you really don't have to leave." Lyndon Johnson cleared his throat, Lady Bird standing behind him. "You can stay on as long as you like."

It had been ten never-ending days since the assassination. The hint of coming snow spiked the gray air, the last forlorn and colorless autumn leaves tumbled about the lawn. I shook my head, smoothed the simple black skirt and jacket I'd chosen for the occasion. "I've imposed on you long enough."

Not only that, but I'd quickly found that I no longer wished to live in the White House. The emotion throughout the entire mansion was so heavy in the air that the mere sight of one person looking tearful set at least two others to weeping. I'd lovingly restored this house, but now the memories it held of Jack inflicted fresh wounds upon me at the most unexpected of moments.

The most recent had been last night when I'd come upon John in his striped pajamas gazing at one of the few portraits of Jack I'd left outside my bedroom. "Good night, Daddy," he'd said, and then tenderly kissed the photograph. I'd barely managed to make it inside my room and close the door before a torrent of tears wracked me until I was gasping.

This house had become a trap, and I was eager to put it behind me. Not forever, but at least until I could hear a motorcycle backfire without being catapulted into that deadly motorcade, when I could sleep through the night without the assistance of a sedative.

"That's very kind," I said to Lyndon, "but the Harrimans have already vacated their town house in Georgetown so we can move in.

We'll stay there until I find a new home for the children and me." I allowed my hand to linger on Lyndon's arm. "Thank you again for the executive orders."

I was truly grateful for Johnson's recent command that had authorized one hundred thousand dollars to pay my household expenses for the next two years. I hadn't worried about money since my marriage to Jack—investment was never his forte and he'd donated his salary to charity while we lived off the Kennedy trust. However, the allotment I was to receive from that same trust as his widow was far from robust; already the arithmetic blared that there wasn't enough to finance the lifestyle that the children and I had become accustomed to.

One thing at a time, Jackie.

Bobby and Teddy loathed Lyndon for his Texas drawl and his coarse manners, but beneath all that, I thought he was a decent man. It was he who had cut the congressional red tape during the White House renovation so I might install a crystal chandelier from the Senate in the upstairs Treaty Room, and his second executive order had already created the John F. Kennedy Space Center during a televised address on Thanksgiving Day, a small step toward honoring Jack's dreams of one day landing a man on the moon. I clasped my hands before me. "I know Jack would be pleased that the space center in Florida will carry his name."

"It's only fitting," Lyndon answered gruffly. "Sweetie, you let me know if there's anything—and I mean anything—else we can do for you."

With nothing left to say, I embraced both Johnsons, then cast a lingering look at the house I'd worked so hard to restore—down to the damaged gold frame of an oil painting on the second floor that I'd had repaired this morning. One careful step after another, I allowed the gilded pages of that chapter of my life to fall closed as I walked down the stairs to where J. B. West and Maud Shaw waited at the car with my children, both little figures dressed against the chill in the same powder-blue coats they'd worn to their father's funeral, an American flag I'd requested tucked in John's hand. For no matter what had happened to their father, I wanted my children to grow up as patriotic Americans.

"The staff asked me to convey their heartfelt wishes," West said with a sad smile. "And to let you know you'll be in their thoughts every day."

John handed his sister the flag, then tugged at the chief usher's sleeve. "What about us, Mr. West? Will they miss us?"

J. B. West hunched down, wide hands splayed on his knees. "The kitchen staff said they'll especially miss you, little chap, and your shop you set up in the corner. They're not sure who will teach them how to use the egg poachers and milk pans now."

John nodded sagely before glancing my way and making a tunnel with his hands to whisper in Mr. West's ear. "Tell them I'll miss them too," he said, so loudly that we all smiled. "But Uncle Bobby says I must take care of my mother now."

"That you shall, young man." J. B. West's eyes were shining as he straightened. "Take care, Mrs. Kennedy. And know you'll all be sorely missed."

I nodded, but like a modern-day Orpheus, I couldn't resist turning to look back at the White House as we drove down the drive. And like the tragic Greek hero, I worried that my time in that otherworldly place—those one thousand and thirty-six days—would forever haunt me.

Eager to help me in any way she could, Lee found me the perfect home at 3017 N Street in Georgetown: a three-story, twelve-room, fawn-colored brick Colonial. Unfortunately, the asking price of $217,000 was too steep for my reduced circumstances.

I'd mentioned the house offhand to Bobby and he'd automatically concocted a solution. "We'll talk down the asking price and authorize the Joseph P. Kennedy Jr. Foundation to front you some cash. How much do you need?"

I cringed. "About a hundred thousand dollars."

It may as well have been a hundred million, with the moon added in for good measure, given my current finances. Yet Bobby only shrugged. "Consider it done."

"Really? It's too much, Bobby, truly."

He'd pressed a finger to my lips, given a rueful shake of his head. "Jackie, you're a Kennedy, the queen of us all. We take care of our own."

Bobby was true to his word. Just days later I received word that the seller would accept $195,000 if it meant helping John F. Kennedy's widow. And just like that, I had a home.

A home without Jack. How is such a thing possible?

Moving boxes were piled around me for the second time in several weeks, and the children shouted with glee down the hall as they unpacked beloved treasures: John's toy soldier armies, Caroline's battery-powered dog, and an electric train set that had never been fully assembled. The children had been so inundated with toys from people around the world after Jack's assassination that I hadn't allowed them to keep most of them, but they'd each kept an oversized rocker—Caroline's was a horse and John's a tiger—that they eagerly installed in their new rooms.

My children are happy. That's the most important thing right now.

Yet I ached with the enormity of all they'd lost.

My heart constricted as I glanced down at the magazine in my hands; the issue of *Look* was a stark reminder of everything that had been destroyed by Lee Harvey Oswald's bullet.

The President and His Son: An Exclusive Picture Story

What had been meant as a lighthearted family article was now a memorial to a fallen father. The camera had caught Jack smiling with our son, John, in the moment just before his young voice pealed with laughter, his hand resting on Jack's shoulder.

I traced the image of Jack's laughing face, that happy moment crystallized in time, before my scalded fingers dropped the magazine into the hatbox where I'd deposited other painful memories—framed photographs, notes in Jack's hand, all the things I didn't have the strength to face but couldn't bear to part with.

I'd thought this house a fresh start, but I spent most nights hanging and rehanging every picture I owned, as if that small act might give me some measure of control over my life. Then I'd set up my easel and paint dark and dreary watercolors until four in the morning, before collapsing into bed, falling asleep only with the help of tranquilizers. When I opened the curtains each morning, it was to find a raucous crowd like a collage of roiling patchwork colors gathered outside. Word of my new address had spread, so gawkers broke their necks for a glimpse of the spectacle of their slain president's grieving widow. Despite the winter chill, they chanted my name and ate their lunches on the curb, leaving a sea of empty Coca-Cola bottles and crumpled paper bags in their wake.

Somehow, I'd become the bearded lady at the circus, the one act everyone in town jostled to see. I hated them for it, and I hated Jack for dying and reducing us to this.

And I hated myself, for letting him die beside me.

"I do wish they would go away," I muttered to Miss Shaw one day while the children were napping, the usual ill-behaved mob gathered on the other side of the muslin curtains. "I know they mean well, but I can't stand being stared at every time I go out on the street. Did you know there was a man peering into the dining room the other day as we sat down for supper?"

"This too shall pass." Miss Shaw poured me a cup of Earl Grey, as if a serving of steam and tannins would solve all my woes. If only it could. "That's what my mother instructed me to remember during trying times."

I gave her a half smile, recognizing the possibility that every day for the rest of my life would be a trying time. "Does it work?"

Miss Shaw gave what could only be described as a very British frown. "Sometimes. In the meantime, perhaps the police or the Secret Service could do something?"

A recent act passed by Congress stipulated that the Secret Service would remain with my children until the age of sixteen and with me until I remarried or died. Those same agents had stopped the more persistent gawkers from climbing the magnolia tree outside my house and told the rubberneckers sleeping in their cars to move along or risk an altercation with the police. My quiet Georgetown neighborhood with its hawkers of cheap Kennedy-related keychains and postcards resembled a hurly-burly Moroccan casbah, a far cry from the oasis of calm I'd envisioned.

I was a prisoner in my own home. I'd sworn to be both mother and father to my children, but I couldn't even be a proper mother, not while we lived in this circus sideshow.

Merde alors. I was so sure that leaving the White House would make things easier, so then why was every minute so goddamned difficult?

Once again, it was Bobby who distracted me from the ancient, inconsolable despair that I couldn't seem to shake. If not for him, I might have ended it all.

"Nothing fun happens in bed, Jacks." He strode unannounced and uninvited into my bedroom one morning. (Or was it afternoon? Difficult to tell when I'd taken to sleeping all day to combat my never-ending crying jags and nightly insomnia.) Bobby threw open the curtains—definitely afternoon according to the blinding glare of sunshine—and glanced in my direction with the edge of a grin, as if it didn't matter to him at all that I looked like I'd been dragged through hell and back ten times. "Well, some fun happens in bed, but you know what I mean."

I burrowed further beneath the rare guanaco fur spread that Jack had given me. I didn't want Bobby to see me like this—didn't want to see anyone ever again. "Go away, Bobby."

"There's not a chance in hell of that happening."

"Aren't you still the attorney general? Don't you have work to do?"

"I'm playing hooky." He lifted my pillow, flung it away. "It's time to face the world."

I glared at him in his crisp Italian suit, looking for all the world like he had everything together. But he was thinner than before—he'd lost more weight than even I had—and those glacial eyes were still ruined lighthouses of despair, haunted with shadows I recognized every day from my own reflection in the mirror.

"I can't face the world anymore," I said to him. "It's too broken. And I'm too alone."

"Bullshit." Bobby threw back the coverlet to reveal my painfully thin body clad in a long silk nightgown that was rumpled from how many days I'd worn it. "You look me in the eye and say that again. He was my brother, for Christ's sake. I worshipped Jack."

I didn't sit up, but I did look at Bobby. Really looked. Perhaps to everyone else, Bobby appeared to be handling Jack's death, but I knew better from the bruises beneath his eyes, the way his suit hung from his bones.

"I'm sorry," I whispered. "I didn't mean it."

Bobby rose and paced the length of my room as if he were a caged wolf ready to pounce. "Do you know what Ethel said the other day? That Jack would take care of the government, because he was up in heaven and knew what to do." Bobby threw his hands in the air. "I'm glad she takes solace in religion, but frankly, right now, I don't know where the hell God is in all of this."

I gaped to hear my own heretical sentiments echoed aloud, then ran a hand through my hair, wondered how long it had been since I'd had a proper shower. I couldn't remember, only recalled Caroline coming to my room earlier and telling me everything was going to be all right.

Get yourself together, Jackie. For them.

Bobby opened my closet and tugged out a blue dress that I'd bought before Jack's death and never worn. "I brought a surprise for you and the kids. Take a shower, then meet us in the children's playroom."

I hadn't felt anything in ages, had entire days where I floated aimlessly, untethered to this world, but my curiosity was piqued at Bobby's command. I took my time in the shower, allowed myself the pleasure of the hot water running through my hair, the fragrance of my favorite Provence lavender lotion after I'd toweled off. I brushed my hair properly and filed down the ragged edges of fingernails I'd bitten to the quick. Still, when I glanced in the mirror, the specter of that November day loomed behind me, my face freshly labored with tiny crack marks like a crackle glaze on porcelain.

One day at a time, Jackie . . .

I arrived in the newly painted playroom with its picture window that overlooked N Street to discover Caroline and John sitting cross-legged at the corners of a red-and-white-checkered blanket, a full epicurean feast of French cheeses and baguettes, platters of fresh fruit, and even a rare bowl of Sevruga caviar laid out for our enjoyment. I was reminded of the time the Kennedy sisters and I had all packed picnic baskets for a summer seaside lunch in Hyannis Port. The plastic coolers that Jack and Bobby's sisters had packed contained hot dogs, potato chips, and beer, while my woven basket was full of Sevruga caviar, French foie gras, and chilled Champagne.

Now Bobby spooned a dollop of the charcoal-gray caviar onto a cracker and offered it to me. "I always liked your picnic baskets best."

It seemed a trait of the Kennedy men to read my mind.

"It's a picnic!" John exclaimed, then clamped his tiny hands over his mouth until we all laughed together.

"Mother has seen it now, so it's not a surprise anymore." Caroline hugged her little brother. "Do you like it, Mommy?"

My daughter's hopeful eyes pleaded with mine, so there was only one possible answer. I was surprised to discover it was the truth. "I love it."

We spent the afternoon sipping Champagne—hot chocolate with whipped cream and marshmallows for the children—while speaking in broken French and pretending we were lying on our backs in Paris and imagining shapes in clouds concocted from shadows on the ceiling—a leaping horse for Caroline, a jet plane for John.

In that hour of bonhomie, I could forget that I was the widow of a slain president. I even surprised myself by laughing when John clambered to the top of the couch and pretended to plant an American flag atop the Eiffel Tower.

We're still a family, I thought to myself as Bobby tossed my son in the air the way Jack never could due to his spinal injuries, Caroline laughing through her fingers all the while. *But their Uncle Bobby will fill in for their father.*

The Jack in my imagination nodded as if giving his seal of approval.

"I wish you were an amoeba," I said to Bobby as the remainders of the picnic were finally packed away. "So you could multiply and then there would be two or more of you."

"I'm not sure how Ethel would feel about that." Bobby grinned, dropped his voice so the children wouldn't overhear. "Good ol' Landslide Lyndon would shit a veritable brick to have to deal with more than one of me."

Winter's purple twilight had fallen by the time we finished playing, yet when Maud Shaw collected the children, I was already eyeing the bottle of sedatives Dr. Jacobson had left for me the last time I'd called him.

Today had been a gift, but I was under no illusion that it had been a cure-all. Night crooked a gnarled finger at me, threatening insomnia and the usual horrors that inevitably followed once I managed to tumble into a tortured sleep. The road before me was still peppered with land mines. One unsuspecting step . . .

"No more visits from Dr. Feelgood, all right?" Bobby rubbed my shoulders as he followed my gaze to the seductive amber-hued bottles. "You need a sedative or you need to talk, you call me, all right? You're stronger than you think, Jackie."

I wanted to believe him. To dare again to *hope*.

Still, malevolent shadows gathered in the corners of the living room, waiting to seize the opportunity the moment the lights guttered.

"I don't want to be alone anymore." I avoided Bobby's gaze, focused instead on lighting an L&M and drawing its smoke into my beleaguered lungs. "I can't bear it."

"There's a simple solution to that." Bobby took the cigarette from my fingers and drew a long drag before handing it back to me, another echo from another lifetime. "Do you want me to stay?"

I let the moment draw out until, so broken and so shattered, I dared to look into the face of this man who might have been Jack's fraternal twin, let myself drown in his eyes. . . .

I didn't want to be helpless anymore; I wanted to *live*.

And so I did.

"Yes." I stubbed out the cigarette. "I would."

And that night when the lights went out, for the first time since Dallas, the nightmares stayed away.

March 1964

Sunday's dawn sky blushed a delicate pink as the night's final stars winked to me their farewell from the other side of the kitchen window. Outside, the world was as mud-luscious and puddle-wonderful as e. e. cummings claimed, with spring mysteriously opening her first roses petal by petal. I marveled anew as I carried the overflowing breakfast tray from the kitchen to the dining room that I could appreciate such simple sights, even take pleasure in them.

"Three cheers for your mother!" Bobby nudged Caroline and John from where he sat sandwiched between them at the table, and all three of them hollered in unison as I set the tray before them. "Hip, hip, hurray!"

That dining room with Bobby's smile and my children's laughter was a lush oasis in the midst of life's otherwise stark and inhospitable desert. Unable to change the past, I could have frozen time and stayed there forever, if only I'd possessed that power.

"I'm going to retire from public life. Maybe open my own law practice," Bobby mused as we all tucked into the waffles I'd prepared. It was a simple recipe I'd once submitted for *The Democrats' Cookbook*: just buttermilk, cake flour, egg whites, and a few other ingredients, but I'd come to savor the simple pleasure of crowding around a table of golden waffles drenched in sticky, sweet syrup every Sunday morning. I mulled over Bobby's announcement as I cut John's waffle into tiny bites, nudged a cup of milk closer to Caroline. "I thought you planned to run for the Senate."

"I don't see how I can go on with a career in public service." Bobby spoke offhand as he spread butter over a waffle, yet he didn't meet my eyes. "Without Jack, that is."

I hesitated, turning over each possible response and inspecting each of its facets as one would a fine gemstone before choosing the one I felt was right. I'd never really given Jack career advice—he'd always told me the one thing a busy man didn't want to talk about at the end of a day was whether the Geneva Conference would be successful or what settlement could be made in Kashmir—but it would have been a true travesty to let Bobby fade into the background, to live a life where he shied away from real happiness and allowed tragedy to over-shadow his every move. Worse, I knew he'd berate himself in the future for taking the easy road.

Kennedys never took the easy road. Ever. I'd learned that the hard way.

"Don't give up, Bobby." I tapped my foot against his under the table. "This world needs someone like you to fight for those who can't fight for themselves."

"I'm only one man, Jacks—"

"One man can make a difference and every man should try. Especially you."

I stood and removed from the ornate mahogany dining hutch a sheath of papers tied with a white ribbon that I'd been safeguarding for a moment like this. My thumb brushed the top page where a foun-tain pen had once scratched the surface—a moment now lost—before I passed the precious package to Bobby across the table. "We'd both be negligent—you and I—in our responsibilities to his memory if we allow ourselves to collapse. Jack would want us to carry on what he stood for, and died for."

Bobby gave me a questioning glance, then untied the package and scanned the top page. "Notes made by President Kennedy at his last cabinet meeting, October 29, 1963," he read.

"I had them gathered up," I answered. "For you."

The children watched in silence as he sifted through the yellow legal pages covered with Jack's scrawling hand before he gruffly cleared his throat and swiped a hand across his nose. All done quickly and efficiently, to tap the wellspring of grief I'd been hesitant to open.

Bobby was my ballast in the storm, a secret rock in the center of my life. I'd push him to follow in Jack's footsteps, just as Bobby had prodded me into the light following Jack's death.

I felt a pang of guilt then, a niggling whisper in the back of my mind asking whether I was being unfaithful to Jack in allowing this sort of intellectual and emotional affair, letting Bobby step into the void his brother's absence had left in our family. Yet I knew Jack wouldn't have wanted us to grieve forever, that he'd have been glad his brother was taking care of his children.

And we would take care of each other, Bobby and I.

"I'm going to have these framed," he finally said. "I'll hang them in my study at Hickory Hill as a reminder."

"And the Senate?" I prodded further.

Bobby sighed, but it was watered down by his smile. "You win. I'll run for the Senate, but only if you promise to help me."

You might be my son's good luck charm.

I recalled Mr. Kennedy's words to me after I'd first witnessed Jack's Senate campaign speech. Knowing that story ended in a tale to rival Shakespeare's cruelest tragedy, I certainly didn't feel lucky, but I gave Bobby what I hoped was a confident smile. "I'll be there every step of the way."

Still, as I hugged him and the children cheered, a cold rash of goose bumps spread up my arms. I couldn't help but wonder if I had just invited history to repeat itself.

Bobby isn't Jack, I assured myself as I breathed in his woodsy Eight & Bob cologne, the same that had once been a gift from Jack. *His story will have a happier ending.*

• • •

bit my lip and scanned the familiar Manhattan skyline as our jet plane touched down in the rain-stricken night at the newly memorialized John F. Kennedy International Airport in New York.

"I wish they'd never renamed the damn airport after my brother," Bobby muttered from his plush window seat next to me. "It's like a knife to the gut every time I fly into New York."

There wasn't much I could say to that, save to silently agree.

This weekend we were taking time to personally thank major contributors to the John F. Kennedy Presidential Library fund before launching Bobby's political career. I might have worried what Bobby's wife would think of my spending a May weekend with her husband, but Ethel—who had taken to calling herself Old Moms now that she was on her way to nine children (including one of whom I suspected of planting marijuana in my garden at Hyannis Port)—was oblivious. In fact, Bobby and I had even taken a recent vacation to Antigua while Ethel and Miss Shaw took our combined ten children skiing in Sun Valley.

For once, I was thankful that the press had always protected the carefully cultivated image I'd projected. There would be no improper speculation about my closeness with Bobby; no one would believe ill of me now, not even if I eloped with Eddie Fisher.

Still, while the press shielded me as their darling, they also made me vulnerable by casting me as a celebrity, and I did worry that this city that I loved might become a sudden twin to Washington, DC, and try to devour me whole.

My skin prickled with nervous excitement when our taxi inched down New York's busy streets lit by garish electric lights, the city seething with life and vitality even at this late hour. Bobby frowned as we passed crumbling tenements where children in hand-me-downs played twilit games of shirts versus skins in the streets, and I rolled down the window to better see the Metropolitan Museum of Art and

Central Park—where two deer that the president of Ireland had given to Caroline and John now lived in the Children's Zoo. I felt wonderfully alive to drink in the smell of wet concrete and green things, the salty aroma of roasted jumbo peanuts and hot dogs sold from pushcarts on the street.

The window rolled down, I pointed to one of the food stands. "Let's get some peanuts."

Bobby laughed. "I never took you for a roasted peanut sort of woman."

"What makes you think you know what kind of woman I am?"

He answered by cocking his head, the question apparent in his eyes. "If I don't know Jacqueline Bouvier Kennedy, then no one does."

Sometimes I still wondered who the true Jackie really was, but Bobby was right, for he had seen me at my darkest hour and hadn't shied away, had instead saved me from myself. He might know me even better than Jack had.

That seemed wrong, and I shoved the unfaithful thought away.

Jack would be happy to see you smiling alongside his brother. Stop feeling guilty for not wallowing in your grief.

Bobby squeezed my knee, then asked the driver to stop and returned with a paper bag chock-full of steaming nuts, his thick hair dotted with glittering raindrops like a golden aureole in some medieval painting.

"I want to soak up everything about this city." I meant every word as I opened my lips and let Bobby feed me the first aromatic nut. It was simple and delicious and utterly New York, which meant I loved it.

"Me too," he said. "That's why I bought a house here."

"Well, that and so you could run for New York's senate seat."

He laughed. "That too."

It was a strategy he'd discussed with his own version of the Irish Mafia, but also with me, moving to New York to try to claim the stalwart GOP seat. Still, Bobby's purchase of a second home in New York made me wonder if that was another escape from the beehive of Hickory Hill, where he and Ethel's children ran rabid with their menagerie of half-wild animals, the television always blared, and every surface was covered with toys and dirty laundry. He was a kind husband and a doting father, but I imagined the time he spent with me was a refuge of peace and tranquility.

"You know." I poked him gently in the ribs. "The entire country already sees you as Johnson's vice president."

The words left a sour taste in my mouth, the very thought of any Kennedy accepting second place. Based on his curdled expression, Bobby felt the same way.

"Let's face it," he said as the cab turned down Park Avenue. "Even if I wanted the position—which I don't—if Johnson had to choose between Ho Chi Minh and yours truly for the vice-presidential slot, he'd go with Ho Chi Minh."

I couldn't disagree. While Lyndon still sought me out, it was an open secret that he loathed Bobby with the fire of a thousand exploding suns. Maybe more.

Now Bobby planned to throw his hat into the senatorial ring, just as his brother had done more than a decade ago.

We were at the St. Regis hotel the following night—Bobby in elegant evening togs and me in a somber black evening gown—when Bobby tapped a spoon on his water glass to get everyone's attention. "I have an important announcement to make." He stood with one hand in his pocket in an unconscious (or was it conscious?) move that aped his martyred brother's. "After much soul-searching and lengthy consultations with my family and advisers"—he glanced at me—"I have decided to resign as attorney general and instead seek the nomination of senator for the great state of New York."

There, I thought to myself as the crowd erupted into applause. *Now it's done.*

"New York invigorates me, makes me feel alive," I said later, tugging closer my black double-breasted Balenciaga coat as we stepped out into the crispness of the spring night air. Sadly, while I still adored Oleg Cassini's elegant creations, I shied away from him and his designs as bittersweet memories I no longer wished to face. "In fact, I think this may be my Mecca."

Truly, for this city of concrete and steel didn't seem to care who I was. People still gawked when I passed them—I doubted I'd ever escape that—but there were far fewer rubberneckers than in Washington, and there were certainly no tour buses that followed me with a deafening clatter of cameras as they did each time I stepped foot outside my N Street town house.

"I'm going to move here," I announced on a whim, and the words felt so, so right.

"I think that's a brilliant idea." Bobby raised his arm to hail a cab, waggled his eyebrows at me. "And you know, your favorite senator will be practically right next door."

Which hadn't been a consideration when the plan had started to take form, but now it was another piece in the puzzle that fit so perfectly. And Caroline was finishing the school year in just a few weeks. . . .

"Done," I said. "I'll put the town house up for auction this summer."

Just like that, I was going to begin a fresh chapter in the memoir of my life. Who would this new Jackie be, the one who could move to a new city in a new state to start a new life?

I didn't know, but I was eager to meet her.

It had been almost a year since the assassination when the Warren Commission Report—claiming that Lee Harvey Oswald had acted alone—was released. I planned to cancel all my newspaper and magazine subscriptions for the anniversary to avoid reliving Jack's death—the inevitable photos of Jack and me alongside each other, the shot of me clambering over the convertible's trunk, which I still didn't remember happening—but I was caught off guard after leaving a lunch meeting with Dorothy Schiff, longtime owner and publisher of the *New York Post*, to find Lee Harvey Oswald's mug shot splashed across every newspaper on every newsstand alongside the image of Jack and me in the motorcade.

The face of my husband's murderer.

Jack's last smile.

Me clambering over the back of the limousine.

Spots blurred my vision and the walls of my lungs caved in, making it suddenly impossible to breathe.

You're not dying, only remembering. Relax and breathe. Count to five, then ten. Then breathe again.

I did breathe, put my head down and stared at the concrete sidewalk as I recalled in my mind the lunch conversation I'd just left.

"I'm weary of being America's widow," I'd said to Dorothy Schiff over oysters on the half shell. "I need a project, one that's all my own. President Johnson said I could have any job I wanted, but I don't want to be ambassador to France or Mexico."

The idea of sinking myself into some type of work held vast appeal, but what could I do?

Schiff topped off my Chardonnay. "You know, you are the most famous and admired woman in the world. It's quite a responsibility." She paused for a moment, as if chewing over some idea. "You could be a columnist for the *Post*, you know."

I perked up at that, for the idea of writing all day—a newspaper column wasn't the great American novel I'd dreamed of as a little girl, but I loved to play with words and paragraphs, to tease nuances from sentences and tug at readers' emotions. I'd recently capitulated and penned a short essay for *Look* magazine to mark the one-year anniversary of Jack's death, knowing the nation would expect something from me and wanting to keep the ball in my court. And I was proud of what I'd written.

I should have known he was magic all along. It was asking too much to dream that I might have grown old with him and seen our children grow up together. Now he is a legend, not a man. . . .

He is free and we must live.

Yet I couldn't base a career on eulogizing Jack. I needed something that was all my own and not hitched to anyone else's star.

"What would I write about?"

Schiff shrugged. "You could just write about events you go to, the people you see—anything you like."

Writing the gossip rags that had buzzed about me like gadflies for so many years lacked appeal, and it seemed cheap to trade on my celebrity for a few columns when what I really wanted, what I needed, was a real purpose.

"Oh, I can't write." I offered the lie as an excuse. "But thank you for the kind offer."

I'd just have to keep searching for that elusive something I craved.

In the meantime, I ignored the Warren Report and did everything in my power to get Bobby elected, letting the campaign distract me from the looming anniversary of Jack's death.

Bobby's Senate campaign was like the second Kennedy coming, the crowds larger and even more demonstrative than they'd been when Jack ran for president. It was all I could do to keep my wits when Bobby recklessly rode in an open-top motorcade down Fifth Avenue alongside LBJ's running mate, Hubert Humphrey. To my relief, women only tossed their shoes into the open car, although one enterprising soul threw her garter belt in as well.

Bordel de merde, I thought to myself when I heard the news. *Is he that eager to follow in his brother's footsteps?*

Didn't Bobby understand that he wasn't invincible? That I was like a ship in an autumn squall, and without his strong, steady ballast to keep me anchored, I'd be inundated by the waves that continued to crash around me?

"What happened?" I touched his cheek one day after we both stoically refused to discuss that display of brash idiocy. I had taken the children to meet him in Brooklyn for a speech event, for although Bobby never asked for it, at more sedate stops I arranged for Caroline and John to pose for press photographs and newsreels with their uncle.

John stood on tiptoes to peer at Bobby's face, which had fresh pink welts all over it. "Did you get into a fight, Uncle Bobby?"

"It looks like it, doesn't it? I'm afraid the last rally ran a little wild." Bobby gave a good-natured shrug as he slipped into Jack's leather bomber jacket with its presidential seal, then held up an empty wrist and gestured to his face. "They made away with one of my cuff links and my watch, and some of their rings and fingernails got me in their enthusiasm. One of them even snagged a handful of my hair."

A clump of Bobby's hair isn't a piece of the cross, I wanted to shout to any-one who would listen. Bobby was his own man, not the ghost of his martyred brother.

Instead, I glanced over the waiting crowd, one hand on each of my children's shoulders until I was satisfied that it was a sedate gathering of mostly Irish grannies with a smattering of children sprinkled throughout.

Bobby is not *Jack,* I had to remind myself as I let my children ac-company him to the lectern. *He's his own man with his own destiny.*

Nevertheless, I breathed a sigh of relief a few weeks later when Bobby was elected in a landslide by seven hundred thousand votes. My heart threatened to burst with pride, but that pride quickly turned to terror when Bobby raised his hand to repeat the senatorial oath of office.

Perhaps it was my imagination, but in that moment, the echo of Jack that had always seemed to follow him solidified even further.

While Bobby had his victory, I had my own as well. I found not one, but two answers to the project I sought. The first— albeit short-term—enterprise was a spectacular fifteen-room apart-ment at 1040 Fifth Avenue.

My first home that's all mine, I thought with a mixture of bittersweet excitement as Nancy Tuckerman and my new household staff helped me unpack the moving boxes and arrange my eclectic library on the floor-to-ceiling bookshelves until they were nearly bursting. *A fresh start in a new city.*

I immediately busied myself decorating the interior of 1040 with cherished pieces I'd collected over the thirty-five years of my life. The Louis XVI bureau on which Jack had signed the 1963 Nuclear Test Ban Treaty complemented an ormolu-mounted Empire fall-front desk that had been my father's, and the walls were hung with small paintings I'd brought back from India. Of course, there were a few new things as well. . . .

"Mommy, may I keep my snake in my room?" John asked on our first day. "Caroline gets to have guinea pigs in her bedroom."

"Of course," I said to John, but offered him my pinky finger as Caroline had taught us both. "But only if you promise to keep the snake in the terrarium."

"Promise!" John's pinky grappled with mine and then he was sprinting toward his room, politely requesting that Miss Shaw help him find the terrarium.

The children settled into 1040 like they'd lived there all their lives. Caroline tacked a world map on one wall and marked with push pins where Jack had traveled during his presidency, and I helped John assemble his drum set in the living room beneath the towering French windows. My children loved the lion and monkeys at the Central Park Zoo and I enjoyed early-morning runs along the park's reservoir, although I could never shake my Secret Service detail, no matter how I tried.

As much as I loved 1040's interior, I could have spent an eternity gazing at the view from the fifteenth floor. Fourteen of my apartment's twenty-three windows overlooked Central Park or the Metropolitan Museum of Art so I had a perpetually stunning view of the ancient Temple of Dendur within the museum's massive glass enclosure. Egypt had gifted and relocated the entire stone structure to America in return for Jack's support in saving the marvelous temple of Abu Simbel from the floodwaters of the newly constructed Aswan Dam. At first, I'd argued to have the temple set up in Washington, DC, as a monument to Jack's presidency, but with a view like this, now I was selfishly glad I'd bowed out of that fight and allowed Lyndon Johnson to award it to the Met.

Of course, 1040 also had the added benefit of being close to Bobby.

Tonight, he burst full of laughter with his cocker spaniel, Freckles, at his heels. "There's Uncle Bobby!" Caroline barely waited for him to set down the plans for Jack's presidential library—my second long-term project—before she leaped into his arms with full confidence that he'd catch her, just as she'd always done with Jack.

"All work and no play makes Jackie a dull girl," Bobby said when I started to unroll the schematics. "Dinner and fun now. Work later."

I acquiesced as John started showing off his new drumming skills for his uncle. After a dinner of truffle soup and tarragon chicken, Bobby gathered both Caroline and John onto his lap, then made room for Freckles atop their laps. "Did I ever tell you about your father learning how to sail as a boy? You know we Kennedys love boats, right?"

To which John only shook his head, absentmindedly rubbing Freckles' ears. "I like airplanes better, Uncle Bobby."

I smiled—thinking wistfully of all the halcyon afternoons when Jack and I had gone boating in Nantucket Sound, the two of us alone on the tranquil sea—and listened to them talk until the Beatles' latest hit came on the radio. I almost died of laughter when John leaped up onto an imaginary stage, swaying his hips and strumming an air guitar while belting out at the top of his little lungs, "She loves you, yeah-yeah-yeah."

How could we not roar with laughter?

Afterward, Miss Shaw ushered the children to bed and the apartment fell quiet save for the theater music playing softly from my new record player; we were undisturbed even by the stifling presence of the Secret Service agents that I'd finally managed to get dismissed during the night hours. Freckles snored by the fireplace while Bobby and I sat on the plush Aubusson rug on my living room floor, half-full glasses of Merlot on the coffee table and small mountains of stubbed-out cigarettes piled in Waterford ashtrays. The detritus of Jack's presidency lay sprawled before us—it had fallen to us to sift through all his papers for his presidential library—as did the bills for that selfsame library that were rapidly piling up.

I'd wanted a project, and I'd finally found one. Or perhaps it had found me.

Still, not everything was roses.

"Tell him we won't take his filthy money."

I made a face as I sipped my Merlot, gestured toward the bills. "We can't afford to turn away a million-dollar donation."

"I don't care if it's ten million," Bobby said. "You tell that Greek we won't touch his ill-gotten gains."

I scarcely refrained from rolling my eyes. We were due the meager earnings of William Manchester's book about Jack's presidency upon its eventual publication and most of our friends had made generous donations, but none had been as outlandishly magnanimous as Aristotle Onassis. I wondered if I might somehow accept the money without Bobby knowing, but it wasn't worth the subterfuge.

I leafed through papers from the Cuban Missile Crisis, letting my finger linger over Jack's doodles and their labels in his compact handwriting of *Khrushchev, serious, Guantánamo, missiles*, when I caught Bobby watching me. "Do you miss it?" he asked, his voice so soft I could barely hear it over the Noël Coward song that played in the background.

"Miss what?" I asked, even though I suspected what he meant.

"The White House." He waved a hand. "Being First Lady. Of course you miss Jack. . . ."

As I took in the tightness around his eyes, I wondered if Bobby struggled with unspoken guilt as I did, whether we'd ever have become this close—somehow more than brother and sister—had Jack still lived.

I shook myself from my macabre reverie, focused on the question at hand.

Do I miss it?

"Do I miss the hundreds of staged events, the thousands of photos I posed for looking empathetic or concerned, the millions of politically opportunistic lies and half-truths that buzzed around my head?" I spoke quickly, unwilling to mine the bedrock of truth that was too fragile to bear. "I can live without politics. I never even voted in a national election before I married Jack."

Bobby set down his wine. "You know, I thought Jack was only kidding when he told me that."

"He wasn't. And I have no intention of casting another vote ever again."

"Except for this last election, right?" Bobby put on a hangdog expression. "Please tell me you at least showed up to vote for me."

"I didn't need to, Mr. Seven-Hundred-Thousand-Vote-Landslide."

What I didn't say was that I hadn't voted during the 1964 election—even for Bobby's senate race—because Jack's name was supposed to be on that ballot, and it wasn't.

As I settled back into my mound of paperwork, a niggling thought wormed its way into my mind. I didn't miss the photos and staged events, the constant feeling of being on stage. Yet there was no denying that those one thousand and thirty-six days had taken on the glittering heat haze of an oasis, all the negative experiences forgotten and replaced by something perfectly magical.

Bobby rose and helped me to my feet. We'd leave the papers where they were; I'd pick them up tomorrow. "What if I were to run for president one day?" he asked softly, so close I could feel the warmth of him. "Could I count on you to cast a ballot with my name on it?"

I turned off the gilded bouillotte lamp, casting a soft darkness over the room's fresh flowers and eclectic mix of Egyptian statuary, carved wooden Cape Cod shorebirds, and Austrian porcelain vases, only the moonlight shining through the many windows. "For you, Bobby," I said, laying my head on his shoulder as we stood looking out over the city, the ancient Temple of Dendur glowing softly below us. "Anything."

. . .

n February, I fled the frigid New York winter for a brief respite: a
five-day cruise to the Bahamas on the *Christina* with Aristotle Onassis while my children enjoyed a jolly visit with their *grand-mère* and my
stepfather in Massachusetts. Had it only been a year and a half ago
since I'd last traveled with Onassis, just after Patrick's death?

It seemed a lifetime had passed. Someone else's lifetime.

As I approached the stark-white yacht that may as well have been
a floating palace, I couldn't resist a roll of my eyes. No one could look
at the *Christina* without being seduced by the pure narcissism shame-
lessly flaunted by its owner, a man with enough riches to bend the
world's economy to his will. Money is power, I'd once heard Aristotle
Socrates Onassis claim, and it was obvious from his yacht that he
wanted everyone to know it.

"Where are the other guests?" I asked one of the white-uniformed
crew members who met me at the gangplank. Lee had claimed she
couldn't come—she and Stas had recently renewed their vows and
things had grown chilly between her and Onassis when he'd again
taken up with his longtime mistress, Maria Callas—but I'd expected
a smattering of natty guests, perhaps a few elder statesmen . . . essentially the same glittering assemblage Onassis always curated for these
sorts of trips.

"There are no other guests," the man said in a deep Greek accent.
"Only you, Madame Kennedy."

Why would Aristotle Onassis invite only me?

I'd thought that Lee's relationship with this modern Odysseus
meant that he saw me as some sort of sister.

Something told me I'd been wrong. Terribly, horribly wrong.

I almost turned and caught the first plane back to New York, my
cheeks burning at the insinuations the press would make, of what
others would think when word inevitably leaked out.

My mind careened toward Bobby, what he would think. Jack's
death meant that my closeness with his brother was a protected cove

made all the safer for the fact that it could never be more than it was, at least to the rest of the world.

There had been no need to keep secret the time we spent together, for we were the two people who had been closest to Jack, so our shared grief had bestowed upon us the gilded veneer of sainthood. Yet if anyone—Ethel or the press—ever insinuated otherwise, I'd be hurled into the whipping winds of a hurricane. It wouldn't matter whether it was true or not—Bobby's career would be ruined.

Was it for Bobby and his career that I walked up the gangplank, to deflect any suspicions the press or Ethel might develop about my relationship with Jack's brother? Was it because Aristotle Onassis had always been nothing but kind to me? Or was there some other reason?

The only thing I knew as I ascended the *Christina*'s silver spiral staircase, wended my way around white marble pillars from the same quarry that built the Parthenon, and sampled the lavish settings of caviar and Dom Pérignon was that it was easy to guess at the cause of Ari's interest in me.

Aristotle Onassis was a trophy hunter, and I was one of the most famous women in the world. A relationship with me would be the crowning jewel in his collection. Still, that didn't mean there would be a relationship, or that I couldn't enjoy his friendship.

After all, Onassis was a kind and attentive host. If not a bit crass.

"Madame Kennedy," Onassis said that first star-filled night while we sat with the warm breeze caressing our shoulders, backs to the bar and elbows resting on the same marble counter where Grace Kelly and Prince Rainier had once toasted their marriage after Ari helped orchestrate their wedding reception. "Did you know you are sitting on the biggest penis in the world?"

Another woman might have balked at the statement, but I'd traveled aboard the *Christina* enough times to know the barstool I sat upon was crafted from the foreskins of minke whales. I suppose I might have been offended at Onassis's crude remark, but instead I laughed at his candor. Who else in the world would dare speak to Jacqueline Bouvier Kennedy in such a manner?

"You're going to have to try harder than that," I said. "Lee told me all about this boat."

And yet, she never told me much about you, Aristotle Onassis. . . .

I still wasn't sure of the depth of Lee's feelings for Onassis, whether it had been lust that faded over time or love that suddenly died when Ari returned to his mistress. I thought perhaps the former, given that Lee hadn't so much as mentioned Onassis in ages, had gone through a string of less illustrious lovers instead.

"How is your sister? Is the princess happy with her husband?"

I searched Ari's face for any hint of malice or even curiosity, but his expression was bland, bored even, as he reached behind him for something on the bar top. Asking about his former mistress was simply Aristotle Onassis's way of making conversation.

"She and Stas are on again, off again. More on than off right now, I think."

"Good. Your sister is beautiful, you know. Of course, the more beautiful a woman is, the more money it takes to keep her interested."

He offered me a golden spoon filled with Almas—Iranian beluga caviar, the most expensive in the world. I didn't move, only arched an eyebrow. "What are you insinuating?"

"Who says I'm insinuating anything?" Ari's eyes sparkled with silent laughter. "Do you not want the caviar?"

I pursed my lips to cover my smile, took the proffered spoon I'm sure he meant to use to feed me, and closed my eyes while savoring the caviar's rich and briny flavor, all the while wondering at Ari's entendre. One taste was enough to tell that the Almas was costlier even than the caviar Bobby had served me during our living room picnic. I opened my eyes, suddenly not liking that I was thinking of Bobby while this enemy of the Kennedys fed me priceless caviar.

It seemed I wasn't the only one whose thoughts veered in that direction.

"You know, I was surprised when you accepted my invitation." This time Ari nudged a fresh glass of Dom Pérignon into my hand. "I was sure your attack dog would have persuaded you to decline."

"My attack dog?"

"Bobby." Ari gritted out the name through his teeth as he stood and leaned against the table, arms crossed before his chest as he looked down his hooked nose at me. "The rest of the Kennedys don't care two shits about you, but he doesn't let you out of his sight, does he?"

I wondered then what Onassis had guessed about my *amitié amoureuse* with Bobby, that simple-yet-complicated relationship that I needed more than the blood pumping through my heart.

"He doesn't guard me," I retorted, but I knew it was a lie before the words left my mouth. Bobby—with his compassionate, unconquerable soul—was my guard, my confidant, my friend. My everything—save for my children—now that Jack was gone.

Still, it wouldn't do to let Aristotle Onassis know that. "Bobby once hiked up my apartment's fifteen flights of stairs during a power outage just to make sure the children and I were safe," I said, mostly to lighten the mood. "Only to accidentally lock himself in the pantry with a month's supply of Cheerios and Yodels."

Ari only rolled his eyes. "That angelic brother-in-law of yours just sees me as a rich prick, you know."

"Does that bother you?"

"Not at all." Ari's teeth gleamed as he laughed into the moonlight. "That's exactly what I am, so in fact, it makes him one smart son of a bitch."

I leaned back, taking full measure of Aristotle Onassis: dark and older, two inches shorter than me, who wore his power and wealth like a snake's second skin, while comparing him to Bobby: golden, energetic, and cut in the image of his martyred older brother.

It would be an interesting battle of wills if these two vastly different men ever came head-to-head.

Ari shocked me with his next observation. "You're sleeping with him, aren't you?"

I blinked, then smoothed my features. I might have affirmed or denied his accusation, but no one—not even Aristotle Onassis—deserved to know intimate details of my private life. Instead, I placed a pale hand with Jack's pink diamond ring over Ari's sun-leathered one. "Bobby's a good man," I said quietly. "He saved me, you know."

My meaning was clear. *And I won't forsake him, not even for one of the richest men on earth. So don't you dare ask it of me.*

"I could bury that sucker, you know," Ari mused in an offhand manner. "I can do almost anything, with my money and a few insinuations here and there."

My heart chilled, then thawed immediately. Jack's assassination and its aftermath had made both Bobby and me nearly untouchable. One glance at Ari's expression told me he was bluffing. "Yes, but then you'd lose the pleasure of my company in the process."

"Thus, your secret is safe with me." Ari gave a wolfish grin, then sealed the promise by tipping his Champagne glass so the golden liquid splashed on the tiled mosaic at our feet, a gesture of all Greeks going back to time immemorial. "To Bobby," he announced as he raised his half-empty glass toward the night sky. "For being a goddamned son of a bitch who at least has the good sense to look out for you."

Then, to my surprise, he tilted his chin down, twining his fingers with mine as he tugged me up into a full-fledged kiss.

To my further shock, I discovered that Aristotle Onassis knew how to *kiss*.

Heat unfurled deep in my belly and I gasped when he released me into the night's embrace with an apologetic shrug. "I once said you had a carnal soul, Jacqueline Kennedy," he said with a smile stolen from the devil. "I hope your boyfriend appreciates that; otherwise, he's a little prick."

Heart still pounding, I gave an evil smile. "That doesn't describe him anatomically."

What the hell has gotten into you, Jackie?

Onassis saluted me with his drink, and I managed to roll my eyes and saunter away on wobbly legs that had nothing to do with the Champagne or the sway of the *Christina* beneath my feet. This was something new, being kissed by someone who could never in a million years remind me of Jack.

I felt Onassis's molten gaze scalding me the entire way back to my cabin.

wanted to shed my widow's skin and move forward as my own woman, but I could almost feel Jack reading over my shoulder the invitation from the Queen of England the following May, his arms crossed and head cocked in a silent demand to explain my reticence.

A dedication ceremony at Runnymede? In my honor? I imagined him asking. *Why wouldn't you go?*

My silent argument felt flimsy. *I'm tired of living in the past, Jack.*

You love England, came the response in my mind. *And the children need to see the world.*

Thus, Maud Shaw and I packed up the children for a trip that I hoped would infuse them with my same sense of wanderlust. As this was a state occasion in honor of a former president, Lyndon Johnson kindly offered us the use of Air Force One, but I didn't think I could steel myself to go on that plane again and asked instead that we borrow the Boeing 707 that looked the least like Air Force One on the inside. Still, John gleefully dubbed the plane "Daddy's airplane" as he crouched down in his suspender shorts to inspect every nook and cranny, including the heaps of candy and chewing gum the crew had fondly set out for the children, and the cockpit, where the pilot let my son take the controls.

So many happy memories, I thought to myself as John donned the pilot's hat, as he'd often done with Jack. *Only there's one person missing . . .*

Miss Shaw remained in the periphery so I could play tourist with my children once we landed in England: witnessing the Changing of the Guard at Buckingham Palace, partaking in a special children's tea party with the chimpanzees at the Regent's Park zoo, and laughing until my sides ached when a uniformed Beefeater had to fish John out from inside a canon at the Tower of London. Still, I dreaded the ceremony at Runnymede, having to face another reminder of Jack's absence.

I will do this. For my children.

"Your father would have loved this," I said to Caroline and John as we walked hand in hand uphill through the scrubby English woodland. A tweedy British historian had informed me that the architect intended for the journey to be part of the memorial, an uphill battle through the muted forest meant to represent life that emerged into the sunlight at the top. "There's so much history here."

John wrinkled his little nose, distracted by a songbird that harmonized overhead. "Because a piece of paper was signed?"

I laughed. I'd explained that this ceremony would also commemorate the anniversary of King John's signing of the Magna Carta back in 1215. Yet my young son cared little for the beginnings of constitutional government, no matter how I dressed it up with the ill-fated Kings' Crusade that John's elder brother, Richard the Lionheart, had fought in.

"The Magna Carta was a very important piece of paper." Caroline straightened the starched Peter Pan collar of her navy dress as she reminded him.

I worried that John would squirm through the ceremony, but he might have been a boy hewn from marble in the grandstand when Queen Elizabeth assumed her place behind the seven-ton white stone in the shade of a towering ceremonial English hawthorn and an American scarlet oak planted for the occasion. With the Thames gurgling placidly in the background, I thought back to a rainy London morning when I'd covered the queen's coronation as the Inquiring Camera Girl for the *Washington Times-Herald*.

Never would I have imagined that she'd be dedicating a memorial to my slain husband more than a decade later.

The memorial stone itself was inscribed with a tribute to Jack and a line from his inaugural address.

LET EVERY NATION KNOW WHETHER IT WISHES US WELL OR ILL,
THAT WE SHALL PAY ANY PRICE, BEAR ANY BURDEN, MEET ANY
HARDSHIP, SUPPORT ANY FRIEND, OPPOSE ANY FOE, IN ORDER TO
ASSURE THE SURVIVAL AND THE SUCCESS OF LIBERTY.

Jack had paid the ultimate price for his country, not for the survival and success of liberty but only because some madman sought to murder him. I knew all the conspiracies that surrounded his death—that the Mafia had arranged a hit on him, that the CIA had ordered the murder—but none of it mattered. Jack hadn't died for some glorious ideals.

He had only died.

My vision blurred and my throat constricted when the dedication ceremony came to a close. For everyone else, Jack had already receded—hence the memorial stone—but to me, no matter what I did, he hadn't receded.

I doubted he ever would. Or whether I wanted him to.

For better or worse, no matter who else I became in the years to come, I would always, *always* be Jack's wife. And so too would I always be his widow.

"Mommy?" I looked down to realize John was tugging on my jacket. "Are we still going to Miss Shaw's house after tea with the queen?"

Miss Shaw and I locked eyes; the white-haired nanny was the first to look away before she bustled Caroline off in the direction of the waiting car, where I'd left a gold-embossed leather-bound scrapbook filled with memories on the front seat. On the inside cover I'd written the following words: *You brought such happiness to all our lives and especially to President Kennedy, because you made his children what they are.*

"Of course, darling," I tweaked John's nose. "You get to spend the entire evening with Miss Shaw tonight. Won't that be fun?"

As John grabbed my hand and planted a kiss there before running after his sister and Miss Shaw, I knew there would be time for tears later.

I'd wanted the children to enjoy this trip, and thus hadn't yet told them that this was to be their last day with their beloved nanny. Caroline and John would be in school this fall and no longer had the need for a full-time nurse, but the real impetus for this change was that

Miss Shaw was contracted to have a book published later this year, a tell-all about her years with Caroline and John.

History books about Jack's presidency were one thing—that was why I'd subjected myself to recounting the horrific events of his assassination in the days after Dallas and approved William Manchester's still-unpublished work that would become the authoritative tome on Jack's presidency—but no matter how affectionate Miss Shaw's book might be toward my children, its very existence was a gross betrayal. Lifting the curtain to allow readers to see intimate scenes, especially without consulting me first, from our family life was wrong.

I'd worried all my years in the White House that we'd be betrayed, but I'd never suspected that the person closest to my children would be the Judas in our midst.

In light of this, I'd calmly told Maud Shaw that I'd continue to pay her a pension, but her services were no longer required after this trip to England. I refused to live in fear of what sort of future stories might be leaked about my growing children by the nanny they loved and trusted.

My children are a source of strength to me. . . .

More than that, Caroline and John were my everything, more critical than oxygen in my lungs or even my own happiness. My children had been rock strong when I needed them most, and I'd sworn to be their ballast until the end of my days, to do everything in my power to ensure they grew up safe while never coddled, aware of their unique place in history while prepared to better the world on their own terms.

If that meant Jacqueline Bouvier Kennedy was never anyone more than Jack's widow, the mother of Caroline and John, I would learn to be content.

September 1966

I t had been almost three years since Dallas and the world around me didn't dare hold still, yet that November day continued to follow me like a dark shadow until I worried I'd never be able to fully shake it.

"That book was meant to be bound in black and put away on dark library shelves," I muttered while Bobby and I watched William Manchester's biplane land at the tiny Hyannis Port airstrip. I'd fired Miss Shaw and voiced my displeasure against other unauthorized tell-alls about Jack, but this new fight promised to be my biggest yet, and one I wasn't guaranteed to win. "Not serialized for all the world to read like some trashy dime-store novel."

Bobby's gaze was inscrutable as the plane landed and he raised an arm in welcome, although I agreed more with his cocker spaniel, Freckles, who growled at the plane and its lone passenger. Bobby had already telegrammed his approval of the 1,201-page tome, *The Death of a President*—which I steadfastly refused to read—before I learned of its upcoming serialization in *Look* for the record-setting price of $665,000, not a penny of which would go to Jack's presidential library but instead was slated to line Manchester's greedy pockets. Those blood-drenched moments in Dallas that I never wanted to relive were poised to be paraded before the entire American public instead of being relegated to a dusty tome meant only for scholars' bleary eyes.

It was my own fault, and I knew it, that I hadn't stipulated the exact arrangements for its publication.

When Manchester's book was serialized in *Look*, it would be like the release of the Warren Commission Report all over again, except instead of Oswald's picture, it would be every detail of the entire gruesome assassination turned over by the masses. I couldn't bring myself to read the book and be dragged once again into the backseat of that motorcade, nor was I willing to let my children endure such a drawn-out spectacle for the sake of the nation's titillation.

"I told him we both had to give permission for the publication of the book, and that hasn't been granted yet." Bobby was on my side, but I knew he'd been prepared to give in to Manchester until I'd decided in no uncertain terms that wasn't going to happen.

"If it's up to me," I said, flicking my cigarette to the pavement and grinding it beneath my Cuban heel, "it never will."

I didn't care when a former aide of Jack's told me that Manchester had cast me as a heroine who held the country together and rekindled our national pride. I was appalled at the personal details the aide summarized for me, including my children's reactions to those terrible days in November and references to my smoking, which, until now, had been a secret kept from the media.

Bobby seemed to understand and had been unbelievably compassionate when I'd argued for this opportunity to persuade Manchester not to serialize, to keep the entire tome together and let it gather dust. With his eyes on the White House for 1968, I knew Bobby had more important grist to mill, that he was doing this only for me.

So I smoothed my green miniskirt and clasped my hands before me as Manchester hopped out of the plane we'd arranged to bring him here. I was prepared to use every weapon in my arsenal—to smile, bribe, cajole, and even threaten—in the name of my sanity and to protect my children from the horrors they'd already survived once.

Yet it seemed we had a Benedict Arnold in our midst.

I spent hours hectoring Manchester and acting every version of Jackie I'd ever played, but still he refused to halt the serialization.

"The information in the book comes from the tapes you asked me to record, Mrs. Kennedy," Manchester repeated calmly, over and over. "The public has a need to know what happened in Dallas."

Fuck the public, I wanted to scream, and barely bit my tongue.

"I only sat down with you on the condition that I could review the book and take out anything I didn't like. I poured out my heart to you. And you included such personal things—his last words to me in Dallas, the copy of my letter to Jack that I put in his coffin—"

"I've told the story in the most respectful way I could manage."

I didn't care if it was true or not. Perhaps I wasn't being rational, but I didn't care. I wanted that part of my life laid to rest, not relived in each gory, blood-soaked detail again and again. But there was nothing I could do to dissuade Manchester.

"I quit." I rarely lost my temper, but barely restrained myself from banging a furious fist on the dining room table. "I'm going to fight and I'm going to win. But right now, I'm going upstairs to lie down."

My gaze snagged with Bobby's, my intention clear in my eyes. *I want this snake gone by the time I return.*

The living room was empty when I emerged before dinner, ragged and wrung out.

"I want to sue." I lit an L&M with shaking hands, but even its acrid smoke curling in my lungs couldn't soothe the trembling rage building within my chest. It was as if every bit of mortar in the walls I'd worked so hard to construct around me, around the children, and even around Bobby was about to be pulled apart brick by brick, leaving us naked and exposed.

"I don't think suing is a good idea," Bobby said.

"You're just saying that because you have an election coming up," I said waspishly, then relented. "I'm sorry. I know that isn't true."

Bobby removed the cigarette from between my fingers and replaced it in an ashtray, where it burned patiently away. "I don't think you want this sort of publicity. The press will make a big hullabaloo about us suing, and then the serialization—and the book—will sell even more copies."

"What I need is for this to all disappear. In order for that to happen, we have to sue. And we need to win."

He seemed to hesitate, then retrieved something from a stack of books and papers on the living room table. "I was going to save this for later, but it seems you could use some cheering up." He handed me a bound stack of printed pages, a manuscript in its early stages.

"'To Seek a Newer World,'" I said aloud as I read the title. "By Robert Kennedy. You wrote this?"

He nodded, subdued but with a somber gleam of pride hidden deep in those ice-blue eyes. "It's just a collection of speeches and essays, mostly about my faith in the new generation's ability to create a society that has learned from the mistakes of its elders." He cleared his throat as if abashed. "The title is from you."

"Me?" Then I realized. "'Come, my friends,'" I started and Bobby chimed in to finish the line. "''Tis not too late to seek a newer world.'"

"'Ulysses,'" Bobby said. "I love that poem."

Among so many other books and poems, I'd recently gifted Bobby a copy of Tennyson's "Ulysses" after he'd been asked to throw out the first ball of the World Series in Yankee Stadium, and Joe DiMaggio—the Yankee's great center fielder and Marilyn Monroe's onetime husband (how many men had that peroxide-doused doxy taken to the altar?)—had refused to shake Bobby's hand because he blamed Jack and, by extension, Bobby, for Marilyn's suicide. Bobby had worried about the negative publicity, and I'd sought to distract him with literature, which had worked.

That Bobby had used my gift as inspiration for his title felt like a gift itself, akin to Jack's precious dedication to me in *Profiles in Courage*. I rubbed my thumb over the plain typescript. "That was one of Jack's favorite poems, you know."

"I know."

They were so alike, Jack and Bobby, yet so vastly different as well. And while both brothers had plenty of relationships with other women, what I had with each of them was special.

"We can't let Manchester's book get out, Bobby. We have to sue."

Bobby sighed at my cri de coeur, and I knew I could have asked for anything—the sun, the stars—and he would find a way to give it to me. "If it's what you want, Jackie, then we'll do it."

Whereas I'd once been America's uncrowned queen-who-could-do-no-wrong, the moment we sued was the moment the media turned into a many-headed Hydra against me—and Bobby. I wanted to scream at the newspapers that all I'd wanted was to protect myself and my children, but we were holding up a hand to an avalanche.

An arrogant abuse of power.

An attempt to stifle America's cherished right of freedom of speech.

Who knew the lady of the funeral could act this way?

I didn't care to see Bobby's name dragged through the mud any more than I wished to parley with the lions' den of reporters waiting to rip me to pieces. So I gritted my teeth and we settled, ending the biggest brouhaha over a book that the nation had ever seen. Manchester's damnable book was serialized and published, albeit with a statement that neither Bobby nor I in any way approved or endorsed the material between its covers. Not even Manchester's donations of the serialization's royalties to the Kennedy Presidential Library could entirely mollify me.

Only a month before the book's release, I stood with Bobby and a coterie of our family in the weak March sunshine to witness Jack's coffin reinterred at Arlington with two heartbreakingly tiny white caskets buried on either side of him. My babies—Patrick and Arabella—were reinterred next to their father at this newly constructed and dignified memorial that I'd ordered. After Eunice Kennedy and her husband had lobbied for a memorial of weeping angels, I'd mandated that there be nothing ostentatious, no statues or colossal buildings that looked like something out of a Dracula horror movie. Instead, simple Cape Cod granite flagstones framed the eternal flame centerpiece that burned steadily above the three pieces so cruelly chipped from my heart.

I was so worn down from the Manchester lawsuit that it was eerie—and even reassuring—to realize while a priest intoned the Lord's Prayer, that I would one day join my husband and children in this hallowed ground.

Hail Mary, full of grace, the Lord is with thee . . .

One day. But not yet.

"I want to finish what he started," Bobby said quietly from his place beside me. "I want to be the man to complete the Kennedy legacy, Jackie. In fact, I want it so goddamned bad I can taste it."

The Kennedy legacy? I thought to myself as I stared at the graves before us. *Camelot? Or the heavy hand of death upon those gone too soon?*

I didn't have an answer, only knew that the happiness of the man standing beside me was paramount to my own.

"Then we'll make it happen, Bobby," I whispered to him. "You just wait and see."

Several weeks later, the television droned in the background at 1040 while I painted a watercolor and the children slept after a long afternoon spent riding the Ferris wheel and gobbling ice cream cones at Coney Island. The sound of Lyndon Johnson's gravelly voice snagged my attention, and I set down my paintbrush just in time for his unexpected announcement.

"I shall not seek, and I will not accept," he said from behind the Resolute Desk, "the nomination of my party for another term as your president."

In one fell swoop, Lyndon Johnson had shocked the nation and given Bobby the greatest gift one political adversary could give another.

Lyndon's somber televised announcement made sense, what with the increasing number of body bags coming home from Vietnam and the recent years of peace protests and race riots, all of which contributed to Johnson's all-time-low approval rating. The Kennedys didn't love Lyndon, but I'd always thought him a decent person, and I believed him when he said he wanted to focus on negotiating a settlement with Vietnam.

A presidency without Lyndon didn't surprise me; it was the idea of who would take his place that had me reaching for a glass of whiskey before the inevitable ringing of the telephone.

"God, you know what this means, don't you, Jackie?" The elation in Bobby's voice might have been heard from Washington to California. Bobby had vacillated on whether to run against Johnson before he declared his candidacy mere weeks ago in the same Senate Caucus Room where Jack had announced his candidacy eight years earlier. "All the things I've wanted to do as senator, fixing poverty in Appalachia or getting us out of Vietnam, now I'm going to do all that and more. The field is clear. Hubert Humphrey knows he can't win against me, and I can trounce Eugene McCarthy. That means it's going to be me against Nixon."

Tricky Dick against another Kennedy, I thought but couldn't speak. *God, how many echoes of Jack can there be?*

"I'm going to do great things," Bobby continued. "Just like Jack. You wait and see."

I'd have laughed with joy for him if I wasn't so petrified. The Greek playwrights of old had surely resurrected themselves to pen this tale of history repeating itself. Even if Bobby had chosen to turn a blind eye, I remembered all too vividly how this story had ended the first time.

"You have to be yourself; don't try to be Jack," I managed to eke out, forcing myself to relax my grip on the telephone receiver. I didn't want him to run, but I wanted him to be happy, so I'd support him as best I could. "Promise me you'll be careful. No more open motorcades."

There was a pregnant pause. "If they're going to shoot," he finally said, "they'll shoot. It's a matter of luck. Look at all the times your pal Charles de Gaulle has managed to stay alive."

The very thought infused my veins with ice. "Bobby, there have been at least six attempts on his life."

"I told you—luck. You can't make it without that old bitch luck."

Somehow, that failed to assuage my fears.

Nineteen sixty-eight lit America on fire.

April was the first conflagration, a raging wildfire that threatened to devour the nation when Martin Luther King Jr. was assassinated on the balcony of the Lorraine Motel for his belief that all men were created equal. I watched the television with fear as America heaved Molotov cocktails and street riots broke out in Washington DC; Baltimore; Chicago; and a host of other major cities. That fear turned to trepidation as Bobby gave a televised impromptu speech urging his supporters to continue King's ideals of nonviolence.

"I need you to attend the funeral with me, Jackie," Bobby said over the crackling telephone line. "Coretta Scott King asked for you specifically."

I set down the pen atop the note I'd been writing him as a distraction: a high-energy milkshake recipe of blueberries, cashews, yogurt, and raw eggs to combat the way he was running himself into the ground with such a grueling schedule. "Can't Ethel go instead?"

Yet I already knew the answer before the words left my mouth.

"It has to be you." There was a pause, for Bobby of all people knew what he was asking of me. "Please."

Please. Because he knows I'd rather hide myself in the deepest, darkest hole than attend another national funeral for a fallen leader.

So I endured the funeral for the fallen civil rights' leader, barely managing to steel myself against the surging crowd and the raw expressions of grief that transported me to another funeral from nearly five years prior.

There is so much hate in this country, and more people hate Bobby than ever hated Jack. How is it possible no one else can see what I so clearly see? Or am I being irrational? Surely lightning can't strike twice.

Thoughts of death plagued me at every turn so that I felt like a bleak and terrible Cassandra, and I feared slipping back into my dark melancholy from the days after Jack's assassination.

My worries made me waspish and I desperately sought a refuge from the sense of all-encompassing dread that dogged my every step as each day dragged us closer and closer to November.

I found my escape in the form of Aristotle Onassis's invitation to a four-day cruise of the Virgin Islands while famed astronaut John Glenn and the entire Kennedy clan were campaigning for Bobby in what everyone claimed was a tight race. While on the early-morning flight, I read that Eugene McCarthy had accused Bobby of being a spoiled little rich kid who couldn't run this race without his dog, his astronaut, or his father's millions. I chortled to read Bobby's reply: "I don't mind McCarthy taking issue with John Glenn or Dad's money, but let's leave Freckles out of this. That cocker spaniel goes everywhere with me."

I asked Ari's chauffeur to pull over on the way to the port so I might telegram Bobby in Portland one last time before boarding the *Christina*.

WEAR A KNAPSACK DURING YOUR NEXT SPEECH. THE WELL-HEELED AND MOSTLY EMPLOYED OREGONIANS DON'T CARE ABOUT CAMPUS RIOTS OR THE VIETNAMESE WAR, ONLY CAMPING.

I knew I should be at Bobby's side, not telegramming him, but I'd made my decision. I tried to shake loose the guilt that settled like fallen ash on my shoulders when I boarded the *Christina* and let Ari embrace me. "I'm glad you're here, *mon ami*," he said.

"And I'm glad to be here," I said softly.

And I was, yet it was all the more difficult to feel guiltless the next morning when the newspapers were delivered with the morning's ripe strawberries and fresh figs, headlines blaring news of Bobby's recent campaign stops while I lounged in the sun on white beach towels emblazed with a giant red *O*.

It's perfectly acceptable that I enjoy a short vacation with a close friend—because that's all Ari is—while Bobby is in the political fight of his life. Soon I'll be back in the thick of it anyway.

"You know," Ari said as he glanced at me in my black bathing suit over the top of his paper, "the only thing JFK and RFK have in common . . . is you."

I sat up halfway, leaning on my elbows. "What do you mean by that?"

But Ari only cocked an enigmatic eyebrow in my direction, settled back into his reading.

I tried to decipher the meaning of his cryptic comment without acting as if it bothered me. Did he mean the brothers' personalities were different? That Bobby was doomed to fail where Jack had succeeded? Or was Ari trying to put my mind at ease, insinuating that Bobby could never share Jack's fate?

"You know, I could take you away from all this Kennedy nonsense," Ari mused offhand a few minutes later. He might have been commenting about the weather, yet I noticed the way he fingered the blue worry beads he perpetually kept in his pocket. "Life on Skorpios is calm, peaceful even. You should see it one day, Jackie, the vineyards and olive groves and stables. It cost me ten million dollars to domesticate its rugged beauty, but it was worth every penny."

Skorpios was Ari's private scorpion-shaped Greek island, for of course a man like him could afford his own island. In fact, a man like Ari—self-made, self-taught, self-assured—could afford everything.

Except me.

"Is that a proposal?" I dropped my fly-eye sunglasses lower on my nose, careful to keep my voice light and playful. Onassis had been courting me with gifts and innuendos for some time, but that didn't change the fact that I could never marry a man like him. Not unless I wanted the American public—and the entire Kennedy clan—to turn on me.

"That, my dear Jacqueline"—Ari's eyes remained hidden behind his gangster-style dark glasses—"depends entirely on you."

He was an Odysseus through and through, every answer a maddening enigma, each question a labyrinthine riddle. And while Ari had more money than God, not even that would be enough to entice me away from Bobby.

Yet I recalled a moment not long ago when the entire Kennedy clan had met at Hyannis Port to discuss Bobby's campaign strategy. "Won't it be wonderful when we're back in the White House?" I'd asked once we were all gathered around the dining room table, like some sort of Napoleonic strategy tent.

Ethel had turned on me, her face drawn in a sour glare as if she'd spent the day sucking on a dozen lemons. "What do you mean, *we*?" She'd made no attempt to mask the vitriol in her voice. "You aren't running. This is our moment in the sun."

I knew her tone and her look, for I'd donned them myself when Marilyn Monroe had dared telephone the White House. I'd always thought Ethel either never cared how much time I spent with her husband or perhaps simply chose to turn a blind—albeit grudging—eye all this time. Yet here she was now, drawing a nonnegotiable line in the sand. Worse still, her outburst had proven that Bobby's likely victory would irrevocably alter the nature of my relationship with him, a relationship that had rescued us both.

Oh, God, I thought. *I'm going to lose him. I'm going to lose us.*

The only question that remained was how far I'd be pushed to the sidelines. Still, I didn't see that there was any other place for me to go. If Bobby won, I'd lose him. If he lost, Jack's dreams and perhaps even his legacy would be lost, potentially forever.

"The press tried to eat me alive during the Manchester suit." I kept my voice light to belie my sadness as I replaced my sunglasses on the bridge of my nose and gazed at Onassis, crossed a nonchalant leg and leaned back in the golden sunshine. "They'd impale me on the sharpest pike available for marrying a decades older, foreign-born tycoon."

Especially one so at odds with Jack's golden Icarus, I stopped myself from adding.

Of course, that was assuming that I even wanted to marry Ari.

Which, although I could see the benefits to such a match, I didn't.
What I wanted was to go back in time to when things were simpler,
although I couldn't imagine when, if ever, that had been.

Onassis snorted, a crude sound. "Perhaps one day you won't care
so much what the press thinks. You'll do what you want, when you
want it."

I laughed. "That day is not today. In case you haven't noticed, it's
an election year and there's a Kennedy on the ballot. That means
we're all under the microscope."

Ari shrugged, nonplussed by my rejection. "You're worth the wait.
And just because we're not married doesn't mean we can't enjoy the
pleasure of each other's company."

His insinuation was obvious, and I chose that moment to flip onto
my front to sunbathe so he couldn't see the flush of pleasure that
warmed my cheeks. Still, I suspected a man like Aristotle Onassis
always knew the effects of his words, especially on women.

Perhaps Ari was right, that there was some pleasure to be had between the two of us. God knew there had been precious little joy in
my life since Bobby had declared his candidacy. And although Aristotle Onassis was an unlikely partner, there was something about
him—the way he wore his wealth and power, his cocksure devil-may-
care attitude—that was vastly appealing.

*God, if only Lee could see me now. She'd never in a million years forgive me if
she could hear my thoughts.*

Yet Lee couldn't hear me and thoughts weren't a crime. Only acting on them.

Still, I arrived home to find an interview Ari had given while at a
Parisian cocktail party in the *New York Times* and the *Washington Post.*
I could hear his voice in my head as I read his response when asked
his opinion of me.

MRS. KENNEDY IS A TOTALLY MISUNDERSTOOD WOMAN. PERHAPS SHE
EVEN MISUNDERSTANDS HERSELF. SHE'S BEING HELD UP AS A MODEL
OF PROPRIETY, CONSTANCY, AND SO MANY OF THOSE BORING AMERICAN

FEMALE VIRTUES. SHE'S NOW UTTERLY DEVOID OF MYSTERY. SHE
NEEDS A SMALL SCANDAL TO BRING HER ALIVE—A PECCADILLO, AN
INDISCRETION. SOMETHING SHOULD HAPPEN TO HER TO WIN OUR
FRESH COMPASSION. THE WORLD LOVES TO PITY FALLEN GRANDEUR.

Why, you little shit, I thought to myself as I twirled my trademark sunglasses in one hand, even as I couldn't help smiling. Because there was no doubt in my mind that Aristotle Onassis planned to be my small scandal.

Apparently, the entire Kennedy clan deduced as much as well.

Both Ethel and Joan showed up in high dudgeon at my apartment that very same afternoon. "Bobby sent us," Joan said as she pushed her way past me. I hung up her wool coat as she perched on my plush couch with her arms crossed against her chest. Joan, who had once been my confidante, was now firmly on the other side of the fence. "To speak to you about Onassis."

"What?"

I was suddenly glad the children were still at Hammersmith Farm with my mother, so as not to witness this particular family interrogation. Ethel kept her brown peacoat buttoned tight and remained by the front door, cast a cursory glance around my pristine apartment that stood in sharp contrast to the bustling home she shared with Bobby at Hickory Hill. That quiet house that I'd designed for Jack and me was now filled to the rafters with their menagerie of dogs, children, and foreign maids—the Irish bunnies, as Bobby called them—that she brought over as hired help every summer. "He wants us to persuade you not to marry him."

"What?" I asked again, keeping my tone as businesslike as possible. *Why did you send them, Bobby? Why didn't you come yourself?*

Yet I knew the myriad reasons why Bobby couldn't come. He had to remain above the fray in case I did drag the family into some peccadillo right before the election. Perhaps more important, he couldn't bear to face the inevitable sundering of our relationship any more than I could.

"If you find it absolutely necessary to marry him"—Joan wrinkled her nose, couldn't bring herself to speak Onassis's name—"and I can't imagine what would possess you to do such a thing with such an oily little shrimp of a man, then you must promise not to do it until after the November election."

"It will look bad for Bobby," Ethel interjected, as if explaining things to a four-year-old child instead of an almost forty-year-old woman. "Such negative publicity would ruin his chance at the presidency."

I didn't speak before Ethel maneuvered to face me. "Bobby may not get a second chance and I'm not leaving until you promise not to sabotage him, Jackie. You owe us this."

She said you owe us, *but what she really meant was you owe* me. Perhaps she was right. Perhaps I owed everyone this: Ethel, Bobby, and even Jack.

Everyone except myself. And I didn't even know what the hell I wanted.

I held up my hands. "I have no intention of marrying Onassis, Ethel. Not now, and not ever."

At least I don't think I do. Do I?

Ethel scrutinized me as if searching for traces of my lie before she finally gave a tight nod. "I certainly hope not." Her lip wrinkled with distaste before she gestured to Joan. "Let's go. Bobby has a fund-raising dinner an hour from now."

Little did I know that Ethel and Joan were merely the beginning of the inquisition I was to face. There was a yap from a cocker spaniel at my door just as twilight's shadows veiled the moon, and I opened the door to face the Grand Inquisitor, his jacket spattered from the light mist falling outside. From the haggard look on his face, I had committed a grievous and unforgiveable sin.

"Did he propose yet?" Bobby's quiet question the moment I closed the door shouldn't have surprised me, but it did. Not even Ethel or Joan had suspected how near Ari had come to asking me to marry him. But Bobby knew.

Of course he did. Because Bobby's soul and mine had been forged together by unspeakable tragedy, until now it was impossible to imagine one without the other.

"Would it bother you if he had?" I was being contrary and I knew it, yet I couldn't help myself as I crossed my arms, as if that would somehow stop my heart from bleeding out.

I'm going to lose you, Bobby. No matter how this story ends, one of us loses. And I'm not sure I can bear to see that happen.

"Goddammit, Jackie. You know the answer to that."

I'd never heard Bobby this angry or this possessive, his shoulders squared and the tension so taut in his voice that Freckles emitted a worried whine from her spot by the fireplace. I tilted my chin in defiance. "He's a friend, Bobby."

"Bullshit. Anyone with eyes can see he wants to add you to his collection."

"So what if he does? And what if he did?"

Bobby's voice was gruff when he finally stopped pacing and looked up at me with eyes so tortured I almost fell to my knees. "I called him, you know. Threatened to have his oil tankers—and their owner— permanently banned from American ports if he doesn't stop talking about you."

My gaze lingered on the framed photograph of Bobby in my living room, signed "To Jackie, my love. Always, Bobby." I couldn't bear to have pictures of Jack around, but here was this image of his brother alongside those of my children. A visitor had once pointed to Bobby's picture and joked that it might give people the wrong impression. To which I'd replied, "Frankly, I don't care what people say about me. I'd jump out of a window for Bobby."

And I would. I'd give up every shred of my own happiness to see him achieve his own.

So now I tried a different tack. "How does it look tomorrow in California?"

Another pause, and I watched Bobby scrub a hand over his face as he compartmentalized his feelings just as Jack always had, rubbing his jaw as he worried about the primary that would make or break his campaign. His expression said *I know you're distracting me, but I'll let you get away with it. For now.*

"It looks good," he admitted. "It looks damn good with Cesar Chavez's voter registration drive and the African American and Hispanic vote out here. I might actually win this thing." His arms fell open at his sides, and in that moment I glimpsed a wider world in his eyes. "But none of that matters if I lose you. To him."

He spoke the last word like it was full of nails and might gut him to spit it out. It occurred to me that not once, but twice I'd gone to Ari and made a Kennedy brother jealous; I wondered what that said about me. I pushed the thought away to walk into the safety and warmth of those arms that had shielded me from the worst storms life had to offer. "You can never lose me, Bobby. Not really."

No, as I listened to his heart and the life beating there, I knew Bobby's victory or defeat in California would usher us—and potentially the entire nation—to the brink of a newer world. Another line from our shared favorite "Ulysses" echoed in my mind.

> All times I have enjoy'd
> Greatly, have suffer'd greatly, both with those
> That loved me, and alone, on shore

All that remained to be seen was whether I'd greet this newer world with those that loved me or alone upon the shore.

woke the next morning to find my apartment empty—Bobby already winging his way to California for its all-important primary—and to the news that artist Andy Warhol was still recovering after being shot in the spleen, liver, lungs, stomach, and esophagus by a paranoid schizophrenic named Valerie Solanas. The artist was still alive—barely—and I wondered if Bobby might now acquiesce to allowing a Secret Service detail, even as I knew he wouldn't for fear of appearing weak.

As if Bobby could ever look weak . . .

To give myself something to do, I ordered a celebratory bouquet and magnum of Champagne delivered to his suite at the Ambassador Hotel in California, then wired a telegram that would make him smile.

YOU AND FRECKLES ARE TOMORROW'S BEST HOPE.

Later that day, I stopped by Bobby's campaign headquarters in New York, where a gaggle of rabid reporters hounded me to answer their questions. I should have left; I knew I should have left, but I thought maybe an impromptu press conference might somehow help Bobby.

"Do you think Bobby will win the California primary today?" one reporter asked.

"I'm keeping my fingers crossed," I answered.

"If he becomes president," queried another, "do you think he'll follow up on the work John F. Kennedy started when he was president?"

"I assume he'll continue some of President Kennedy's programs, but I'm also certain he'll undertake a number of his own. The country faces a whole new set of problems."

A third journalist joined the fray. "Are you planning to marry Aristotle Onassis?"

Va te faire foutre, I wanted to say, but reminded myself that cursing for Jacqueline Kennedy was only acceptable if it remained silent, even if it was in French.

Instead, the look I gave the nosy reporter might have shredded steel. "I'm here today in support of Senator Robert F. Kennedy. I haven't given any thought to my own future plans," I lied. "I just want Bobby to win—first the California primary and then, hopefully, the presidency."

With that, I excused myself to attend another rally in front of the United Nations, then returned to my apartment to watch with a conflicted heart as Bobby was declared the winner of the California primary. Whether I liked it or not, his campaign was now poised to win it all.

I told myself I was happy for him. Terrified, but content to see his dreams coming true. To see Jack's legacy being protected and fulfilled.

Bobby was due to take the podium at midnight Pacific time for a victory speech—one in which I knew he planned to thank both Cesar Chavez and Freckles—but it was already nearly three in the morning on the East Coast and I was craving my bed. I imagined him lighting a cigar and popping open the bottle of Champagne I'd sent him just as the phone rang.

I thought it would be Bobby, but instead it was Steve Smith, his brother-in-law and campaign manager. "Bobby asked me to call you, to tell you the good news." There was cheering in the background over the crackling static on the line. Suddenly I wished Bobby could be here, in my apartment, so I might congratulate him in person. "He's won South Dakota, too, with a two-to-one lead."

"That's really wonderful," I said softly. "Tell Bobby I love him."

I hung up and switched off the television, planning a congratulatory phone call for the morning.

I drifted into a light sleep, only to be woken in the dark of night by the flashing of the light on my bedside table telephone. A glance at the clock showed it to be almost four a.m.

It was Stas, Lee's husband, asking about Bobby.

"Isn't it wonderful?" I asked, still groggy from sleep. "He's won. He's got California."

"But how is he?"

"Oh, he's fine," I said, as I sat up. "He's won."

But there was something more in Stas's voice, a hint of urgency that plunged a hot-cold feeling through to the marrow of my bones and a violent shock of gooseflesh rippling over my skin.

There was a moment of hesitation from Stas's end. Then, "You don't know, do you? Why, Bobby's been shot."

No. I felt such a sudden pain in my chest that it seemed my very body might fly apart. I shook my head, the telephone receiver still pressed to my ear. *It can't have happened. Tell me it hasn't happened.*

But it had. My worst fear had suddenly come true.

I listened in numb silence as Stas relayed the rest of the horrible news. "He was in the kitchen of the Ambassador Hotel right after his speech. Some Palestinian terrorist shot him at close range."

"How many times?" I managed to whisper to Stas. "How many times was he shot?"

"Three," came Stas's reply, and I thought, *Of course it was three.* "They're saying he took a bullet to the head, Jackie."

I pressed a fist into my mouth to block the scream of agony that threatened to tear me in two. Which was worse? Being beside Jack so I could feel his soul being ripped from his body, or being on the far side of the world, alone and unaware, as Bobby met the same fate?

But if Stas had been asking about Bobby's condition, that meant there was still a chance, that there was still hope. . . .

I had no idea what I packed, only that I threw things into an overnight bag and called someone to arrange for a limousine to drive me to the JFK airport and a private jet to fly me to Los Angeles. It was there that I numbly learned of how Bobby had lain in an everwidening pool of his own blood after he'd been shot by Sirhan Sirhan, a Palestinian who faulted Bobby for his avowed support of Israel after the previous year's Six-Day War. I swayed in my limo seat to learn that Bobby had still been cognizant after he was shot, had clutched a rosary someone pressed into his hands and whispered to the ambulance attendants not to lift him onto a gurney before he finally lost consciousness.

He was awake. Dear God, he was awake after it happened.

I wondered how much pain he'd been in, whether his injuries were something he might still survive. I arrived bleary-eyed at the city's Good Samaritan Hospital to find Chuck Spalding, a family friend and Kennedy aide, waiting for me.

"How bad is it?" I tried to radiate calm even as I clutched my handbag, dreading the answer. "I want it straight from the shoulder."

Chuck seemed to shrink before he found the courage to answer. "He's dying."

I closed my eyes and drew a ragged, steadying breath as the whirlpool of hope within me suddenly went still. I'd done this once before, bid good-bye to a man I loved amid the fluorescent glare of hospital lights and the astringent smell of antiseptic. All because of an assassin's bullets.

Every step saturated with dread, I found Bobby's room in the intensive-care unit and suddenly my entire world narrowed to that lone hospital bed, to the brave, bold man lying on it. Bobby's head was bandaged and his eyes blackened, his body trapped in a terrible tangle of medical equipment. His chest beneath the white hospital johnny was rising and falling as the respirator forced air into his lungs. He was breathing, and that meant he was still alive. That there was still hope.

But Teddy gave a minute shake of his head when I dared voice that thought.

"There's no brain activity," the youngest Kennedy brother explained as he rose from the foot of Bobby's bed, a rosary pinched tight between his fingers as he scrubbed a fist over puffy eyes. "They say it's irreversible, that the machines are keeping him alive."

I blinked as those words penetrated my mind and my vision expanded to encompass the rest of the room. Ethel—red-eyed and heavily pregnant with their eleventh child, the final for Bobby's football team—sat next to Rose at his bedside. Bobby's wife lifted her sodden gaze to mine, then stood and held open her arms in an unexpected gesture.

"Jackie," she said as I walked mechanically into her wooden embrace. "I'm so glad you're here."

I was shocked into stillness by her response, more so when she wiped her eyes. "You've come all this way—you probably want to spend a little time alone with Bobby."

It was a surprising gift I probably didn't deserve, but I wasn't going to question Ethel's sudden generosity as everyone somberly filed from the room—Rose pausing to touch my elbow in silent communion—until only I remained.

Alone on the shore.

Irreversible brain damage meant that Bobby could remain hooked to these machines until the end of time, that they would keep the oxygen flowing into his broken body perhaps even after the rest of us had passed to our graves.

"You'd never want that." I touched Bobby's hand as I once had Jack's. There was still life there, but I knew Bobby was gone then, just as I'd known when I'd lain sprawled over Jack's broken body in the back of a speeding midnight-blue Lincoln. I swallowed a mangled sob, knowing that once that dam shattered I'd never be able to piece myself together again. "Why couldn't you have just accepted the Secret Service detail? Why the hell did you have to be so goddamned stubborn?"

Bobby didn't respond, only laid there, immobile. It was unthinkable to imagine my life without his laugh, his bluster, his dreams.

Without him.

I can't do this without you, I thought as I clung to his hand, a familiar cold numbness spreading like winter's first frost around my still-beating heart. *My life . . . it's only because of you that it became bearable.*

When I looked up through bleary eyes, I imagined Jack sitting beside me, his silent presence giving me strength. "What do I do?" My whisper reverberated off the walls, punctuated by the steady metronome of Bobby's heart monitor.

I imagined Jack's gray-green eyes growing infinitely sad. *You know what you have to do.*

No matter what the poets say, a human heart cannot break. If only it could.

I couldn't leave Bobby hooked up to these machines, yet it wasn't my place to make that decision. Still, no one else had the courage to do what needed to be done, even after everyone filed back into the room and a full panel of physicians confirmed what Teddy had said.

I stood tall at the head of Bobby's bed, my voice level and my hands clasped tight before me. There would be time to fall apart later. There would be forever for that.

"Is there any hope?" I asked the lead physician.

"I'm afraid not, Mrs. Kennedy."

"Has he already had last rites?"

Teddy nodded. Beside him, Ethel gave a sharp intake of breath. "What are you trying to say?"

I straightened my shoulders and closed my eyes, rubbed the bridge of my nose. "I'm saying that by keeping Senator Kennedy tethered to a respirator, we're only prolonging the inevitable." Each word stole something precious from me. "But neither I nor any physician can tell you what to do."

Teddy refused to meet my gaze, and even Rose shook her head violently.

There was a long, timeless pause before Ethel gave a slow, stoic inhale, as if gathering the strength to say the words. When she finally spoke, her eyes bored into mine. "Will you do it, Jackie? I can't." Her hands rested on her swollen belly, the diamond wedding ring Bobby had given her shining dully. "I just . . . can't."

Dear God, I silently screamed to myself as my whole body began to tremble. *Why does it have to be me? Haven't I endured enough already?*

It seemed the answer to that question was a resounding no. Of all the red-blooded, larger-than-life Kennedy clan, only I had the strength to tell the doctors what had to be done.

"It's time to let Bobby go." Each word I spoke to the physician was a garrote around my throat, and I knew this scene would follow me into my nightmares.

He glanced around the room. "Are you speaking for the family?"

I looked at everyone in turn, waited for any dissent. There was none.

So it was my quaking hand that signed the stark consent form, my unblinking eyes that witnessed the somber attendant turn off the cold, unfeeling machines one by one, and my scarred soul that shattered anew when Bobby's chest fell for the last time. To me, it seemed a sigh of relief.

Rose dropped her head into her hands and we all held our breath as the heart monitor continued its measured cadence. Then . . .

It stopped.

Just like that, the heart that had bled for the plight of his fellow Americans, that had beat faster at the sight of me, that had grown with love to encompass the children of his slain brother . . .

It just stopped. And Bobby was gone.

"Well, now we know death." I hardly knew what I was saying, only heard the way my voice rung hollow as I spoke to Ethel. For the second time in my life, I found myself wishing that I, too, could die and leave all this behind. "In fact, if it weren't for our children, we'd welcome it ourselves."

Ethel seemed to understand, silent tears streaming down her cheeks as she gave a tiny nod acknowledging that we were now unlikely sisters in this miserable task of surviving.

"Thank you, Jackie," Rose said from her chair by the wall. She looked smaller than usual, frailer with her rosary tangled between her age-gnarled fingers. This was her fourth child to die, and had I not felt so numb myself, my heart would have bled for the woman who averted her eyes when her son breathed his last. "For doing what none of the rest of us could bring ourselves to do."

I only nodded, dreading the hours and days to come, for this time there was no one to put me back together.

Bobby is dead.

Bobby is dead.

Bobby is dead.

My heartbeat drummed the words, but my mind struggled to make sense of them even as the attendants came and carefully—reverently—took Bobby away. It was the same story over again, yet it was impossible that Bobby was gone. There was no blood on the front of my suit to make it real, only a now-empty hospital bed and a funeral to plan.

This was an abyss from which I might never return.

PART FOUR

. . . . .

June 8, 1968

The bronze bells had already tolled the nine o'clock hour by the time the journey ended beneath a bruised night sky scattered with pinpricks of stars. Throughout that humid and joyless day, the heavens had hung heavy with dull clouds while the somber funeral cortege traveled by train from New York's St. Patrick's Cathedral to that familiar grassy knoll in Arlington. The four-hour trip to Washington took twice as long to accommodate the thousands of tear-stained mourners— dirt-smudged farmers holding signs of condolence and weary factory workers with vacant eyes, wimpled nuns crossing themselves and young girls blowing sorrowful kisses—who wished to pay their solemn respects and bow their heads to the martyrs' widows as they acknowledged them from the observation deck.

It was all to be expected, until just outside Washington, when a press camera gave a lurid flash in the muffled darkness at the exact moment something thudded hard against the train carriage.

"Is someone shooting at us?" The first widow's young son clung to his mother's maid, his child's voice frantic and his small hand reaching for hers in the shadows. "Are they coming to get us next?"

In the darkness of the vestibule, the former First Lady's decaying heart crumbled further to overhear her son's question, and once they had arrived at Arlington, she welcomed the familiar numbness that chilled her gray soul. Flickering candles held by hundreds of mourners cast a yellow haze upon the cemetery's undulating sea of diminutive crosses. Some of the black-clad children held wilted flowers, others clasped rosaries.

The widow's hands were empty.

The former First Lady's lace veil obscured her face from curious onlookers, but her wince was palpable when the American flag that had draped the slain senator's African mahogany coffin was tucked away with pristine folds and placed into the youngest brother's open and trembling hands.

Only one Kennedy brother remained. There were whispers now that the family was cursed.

Mourners approached the coffin one by one, knelt and murmured their final words to the fallen. The widow's children clasped her hands tighter, her pale wisp of a daughter on one side and her raven-haired son on the other. Even in the gloom, they were twin blooms of light and hope. The girl—dressed in a pale blue English frock with puffed sleeves she didn't care for but had chosen because she knew how much her mother loved it—willed such steel into her spine that several onlookers muttered among themselves that no ten-year-old should be so accustomed to death as this.

The former First Lady watched her children bid good-bye to their favorite uncle; then she pushed aside her veil with black-gloved hands. It was a wonder to watch her infuse her very skin with dignity and force a queen's grace into each step she didn't wish to take as she approached the coffin. She spoke no words, only kissed the foot of the casket in an echo from another slain hero's funeral.

The only difference between this night and that November evening five years ago was the light overhead, the dying harvest moon replaced by a pregnant midsummer moon muted by roiling gray clouds.

Afterward, there was a second grave to visit, the family's short walk up the night-blackened hill guided by a dim beacon of flickering golden light from the eternal flame. There she bore tearful witness as her children knelt and said good-bye to their father once again.

When it was over and her children broke into wild and discordant sobs in her arms, she swore a bitter oath under her breath to them, to herself.

We will never do this again.

CHAPTER

19

June 1968

To everything there is a season: a time to be born and a time to die, a time to plant and a time to pluck up that which is planted. I knew the Bible verse from Ecclesiastes, but the days following Bobby's death were a time to mourn and a time to hate.

I mourned Bobby and I hated America. If my country had lain any claim to me after Jack's assassination, Bobby's murder had forfeited those ties. America and the Kennedys could keep the pieces of their shattered dreams; I wanted nothing to do with castles in the clouds, or with politics, ever again.

I knew I had to do something the afternoon I came home to find John sitting cross-legged on his bedroom floor, a pile of library books scattered around him. He was immersed in the open children's book on his lap, and I watched him dog-ear a page—a crime for which he'd usually be reprimanded—before he glanced up and blanched in alarm.

My skin prickled. "What are you reading?"

He slammed shut the book, then hid it behind his back before squirming away until he was pressed against his bed. "Don't look, Mommy."

"I'll never get upset at you for reading," I gently chided. "May I see?"

He removed the book from behind his back, the reluctant motion weighed down as if he were underwater. "Close your eyes, Mommy."

It was a children's history book containing a spread of important American events: the signing of the Declaration of Independence, Lincoln giving the Emancipation Proclamation, and Rosa Parks refusing to give up her seat at the front of the bus.

The dog-eared page showed Jack in a motorcade in Dallas, me beside him in a pink suit, and both of us waving in the moments before he was shot. I heard a roar in my ears as John covered the page with his little hands before I could read the text. "Don't look, Mommy," he repeated.

Even worse, my panicked heart thundered in my chest later that day when a somber Clint Hill informed me that the FBI had received death and kidnapping threats about both Caroline and John. "They started after the president's assassination." Mr. Hill's hands were clenched together so tightly that his knuckles were white. "The threats subsided, but a new wave has cropped up following his brother's murder. We don't find them to be credible, but . . ."

Every bone in my body was cracking with the need to escape all of this. If they were killing Kennedys, then my children were number-one targets.

I refused to allow my children to live in this poisoned country anymore. I wanted out of America.

Is it any wonder that two weeks after Bobby's funeral, I accepted Aristotle Onassis's offer to visit, even invited him for an overnight trip to meet my mother at Hammersmith Farm?

My mother, who loathed Ari for his scandalous relationship with my sister and had shuffled Lee out of Hammersmith so our two visits wouldn't overlap, who was even more disinclined to like him now that she suspected the designs he had on her eldest daughter . . .

We three sat on opposite ends of the sofa in the Deck Room after the children had trundled off to their baths, worn out from the toys Ari had brought to distract them from their grief over Bobby: a radio-controlled yacht for John and a first-edition copy of *Black Beauty* for Caroline. They'd both marveled at Ari's newly purchased cassette-tape contraption, and I'd managed a ghost of a smile while Ari ex-

plained the built-in microphones to my mother. The tinny notes of
Chopin and Tchaikovsky had transported me away from my troubles,
if only for a few minutes, but in the silence that followed, I drew a long
drag off my menthol Newport—I'd recently switched from L&Ms in
an attempt to be healthier—and pinned my bleary gaze on the stuffed
pelican hanging between the teak rafters.

"There was a time when Bobby meant more to me than life itself."
I heard the bitter note to my voice and recognized how easy it would be
to lock onto that tone forever, to stay in this place that was angry and
morbid for the rest of my days. I should be talking about something—
anything—else, but with Bobby gone, I was bruised and so damn
vulnerable, so *broken*.

My mother's frown was likely caused by a combination of my sat-
urnine mood, my smoking, and Ari's presence. "You have your children, Jackie. They will always be your life."

I scarcely startled when Ari plucked the cigarette from my hand
and stubbed it out in the ashtray. My mother cocked her head at him,
her tone frosty. "That's the third time you've done that to Jackie's
cigarette today, Mr. Onassis. Would you mind explaining why?"

Here we go . . .

A smile deepened the creases of his craggy face. "I don't mind if
women smoke, but I don't believe they should be seen smoking, don't
you agree, Mrs. Auchincloss?"

"Indeed." My mother nodded slowly, as if truly seeing Ari for the
first time. "In fact, I used to take Jackie's cigarettes away when she
was in the White House."

Ari smiled, neatly stacked the cassette tapes on the low coffee table,
and offered them to her. "You seemed most intrigued by this new
contraption earlier. It's yours."

My mother appeared taken aback at his generosity. If only she
knew how Ari had hidden a freshwater pearl the size of a grape in my
napkin at dinner. "No, really. I couldn't."

"I insist," Ari responded. "Think of it as my gift to this week's very
generous hostess."

My mother thanked him profusely, then rose. "It's getting late and Hughdie is waiting for me. Don't you two stay up too late."

We won't, Mummy, I thought. *Then we'll remove ourselves to the separate bedrooms you assigned us on opposite ends of the house.*

"You've accomplished the impossible," I said to Ari as I watched my mother depart with her new cassette player, the door to the deck room left gaping wide open behind her as if we were teenagers. "No one has managed to tame my mother so quickly."

"That's only the first Herculean task I mean to accomplish to-night," he said from his side of the couch. "I want you to marry me, Jackie."

Just like that. No romance or frills, only a matter-of-fact proposal, as if this was a business deal. It was only when Ari removed a black velvet box from his jacket pocket that I knew he'd been planning for this moment, perhaps for some time. I gaped at the contents, for in-side was the largest diamond I'd ever seen, a colossal dazzling mar-quise at least forty carats in size.

"The Lesotho III," Ari said offhand, as if he was speaking of the weather. "Cut from the largest diamond ever discovered by a woman. It's rare and beautiful, as is the woman who should wear it."

A freshly sharpened pickax of guilt stabbed me as I considered his proposal. How many people would I betray if I accepted? Surely Jack and certainly my sister. Bobby too? The entire Kennedy clan?

Yet Ari's next words eclipsed all those worries. "Let me take you away from all this. You know I'm the only one who can protect you, and your children."

"I don't love you," I said, even as my resolve weakened. I wasn't going to enter into this union under false pretenses, wasn't sure if I ever wanted to love again now that I'd twice experienced the heart-break that inevitably followed.

Ari merely shrugged. "No, but you're intrigued by me, and you like my money and the protection I can give you. That's a start."

There was only one thing I could say to that.

. . .

told the news only to my mother and a few close friends.

I waited to break word of my engagement to my mother over the phone; I lacked the courage to speak the words vis-à-vis and hadn't wanted to interrupt the lecture she was attending at Stratford Hall, but Ari and I had decided to be married on Skorpios in two days, so there wasn't time to waste. After a long pause, she had only one sharp question to ask over the crackling line. "Why are you going through with this tragedy, Jackie?"

I winced. I'd believed Ari had won my mother over, but I should have known it would take more than a gadget and a well-oiled smile to buy her acceptance. "I have no choice. They're playing 'Ten Little Indians.' I don't want the children to be next."

"You're not thinking straight. Aristotle Onassis is old enough to be your father and a well-known philanderer to boot. Do you even know for certain whether he ended his relationship with Maria Callas? Because he certainly carried on with her publicly when he was married to his first wife."

And even when he was with Lee . . .

"That's ancient history, Mother." I *had* asked Ari about Callas and even his first wife, who was still living, and he'd assured me they were over and done with. I wanted to believe him, so I did.

My mother cleared her throat. "It seems I'm forever doomed to watch you throw yourself at one man after another who can't truly love you, to see you make the same mistake I did with Black Jack Bouvier."

"This isn't about you, Mummy." The beginnings of a headache pounded at my temples. I imagined my mother off to the side when I walked down the aisle with Ari, repeating herself like a perfect Greek chorus: *All men are rats. All men are rats.* "This means getting out of America and protecting my children. If anything happened to Caroline or John, I would never forgive myself. And I would never survive it." My voice caught in my throat. "I simply would not survive it."

My mother's voice was so quiet I had to strain to hear it. "A marriage is supposed to be about happiness and love. Not the size of a man's bank account."

"Ari's money can keep the children and me safe." I ground out each word, struggling to keep my tone level. "That makes me happy."

What I didn't mention was that after I'd told Caroline I was planning to marry Ari, she'd curled up in her room, shoulders heaving with sobs next to the framed picture of Jack she kept by her bed until I asked the maid to help her pack.

My mother's sigh was heavy with resignation and disapproval. "I hope you're right, Jackie. And you need to speak to your sister."

I thought of my sister's affair with Ari but pushed the thoughts away, that is until Lee called me following the publication of a photograph of Ari and me in the *New York Post*. "If you marry Ari," she warned, "you're going to fall off your pedestal."

White-hot jealousy and anger threaded between her every word, yet I couldn't allow Lee to dissuade me now that I'd made up my mind. "It's better to fall off than be frozen to it."

It was flippant and I knew it, but I was preparing to marry my sister's former lover and was at a loss over what to say to her. Should I apologize? Ask her permission?

"The Kennedys will never forgive you." She spat out every word so her voice piped through my bones. "I might not either."

"I'm sorry, Lee." I swallowed, hard. I didn't wish to damage the Kennedys or my relationship with my sister, but things had changed with Bobby's death. I had to do what was best for my children and myself. Why couldn't everyone understand that? "Those are chances I have to take."

Lee was right. Ari called me to boast that the Kennedys had sent Teddy all the way to Greece to dissuade him from marrying me, all to no avail.

We married amid a chilly drizzle—considered good luck by the Greeks—on Ari's private island of Skorpios, almost as far away from America as I could manage. Outside the rain pounded this island stolen from an Old World fairy tale and a chill permeated everything—even my knee-length Valentino cream lace dress with bishop sleeves and delicate accordion pleats—inside the tiny stone Chapel of the Little Virgin.

"This is nothing like your wedding to Jack," Lee said under her breath as she handed me the bouquet. She'd deigned to be my matron of honor, and I knew I'd earned every bit of her frosty demeanor, which left me feeling as damp and cold as the weather. I'd have borne it if she'd abandoned me, as I'd done with everything else in this life, but I was grateful it hadn't come to that.

"I know," I said softly. "And I'm glad of it."

My mother had organized the processional line—both Caroline and John carried six-foot beeswax candles to place at the altar—and now she maneuvered Hughdie to my side, then leaned close to whisper in my ear. "You don't have to do this, Jacqueline."

"Stop it, Mummy," I said. "Or I will never speak to you again."

I ignored her pursed lips to follow Lee as the eerie harmonization from the trio of Byzantine choristers reverberated off the church's stone walls. Hughdie offered his arm to walk me down the aisle, the only echo from my first wedding. My stepfather sniffed, touched his nose with his handkerchief. "You deserve happiness after all you've been through," he murmured to me. "I hope you can find it now."

I squeezed Hughdie's hand when he handed me off to Ari. *I hope so too. . . .*

"All hail Queen Jacqueline!" Ari spoke loud enough for everyone to hear when I assumed my place beside him at the end of the aisle. My groom stood shorter than me in a midnight-blue suit with a fiery Pompeiian red rose at the buttonhole, his black hair brilliantined to a high shine so sharp the smell of his hair tonic tickled my nose. I couldn't have found a man more different from Jack, or Bobby.

Still, I cringed to think how Bobby would have lost his temper to see me standing upon this altar, offering myself to Aristotle Onassis. I didn't dare imagine what Jack would have thought.

Ari was exactly what I wanted. What I needed.

Yet, as we repeated our vows to the bearded Greek Orthodox metropolitan, our future didn't look perfectly becalmed. While Caroline and John stood silently on my side, Ari's grown children—his heir, Alexander, and daughter, Christina, whose unevenly lined eyes made her appear off-kilter and whom he'd named his boat after—glared at me from their corner with angry, unhappy faces.

It was no secret that they'd held out hopes that Ari would reconcile with their mother, had called me a gold digger when Ari told them of our engagement despite the fact that I'd accepted the barest prenuptial agreement with their father—a mere $3 million of Ari's $500 million fortune—against my financial adviser's vociferous protests. But I didn't care—Ari's children would come around, and in the meantime, my own children would be safe.

After we finished walking around the altar three times, Ari slipped his ring on my finger. In that moment, a rusty chain around my chest loosened; I was suddenly released from being a slain hero's widow.

I molted away my old life in that single moment, transformed from Jackie Kennedy into Jackie O.

"*Na zisete!*" the guests cheered. *Long life to you!*

Back on the *Christina* for the reception, boisterous Greek music played from the main deck while Ari presented me with my wedding gift of a spectacular ruby jewelry set worth more than a jaw-dropping $1 million before guiding me effortlessly around a dance floor bathed in the softest moonlight. I'd changed into a comfortable yellow evening gown with glass beads around the neck and slits up the sides; occasionally Ari rubbed my back in a reassuring manner, although it was the distance he put between his yacht and the press boats that I found even more heartening. Ari's children stayed as far from me as they could manage, but Lee approached between songs when Ari had gone to find us glasses of Dom Pérignon.

"You seem happy," she bit out grudgingly.

"I am. At least I think I am." I clasped her hand. "I need this, Lee. I hope you can understand that."

She blew a puff of air so forceful it lifted her hair, which wasn't easy to do considering the amount of lacquer in it. "I know you do. And I suppose you should have it. You are my sister, after all, and the map of love is uncharted."

I hugged her then and couldn't fault her when she excused herself as Ari approached, two gleaming Champagne flutes in hand.

"I still say there's something mystifying about you, Jackie," he murmured in my ear. "You're willful and provocative."

"Mystifying, willful, and provocative?" I felt a familiar flush of pleasure at Ari's words as I let him lead me to the edge of the deck, our guests still swirling around us in an effervescent cloud. "The mind reels at how one might accomplish such a contortion of character."

"It's simple." He balanced our drinks on the railing, clasped my pale hands in his sun-leathered ones and lifted them to my sides. "You look Greek but behave like an American princess."

"A princess or a queen?" I teased. "I can't be both."

"Princess, queen, sultana, empress . . . Does it matter?" My self-styled Sun King shook his head, smiled, and dropped my hands as he removed a fresh Montecristo from his jacket pocket. "And now that we are married," he said as he bit the end from the cigar, "you are the final diamond in my crown."

I flinched at the twinge of memory, of the Kennedy men once discussing my potential contributions to Jack's career as if I were a thing. But I kept my tongue as Ari lit his cigar, and I forced myself to relax in his arms. I reminded myself that we would be happy together in this mutually beneficial relationship, that the world would understand my decision to fly free from my cage.

To *live*.

After reading the headlines the following morning, I realized I'd misjudged the press. And the world.

"JACKIE SELLS OUT," yelled the *Los Angeles Times* from its front page.

This was followed by "WHY, JACKIE" and "JACK KENNEDY DIES TODAY A SECOND TIME," shouted from several other American papers.

"JACKIE, HOW COULD YOU" came all the way from far-flung Stockholm.

Even the Vatican denounced me as a public sinner because of Ari's scandalous divorce from his first wife.

"It seems I found my peccadillo," I said to Ari as I refolded the offending papers and pushed the stack as far beyond the breakfast trays as I could reach.

He waggled two thick eyebrows and passed me a croissant liberally slathered in quince preserves. "Indeed you did. And doesn't it feel grand?"

He was right; I was already starting to breathe easier. With my marriage, my Secret Service detail had been terminated, and I'd bid a fond farewell to Clint Hill just the night before. Although the children still retained agents for their protection, after eight long years, I no longer had the shadow of a black suit following my every step.

Ari and I behaved like teenagers on our honeymoon—I was only slightly scandalized that he'd made us our own private plane by having the first-class seating removed from an Olympic Airways jet and replacing it with a king-size bed—so I even managed to ignore the news when Richard Nixon was elected president back home, further proof that Bobby's death had irrevocably changed the course of the nation.

Like my first honeymoon, the second one ended all too soon.

In a fit of dramatics one night, Alexander, Ari's son and heir, loudly proclaimed when I asked him to stay for dinner, "Since my father married, I have no home."

He gave me a pointed stare—as if daring me to justify such horrific manners with a response—then Ari's son swiveled in a move worthy of the stage at Versailles and stormed toward the door. Christina, who had just come down from upstairs, glared in my direction as if she might spit and gathered up her handbag. "Good night, *kyría*."

Kyría. Lady.

I supposed that was kinder than the other nicknames she and her brother whispered about me: Gold digger. Widow.

Still, I barely kept my jaw from hitting the floor when she made a sign to ward off the evil eye. I waited for Ari to rebuke his grown children, but my husband scarcely looked up from his accounts as they stormed away.

Alexander was Ari's alpha and omega—the golden heir-who-could-do-no-wrong—and I'd been warned to tiptoe around his daughter's moods, which often swung toward dangerous depressions, but had they been younger, I'd have thrown them over my knee and spanked the lot of them. Instead, I could only assume that their every whim had been indulged since birth, that Ari's vast wealth had spoiled them in more ways than one.

But that didn't mean I was going to turn a blind eye.

"I don't know why your children are so rude to me," I said to Ari after the front door had slammed behind them. A sputtering roar came from the direction of Skorpios's private air strip a few moments later, Alexander's ancient Piaggio coming to life before it could whisk them away from me. I wondered what had happened to the young man famed throughout Greece for helping people ill or stranded in remote areas; most recently Alexander had rescued a fisherman's son whose hands had been blown off by dynamite, yet he treated me worse than a leper.

"Worry about your own children, not mine, dear," he said. I didn't like the nasty undercurrent to his tone, but we were new at this, so I bit my tongue and went upstairs to read with Caroline and John. Passing my bedroom, a strange scattering of something that glittered like old snow on the carpet caught my attention.

Salt, I thought as I touched the ground, the crystals hard and scratchy against my palm. No doubt left behind by Ari's vindictive daughter.

Perhaps Christina didn't realize that I knew the Greek superstition of using salt to drive away an unwanted guest. Or perhaps she wanted me to know where I wasn't welcome, as if she and her brother hadn't already made that perfectly clear.

Ari's children stayed away, and I floated listlessly from one sun-drenched day to the next. To my growing consternation, Ari kept me at arm's length whenever I asked about his businesses, beginning with his Project Omega deal with Greece's current dictator, Giorgios Papadopoulos. "You'd be bored," Ari claimed one night as he inspected the ledgers for Olympic Airways onboard the *Christina*, as if I was too simple-minded to understand business or government. "How is your Greek coming along?"

"Fine," I answered, for I'd taken to learning how to conjugate Greek verbs alongside Caroline and John, determined to master my new husband's native tongue. Still, learning a new language came easily to me, and my days confined to the island were lackluster—and I rarely left. To my dismay, Ari's protection from the lenses of the paparazzi didn't extend beyond Skorpios and the *Christina*. While Ari often traveled to Paris for business, I'd found myself missing my apartment in New York, the food carts near Central Park, the museums and concert halls that had once thrilled me.

So I was enthusiastic when NBC called to offer me a lucrative position anchoring a television show about Venice and Angkor Wat. I was intrigued and excited about the idea, but I'd waited to mention it to Ari. Now I dared broach the subject, and immediately wished I hadn't.

"What are they thinking?" he huffed into his ouzo. "No Greek wife works."

Yes, my dear, I wanted to say. *But I'm not Greek.*

Yet I knew better than to push, especially considering that Ari had dipped into his extensive liquor cabinet, and I could see from here that Olympic was operating in the red this month, a combination guaranteed to make him fractious. "I saw your little tour of the White House," he said, surprising me as he tapped a pencil over the ledgers. "Why don't you busy yourself with redecorating my Pink House on Skorpios? Spend as much as you like."

This, from the man who refused to let me so much as move a

framed photograph onboard the *Christina*, where he continued to eat most of his meals and sleep most nights. I almost laughed, thinking Ari spoke in jest, until I realized he was serious.

Does he really think changing wallpapers and settees in his villa compares with my renovation of the White House? And does he truly think I can be happy when my whole world has been constricted to this one tiny island?

However, I wondered if Ari's suggestion was a sort of peace offering. There was no denying I loved to decorate and change things, and I was going to start climbing the walls if I didn't do something. I wanted my houses to express my personality in everything I used in them. There were so many things in this world I couldn't change, but when it came to furniture and draperies, paintings and flowers . . .

So I did as Ari suggested, working to fluff up the pink villa atop Skorpios's highest hill. It was lovely, really, a gem set amid the island's lush greenery, where every morning I breathed in the rich scents of eucalyptus and jasmine that swirled in the briny sea air. As a tribute to the memory of his grandmother, Ari had planted around the island trees of the Old Testament: almond, fig, cypress, and pine, and he'd installed a six-horse stable reminiscent of Hammersmith Farm, which piped in classical music to keep the Shetland ponies calm. The entire island was a juxtaposition in opposites, melding the rugged beauty of miles of empty riding paths with a decadent palace staffed with waiters in white gloves serving Dom Pérignon and beluga caviar at dinner.

I can be happy here, I thought to myself. *I will* try *to be happy here.*

If not happy, I would at least be content, safe in the knowledge that my children and I were protected and that we would never again want for anything material. On that idyllic island, perhaps we might even forget for a while that we were Kennedys.

For a little while, at least . . .

I t was more than a year after Bobby's assassination when the children and I gathered around the Pink House's freshly unpacked RCA New Vista color television to watch in awe as Neil Armstrong landed on the moon. Ari was in Paris—staying at his daughter Christina's apartment while he conducted meetings for Olympic Airways—but Caroline, John, and I had grown accustomed to his frequent absences.

"One small step for man," John repeated, cheering as we held hands and witnessed the breathtaking moment in history. "One giant leap for mankind!"

"That's what Daddy promised, wasn't it?" Caroline asked quietly as eight-year-old John leaped across the shining living room floor as if it were the dusty moonscape, scarcely keeping his balance when he slipped on one of the new flokati rugs I'd ordered. "To put a man on the moon?"

"It is." I stared at the screen with no small amount of awe. I still remembered the day Jack had given the speech at Rice University that claimed America would go to the moon before the decade ended, *not because it is easy but because it is hard*. And I recalled the way people scoffed and said it couldn't be done. "America did it."

That was the first moment since Bobby's assassination that I was proud of America. That I missed its bold daring.

Caroline settled back into the settee's cushions while I unwrapped a box Ari had left for me, its note instructing that it be opened only after the moon landing was complete. Inside dangled a pair of solid gold ear clips shaped like tiny moons, their hammered surfaces cratered with chips of rubies and suspended from space capsules. And a note that read *Next year, if you're good, I'll give you the moon itself*. I replaced the note and earrings in their box. Maybe I'd wear the gaudy trinkets one day, but not today, not when Jack's memory was so near.

Caroline cleared her throat, a copy of *The Jungle Book*—one of my childhood favorites—waiting on her lap to transport her to Mowgli's jungle. She would happily spend the afternoon reading, but I guessed John would play at being an astronaut until he collapsed into bed tonight, probably while mumbling *the Eagle has landed* into his dreams. Caroline touched my hand to get my attention. "When are we going back, Mommy?"

"Going back where?"

"To America. And the White House." She glanced at her brother and whispered, "John doesn't even remember it. And he lived there."

I bit my lip, realizing that no matter how I'd sought to protect my children, it wasn't enough to run away, that I'd been a fool to think we could hide from being Kennedys. Borrowed dreams in the Pink House on Skorpios were only that: dreams. The time had come for us to confront certain ghosts, no matter how I trembled at the thought.

Not because it is easy . . . I heard Jack's New England drawl echoing in my head as I gazed at his children, more precious to me than life itself. *But because it is hard.*

I t had taken me more than half a decade to return to the White House. I might have stayed away forever, but Caroline and John deserved a chance to see the places where they had lived with their father. So when Pat Nixon—who had condemned my fashion choices when our husbands ran their cutthroat race for president—extended an official request for me to view the unveiling of Jack's and my official portraits by Aaron Shikler, I mustered my courage and accepted, although it would have been far easier to make the same excuses I had for the myriad other events I'd refused to attend at America's *Maison Blanche* over the years.

When I arrived with the children—Ari had tactfully declined to accompany us—I was surprised to discover the White House a veritable ghost town. "This is odd," I said as Caroline and John climbed out of the limo behind me.

"What is?" John asked. He was nonplussed about the entire event, but Caroline had fallen silent since we'd pulled onto Pennsylvania Avenue, so I wondered what sort of forgotten memories were swirling in her mind.

"No tourists, not a camera in sight. I've never seen it this way." My heart fluttered like a trapped songbird as we stepped into the pillared South Portico, where Jack and I had so often greeted foreign heads of state before welcoming them into an elegant dinner party, violin concertos playing in the background and *filets de sole Normande* waiting to be served. It didn't matter that this time I was the guest; if I closed my eyes, I could imagine Jack in the alcove dressed in his finest tuxedo, nodding to me so his hair fell over his forehead. *Welcome back, kid.*

Part of me wanted to run, but I anchored myself by holding tight to my children's hands. Caroline and John were my ballasts now, forever and always. "No matter who lives here," I said to them, "remember that this will always be your house too."

Not a single soul bustled in the echoing corridors as we were led by the new chief usher—sadly, J. B. West had retired two years prior—into the cheery Diplomatic Reception Room.

"We're so glad you're here." Pat Nixon greeted us warmly alongside her grown daughters, Tricia and Julie. Her pleasant greeting was a total about-face from when her husband and mine had faced off for their presidential debates, but that seemed a lifetime ago, and we were different people now.

"It's so quiet," I marveled after I'd introduced my children, both of whom offered the First Lady their finest handshakes with such pristine manners that I fairly beamed at them.

"The White House is on lockdown for the duration of your visit," Pat informed me in a gentle voice. "No interruptions or disturbances."

My shoulders relaxed and I smiled my thanks. Perhaps I shouldn't have minded the potential interruptions, but I had no desire to share this sacred moment with members of the gawking public or the paparazzi.

Pat pointed to the chandelier overhead. "It's an antique, English Regency," she said, and I recognized the tactic to make me feel at ease. "Lady Bird and I have done our best to follow the guidelines you set for each room with your restoration."

"It's perfect." It may have been hubris, but I enjoyed the idea that my work on the White House restoration might inform other First Ladies' decorating for years—perhaps decades—to come. I couldn't stop myself from reaching out to touch the striking panoramic wallpaper I'd installed back in 1961, the images of the Natural Bridge of Virginia and Niagara Falls.

This isn't a dream, or a nightmare. Just another scene in the extraordinary story that is your life.

Tricia Nixon knelt next to Caroline, who had dressed for today's momentous visit in a gray jumper and jacket topped by a jaunty red beret and brushed camel topcoat. "Would you like to go up to the Solarium?" she asked. "I believe that's where you had your first school."

Caroline looked to me for permission, which I was happy to give. "Your kindergarten was on the roof of the White House," I said.

Her face lit at the memory. "I remember. We used to sculpt clay animals and sing the alphabet song while we ate graham crackers. Sometimes you came in and taught us poetry."

Together, we traipsed upstairs, where both Caroline and John took in the view of the National Mall from the Solarium. I pointed out the holly trees that had once hid a trampoline I'd installed for exercise, where the children had sometimes come to bounce with me in the mornings. All traces of Caroline's kindergarten were long since removed, but ghosts still whispered to me from the walls.

Jack toweling his still-damp hair after his afternoon swimming lesson with Caroline.

John taking his first wobbly steps in the Lincoln Bedroom.

Bobby leading me downstairs to Jack's casket to say good-bye.

My mind became so mired in the past that I scarcely heard John ask the question that must have been at the forefront of his mind since we'd arrived. "May we see the Oval Office?" he asked Pat Nixon. "I remember playing with my father there."

I ran out of planes in my drawer for him that day. So we turned the Resolute Desk into a cave.

"Of course," she responded. "I asked Dick if he could work somewhere else this afternoon, just in case you wanted to visit." I was touched by the Nixons' thoughtfulness as Pat and her daughters led us to the West Wing, where she held open the door to the president's innermost sanctum. "We'll wait outside."

The Oval Office belonged to Richard Nixon now—and it was his memorabilia and family photos scattered about the desk and shelves—but Jack was still everywhere: standing in the shaft of February sunlight that streamed through the windows as he pondered the escalations in Vietnam, crouched in the chair behind the Resolute Desk with his hands in his hair as he agonized with Bobby over the puzzle that was the Cuban Missile Crisis, crawling on the carpet as he played planes with John.

I swayed on my feet, steadied only by my son's hand at my elbow.

"He loved this place, didn't he?" John asked quietly, as if he, too, was afraid of disturbing this sacred space.

My only reply was a tearful nod.

When we finally backed out of the room, the Nixons silently ushered us to Jack's new portrait in Cross Hall. The moment I saw it, I wanted nothing more than to reach out and touch that bumper crop of sandy hair I'd always loved. It was I who had commissioned Aaron Shikler after he had painted portraits of the children and me, and my only stipulation was that he not paint Jack the way everyone else made him look, with bags under his eyes and a penetrating stare. Art could preserve the best of the past, and Shikler had rendered the best of Jack with his head bowed, caught in a moment of contemplation so unlike all the other godforsaken postage-stamp presidential portraits hanging in the White House. Jack hadn't been a perfect man, or even a perfect president, but this portrayal of him was without fault. I swallowed over the lump in my throat. "Thank you for displaying his portrait so prominently," I managed to say to Pat.

"Of course." She gave a sad smile. "Both Dick and I agree that a great light went out when America lost him."

I nodded, but I suddenly worried that I'd made the wrong decision in bringing the children today, that seeing their father's office and portrait were burdens too heavy to bear. They might have thought the same of me, for both turned to me with shining eyes. "It's a good portrait," Caroline said to me, and the way she tilted her head reminded me of Jack's inquisitiveness, the way he scrutinized everything.

"Father would have liked it," John agreed.

And that was that.

Afterward, we meandered to the Family Dining Room on the second floor, where Tricky Dick himself joined us, accompanied by a barking medley from a French poodle, a Yorkshire terrier, and an Irish setter named King Timahoe that Caroline took an instant liking to. "Welcome back, Mrs. Kennedy," Nixon said as he motioned—without success—for the dogs to sit. "The girls and I are so glad you could come. Were you able to see everything you wished?"

"Just Jackie, please," I said. "And yes, everything today was just perfect."

"I hope you like meatloaf and spicy pepperoni salad." Nixon spoke equally to the children and me, and while they responded politely—Caroline wasn't a picky eater and John would eat anything—their eyes strayed eagerly to the dogs. "I know," the president said with a laugh. "My dogs are far more interesting that I am. Go ahead."

"He reminds me of Pushinka." Caroline giggled when Tricia Nixon fed King Timahoe a slice of meatloaf as it was served, putting one finger over her lips as the dog lapped up his clandestine treat. I smiled, wishing I had a camera to capture so many images: the way John's legs swung happily beneath his chair, the rich taste of the Bordeaux (real Bordeaux, not the cheap bottles I'd heard Nixon usually served to guests with a towel wrapped around the label), and even the dining room wallpaper that still bore images of diminutive British redcoats at the battle of Yorktown, which I'd chosen as one of America's most historic moments in battle.

I listened in utter contentment as the current president of the United States regaled my children with stories of the one-lane bowling alley he'd had installed beneath the North Portico of the White House, with invitations for a competition after the strawberry shortcake was served. It was as if we were at any family dinner, no longer bogged down in a quagmire of former feuds, painful memories, or echoes of an incomplete presidential legacy from long ago. I had faced my ghosts so my children might rediscover their childhood and thus had witnessed a day I always dreaded transformed into one of the most precious memories of my life.

As we waved good-bye to the Nixons later that evening (after a round of bowling that John won, although I suspected the president had purposefully aimed for the gutter), I recognized this bittersweet day for what it truly was.

A gift.

CHAPTER

20

August 1971

Once I returned from the White House, my days with Ari settled into a peaceful routine, tranquil on the surface, so long as no mention was made of his failing business enterprises. We would read in the morning, swim and take meandering sunset walks on the beach in the early evening. Some days we skimmed over the waves of the Aegean on the *Christina* to visit crumbling temples on Rhodes, Patmos, and Corfu.

In my studies of everything Greek, I'd read with rapt attention the travails of Odysseus against Charybdis, she of the churning whirlpools intent on swallowing ships whole. Little did I know my Montecristo-smoking Odysseus was his own Charybdis, lurking just beneath the restful surface of our lives.

One rainy evening in Glyfada, I was sitting with Ari and a triumvirate of his business associates, one ear pricked while pretending not to listen to their heated discussion regarding Ari's struggling Project Omega. The enterprise was meant to build up Greece's oil refineries and aluminum smelters but was failing in the face of Greece's recent military junta. Ari became more and more agitated so that I almost intervened to change the subject. Fortunately, the talk veered away from business and more toward crass jokes about Ari's business rivals, and I let myself fall into reading a biography about Socrates. I'd kept up my studies of all things Greek until it felt as if I knew more about the country's history than my Greek-born husband. My wine forgotten, I'd become so engrossed in the pages on the trial that led to Socrates's death that I didn't notice Ari trying to get my attention.

"Honey." His ouzo sloshed over the edge of its glass, and I balked to see how much liquor the men had already packed away. I recalled the copious amounts of alcohol my father used to drink, but Black Jack Bouvier was an affable drunk. Ari, on the other hand, was less agreeable after he'd tippled too much. "Did you know a woman is like the world?"

"Oh really?" I kept reading, listening with only half an ear. "How is that true?"

"At twenty years, she is like Africa. Semi-explored. At thirty years, she is India. Warm, mature, and mysterious. At forty, she is like America. Technically perfect. At fifty years, she's Europe. All in ruins. At sixty years, she is Siberia. Everyone knows where she is, but no one wants to visit her."

I was forty-two and could think of little to say in the face of his boorish tirade. Instead, I used my reading glasses to mark my page and closed the book in my lap. "Do you think Socrates really existed?" I asked Ari's nearest friend. It was a blatant attempt to redirect the conversation, but also a question I was truly interested in discussing. Either answer seemed plausible to me; after all, even Homer's and Shakespeare's existence had been called into question at one time or another. "Or do you think he was an invention of Plato, created to represent all the Athenian philosophers of the day?"

Ari's friend opened his mouth to answer, but my husband had had too much ouzo, or perhaps too much of a woman who didn't fit his expectations of how a good wife should act. Namely, that I should remain silent and content myself with being the largest diamond in his crown.

He leaped from the sofa, going purple in the face in a way I'd never seen. "What is the matter with you?" he actually screamed, and I lurched back in surprise and to avoid the spittle leaping from his mouth. "Why do you have to talk about such stupid things? Don't you ever stop to think before you open your mouth? Have you ever noticed the statue of a man with a mustache that is in the center of Athens? Are you too stupid to know that is a statue of Socrates?"

Hot tears of anger and humiliation welled in my eyes at his tirade, but I refused to let them fall, even when I felt the gazes of Ari's guests slide away. My cheeks burned to realize they were embarrassed for him, for me.

Wordlessly, I stood, muttering to myself in French. *"Oui, bâtard. Je le sais."*

I scarcely restrained myself from lobbing a further grenade of angry words at him, wasn't surprised when Ari didn't apologize as I donned my jacket and escaped outside in the rain. I lifted my face to the weeping sky, willing the raindrops to cool the rumbling Vesuvius of my boiling rage.

What on God's blessed earth have I gotten myself into?

I didn't care that Ari's business projects were struggling or that he had certain expectations that I'd be a quiet and unassuming wife. It was unacceptable—unforgiveable, even—for him to snap as he had. I understood the need to change costumes depending on what role was necessary in the moment, but I worried that this turbulent, crude peasant of a man was the real Aristotle Onassis, and the one I'd married had been a façade, an impresario of a grand circus act meant to lure me in.

And there were more potent deceptions to come . . .

ow many times has Ari traveled to Paris since you were married?" Lee had barely said hello before she launched into her query one afternoon just as I'd sat down to a lonely lunch of *dolmas*. With the children at school and Ari and I scarcely speaking, the Pink House seemed smaller now every time I returned, as if the walls had moved a few feet in the time I'd been gone. I'd been planning to go riding to clear my mind and considered begging off from talking to Lee; telephone conversations with my sister were stilted these days, but she'd forgiven me for marrying Ari, which meant my afternoon ride would have to wait.

So I set aside my untouched plate of stuffed grape leaves, found myself worrying the extravagant gold bracelet at my wrist that had been Ari's wordless apology for his outburst about Socrates. He'd left the flashy bauble on my nightstand before he'd left for France for the weekend, supposedly for something about Olympic Airways.

Merde alors, I thought to myself. *What is my sister up to now?*

"I don't know," I said. "I suppose he's gone a handful of times. He often meets his daughter there."

"He's cheating on you, Jacks." Lee's words possessed the ruthless- ness of a blood-spattered guillotine. "All those supposed business trips? They're fronts so he can be with Maria Callas. A friend of mine saw him leaving her apartment yesterday morning. He was wearing his opera clothes from the night before, and Maria . . . Let's just say she was in a state of dishabille."

A cold stillness settled over me at the cruelty of Lee's details, the certainty that I'd acted—and that the curtain had fallen on—this scene before in my life. *Fin.*

Except suddenly all the disjointed pieces made sense: Ari's coldness toward me, the late-night telephone conversations that abruptly ended when I walked into the room, the ever-more-frequent trips to the City of Lights, and his refusal to elaborate on the business he did there. Surely I'd recognized the signs . . . had I simply refused to see the evidence staring me in the face?

"Are you sure, Lee?" My stomach clenched with the question. "Are you positively sure?"

Lee interpreted my shock as permission to vent her frustrations, which had likely accumulated since my marriage to Ari, each word becoming an angry jab in the air. "Did you really think you'd be im- mune just because you're Jackie Kennedy? Ari only cared about add- ing you to his collection; he lost interest the moment his ring was on your finger."

That ring was supposed to set me free, not lock me in a gilded cage.

"What is wrong with me?" My voice cracked as I yanked Ari's heavy golden bracelet from my wrist, snapping its clasp before I flung it into the bottom of a dresser drawer. While I appreciated the security Ari gave me, I didn't love him—not really—but that didn't mean I enjoyed being humiliated like this. "For my husbands to treat me like this?"

"It's how men—especially the powerful ones—are." My sister gave a high bark of laughter, so I could imagine her throwing her hands in the air. "Look on the bright side: at least you wheedled a ring from Ari before he climbed back into Maria's bed, which is more than I ever managed."

I winced at her crassness before sliding down the wall and bracing my aching head against my knees. With all the tragedies in my life, I felt as though I'd walked through every street in hell, had believed I'd finally escaped into a life of ease—if not love—by marrying Ari.

Instead, it seemed I'd found myself back on a familiar road of public and private humiliation, still as fiery and filled with brimstone as ever.

Bordel de merde.

I t was almost with relief that I received a phone call from Rose Kennedy one sunny November morning. The children had joined us for a long weekend from school, and I'd been cheering Caroline as she made jumps on the white pony Ari had recently given her, perhaps as a sideways apology to me for his recent transgressions, although I had yet to confront him about Maria Callas. John was with Ari; the boys had taken the *Christina* for a jaunt to Athens with plans to see a picture show before returning late this evening. Ari was a decent stepfather to my children, but that was no longer enough for me. Unfortunately, I didn't know how to untangle the never-ending skein of this problem.

See no evil, hear no evil, speak no evil. Except I've already heard it and now I can't unsee it everywhere I turn.

So it was that I welcomed the distraction of Rose's call. But I wanted to unhear the reason why she called the moment she began to speak.

"He doesn't have much time left." The bad connection was full of crackling delays, but waves of gooseflesh still rolled up my arms. "You should come, Jackie. I think he's waiting for you."

How many Kennedy men was I destined to bid farewell to? Yet this was one I'd been preparing for since the stroke had nearly felled him almost eight years ago.

"I'll be on the first plane out of Greece," I assured her. "Tell Mr. Kennedy I'm coming."

I hung up with a feeling of remorse, stood staring at the empty horizon until Caroline burst inside, her cheeks pink from the exertion of riding. Her brows knit with concern as soon as she saw my face. "What's wrong, Mom?"

How I wished my children had known Jack's father before he'd been ill so they would possess memories of the vibrant, witty colossus that Mr. Kennedy had once been. Instead, they'd only ever known their grandfather as the broken man who remained mostly in bed and required a pad of paper to write in a trembling hand whatever it was he wanted to say to them.

"It's your grandfather," I said, holding out my hand for her. "It's time to say good-bye."

We flew to his side, all three of us Kennedys. Ari offered to accompany us, but the idea of him at Mr. Kennedy's bedside while surrounded by Jack's remaining siblings seemed like the worst sort of trespassing. Still, he was kind and solicitous, arranging for all the details of our transportation without being asked.

"I'll be waiting for you." His hand lingered on the small of my back as the Olympic Airways staff wheeled the metal gangplank into place. "Hurry home."

Try not to enjoy yourself with Maria Callas while we're gone, I thought, but managed to bite my tongue. *Speak no evil, Jackie, and everything remains status quo.*

The only problem was, I wasn't sure I was willing to settle for the status quo. I'd think about that another day.

The compound in Hyannis Port was somber when we arrived, a stillness to the very sea air as if the old clapboard house was holding its breath, waiting for its revered patriarch to pass the torch to a new generation.

Yet who would lead the Kennedys now that their uncrowned queen had fled the kingdom and their old emperor lay dying?

Without Jack or Bobby, that heavy mantle would fall to poor, unfortunate Teddy. Their scapegrace younger brother had a heart cast from gold, but his life was in shambles after he'd recently caused a young woman's death after driving their car into a lake and then fleeing the scene. I didn't envy Teddy; at least I'd had the ability to fly far away from this place that held so many memories, yet so few remaining living ties.

Some were not so lucky.

As was tradition stretching back to time immemorial, Rose awaited our greeting on the porch, her face etched with fatigue. "You children can settle into your rooms upstairs," she said kindly after both Caroline and John had kissed her cheeks. A maid dressed in somber gray and white opened the front door and wordlessly ushered us into the foyer. "*Midnight Cowboy* will start in the basement theater at eight o'clock sharp."

John's face lit at the mention of a movie, but Caroline gestured to a lopsided mountain of stamped envelopes in a basket on the hall table, so out of place in a house where Rose maintained absolute order. "Do you want me to take those to the mailbox, Grandma?" Caroline asked. "There certainly are a lot of them."

"That's very kind, but I'll take them myself in a moment," Rose answered. "I write so many prayer cards these days. I respond to every note I've received about your father and uncle."

Oh, Rose, I thought with a shudder. *I'm not sure whether to pity or revere you.*

Rose Kennedy turned to me as my children filed upstairs, followed by the butler and maids with all our luggage. "Jacqueline, will you walk the perimeter with me?" She held up a hand with two rosaries woven between her gnarled fingers. "I thought we could pray together."

I recognized the command couched as a question, so I accepted the second rosary and walked in silence alongside Jack's mother as the sun sunk toward the horizon. We paused to deliver the basket of prayer cards to the mailbox, but only once we finished reciting all sixty-plus prayers and arrived back at the main house did Rose stop me with a frail hand on my arm. "I've always admired your dignity, Jacqueline." Her voice quavered, then recovered. "I'm glad you've come, if only so I can borrow from that well of strength."

It occurred to me then that Rose Kennedy, who managed every minute detail of every day, did so because there were few other things she could control in a life where so many things—so many people, including her husband who lay dying inside and the four children she had already buried—had spiraled beyond her reach. I thought of the way I'd hung and rehung pictures in the days after Jack's death, how I still loved to rearrange my art collection or reorganize a closet in the middle of the night. Perhaps Rose and I weren't so dissimilar after all.

In fact, Rose might be the toughest Kennedy of them all.

She walked me to the first-floor space that had been converted into a makeshift hospital room so I might have a few moments alone with Jack's father. Outside on the lawn where I'd once played football with Jack and his siblings, Teddy now chased Caroline and John and all their cousins in a raucous game of tag.

Life would go on. Somehow, it always did.

Yet, inside, everything was stillness. Not for the first time, I wondered what Jack's father could ever have done to deserve such a long, lingering death. While this might be the end, the truth was that Mr. Kennedy had been slowly sliding away from us since the day of his stroke nearly eight years ago.

The door scarcely made a sound on well-oiled hinges as I opened it to reveal a room muted by gray. The sleeping figure shifted on the bed as I approached and Mr. Kennedy's eyelids flickered open to reveal rheumy eyes. Was there recognition as I released the bed's metal railing so I could sit next to him and clasp his dear, age-spotted old hand to my cheek? "Oh, Poppy Doodle," I murmured. "How weary you must be."

His fingers fluttered against my temple and his eyes closed, but I had the sense that those keen ears with his even keener mind were still listening, still waiting . . .

So I began to talk, as I had that day after Jack's death. This time, I recited to Mr. Kennedy only the happiest of memories.

Of the time he'd first welcomed me to Hyannis Port, how he'd put me at ease by calling me "kiddo."

Of Jack saluting his father at his inauguration, his eyes sparkling with pride.

How we'd once stopped at a snake farm on our way to Camp David so John could pet a tame cobra named George.

Of Caroline and John bursting in to surprise Jack in the Oval Office that last Halloween together, Caroline dressed as a witch and John as a goblin.

Bobby teaching my children to fly a kite they'd designed together to look like Air Force One.

Of our recent trip to the Caribbean, the children shrieking in the rollicking turquoise waves as they tried to bury each other in the sand.

I couldn't tell how much Mr. Kennedy heard or understood, but I kept up the steady stream of joyful memories until night had fallen outside and Teddy appeared next to me, a green sleeping bag in hand. "I thought I'd sleep in here tonight," he said as he offered me a pillow. "You're welcome to stay too."

The children came then to bid their grandfather good night—good-bye—and again, Mr. Kennedy's eyelids fluttered at their voices before he settled back into stillness. I left his bedside only to tuck them in and join their prayers for their grandfather before resuming my vigil next to Mr. Kennedy's bed. Throughout the dark night I barely dozed, waking at the slightest rustle or change of sound while listening to Teddy snoring on the floor.

I'd witnessed death come to collect the souls of three Kennedy men: first Jack, then Bobby, and now their father. For finally, as the sun rose on November 18, four days shy of the sixth anniversary of Jack's death, Mr. Kennedy slipped peacefully away.

"Rest well." I touched Mr. Kennedy's stilled hands just as I'd done his sons', then bent to press a kiss onto his forehead. "Go to them now. Go to your boys."

Tell them Jackie says hello.

January 1973

n the years that followed Mr. Kennedy's death, I managed to avoid some—but not all—of Ari's squalls of temper by escaping home to the comforting bustle of New York City as often as possible, especially as my children remained enrolled in schools there. The quiet oasis of my apartment at 1040 welcomed me back whenever I returned, and it was there that I found an unlikely distraction from my grief and marital woes when I picked up the *Times* one morning to the headline "City's Naming of Grand Central as a Landmark Voided by the Court." I grew more and more enraged with each word of the story, for not only was the historic train station's landmark status being voided, but the entire Beaux-Arts terminal was going to be torn down and replaced by yet another soulless skyscraper.

Choose one thing and do it well. . . .

There was no denying that the graceful old building had fallen on hard times—its waiting room was now a homeless camp commuters did their best to avoid, and the only retailers were a couple of stands that sold near-poisonous sandwiches—but I recalled walking hand-in-hand with my father beneath its yawning cerulean ceiling studded with a golden zodiac and imagined that beauty lost forever, all its history gone with a few swoops of the wrecking ball. . . .

Not if I can help it.

I didn't mention the project to Ari or anyone else, just placed a few phone calls that morning to the preservation society and the Municipal Art Society, laughed silently to myself when I heard a secretary's muffled voice say to her boss, "I know you won't believe me, but there's a woman on the phone who claims to be Jackie Kennedy."

Needless to say, he took my call.

When I hung up, it was with future meetings already penciled in on the calendar and a fresh outlook of enthusiasm and anticipation I hadn't felt in a long time, since before Bobby's death at least. This project was something to follow in the footsteps of Lafayette Square and Abu Simbel, even the White House restoration, and I was excited to dust off my role of Jackie, historian and preservationist, even more surprised to realize how much I'd missed her.

But I was still Jackie, wife and stepmother. And family came first when Ari received word that his son, Alexander, had crashed his elderly beloved Piaggio, and was now lying in an Athens hospital with irreversible brain damage.

dropped everything and flew with Ari to Athens where a gray-faced Christina met us in the hospital room where her brother lay unconscious. "If I give you my entire fortune, can you save my boy's life?" Ari begged the neurosurgeon after arranging for the sacred icon of the Virgin Mary to be flown in from the island of Tinos, a place where the sick and dying made pilgrimages. Only one thought came to me as I took in the young man's shattered face, the concavity of his skull that no neurosurgeon could possibly repair.

There is no way he can survive this. This will break Ari.

And it did.

The strong, irascible Greek I'd married could barely sign the necessary paperwork and crumbled to the floor the moment the doctor cut Alexander's life support. A memory hit me—of another set of machines echoing another man's final heartbeats—but I put my guard up before the blow could land. Instead, I watched as Ari became a husk of himself, an old man who couldn't stop crying over the loss of his boy.

Something glass-fragile shattered inside me in that hospital room. I'd barely survived the deaths of my three infants who had never been given the chance to live, but now Ari was being forced into every parent's darkest nightmare.

"My son is dead," he muttered over and over, rocking back and forth on the cold hospital chair as they wheeled Alexander's body away. The gurney squeaked as it passed, a damaged wheel spinning listlessly out of control.

Ari was still muttering those same words to himself a month later after the funeral had finally taken place. All our prior animosities set aside, I worried for him and even for Christina, whose moods often plunged toward dangerous depressions and who had been so close to her brother. Both had refused to let Alexander be buried in his gold-plated casket, but I finally persuaded Ari in a moment of lucidity to let his son be at peace in a quiet plot beside the tiny stone chapel where Ari and I had been married on Skorpios.

No parent should ever have to watch their child be buried, to witness that precious part of themselves consigned to dust and darkness. Yet I was helpless to protect Ari from bearing that terrible burden.

Filled with a fierce need to protect the father in Ari who was living a tragedy I knew I'd never have survived, I slipped back into the part of an obedient Greek wife, spent my days after the funeral anticipating Ari's every need while assembling a monumental scrapbook during his naps each afternoon. The book was the story of Ari's entire life that included highlights with Alexander but set to the tune of *The Odyssey*, a colossal story for a colossus that I painstakingly told through a collection of Greek quotations, my own poetry, and watercolors.

"Oh, that's very nice, Mummy," Ari said absentmindedly when I presented it to him during a picnic lunch with Christina outside Alexander's marble mausoleum. My husband's visits to Alexander's gravesite were becoming more and more macabre with each passing day, usually accompanied only by a stray dog, but today I'd tried to set a happier tone by having an outdoor table set with a linen cloth, silver, and glass. I frowned as Ari ignored the tomato ricotta tart and pear sorbet I'd had the chef specially prepare; instead he became more and more weepy as he insisted on drinking copious amounts of ouzo and poured out several glasses to toast his son. I'd hoped the scrapbook might remind my husband of what he had been—what he could still be—but unlike Bobby's living room picnic that had reminded me not to linger too long in the rubble of my grief, Ari seemed intent on languishing in that same darkness forever.

I felt a brief moment of hope as Ari opened the scrapbook's cover before he glanced at Christina. I scarcely caught the minute shake of her head before he set the book aside and ignored it entirely.

"We'll see Alexander again," Christina reassured her father. She clasped his hands, turning her father so he faced only her haggard expression with the dark shadows under her eyes. "He's with God, but one day we'll meet him somewhere."

"No, I don't believe what you're saying." Ari gave a violent shake of his head and pushed Christina away. "My son is dead. Gone."

I knew all too well the need to hold tight to memories of loved ones, but so too did I know that sometimes those memories could be the most pointed weapons aimed against us. I ignored the dagger looks Christina hurled in my direction as I came around to Ari's side of the table, crouched next to him.

"Sit in the garden with me." *Away from this mawkish mausoleum*, I wanted to add. "We can have another table brought out and play poker if you'd like."

Ari clasped his tumbler of ouzo so tight I worried the glass might shatter. "This is where I want to be. You can sit elsewhere if you like."

I ignored Christina's smug expression as I stood and went back to my seat, wishing I'd brought a book or even my watercolors as a distraction. Instead, I sat in heavy silence while Christina regaled Ari with story after story of growing up with Alexander, each reminiscence adding further polish to the halo Alexander had acquired in death.

Later, I wished perhaps I'd interrupted, that I'd tried harder to distract Ari somehow.

As I was packing up the picnic basket and the forlorn scrapbook, I caught Christina and Ari whispering, their backs to me as they faced Alexander's mausoleum. Two phrases caught my attention.

Divorce writs.

The Widow.

A chill went through me, for Alexander had been unmarried and Christina had taken to referring to me as the Widow when she thought I wasn't listening. In the face of their grief, I'd been willing to forgive Ari and Christina their crimes against my marriage—it wasn't lost on me that Ari had stayed at his daughter's house on all those supposed business trips to Paris, that she'd likely been his willing accomplice in trying to shoulder me out of what had once been their happy triad. With Alexander's death, I'd been willing to let bygones be bygones, but it seemed I was alone in that.

While Ari now referred to divorce writs in Greek, Christina was speaking in her accented English, so I knew she wanted me to hear.

Wanted me to know this was the beginning of the end.

Ari patted her shoulder and she returned the gesture with a fierce hug before releasing him to shuffle back toward the house. My hands shook with anger as I gathered up the scrapbook and tried to piece together my thoughts.

"*Atyhya*," Christina muttered when she passed me on her way back up the stone pathway to the Pink House.

"What did you say?" I asked her in competent Greek, but she only wrinkled her nose—newly sculpted via plastic surgery to reduce the beaklike hook she'd inherited from Ari—and looked at me as if I were something contaminated.

"You heard me, *kyría*," she said.

Christina was right, I had heard her.

Atyhya. The curse.

She gave a haughty tilt of her head, the same I'd seen Ari give when facing down Bobby and his other opponents over the years.

"You've been a curse from the moment I first saw you with my father. We were strong before you came along. Now my brother is dead, Olympic Airways is slipping away, and so is my father."

Her accusations would have been laughable, had it not been apparent that she believed we were doomed characters in some ancient Greek tragedy.

I straightened to my full height and looked down my nose at her, needing to defend myself from these ridiculous accusations. I wasn't a curse. Was I? "I have nothing to do with Olympic Airways, nor was I responsible for your brother's plane crash."

"You were by your husband's side when he died. . . ." She drew strength from my wince, leaned closer so I could smell the mint on her breath. "Now the curse is part of our family, and before long it will kill us all."

"You can't honestly believe that," I said, but I knew she did.

Stupid girl, with her stupid Greek superstitions.

Like her brother, Christina had hoped that her mother and father might have reconciled and she blamed me for shattering that dream, believed that I was merely a gold digger who had never cared about her father. Ari's unstable daughter was so warped by hate and grief that she wanted to tear me down as well. There was no doubt she was a poisonous asp whispering in Ari's ear at every opportunity, seeking to turn him against me.

I did what I could to combat Christina's venom, but it should have come as no surprise when, on my way to bring Ari a lunch of sautéed scallops Provençal one day, I found a half-finished letter in my husband's handwriting that had been left out on his desk. Water ran in the adjoining bathroom and I heard Ari gargling as I scanned the scrawl of his handwriting, its words informing his daughter that he'd rewritten his will to leave everything to her and instructing her that she was to carry out its provisions.

The water turned off and I retreated with the lunch tray on silent feet, my heart pounding.

Ari and I had signed a legally binding agreement before our marriage, but there was no doubt I was being cast off and cut off, one thread at a time.

That night I told Ari I was returning to New York to be with my children. There was nothing I could do to stop him from divorcing me, but I sure as hell wanted to consult with my own lawyers before it happened.

Christina claimed I was a curse. I wasn't one to believe such superstitions, but then I'd married Ari to protect myself and my own children. They were both healthy and happy teenagers now—Caroline was a studious sixteen-year-old and John was all lanky arms and legs at fourteen. No matter what came of my second marriage, my sacrifices for Caroline and John had been worth it.

Even if there was a curse, I was not its root. Caroline and John were proof of that.

Then came the day that Ari fell ill.

was lying abed late one morning, indulging in the rare pleasure of staying nestled beneath a down comforter while the children were at school. I'd been happily immersed in a travelogue about Russia, savoring each sparkling description of the swirling snow and beshawled babushkas, and thinking how I'd like to visit there one day, and so I ignored the ringing telephone.

"I'm sorry to bother you, but that was Miss Onassis." My secretary appeared in the doorway to my bedroom, her lips drawn taut as she recited the message jotted onto one of my yellow stenographer pads. "She wanted you to know that her father needs emergency surgery in Paris to remove his gallbladder. Apparently, he collapsed while alone in Glyfada; Miss Onassis made it very clear that I convey that she felt her father should have had someone with him so soon after being released from the hospital."

Because Ari had just been diagnosed with myasthenia gravis, an

incurable neuromuscular disease that meant he now required cortisone treatments to counter his decreased adrenal function and stiff
plaster to hold up his drooping eyelids.

Myasthenia gravis.

Gravis. Grave.

I'd refused to think on the other, more permanent definition of that
word, even after Ari forbade me to return to Greece on his account.
It was true that we'd grown apart, but this was a stark echo of a different man in a different hospital, who had also hated anyone—even
his wife—seeing him so weakened.

*Of course. Now Christina blames me for not being there, but if I'd been there
to catch him, she'd claim that I shouldn't have let him get sick in the first place.*

It didn't matter what Ari had forbidden; instead of Russia with its
fairy tales of fire birds and Baba Yaga, now I winged my way to Paris
on a steel Olympic Learjet. I landed in time to help guide Ari through
the swarm of locusts disguised as paparazzi waiting outside the hospital on the morning of his surgery. I scarcely recognized the wreck
of a man who had replaced the wily business magnate I'd married;
dark sunglasses meant to camouflage his ruined eyes dwarfed his
gaunt face and his Italian suit hung from his bones, for he was nearly
forty pounds lighter than when I'd seen him last. Yet my husband's
silver hair was stubbornly slicked back above ink-black eyebrows and
he still brayed like an ill-tempered mule.

"I don't want those sons of bitches to see me being held up by a
couple of women," he snarled when I tried to place my hand beneath
his elbow. Christina flanked his other side and I half expected her to
serve me with divorce writs at any moment, but instead we studiously
ignored each other as a cascade of flashbulbs went off, unwilling to
hand-feed the reporters any salacious tidbits about the chasm between the Onassis women.

The surgery prolonged Ari's life, but not its quality. His ruined
gallbladder removed, my husband became a victim of his own failing
lungs, a complication of his myasthenia gravis. For the next five
weeks, he remained mostly unconscious while a ventilator filled those

same beleaguered lungs with oxygen and an IV kept him fed and hydrated. During each day's non-visiting hours, I trod a familiar path to Notre Dame to light a votive candle and pray for him.

How do you pray for a dying man? A rosary hung limp in my hands one morning; the Lord's Prayer hadn't brought me solace in ages. Instead, I sat in silence, witnessing the slow passage of time as a shaft of rainbow-colored light from the stained-glass window changed its angle into the cathedral's gloom. *Peace*, I finally thought. *I wish for peace for Ari. And the ability for those of us he leaves behind to finally forgive.*

"When will my father recover?" Christina asked the lead physician on Ari's team upon my return late that afternoon. I pitied her then, this grown woman trapped in a child's fantasy world. Her sleepless eyes were ringed by dark bruises made worse by thick lines of liquid eyeliner, her dark hair limp from lack of washing since her father had fallen ill. I allowed the doctor to usher her back to reality.

"I'm afraid your father won't recover," he said kindly. "Mr. Onassis is stable, but the best we can do is make him comfortable."

I closed my eyes, tried to draw strength from the very air as yet another man I cared for lay dying in a hospital bed. "How long does he have?" I finally asked the doctor.

"It's difficult to guess in cases like this." He rubbed his chin. "Optimistically? Several months at least."

Christina bristled. "You're wrong. My father is going to be fine. One day he'll walk me down the aisle and laugh in your faces while he's holding his grandchildren."

You poor delusional child . . .

"You should go back to the hotel," I said to her. "Try to rest."

She shook her head vehemently, the golden bangles hanging from her ears shaking like angry fists. "I'm not leaving him."

I know how you feel, Christina. Truly, I do.

I directed my gaze at the doctor, unwilling to engage Christina in an argument. "My children are alone in New York with only my household staff and their Secret Service agents." Not only that, but the Grand Central preservation project had moved forward without me and was in dire jeopardy, although I knew exactly how to save the building. I wanted to stay by Ari's side—truly—but there were so many strings tugging me back to New York and only one frayed knot to keep me tethered here. I knew Ari would understand, for after all, before we married it was he who had reminded me to live.

"Go," Christina said.

And never come back, I knew she wanted to add.

I ignored her to run a hand over Ari's tepid forehead, smoothing his thinning hair back before dropping a kiss there. "I'll be back," I promised. "I'll be here when you need me."

I only wondered if he could hear me.

I arrived in Grand Central's lower-level Oyster Bar early one foggy morning dressed in an elegant two-piece tan dress adorned with a single gold chain. Other prominent New Yorkers—the mayor and the president of the Municipal Art Society—filled the restaurant, which might have passed for a medieval catacomb, along with hundreds of guests and reporters, but as America's former First Lady, I was the guest of honor.

It had been so long since I'd done something of substance, I wanted everything today to be just right, to have a lasting impact.

I smiled serenely at the throng of press as everyone clustered around plates filled with oysters and bagels while sipping steaming mugs of coffee. It was my hand that had gathered reporters from every major city in America and even the London and Parisian presses, and we'd planned the event for early in the day so the story that was about to unfold could run all day tomorrow on television and radio so we might garner support from far and wide. Caroline and John and I planned to watch over breakfast, before they went to school.

The event began with a twenty-minute narrated slideshow that highlighted Grand Central's irreplaceable architectural heritage: her golden stars twinkling in the ceiling and an explanation of how great trains all over the country were aimed straight to her heart. And we cast a spotlight on her memories: the way the rails sparkled with ice chips used to clean them between trains, how the red carpet unrolled daily to greet passengers bound for the glittering gem of the 20th Century Limited to Chicago, and even how my own father—Black Jack Bouvier—had once brought me to marvel over the station.

The lights came on when the show was over. Then it was my turn to take the stage.

I imagined for a moment how Jack and Bobby must have felt standing before a crowd like this, their skin prickling with excitement and history in the making. "Europe has its cathedrals and we have Grand Central Station." I knew that every word I spoke into the bank of microphones mattered, that the short, punchy speech I'd labored to write on the flight from Paris would be more effective than an hour-long diatribe. "Is it not cruel to let our city die by degrees, stripped of all her proud monuments, until there is nothing left of all her history and beauty to inspire our children? If we don't care about our past, we can't have very much hope for our future. We've all heard that it's too late, or that it has to happen, or that it's inevitable. But I think if there's great effort, even if it's the eleventh hour, that you can succeed and I know that's what we'll do."

When I finished to thunderous applause, I knew papers the next day would be filled with photographs of me in front of Grand Central, that money for the project would begin pouring in just as it had when I'd urged Jack to come out in support of saving Abu Simbel.

In one morning, I saved Grand Central, but I broke something even more precious.

A promise.

For I'd promised Ari I'd be back, that I'd be there when he needed me.

Instead, I was an ocean away.

Ari died just after my Grand Central denouement, felled by the pneumonia that had crept stealthily into lungs beleaguered from a lifetime of smoking Montecristo cigars. Christina was the only person at his side, but I suspected that was exactly as they'd both wished it. Then came the added cruelty of the gossip columns that catcalled after me.

Aristotle Onassis Is Dead at 69

Jackie O Far from Husband's Deathbed

Dressed in widow's black again, I boarded a jet at New York's airport named for my first husband so my children and I might attend the funeral for my second.

"Why are all these people here?" Christina—sedated to smooth the ragged edges of her grief—asked loudly of the paparazzi gathered in front of the eighteenth-century Chapel of the Little Virgin on Skorpios for the funeral. I remembered a day from seven years prior when my self-styled Sun King and I had exchanged holy vows inside the same church that now cast its shadow over us. Christina's black hair snapped in the wind, her skin was a sickly yellow hue as we passed pink and white hyacinth wreaths from Swiss banks and another whose card read *To Ari, From Jackie*.

"Get them away!"

"Easy," I crooned to her as my own children walked behind me. I'd once sworn to spare them further grief, but here we were, clad in black again and walking these all-too-familiar steps toward another funeral.

How did I fail them? How did I fail Ari? Or, for that matter, Jack or Bobby?

I sniffed, knowing it wouldn't do to delve into those morose questions under the glare of the flashbulbs. "Your father once said that people throughout the world love fairy tales, especially those related to the lives of the rich," I said to Christina in an effort to calm her, silently musing to myself that perhaps Lee had been right instead. *Living in a fairy tale can be hell.* "This will soon be over and the reporters will leave then."

Her squeeze of my hand gave me hope that we could put our former animosities behind us and honor Ari together. Once inside the chapel with its decorative columns and arched niches painted a sky blue, the bearded Orthodox priest bid us all to kiss Ari one last time. Christina swayed on her feet when it was her turn, so John had to help her back to her pew. The simple wooden coffin was cool against my lips as I placed one white orchid on its top to join fifty-nine others.

"Good-bye, Ari," I whispered. "Your odyssey is finally over."

Standing in the outdoor courtyard after the service, I removed my trademark fly-eye glasses and witnessed Ari's silver-handled coffin being lowered into the vault beside Alexander's, a twisted cypress tree towering over both of them as Christina dropped a forlorn handful of dirt onto her father's grave. When it was over the mourners began to drift to the yachts and small planes that waited to take them to the mainland. That was when I heard Christina—whom I pitied, and wanted even more to forgive—whispering with a clutch of lingering Greek women while they all cast glances in my direction.

"*Atyhya*," one said.

"A widow for a second time."

Atyhya. Curse.

It was impossible to miss the way their eyes flicked toward me, how they tugged their black shawls a little closer to their bodies.

Bordel de merde. So much for putting our animosities behind us.

I schooled my features into a smile borrowed from the *Mona Lisa* and busied my shaking hands with straightening the red velvet that draped the decorative pots of lilies laid out for the service. I'd always believed that people with wonderful manners actually protected themselves from a lot of things, and right now it was only a thin veneer of decorum that kept Christina safe from a potted lily being hurled at her head.

She's a young woman still bruised from her brother's death and now grieving her father. You have to be the magnanimous one, Jackie, even when she makes you want to spit nails.

"I'll always keep the Onassis name," I assured her in a final attempt at decency and forgiveness when the last of the guests had finally left, the howling wind whipping the hair around both our faces. The decadent yacht named after her waited at anchor in the distance, the *Christina*'s crew dressed in black and its flag at half-mast as Skorpios's bell tolled into the damp, wet air. "As a tribute to Ari."

And because my years with Ari had been a part of me, the moment I'd tried to break free of the Kennedys' heavy mantle. I meant it as a kindness, but she interpreted it as a taunt.

"Don't bother." Her chapped lips twisted like two thin ropes. "Keeping my father's name won't get you a single cent of his money. He changed his will months ago."

I know, I thought to myself. I also knew my lawyers were prepared to fight for my part of Ari's fortune, however small it might be.

"I'm sorry for you, truly I am." I wondered what would become of Ari's broken, poisoned daughter, even as I hoped I'd never have to revisit her or this chapter of my life again. "I was his wife, Christina, and he rescued me at a moment when my life was engulfed with shadows. Nothing will change that, nor the fact that you were his daughter."

I strode away before she could respond, unwilling to linger a moment longer. In marrying Ari, I'd removed myself from the world, used his name and wealth to protect myself and my children behind invisible barriers.

Now Caroline was eighteen and John was growing fast. My children no longer required my protection, and the world was less enamored with the forty-six-year-old widow of a bygone era.

With Ari's death, I was no longer Jackie Kennedy, or Jackie O.

I was just Jackie.

CHAPTER

22

March 1977

The terms of the settlement state that you'll receive twenty million dollars, plus Caroline and John will each receive payments of twenty-five thousand dollars per year until they turn twenty-one." Maurice Tempelsman, my gentle giant of a financial adviser pivoted the slim stack of papers and pushed them across his desk so I could read them.

"And in return, all I have to do is renounce my twenty-five-percent share in Skorpios and the *Christina* and vacate my position on the board of the Onassis foundation?" I popped a piece of spearmint gum in my mouth—a recent diversion to cut back on my smoking—and chewed thoughtfully. This settlement had Christina's hand all over it, effectively cutting me off from Greece so I'd never have any reason to return. I raised a skeptical eyebrow. "This seems too easy, M.T."

"Easy?" Maurice—M.T., as I'd taken to calling him—scoffed and tugged the tan lapels of his double-breasted suit that was too broad in the shoulders. I was going to have to buy him something that fit better if he was going to keep squiring me around New York. "Maybe you've forgotten how we've been fighting this battle for the past two years."

"A selective memory proves useful sometimes."

"I suppose." Maurice rubbed his eyes before handing me a pen. A Belgian-born international diamond trader, he had been imposing once—I recalled him from a state dinner for President Ayub Khan of

Pakistan that Jack and I had hosted at Mount Vernon back in 1961—but now he was my kindly financial adviser who was fluent in Yiddish and several other languages, loved the theater, and had made me a substantial fortune worth millions by investing in gold futures. "That includes the profits, pension, and medical insurance policies that come with the foundation position."

I uncapped the fountain pen. "I can't sign this fast enough."

"Ready for this all to be over? Me too." Maurice had been by my side for the entire fight, for as Ari's widow, I refused to allow Christina to cut me off entirely from his $500 million empire. I wasn't the gold digger that she'd so often claimed—I still resorted to selling Halston tops and Valentino gowns to the Encore resale shop in Manhattan—but nor was I willing to be penniless, especially as I was cut off legally from any further Kennedy financial support since my marriage to Ari. Self-reliance was the last gift Ari would give to me, and I'd been willing to fight for it.

One scrawl of my signature and I was a free woman.

"So," Maurice asked over a celebratory toast of Scotch. "What do you plan to do now?"

I glanced at the framed world political maps that lined his office's expansive walls. "I'm going to Russia."

Maurice coughed in surprise, then glanced about as if I might be trailing KGB spies. "Not a permanent relocation, I hope? After all, I thought we had tickets to see *Chicago* next month."

"It's for a book I'm editing, my first for Viking: *In the Russian Style.*" I found it impossible to keep the pride and enthusiasm from my voice, but really, why shouldn't I be proud? I was forty-seven—and each of those years was starting to show on my face—but this editorial position was my first job since Jack had proposed to me back in 1953. I couldn't help adding, "Its publication will coincide with an exhibit on Russian costumes from the eighteenth and nineteenth centuries that the Met is hosting. I'm also preparing an anthology of Russian fairy tales."

"Ah, yes." M.T. cleared our empty glasses. "How is the new position treating you?"

"Being a consulting editor is difficult but fulfilling."

To me, a wonderful book took me on a journey into something I didn't know before. With this career at Viking, I was on a new and wonderful journey every day.

If a person produces one book, they will have done something wonderful in their life.

I'd said that to Jack to encourage him to write *Profiles in Courage*, and now I was slated to edit and help produce more books than I could count. More than that, being an editor gave me a purpose. I refused to be a dilettante, had instead exchanged my bouffant hairstyle and pillbox hats for soft bell-bottom jeans and snug Henley sweaters to arrive at the office via taxi every weekday by 9:30 a.m. sharp. Once there, I poured my own coffee before diving into a wire in-basket stuffed with manuscripts, shocked to discover that sailing on a yacht and buying couture clothes in Paris were less sustaining than going into the office and drinking coffee out of a foam cup. This was my job: to acquire books in the search for literary gold, spot fresh talent, and bring ideas to the table. They were tasks I excelled at, and ones I felt I'd been preparing for even since my days as the Inquiring Camera Girl at the *Washington Times-Herald*.

Maurice smiled, a jolly grin that could have been stolen straight from Saint Nicholas. "I know one of the senior editors. Do you know what they're saying about you there?"

"I'm not sure I want to know." I cringed to recall my first morning there, how I'd had to sneak in a few days early to throw off the mobs that had started gathering in anticipation after word had leaked out. But Tom Guinzburg—a senior editor whose office had a dartboard taped with photographs of agents and reviewers who annoyed him— had reassured me that the press's fascination with my day job would wear off. Eventually, it had.

"Public opinion is you're not merely a Hollywood type of star, with a double doing the hard part of the job." Which was true, given the number of my suggestions—including a junior archaeology book with hinged pages and a coloring book tracing the history of gold around the world—that had been rejected at editorial meetings. Maurice raised his glass to me. "It sounds to me like you've made a whole host of new fans."

After the terms of Ari's will were settled, I flew to Paris to meet the Met's director as we began our search for European costumes to complete our exhibit and was appalled to find that the doorman at my hotel had informed the press of my arrival. "Jackie!" screamed the cameramen gathered outside the Left Bank restaurant where we'd planned a quiet evening, their flashbulbs exploding like a cacophony of distant stars going supernova. *"Jack-ie!"*

I held up a hand to block their pictures and avoided eye contact, instead chattered blindly with the Met's director to make it impossible for any of the paparazzi to interject with an awkward question I'd be forced to answer.

Some things never change. . . .

"I should have warned you that lunch with me is sometimes akin to taking King Kong to the beach," I joked to the director, but he only gaped at the melee, his eyes like saucers.

Once we were settled into the back of the restaurant, the poor man shook his head as if to clear it. "You must have the most famous face on earth. I'd bet you could parachute into the wilds of Madagascar, Murmansk, or Mozambique and there'd be a crowd just as wild clamoring for photos and your autograph."

"I don't know about Mozambique, but the crowd in Mumbai was just as big," I answered as I settled the linen napkin on my lap. "Thank goodness the state controls the press in the USSR. They'll take one picture when I arrive and one when I leave. *Spasibo* and *da svidaniya.*"

Really, there were some advantages to being Mrs. Onassis Kennedy, as the Russians insisted on calling me upon my arrival in Leningrad. "I'd love to have the costumes of Czar Nicholas and Czarina Alexandra," I informed the Communist bureaucrats at the Hermitage as I attempted to arrange my own détente. "For the Met's exhibits, of course. They would make a perfect spread in the book."

"*Nyet*" came the answer from the Hermitage's stern-lipped Communist director. Given that their beloved Comrade Lenin had ruthlessly ordered the executions of Nicholas and Alexandra, I expected the Russians wouldn't be keen on featuring their highnesses' imperial clothing. Yet the woman paused, her face softening as she drummed well-manicured fingernails against the desk. "But perhaps we let you have something from Princess Elizabeth."

I was quite pleased with the mothballed green velvet upholstered sleigh and lap robe she produced from a cupboard somewhere, for Princess Elizabeth had been the daughter of Peter the Great. Just as my prior hosting of the *Mona Lisa* had bridged tensions between America and France, so too was I now making inroads with Russia, all while our two countries were shivering in the midst of the Cold War.

Perhaps I'd go to Cuba next, arrange to display their cultural treasures so Americans might learn from them as well. *The sky's the limit, Jackie. Maybe beyond that—the moon at least.*

That was how it seemed, especially when both *In the Russian Style* and the Met's corresponding exhibits were hugely successful. I drank up the moment while standing in the receiving line at the opening night party, dressed in a white strapless Mary McFadden dress while everyone moved about in a cloud of Chanel's Russian Leather perfume.

You don't just turn everything beautiful; you turn it to gold. If I closed my eyes I could almost hear Jack's voice. *Buttons, your mother is a veritable Rumpelstiltskin, did you know that?*

I smiled at the remembrance, didn't push it away as I had so many others over the years. *I hope you're proud of me, Jack. And I hope you can see the other projects I'm turning into gold.*

The first was saving Grand Central Terminal in New York. I'd shared a glass of celebratory Champagne with M.T. when I received definitive word that the historic station would be saved from the wrecking ball, a cultural treasure preserved for future generations to enjoy, just as I'd helped restore and protect the White House, Lafayette Square, and Egypt's temple of Abu Simbel.

My second golden project was the opening of Jack's presidential library.

Jack had looked forward to retiring to his library after his term in office was up, of making his headquarters there, but such a dream wasn't meant to be. Instead, after nearly sixteen years of poring over schematics and hosting fund-raising specials on C-SPAN, I'd finally pulled together the funding, documents, and construction of the building itself to create the capstone of Jack's lasting legacy: the library that would forever safeguard those one thousand and thirty-six days of his presidency.

Jack would have applauded the location we'd chosen on Dorchester's Columbia Point peninsula, nine-and-a-half windswept acres with a view of Boston's skyline and the Atlantic's argent waters. I smiled to watch sailboats ply the choppy waves, reminded of all the times Jack had sailed the *Victura* and the *Honey Fitz*, how he'd hunted with Caroline and John for purple sharks with our socks. I'd expected those little remembrances to fade as the years went on, but the tender reminders I imagined came from Jack remained constant, and for that, I was grateful.

This library would not be a dead place or merely a depository for dusty relics and yellowing papers of the past. That wouldn't be a fitting memorial for Jack, who was so intensely involved in life. This beautiful nine-story concrete-and-glass building we were dedicating today would grow and change with time.

Dressed in a gray turtleneck suit with practical black calfskin gloves, I reveled in the wind whipping my hair around my face as I walked purposefully past the clapping crowd that included President Carter, Lady Bird Johnson, and countless other dignitaries, and toward the dedication stage with Caroline and John at my sides. Despite everything they'd been through, my children had grown from babies who tugged my pearl necklaces during photo shoots into grounded, level-headed adults who sought to leave this world a better place than they'd found it. I'd raised Jack's children for the both of us, so that together the three of us might honor his legacy.

Worn beneath one of my black leather gloves that afternoon was the pink diamond ring Jack had planned to give me for Christmas in

1963, and in my children's pockets were two emerald solitaire bands I'd given them in the car on the way here, keepsakes crafted from the eternity ring Jack had given me on our ten-year anniversary. Perhaps Caroline would one day wear hers on her wedding anniversary; John might give his to his future wife. Maybe they'd even give them to their own children one day. Only one thing was certain.

Life would go on.

I'd seen the worst of everything and I'd seen the best of everything, but I couldn't replace my children. They were my greatest victory in this life, my vengeance on a world that had sought to defeat me more than once.

A line from "Ulysses" tickled my mind, made me think of Bobby.

> *Tho' much is taken, much abides; and tho'*
> *We are not now that strength which in old days*
> *Moved earth and heaven, that which we are, we are.*

Much had been taken, but my family still abided and now, together, we sat in the front row as the celebration of their father's library dedication began.

We are . . .

My heart nearly burst with pride when the rousing operatic "Overture" from *Candide* wound down and Caroline opened the dedication and introduced her brother in a steady voice that would have made her father proud. John—who shared my love of poetry—read excerpts of Stephen Spender's "The Truly Great" in celebration of his father before offering the lectern to a windblown President Jimmy Carter. "I am honored to be here at this occasion, at once so solemn and so joyous," the president said, his tone frank and measured. "Like a great cathedral, this building was a long time coming. I didn't know John F. Kennedy, but I do know he loved politics and laughter. At a press conference in March 1962, when the ravages of being president began to show on JFK's face, he was asked, 'I wondered if you could tell us whether if you had it to do over again, if you would work for the presidency, and second, whether you would recommend this job to others.' To which John F. Kennedy replied, 'Well, the answer to the first question is yes, and the second is no, I do not recommend it to others.'" Carter paused here for comedic effect just as I remembered Jack doing. "'At least for a while.'"

The crowd laughed and I smiled that Jack's wit and wisdom were once again on display for all the world to see and hear, sixteen years after the fact.

I'd been offered the opportunity to give a speech but had demurred and handed over that weighty responsibility to Teddy, who now assumed the stage. Jack's brother wore the evidence of recent years in the lines on his face, so I could imagine how his martyred elder brothers might have looked had they survived to achieve middle age. Teddy spoke a few minutes about his brother before offering my favorite line in the speech he'd shown me ahead of time. "In dedicating this library, we honor Jack, and in honoring Jack, we honor the best in our country and ourselves."

That was what I'd tried to do in every decision I'd made after Jack's death: honor him, his family, our children, and finally, myself.

After the ceremony, I wandered the museum exhibits on the bottom floor, indulging in a trip down memory lane. I almost wished the rest of my remaining family might have been here today, but my once-indomitable mother was growing frail and Lee was in the midst of a massive hotel decorating project—interior design was her current passion and I was glad she'd found something to enjoy that was all her own. Thus, I wended my way through the exhibits alone, smiled to see the coconut shell Jack had inscribed with a rescue message after his PT boat accident—the same he'd kept on his desk in the Oval Office—and my eyes misted when a blinding sparkle of emeralds and diamonds caught my eye, for I'd donated my engagement ring to the library. I had so many glittering jewels Jack had given me, but my memories were even sweeter. I thought it fitting that some of my treasures live here, so every American could experience a little bit of that magic that had been our Camelot.

Lady Bird Johnson found me in front of the massive Kennedy family Bible Jack had used to swear his presidential oath of office. "This must be both a proud moment and an emotionally exhausting day for you." Her soft Texas drawl reminded me of her many kindnesses to me over the years, from the early days of campaigning when I was pregnant with John all the way to that terrible day in Dallas. Lyndon had passed back in 1973—only two years before Ari—but Lady Bird and I had maintained sporadic contact over the years. "Do remember there are so many people wishing you happiness and contentment. Count myself among them."

I smiled at the former First Lady as Caroline and John came up behind us. "Thank you," I said, and together we gazed at a framed photograph from the morning we'd received word of Jack's election, me seated in the Kennedy living room between Rose and Ted with Jack, Bobby, and Mr. Kennedy directly behind me. Everyone was grinning wider than Halloween jack-o'-lanterns, waiting to greet the tempestuous future that was then still to come. Funny, I remembered worrying in that moment that the White House might ruin my marriage to Jack, but we'd ended up so happy there. It just went to show that you never could know what will be best for you. "It's taken many years"—I reached out to touch the photograph, to connect with that glorious past—"but I am finally content."

I felt Lady Bird silently leave us as both Caroline and John wrapped their arms around my shoulders. They leaned their heads there—no mean feat as Caroline was shorter than me and John had bypassed six feet several years ago—so I was reminded of an unbreakable nautical rope. "You've done so much, Mom," Caroline murmured. "Dad would be so proud of you."

"Grandpa Joe and Uncle Bobby too," John added.

My children were probably right, for I was no longer a ghost forgotten in time, searching for my long-dead companions and crawling around the ruins of a life. Instead, I'd quietly patched up the foundations that had been shaken, lovingly rebuilt the walls that had fallen in, and let the soft sunshine filter in.

And I'd done it all for these two wonderful human beings standing next to me, and to safeguard the legacy of the men I'd loved. I'd done all I'd set out to do.

I'd been the devoted wife of one of America's greatest presidents, the cosmopolitan Queen of Camelot in the pillbox hats, the amateur historian who gave to the White House its rightful role as America's historic home. A dignified widow who taught her country how to grieve, the loving sister-in-law of America's last prince, the willing wife of a Greek shipping tycoon.

My life had been filled with adventure and wisdom, laughter and love, gallantry and grace.

Now I was just Jackie, mother of two courageous children and dedicated book editor.

And that was enough.

AUTHOR'S NOTE

First and foremost, this is a work of fiction. While I strove to be as faithful to the historical record as possible, this is most certainly a fictionalized account of the life of Jacqueline Bouvier Kennedy Onassis.

Jackie Kennedy is best known for her grace and style during her years as First Lady, and also for that fateful day in Dallas when her pink suit and trademark pillbox hat would be forever seared into our nation's memory. However, what surprised me most as I began researching this amazing woman's story is that so much of her everyday strength and tenacity has been forgotten. Jackie was a wife and mother who was forced to deal with her husband's rampant affairs (JFK once commented to a friend that the reason he needed to sleep with so many different women was to avoid headaches), lost three children to miscarriage or death, and grappled with what we now recognize as postpartum depression and post-traumatic stress disorder. Yet, despite these struggles, Jackie triumphed to renovate the White House into a living museum, garnered international accolades for her wildly successful goodwill trips abroad, and rescued both Egypt's Abu Simbel temple and New York's Grand Central Terminal from destruction.

My aim in writing this novel was to shine the spotlight back on this iconic First Lady's heartaches and triumphs, especially as time moves us further away from the years when Jackie's name was consistently in the newspapers. While all of the characters and major events in this book are lifted from history, to include everything in Jackie's well-documented life would have required a one-thousand-page tome. This means that although I did my utmost to be true to what could have happened and not to blatantly rewrite history, there were occasions when I had to make decisions regarding conflicting evidence, missing accounts, or incidents that were drawn out over long periods of time.

I was shocked (and sometimes dismayed or delighted) that some events of Kennedy lore that one would imagine were well documented are, in fact, murky at best. (Some sources even bicker over the color of JFK's eyes!) The most mind-boggling of these foggy moments in history was how Jack actually proposed to Jackie. I came across several versions and potential dates—possibly booth number three in Martin's Tavern, maybe table forty at the Omni Parker House, or perhaps even via telegram while she was in London for Queen Elizabeth's coronation. Since no one can agree, I chose the version that worked best for this story.

I did my utmost to tell this story as Jackie might have told it, meaning that readers may occasionally discover a blind spot in the telling. For example, Jackie never remembered climbing over the back of the Lincoln limousine toward Clint Hill immediately after JFK was shot, yet we have photographic evidence that she did. Initially, Jackie recalled three shots, and later, only two. (Other witnesses were also split on the number of shots, given the sounds of engines backfiring.) President Kennedy was struck by two bullets, including the fatal wound to his head.

Jackie Kennedy was a very private person, and as this novel is told from her point of view, I made a conscious decision to let readers draw their own conclusions about her relationship with Bobby Kennedy after JFK was assassinated. By all accounts, Jackie and Bobby were incredibly close after the tragedy, and biographers are evenly split over whether the two had a long-lasting affair. I doubt we'll ever have a definitive answer to that question, which I suspect is the way Jackie would have preferred it.

I also freely admit to tugging some events slightly off the actual historical time line. For example, I moved slightly forward the date of Lee's engagement to Michael Canfield, while combining a few others, such as two of Jackie's early trips to Hyannis Port, which included her introduction to the Kennedy family with the *Life* photo shoot that Jack's father arranged. By his own admission, Oleg Cassini met Jackie a few weeks after her wedding in 1953, but he didn't officially begin to design for her until after the birth of John Jr., hence my introduction of him then. My biggest historical swap involved the death of Alexander Onassis, as that tragedy actually occurred two years before Grand Central's landmark status was voided. However, in a story fraught with deaths, I felt that giving Jackie the small new hope of saving Grand Central was warranted between the bookends of Joseph Kennedy's and Alexander's death, especially as her marriage was unraveling at the same time.

Some events that took several days or even longer were slightly compressed for the purposes of pacing. Once Jack was elected president, J. B. West actually informed Jackie that Mamie Eisenhower had a wheelchair waiting for her two months after their initial tour, not on the same day. Both the Bay of Pigs and the Cuban Missile Crisis unfolded over a span of many days, but for the sake of pacing, I decided against a blow-by-blow retelling. (I borrowed Jackie's pink-and-white straw lace Cassini gown worn during the Bay of Pigs incident that was actually for a gala reception of members of Congress held during the crisis.) I also swapped the time line on Marilyn Monroe's scandalous "Happy Birthday" song and Jackie's dinner with Arthur Miller for better narrative flow. (Both happened within a scant eight days of each other.) In a story fraught with so much tragedy, it seemed best to combine a private Mass given for JFK after his assassination with an interlude that took place the following day when Jackie prayed alongside Caroline and they tucked special items in JFK's coffin.

Sometimes it was also necessary to move historical figures around on the chessboard of this novel as I juggled history. For example, I maneuvered Mr. Kennedy into the room when discussing whether Jack would campaign for vice president in 1956; in reality Bobby called him after Jack had declared his candidacy and Joe cussed out both of his sons with what was called "blue language." According to Jackie's own words, Jack slept in a different bedroom the night that he was elected president, but I put them in the same room so they could share that historical moment together, just as I placed Bobby in the room when JFK broke down following the Bay of Pigs incident. (Jackie's interview with Arthur Schlesinger says Jack was just with her.) After that terrible November day in Dallas, Aristotle Onassis did attend a wake for JFK before his funeral, but I couldn't find any definitive record of him attending John Jr.'s birthday party. However, he and the Kennedy brothers did share a healthy loathing for one another and had it out both on and off the Senate floor.

In an effort to keep the cast list of this novel from resembling that of both houses of Congress, I combined one of JFK's closest friends, Lem Billings, who warned Jackie regarding Jack's taste for women, with that of a mutual friend, John White, who bet Jackie one dollar that the wedding wouldn't take place. Both of these incidents were rolled into my version of Bobby Kennedy.

Immediately following JFK's assassination, Jackie met with Theodore White of *Life* magazine and gave three interviews total (including those with William Manchester in 1964) about that fateful day in Dallas in order to ensure the events were correctly recorded for posterity. While Jackie didn't take umbrage toward White's authorized story, she did sue Manchester against the serialization of his book as she didn't want the horrific events dredged up and sensationalized in *Look* magazine. I combined her interviews with White and Manchester to better focus on the later lawsuit and its negative impact on Jackie's public image. Also, it was Jackie and Richard Goodwin who met with Manchester at Hyannis Port to try to stop the serialization, not Jackie and Bobby.

Scattered throughout the novel are lines of dialogue recorded by

Jackie, her family, and her friends, yet there were occasions when I borrowed famous quotes for specific events that were said by or to historical figures that didn't make the cut for this story. For example, Black Jack Bouvier's comment to Jackie about life enhancing and life diminishing people was actually said to Lee by art historian Bernard Berenson. The conversation Jackie has with her mother about worrying for Bobby's safety was one she had with Arthur Schlesinger at a fund-raiser dinner shortly after Martin Luther King Jr.'s assassination, while the line about playing "Ten Little Indians" was spoken to her friend Bunny Mellon, not Janet Auchincloss. I also combined Jackie's speech at Grand Central with architect Philip Johnson's comment about Europe having its cathedrals, as that seemed like something Europe-loving Jackie herself could have said.

I could never have tackled a story of this scope without a whole host of enthusiastic cheerleaders who cheered on all the necessary marathons of researching, writing, and revising. I owe a huge debt of gratitude to Stephanie Dray for several late-night telephone conversations that kept me from wanting to hop a time machine so I could throttle Jack Kennedy for his tomcat ways. Kate Quinn deserves the shiniest of gold medals for her uncanny ability to dig straight into my characters' heads and tell me exactly what they're thinking. My agent extraordinaire, Kevan Lyon, was the first person who didn't scoff when I said I wanted to take on Jackie Kennedy's story, and my editor, Kate Seaver, is the one who helped turn this story into reality. A huge debt of gratitude goes to the entire team at Berkley who have been cheering on my novels about America's leading ladies: Claire Zion, Jeanne-Marie Hudson, Fareeda Bullert, Craig Burke, Danielle Keir, Loren Jaggers, Sarah Blumenstock, Megha Jain, Heather Lewis, Anthony Ramondo, and Emily Osborne.

To my friends—I'm looking at Megan Williams, Kristi Senden, Claire Torbensen, and Nicole Smith—for their unwavering enthusiasm about Jackie, and a special thank-you to Nicole Ayers for double-checking my French. (All errors are, of course, my own.) Also, to my family—Tim and Daine Crowley, Hollie Dunn, Heather Harris—for keeping up a steady stream of encouragement as I breathed and ate (and even dreamed!) about the Kennedys for these past years.

Thank you also to all the readers, bloggers, and reviewers who have tweeted and messaged about your excitement for this book and my others, specifically Erin Davies, Audra Friend, Samantha Talarico, Magdalena Johansson, Megan Wessell, Clarissa Devine, and Ashley Hasty. I'm so glad you love to read my stories!

Most especially, to Stephen and Isabella. I love you more than words can say and could never do any of this without you both at my side.

ADDITIONAL READING

Baldrige, Letitia. *In the Kennedy Style: Magical Evenings in the Kennedy White House.* New York: Doubleday, 1998.

Bradford, Sarah. *America's Queen: The Life of Jacqueline Kennedy Onassis.* New York: Viking, 2000.

Brower, Kate Andersen. *First Women: The Grace and Power of America's Modern First Ladies.* New York: HarperCollins, 2016.

Cassidy, Tina. *Jackie After O.* New York: HarperCollins, 2012.

Cassini, Oleg. *A Thousand Days of Magic: Dressing Jacqueline Kennedy for the White House.* New York: Rizzoli, 2015.

Condon, Dianne Russell. *Jackie's Treasures: The Fabled Objects from the Auction of the Century.* New York: Clarkson Potter, 1996.

Dehême, Jacqueline. *Mrs. Kennedy Goes Abroad.* New York: Artisan, 1998.

Heymann, C. David. *Bobby and Jackie: A Love Story.* New York: Atria Books, 2009.

Hill, Clint, and Lisa McCubbin. *Mrs. Kennedy and Me.* New York: Gallery Books, 2012.

Kashner, Sam, and Nancy Schoenberger. *The Fabulous Bouvier Sisters: The Tragic and Glamorous Lives of Jackie and Lee.* New York: HarperCollins, 2018.

Kennedy, Caroline. *The Best-Loved Poems of Jacqueline Kennedy Onassis.* New York: Grand Central Publishing, 2001.

Kennedy, Jacqueline. *Historic Conversations on Life with John F. Kennedy.* New York: Hyperion, 1964.

Leaming, Barbara. *Jackie Bouvier Kennedy Onassis: The Untold Story.* New York: Thomas Dunne Books, 2014.

McKeon, Kathy. *Jackie's Girl: My Life with the Kennedy Family.* New York: Gallery Books, 2017.

Mills, Jean. *Moments with Jackie.* New York: MetroBooks, 1999.

Sgubin, Marta, and Nancy Nicholas. *Cooking for Madam: Recipes and Reminiscences from the Home of Jacqueline Kennedy Onassis.* New York: Scribner, 1998.

Shaw, Maud. *White House Nannie.* New York: Signet Books, 1965.

Sidey, Hugh. *Remembering Jackie: A Life in Pictures. Life Magazine.* New York: Warner Books, 1994.

Smith, Sally Bedell. *Grace and Power: The Private World of the Kennedy White House.* New York: Random House, 2004.

Smith, Stephen Kennedy, and Douglas Brinkley. *JFK: A Vision for America.* New York: HarperCollins, 2017.

Taraborrelli, J. Randy. *Jackie, Janet, and Lee: The Secret Lives of Janet Auchincloss and Her Daughters Jacqueline Kennedy Onassis and Lee Radziwill.* New York: St. Martin's Press, 2018.

———. *After Camelot: A Personal History of the Kennedy Family—1968 to the Present.* New York: Grand Central Publishing, 2012.

AND THEY CALLED IT CAMELOT

·····

A NOVEL OF
JACQUELINE BOUVIER
KENNEDY ONASSIS

STEPHANIE
MARIE
THORNTON

INTERVIEW WITH THE AUTHOR

What inspired you to write about Jackie Kennedy?

After writing *American Princess*, I knew I wanted to write about another iconic American woman and immediately thought of Jackie Kennedy. I discovered that while most people think they know her story, many of the details of her life—the deaths of her children, the monuments she saved, her many tumultuous family relationships—have already started to be forgotten. Also, while there are enough nonfiction books about her and the rest of the Kennedys to fill an entire library, I quickly realized that there was an opportunity to transform her momentous life into historical fiction. While I love a good nonfiction read, there's something special about experiencing life through the eyes of the person who lived it. (I often joke that historical fiction is the closest thing to a time machine, but it's true!) I loved being able to transport readers to see what it would have been like to be the one and only Jackie Bouvier Kennedy Onassis.

In your previous book, *American Princess*, you profiled the life of Alice Roosevelt, another iconic woman from a well-known political American family. What similarities and differences did you find between the two women?

The first thing that struck me as similar, especially as I wrote about the early days of these women's marriages, was how political wives of America's twentieth-century upper class were typically expected to put up with their husbands' bad behavior while remaining morally impeccable themselves. In fact, it seemed almost expected that men would cheat on their wives. It was an unfair double standard and both Alice Roosevelt and Jackie Kennedy had to find ways to keep their tumultuous marriages from ruining their lives.

The biggest difference between Alice and Jackie was probably how dearly Alice loved the White House, while for Jackie it became the centerpiece of many painful memories. Alice dove into being First Daughter with gusto (as she did with everything in life), and after her father's presidency, she did everything she could to return her immediate family to the White House. Jackie was relatively slow to embrace her role as First Lady and, understandably, it took her years to return to the White House after JFK's assassination and to accept that those one thousand and thirty-six days had been among the happiest of her life. However, it seemed that both women came to treasure their years spent in the White House.

You've done so much research on Jackie's life. You know so much of it intimately and yet she was such a private person. If you could ask Jackie one question about her life, what would it be?

So much of Jackie's life is meticulously documented, down to what jewelry she wore and which wine was served at certain events, but there are some telling gaps too. I'd never dare ask her what part of me really wants to know—what the true nature of her relationship was with Bobby Kennedy—but I'd certainly ask whether she felt the spectacular triumphs of her life were worth the many tragedies she endured. Jackie is America's most memorable First Lady, but I've always wondered if she wished perhaps that she and JFK could have lived more mundane yet longer lives together or whether she had accepted the fact that their White House years were reminiscent of the Greek tragedy of Achilles: brief but filled with glory.

Jackie was an amazing, loving mother. What do you think drove her devotion to her children? She spent more time with her children than most mothers of her socioeconomic class at the time. Why was she willing to break from that convention? It doesn't necessarily feel like behavior she learned from her own mother.

I believe Jackie truly wanted to be a mother and not only that but be the best mother possible, especially after the heartache of a miscarriage and stillbirth during the early years of her marriage to JFK. After all, this is the woman who once said, "If you bungle raising your children, I don't think whatever else you do matters very much." Jackie's devotion and her place in society meant that she could reject the conventions of upper-class America, especially how much time she—rather than the nanny—spent with Caroline and John Jr.

What's the biggest takeaway about Jackie as a woman that you would like readers to glean from reading about her life?

My entire goal in writing this story is that readers come to realize just what a survivor Jackie was. No matter how much tragedy she endured—and there was plenty of it—she never gave up on love and she always managed to find the beauty in life. I think that's a true testament to her character.

There's a line in the novel when Jackie says she wants her husband's presidency remembered as a "shining city upon a hill where valiant men danced with beautiful women, when hope reigned and great deeds were done." The Kennedy administration has gone down in history as a time when Camelot was

reborn, but where did this idea really come from? Is it a fitting tribute to the Kennedy years?

This romantic idea of Camelot was created by Jackie during her 1963 interview with *Life* magazine immediately following her husband's assassination when she was inspired by a line from the musical *Camelot*: "For one brief shining moment there was Camelot." Even in those horrific days so soon after Dallas, I suspect Jackie sought to protect JFK's legacy and shape the public's image of his presidency, to cast his years in the White House in a positive light and enshrine them in legend. America still identifies the Kennedy years with the ideas of hope and youth and passion; however, as time passed, Jackie reputedly conceded that Camelot was "overly sentimental." Still, she never backed down from the characterization as she believed those one thousand and thirty-six days were a period that would never be repeated.

What are you working on next?

I'm returning to roughly the same time period as Jackie Kennedy's life, but my next story will be one of spies, romance, and intrigue during the early days of the Cold War!

DISCUSSION QUESTIONS

1. As a young woman, Jackie refuses to repeat the mistakes of her parents' marriage even though she realizes she must marry well in order to avoid living off her stepfather's charity. Just after meeting Jack, Jackie recognizes that he's cut from the same cloth as her philandering father, Black Jack Bouvier. What was Jackie's biggest motivator in choosing to marry Jack? Did she make the right choice?

2. Jackie and Lee start out as the Whispering Sisters, but then their relationship takes many twists and turns throughout the novel. What did the Bouvier sisters share, but what also set them against each other? What do you think it was like for Lee, unable to escape the shadow of being Jackie Kennedy's little sister?

3. Lee once remarks to Jackie, "Living in a fairy tale can be hell. Don't people know that?" Was this true for the Bouvier sisters? To what extent was Jackie's life a fairy tale and to what extent was it hell?

4. Jackie endures two miscarriages and Jack's cheating on two separate occasions before he runs for president. Given the attitudes toward divorce in the 1950s, do you think she made the right choice in staying with him?

5. Jackie was known as one of the most elegant women in the world at a time when beauty was often viewed as a woman's greatest accomplishment. What did you think of her comments regarding her strict beauty regimen—the "legion of horrors"—and also her attention to designer fashions?

6. Multiple celebrities and well-known politicians make cameos throughout the course of this story, including Winston Churchill, Frank Sinatra, Marilyn Monroe, Richard Nixon, and Lyndon Johnson. Was there anything that surprised you in reading about them?

7. Immediately following Jack's assassination, Jackie records her memories and is inspired by a line from the musical *Camelot*: "For one brief shining moment there was Camelot." Based on what you know of JFK's administration and perhaps later politics, was his presidency Camelot? Will there ever be another presidential administration that can compare to the glitz and glamour and hope of the Kennedys?

8. Jackie and Bobby became extremely close in the aftermath of JFK's assassination—some of their contemporaries and biographers believe they actually had an affair. Do you think they would have had such a close relationship had Jack survived? How does grief sometimes work to bring people together?

9. Jackie was reviled for her marriage to Aristotle Onassis, who had also had a long-lasting affair with her sister, Lee. What was your take on their tumultuous marriage? Do you think Jackie made the right decision in marrying Onassis?

10. As First Lady Jackie restored the White House and made it a tribute to American history. She also helped nurture foreign relations with her international goodwill trips and by facilitating cultural exchanges. How do you think she is similar and different from other First Ladies? Has the role of First Lady evolved since the 1960s? Do you think it has changed as the role of women in society has changed?

ABOUT THE AUTHOR

Photo by Katherine Schmeling Photography

STEPHANIE MARIE THORNTON is a high school history teacher by day and lives in Alaska with her husband and daughter.

Ready to find
your next great read?

Let us help.

Visit prh.com/nextread

Penguin
Random
House